UPROAR

DRAGON BONES BOOK III

CELESTE HARTE

IMMORTAL WORKS
SALT LAKE CITY

Immortal Works LLC
1505 Glenrose Drive
Salt Lake City, Utah 84104
Tel: (385) 202-0116

Cover Art by Ashley Literski
http://strangedevotion.wixsite.com/strangedesigns

ISBN 978-1-953491-76-3 (Paperback)
ASIN B0CV6242YV (Kindle Edition)

This book is dedicated to the Kings and Queens of our generation. These pages are instilled with love and passion for storytelling, a need to be heard. A need to be loud. This book shouts from the rooftops, and this book is dedicated to those that have always felt silenced and hushed.

I hear you, I see you. So come with me into these pages, where we can shout as loud as we want, and know what it feels like when someone hears.

PART I:

CLAWS

OCEAN

Jashi Anyua-Omah

Ever since being taken from the palace, I could only take in my surroundings between bouts of consciousness. I was bound and gagged, jostling as I lay on a hard floor, and I felt like I was constantly moving. A car. I was lying in the back of a hovercar, I realized.

All the while, I heard — no, *felt* — a voice tugging at my senses.

Hold on.

I'm coming.

Hallucinations. I had to be hallucinating.

Stay awake, the voice insisted. *WAKE. UP.*

That somehow cleared the fog a little. I opened my eyes, and the world stopped swimming for a moment. I looked around at the vehicle I was traveling in. Too big to be a hovercar. Most likely a hovervan or something slightly bigger. I remained still but chanced a glance behind me, where I heard movement. Two men sat at the front of the hovervan, and even from behind, I recognized the one driving as Attican. There was no mistaking that silvery-blond head of messy hair and stiff fingers maneuvering about the controls. The other, I didn't know.

Not seeing Talad, I supposed they must have parted ways with him once I'd been captured.

A sting of hurt flashed through my mind. Talad *helped* them capture me. Kahmel and I knew the Zendaalans wouldn't sit quietly on their hands as we came closer to connecting with the Dragon Kings and revealed ourselves to our people at the same time. In fact, Averton warned us as much—which was the only reason I knew I wasn't without hope. Because of his warning, I was able to think quickly and slip the hairpin Kahmel had given me into the curls of my hair, knowing there was a tracking device installed on it.

When my parents were moved into the palace, we knew they could only be there to sabotage our efforts. I never expected *their* presence to be friendly. But Talad? He'd had an attitude the last time we met, but *this...* I still didn't know how to process what'd happened.

From the undignified position of lying on the floor, I could see the stars passing in a blur through the car window. I had no way of knowing how much time had passed since I was taken, but it felt like I'd slept for a while. The hunger aching in my belly confirmed that. With the drugs I was being given, I might have been asleep for a day. Maybe even more.

The clip in my hair. Did they pat me down when they brought me to the car? I was sure they did, but had they thought to check my hair? Hell, I lost pins in my own hair all the time. I rolled my head to the side, relieved at the comforting pressure of the clip against my scalp. They hadn't noticed. Wherever they took me, Kahmel would be able to find me.

But the question remained. Where were they taking me?

"Did you hear something?" the unknown man asked in a startlingly deep voice. My muddied mind barely registered what he'd said. He was speaking Zendaalan.

Quick, don't let them see you're awake! the voice from within said, and I was convinced whatever Attican and his friend had slipped me had been some powerful stuff. My hallucinations were trying to be helpful now.

Attican turned and looked at me, and I wished I'd pretended to be asleep. "She's awake," he replied in the same language. "I'll take care of her."

He produced a small cloth and held it over my face. I held my breath, struggling for as long as I could manage. But when my lungs burned for air, an involuntary inhale had the world blackening around me again.

$$\text{\textbf{W}}$$

THE NEXT TIME I woke up, I jumped when my eyes opened to the other man crouched in front of me—not just because he stared right at me, but because he was K'sundii. Except, just like the Zendaalans, he had cybernetic implants. Even more than most of them, actually. His left shoulder, jaw, and what I could see of his hands were all covered in gleaming metal and glowing seams. The skin that remained was a grayish brown, like it was devoid of life or blood. Something about him was...off.

The most shocking part of it all was his eyes. They were an intense orange. Almost red. He was dragon tribe, on top of everything else.

"Eat," the man said in a clipped tone, and his deep, robotic voice took me aback once more. It rumbled like a deep growl, something predatory and vicious. I knew some Zendaalans preferred their cybernetic implants that way, like the president with his six arms and freakish face. But a K'sundii man with cybernetic implants following Zendaalan trends? Could he be mixed? K'sundii people were rarely sick enough to need the cybernetic parts the fragile Zendaalans did to sustain their bodies. Of course, he could have simply chosen to look this way, though I couldn't imagine why.

I was so busy trying to puzzle out this strange K'sundii man that he had to growl and repeat himself for me to register that he was reaching for me with a bowl of some kind of hot mush. It was the color of wheat, hot steam and the smell of burnt rubber wafted from it. I didn't want anything to do with it, but for the lack of strawberry ice cream, I supposed it was as good as I was going to get. I nodded, accepting his offer to feed me, and at first I stared at him, confused, trying to piece together a likely set of circumstances that would result in the man that crouched before me. And then, as the waves of fog receded and clear thoughts flowed back, I became furious. This man was K'sundii—halfway, all the way, I didn't care—I was his Faresha. Attican's actions, I understood. The Zendaalans hated us because we were a threat to their rule, and, I'd found through the Dragon Kings, that hatred stretched even beyond the history I was familiar with, going all the way back to our connection to the dragons and the Zendaalans' lack thereof.

But this man? What interest did this man have in my capture? It was like having Talad sitting here in front of me. What could the Equalizers have promised him and Talad to make them turn so blatantly against their people's throne like this?

I sat up as the man set down the bowl and strode around behind me, unlocking my handcuffs moments after. We were alone, I realized belatedly. Attican must have had better things to do than feed the captive.

"I've never seen a K'sundii dressed so primly like an Equalizer," I drawled, letting bitterness be my companion in this humiliating position, betrayed by everything meant to protect me—my friend, my parents, and now this freak. "The Peace-Makers must be impressed."

I knew I could have gotten hurt for such a comment, but anger filled me with a brazen bravery. I supposed I had to pick up something from being married to Kahmel for a year. But to my surprise, the assault never came.

The K'sundii man gave a rough laugh. "I suppose that's what I look like, yes."

Surprised at his response, I forgot to snap something angry in return. Instead, I rubbed the raw skin around my wrists, trying to get feeling back into my arms. How long had I lain in the same position?

"Eat," he barked, giving me the bowl and a plastic spoon to go with it.

There was no gun to my head, no threat. I supposed no threat was needed. It was clear I had nowhere to run. The doors in the back of the van were likely locked, and I assumed we were in Zendaal, the one place Kahmel couldn't reach me.

A thought floated through my mind. A defeated, crushed, futilitarian thought that all the effort I made to take Kahmel's hair clip might have been useless. But I pushed that thought away, summoning that brazen bravery again. One problem at a time. The most present one was hunger.

Just as I picked up the spoon, the voice came back.

Keep talking to him, it hissed. The thought sliced through my mind with an aggressive need to be understood, shaking off any traces of the grogginess I felt. Maybe this voice was something more than just a result of being drugged.

Feeling like a lunatic, I ventured into my own mind. *What do you mean?* I asked.

The voice responded. *Ask him more questions. You need to know who he is.*

I felt rage—but it wasn't coming from me. It was like my body was a bottle, and the emotion siphoned in from somewhere else. And once it was mine, an entire onslaught of feelings descended. The rage boiled in my gut, only to be smothered by something else—reason. The necessity to contain one's emotion. The need to concentrate on a more important task.

I could differentiate between my emotions and these foreign ones. These added thoughts came in waves and then receded. This experience was somewhat...familiar.

"Are you just going to sit there and starve?" the K'sundii man muttered, and I forced myself to push the gray foodstuff between chapped lips, finding it tasted as good as I expected it to.

Instead of focusing on the unflavored glop, I returned my attention to my own mind. *Ocean?*

Of course! my dragon exclaimed. *Who else would it be? Now hurry, before you finish eating. Keep him talking. You have to learn who he is.*

I tried to wrap my head around what was happening.

Assuming I wasn't, well, losing my mind, Ocean—the deep blue adolescent dragon I drake-bonded with in Vahdel and brought back to K'sundi—had somehow broken free from our stables and followed me all the way to wherever the hell I was.

The Drake Bond. The idea seemed preposterous, but I remembered when I flew Ocean over attacking Zendaalan officers how her feelings blended with mine until I barely knew which was which anymore. When the Zendaalans hurt her, I *knew*. Not just that she was hurt, but where the damage was done, how much it hurt, whether she could keep going or not. The information merged into my consciousness seamlessly, like there was no gap between me and her once we were bonded.

The Drake Bond not only freed her from the ZST training that I'd rescued her from—it connected our *minds*.

Keep talking to him, Ocean insisted, sensing my confusion and fighting to keep me focused. *Before the other one comes back.*

She meant Attican. She wanted me and the K'sundii man to talk alone. Why? Did she somehow know who this man was? Why couldn't she just tell me? I reasoned that if she could tell me directly, she would have already. Not to mention the possibility of this just being a hallucination was still on the table. But I was just mad enough at this K'sundii traitor to have a few questions I wanted answered anyway. Just me and him. I knew why Attican was here. But this man's presence was a disgrace that demanded an answer.

"So," I said, cocking my head to the side, considering him, "how much does it cost for a K'sundii to sell out their Faresha?" I shrugged. "What are you getting, a position in the Court? Status for your clan's family? Assuming you have a family clan. I hope you set a high price. The Zendaalans would have paid anything." I smiled with the grim audacity of someone to whom the worst had already happened. "They're more scared of me than I am of you."

Traitor, I hissed internally.

Ocean repeated, *Yes, traitor.*

Confused, I wanted to ask her what she meant, fairly certain my dragon—assuming I was talking to my dragon and not just echoes of my mind—wasn't thinking about K'sundii politics.

The man responded, "What spirit." His low, crackly voice purred, and the way he looked at me made me shiver. He marveled at me, making no move to attack me, like we were just having a particularly interesting discussion. It was quite unlike when the Zendaalans had me under their thumbs a year ago, when I was slapped just for asking questions. "But you've lost, little dragon," the man added, almost sympathetically. "It's best to wait for your husband to concede his throne and then retrieve you. He has no other options."

I seethed at being called *little dragon* but bit back the insults that rose to my tongue. I'd reached my limits with this captor, thinking I'd only live up to the stupid nickname he gave me if I started puffing fire through my nostrils.

Of course their plan was to force Kahmel to abandon the throne.

As I tried not to taste the mush going into my mouth, I wondered what Ocean wanted me to glean from this conversation. *Something* about this man was perplexing—aside from his Zendaalan machinery. The way he studied me as I ate sent a chill down my spine. There was no malice in his gaze. I'd been so distracted by my own scalding hatred that I didn't realize until now that his own eyes were devoid of it. Like he didn't even regard me as an enemy. I wasn't sure if those almost-red eyes really regarded me at all. He looked beyond me. At what I *represented*, rather than who I *was*. An inconvenience to be removed; nothing less, nothing more.

His gaze was more than that of just a henchman, like Attican. Attican didn't care about me one way or another. He was just doing his job. Frustrated when I spoke above my place as a bug needing to be crushed. This K'sundii man was different. Seeing beyond me didn't mean he underestimated me. It was quite the opposite, it seemed. He knew I was dangerous. That was why I needed to be removed. He regarded the fact simply but not carelessly.

The thought made me straighten rather than hunch over the slop

I'd been given, despite how hungry I was. For the first time, I realized I was dealing with a player to this game that may have been more instrumental than I first assumed. One that came to deal with me personally once I was successfully captured. Like he wanted to finally see first-hand the threat he'd been facing.

"Well?" I challenged, feeling deep in my gut I was right. "Am I everything you expected me to be?" For a moment, I thought he would dismiss me. Shrug off the comment and tell me to finish my food.

But instead he grinned, revealing stark white teeth, though several had been replaced with silver ones. "No, not at all," he said. "I think I like you."

His words, his eyes, sent ice down my spine, and suddenly I couldn't bring myself to finish my food. A rap on the door came at that moment, and the K'sundii man's face fell. Actual disappointment. "Seems we're out of time, little dragon." He yanked my hands away from the bowl, niceties over, and handcuffed me again. "I hope your Faresh takes his time in giving in, though. I think I am enjoying this."

I didn't have time to ask Ocean why in the world she wanted me to speak with this terrible man—this monstrosity of a person—before a cloth was pressed to my mouth and nose, and the world faded.

WHEN EVERYTHING CRUMBLES

Kahmel Axon Kai of the Omah Clan

Too fast. Everything had moved too fast. Time slipped away from me. Jashi slipped away from me. And I'd had enough.

In the dead of night, I moved through the corridors of the palace like a shadow. The days since Jashi's disappearance trickled away like water, and I wasn't sure how many had passed. Long enough, though, for my rage to boil over with the gentleness of a spewing volcano. It was time to make my move.

It was clear the Courts were going to make their decision, so I was making mine first. Most of the preparations were made at this point. There was only one more thing left to do. Dressed in camouflage hoods that cloaked us from prying eyes, Rand, Arusi, and I made our way to the dragon stables.

I was giving up.

I never wanted things to get to this point; obviously that didn't matter. As much as I wanted a reformed K'sundi, K'sundi wanted nothing to do with my dreams for its future. This result was inevitable. Jashi was gone, and so was my patience and forgiveness.

Sleep escaped me these days, and the few moments my eyes drifted closed were filled with terrible, vivid nightmares. Even now, as I moved softly through the halls of the palace with my men, the memory of those dreams flashed in my mind, of dragons and fire and burning sensations. Indicative, no doubt, of my mood. I had become the dragon. Fearsome, a stranger to silly concepts like mercy.

This was poetic justice. It was because of how little this country cared for its royals in comparison to their precious saviors that the Zendaalans were allowed to infiltrate as much as they had into the palace. Jashi and I were torn apart; K'sundi was tearing itself apart. But unlike K'sundi, I was willing to save Jashi.

I no longer wanted anything to do with saving this country. If they wanted their Equalizers so badly, they could have them from now until forever. I'd done what I could. I was finished.

A pair of Zendaalan guards flanked the entrance to the stables. From where we stood around the corner of the palace walls and dressed in camouflage gear, they couldn't see us.

Before I could move, Rand's hand pressed on my shoulder. "Are you sure you want to do this?"

Am I sure?

At another moment in my life, the question would have been reasonable. I might have even appreciated it. But not now.

Jashi was taken a few weeks ago. I didn't have time to investigate —it was pointless to do so anyway. I had a feeling they'd eliminated most, if not all, leads in this case. It was clear they had inside help and a lot of it. I was in high demand from my council and the Court. Jashi and I hadn't attended the summit the Zendaalans had "invited" us to in Zendall, now K'sundi was heading for the rebel country list.

Asan had tried to argue to them that Jashi went missing and there was no way I could go without her, but the Zendaalans quickly blamed Jashi's unpredictable nature as the reason for her disappearance, saying she didn't want to answer for her strange abilities and thus ran away. Asan was livid. Oddly enough, I wasn't. They laid this trap; there was no way they would have initiated it without having done the proper preparations. Averton was right. There was nothing we could have done to avoid this, even if we'd known about it in advance. They had us cornered and outnumbered.

I'd seen enough battles to know a victory when I saw one, and this was theirs.

So to avoid being put on the rebel list, the Court was going to try to depose me from the throne. It was all but certain.

I'd lost Jashi, and I was about to lose my country. I had nothing left to lose. The question "are you sure" was insulting. What the hell else would I be? I'd been dealing with accusations, ridicule, distrust, and betrayal since the beginning. From friends, family, and as much as I loved her, even Jashi. I'd *wanted* to do this from day one. But back then, I loved my country too much to truly let them down, regardless of what they thought I was actually doing.

But all that changed.

"Let's go." I turned my back on him. He stiffened behind me, and part of me recoiled at that. Rand and I hadn't been on the same page about this like we usually were. I knew he could sense the change in me. I didn't even know what was happening to me. But I wasn't fighting it.

For once, I couldn't even claim to be angry—the result of reaching such an intense anger that one no longer felt anything else, including the anger itself. It all led up to today, and I was hopelessly numb to everything happening around me. It was like I was only half-watching a movie, only tuning in when important details were mentioned, zoning out for the rest; catching glimpses here and there to get the gist of what was going on, but never fully engaged.

I was engaged for this, though.

Everyone around me looked at me warily, like they were worried about me, and I didn't understand that. *I* wasn't worried about me. Whatever you wanted to call the state I was in—unfeeling? Robotic? Detached?—it didn't matter. I wasn't uncomfortable with it. In fact, I was seeing things clearly for the first time in a while.

The only person worth my attention, my compassion, my concern, was Jashi. She had my heart, the most authentic part of me, the vulnerable part of me. The moments we shared weren't always happy, but if anything, that was what made them invaluable. We'd seen the truest parts of each other. At our worst, at our best, we'd been through it all. Jashi was my world now. I'd protect her with my dying breath.

The rest of the world could *burn*.

So, I changed the plans a bit. I first told Rand, Arusi, Asan, and Khes. They tried talking me out of it, but I wouldn't change my mind. To be honest, I told them as a courtesy. Regardless of what K'sundi decided to do with me as their Faresh, I was still the rebel leader, and they all knew it. So they backed down.

And now we were going with my new plan: screw everything.

We stepped out from around the corner, closing the distance between us and the guards. With the pent-up fury from years of ridicule and distrust, I volleyed a ball of flames that burst when it came in contact with the armored suit of one of the guards, catching the man next to him as well, sending them sprawling. Fire exploded from my palms as I directed the blaze toward the control panel beside the guards, breaking the automatic lock. The fire warped the metal like it was ice cream.

Before the guards could regain their bearings, Rand and Arusi moved like two blurs. The technological interface that was weaved throughout most Zendaalans' systems allowed them to easily control their armored suits like they were simply extensions of their bodies. For some, they literally were. But though this interface made the suits easy to control, it also made them easy for us to disable. I wasn't sure what it felt like to short-circuit; unlike them, I wasn't a microwave. But our Zendaalan friends found out as Rand and Arusi made quick work of them with their tech-disabling wands. With a few quick jabs to essential control centers—the left part of their chests, their necks, and stomachs—the robot men were taken down. They were still conscious, but their bodies were unable to move anymore. Like a toy with the battery taken out.

With the Zendaalans down, we strode into the dragon stables.

We were already wearing protective ear pieces, and it was a good thing too. Huntress and Comet roared as soon as we entered the room, scratching at the ground and whipping around frantically. The dragons were antsy. The Zendaalans had prevented us from letting them out at all these past few weeks, and frustrated dragons were never a good thing. The hardest part in all of this, as usual, was more the dragons themselves than the actual task of breaking them out. I wasn't sure how we were going to get them calm enough to get them out of here without killing us.

I did a double take. Wait, only Huntress and Comet?

But sure enough, only the onyx and electric-yellow dragons were in the room. The third forcefield chamber was empty, a small hole in the wall just above the ground.

I was a little tired—lack of sleep and all—so the realization hit me slower than Rand and Arusi, who gave each other worried glances as I eventually came to the same conclusion as they. Huntress was my dragon, Comet was Jashi's, and Ocean was the latest dragon we'd acquired, one Jashi tamed herself. Jashi figured out how the Drake Bond worked and used it to bond with the azure-blue dragon we found in Vahdel. Ocean wasn't a big dragon like Comet or Huntress. Dragons took a long time to reach maturity. It took them as long as fifteen years to be considered a full adult. Ocean couldn't have been older than maybe eight. The hole she'd made in the wall was just big enough for her to squeeze through.

Ocean had escaped—some time ago, from the looks of things— and no one told us. Unlike the floor beneath Huntress and Comet, which was fresh with scratches and scrape marks, the floor of Ocean's stall was covered in a thin layer of dust and dirt.

Rand and Arusi looked at me like I was a grenade with the pin pulled out. But I simply breathed out, embers flying. "Well then," I said, because there was nothing else to say. "Let's let them out. We have to get out of here."

Arusi and Rand wordlessly used their disrupter wands to break the shielding interface panels that kept the dragons inside. Arusi and Rand knew how to handle themselves around rogue dragons. As soon as the shields were down, they pulled out laser whips set to stun, taking wary stances, their backs to the wall so they could keep an eye on both dragons at the same time. Normally these dragons were our friends, but right now, their extended confinement might have made them more wily than usual.

I took no such precautions as I made my way over to my deep black dragon empty-handed, the wingless creature hissed at me with a look in her eye she rarely ever showed me. A warning look. Right now, she was dangerous, even to me.

"Kahmel, be careful!" Arusi warned.

But in this state of mind, I knew how dragons worked. Maybe a little more than my friends did right now.

Dragons respected power, and their favored form of asserting dominance was intimidation. The dragon snarled at me and charged. Arusi and Rand called out just as she stopped a few steps in front of me. She looked me in the eye. A moment passed as she stood there. Then she recoiled, backing away, an almost fearful look in her eye.

I didn't blame her. I was different, and she wasn't used to it yet. She would be, though.

Slinging myself onto her back as Rand and Arusi stood in silence, I said, "Let's go. The dragons were the last thing we needed. Now we have no reason to come back here."

Everything was moving *so* fast. Jashi was gone in the blink of an eye. And from now on, everything was going to be turned on its head because I was pulling a full reverse. But none of that mattered.

I sensed the argument rise up in the set of Rand's jaw, but he clamped it down, saying nothing. I knew his feelings on this; he hated this plan, but he knew I wasn't going to change my mind. There was only one thing I was worried about. I just hoped Jashi would forgive me. The man she loved had to take the backseat for a bit. He'd be back when we were able to be together again. Until then, I was someone else. Even *I* wasn't sure what I was capable of at this point. And the scariest part? I didn't care.

PATIENCE GAME

Jashi Anyua-Omah

For a minute, I was back at the palace, warm and in Kahmel's arms. He ran his fingers through my hair and kissed my head gently. I leaned into his embrace...and my mind stirred, the cocoon of comfort fading as reality took over again. My back pressed against a hard surface, my mouth was gagged, and my arms ached as they knocked awkwardly on the floor, restrained by the handcuffs that held them in place. Hunger racked my insides.

I was captured.

Kahmel was gone. For the first time since we'd been married and I ran away from him what felt like decades ago, I was alone. No one was here to save me. He could try. He *would* try, because he was Kahmel, and he wouldn't let me go without a fight. I knew. He would burn the world for me. But even that wouldn't save me. The reality started to sink in as my head rolled to the side, my eyes heavy.

I wanted to stay focused on the present, but being left on the floor with nothing to do but think, my mind couldn't help but drift to thoughts of futility. Zendaal was the one place in the world Kahmel wouldn't be able to come and get me from. Frustration gnawed, clawed at my insides.

The Zendaalans protected their borders viciously. The details danced just out of my focus, but I remembered Kahmel telling me about it, and the thought of his soothing voice settled my mind better into the memory, a minuscule safe place for my thoughts to rest in for a moment.

It had been when we were having a rare conversation about the reality of waging a war with Zendaal. Those kinds of conversations were few and far between because the threat of being overheard was even more lethal than our other blasphemous discussions.

Kahmel had said getting to Zendaal would be near impossible for the rebels, which was why we needed the help of dragons to hope to oppose them in war. More dragons than we could tame on our own because it would take too long to find enough for the scale of battle he was proposing. We would need the dragons on our side just to get over the border.

Factions of the rebellion were nonexistent in Zendaal. And the border was hard to cross, even legally. The Equalizers didn't allow any international travel without proper visas, not even for overnight stays. The visas were notoriously hard to get. Most people got denied unless they were in Zendaal for work. And even with that, the waiting list for approval took so long it was hardly worth it.

Back when Kahmel and I went to Vahdel, a country given the label of rebel, it took months to arrange for all of the inside help we needed to perform the operation from K'sundi. But for Kahmel to arrange a trip to Zendaal...if he thought we needed all of the dragons in K'sundi put together just to get in, there was no way he could come for me.

In the swampy mess that was my drug-addled mind, I tried to fish for any scrap of information I could remember about the Zendaalans. Something I could use to my advantage. They used cybernetic technology for a reason. They weren't like other Hemmorans. As much as I hated world history class in school, even *I* remembered the history of the Zendaalans. How they were a race that nearly died out almost a millennium ago, ironically enough, because of their own crude practices. Zendaal once had royalty, too. And to maintain their supposedly "pure" bloodline, they took up the practice of marrying cousins to one another. Sometimes the relatives they married weren't even that far apart. The royalty's practice and their purist mentality spread to their people until, as disturbing as it was, it was almost unheard of in the country to marry outside of the family. But history was weird and creepy like that, and that was what birthed the purist mindset of the Equalizers, the obsession with borders and labeling people as acquiescing or not. Unable to deal with or tolerate anyone that disagreed with their way of thinking. They only ever married family, people who never disagreed with them or thought differently than they were used to.

As could be expected, their marriage practices made their lineage weak over the years, dipping into the same tired gene pool over and over. Weak and susceptible to the disease that nearly wiped their entire country out. One that made their bones brittle and shut down their organs one by one, like a wicked entity that decided they truly were machines and set to turn them off, one system at a time. When other nations learned of the disease ravaging the Zendaalans, the roles of today were reversed, and the Zendaalans found themselves without a friend as the world's borders closed to them for fear of the sickness's spread.

The Zendaalans struggled to contain the sickness, later called the Withering, but to no avail. Because, as they were discovering, the Withering wasn't *caught* but *passed down*. It was a sickness that had slowly developed in their bloodline over decades, turning up as a family member here or there who was known to be sickly. The illness grew to take its ultimate form once it was too strong to stop. The disease, fully developed, could manifest itself in a Zendaalan's life at any age, lying dormant in their blood until that moment. It turned each Zendaalan into a virtual ticking time bomb, no idea when their life was destined to meet a sickly, broken end.

Around that same time, though, their researchers were developing the world's first automated technology. And out of desperation for a solution to somehow survive as a race, they used their automations to replace body parts that no longer worked on their own.

The development of the technology went slowly as they learned how to make their prototypes stable and get human physiology and machines to work in tandem. By the time the technology functioned reliably, the sickness had ravaged nearly every Zendaalan in the country. It was now hereditary for all of them.

But then the technology was completed. They were able to replace nearly anything that was no longer working, and the Zendaalans were reborn with the Withering in one hand and their cybernetic solution in the other. Cursed to live with both.

That was around the same time the idea of the Equalization took form. As the technology to save their race developed, they realized another problem that came along with it—the likelihood of fighting breaking out over it. Zendaal wouldn't survive a civil war. The royals, because they were royals, got a hold of the new technology first. They came up with the simple idea that peace had to be agreed upon for it to be maintained. And any who disagreed were labeled rebels, turning them into targets for all the people to take down in order to maintain the peace they so desperately needed in order to survive long enough to see the new technology save them all.

When the world finally reopened their borders to the newly made cyborg race, they opened it to a people that had not only miraculously recovered with impressive new technology, but had mastered the art of peace. Violence dwindled into almost nothing in Zendaal, and their desperation resulted in amazingly quick technological development. And suddenly, the world went from shunning them to hungry for answers on how it was done. The Zendaalans, changed in practice but not mind, were all too happy to share their beliefs the only way they knew how—stripping away anything they didn't recognize as their own, assimilating others to their way, and treating the noncompliant as enemies only fit for destruction.

My head rattled as the hovercar passed through turbulence. Thoughts tumbled through as well. The grogginess was dissipating, and I felt like I'd struck upon something important in my ruminating. There was something there, something in their history that didn't quite make sense. Maybe I'd been around Kahmel too long, turning me into a sort of scholar of my own. I never thought I'd be poring over all the details of history texts in my head, but here I was.

A thought occurred to me—what if their history *did* make sense, but it was the *present* that didn't? The world had agreed to the Zendaalans' idea of peace. Blinded by technological advancements and pretty words, they ignored the fact that the sellers of this peace had caused their own catastrophes, and the way they solved social problems was to eradicate people's identities in order to make them easier to deal with.

But then, why would Zendaal monitor their Equalized nations so heavily? Why so many threats when the whole world went willingly into their Equalization? And ultimately, why protect their borders so viciously when no one would dream of doing their precious Equalizers harm?

The thought crept up like a lizard sneaking out of a crevice to peer at the sun, test the air, and see if it was warm enough to come out.

Half-Drac! came Ocean's frustrated voice.

I'd been so deep in thought I didn't realize she'd been trying to talk to me this entire time. I took a breath as best I could through the gag. Was I really convinced my dragon was talking to me in my head? On one hand, I was probably on enough sedatives to take down a horse and shouldn't pay anything in my headspace too much mind. But if I wasn't hallucinating...this could be advantageous.

I'm sorry, what is it, Ocean? I conveyed.

Now that I was paying attention, her panic poured into me with such overwhelming strength, the lines between my emotions and Ocean's blurred, infusing me with cold fear that made my heart pound and my face sweat.

Ocean was fervent. Antsy, itching, and desperate for me to be *anywhere* but where I was. The fact that I wasn't free right this instant gnawed at her like a parasite, urging her to do something about it.

We have to get you out of there, Half-Drac.

I stifled a cry as the hovercar jerked and my head bounced against the floor. Cautioning a glance upward, I saw Attican and the K'sundi man watching the sky. I shut my eyes, a small strategy forming beneath the waves of panic and confusion from my and my dragon's combined emotions. I would have to practice steady breathing while pretending to be asleep but *absolutely not* sleeping for as long as I could manage. Ocean projected her enthusiasm through our bond, but even if she could rip me out of this car, I recognized the bulky protrusions in the sides of the vehicle. Laser cannons. They would shoot at her if she took to the skies to come get me. Dragons without riders were wily. They didn't have the strategy riders could implement. Dragons fought headfirst. That sort of plan worked when dragons unleashed an onslaught with numbers on their side but didn't work as well when they were on their own. And Attican and the K'sundi man both had laser guns at their sides, along with rifles. My captors were armed to the teeth. Ocean didn't stand a chance.

Let's think this through, I reasoned calmly. If she could send me panic, maybe I could send her comfort. Something we both needed right now. *Where will we go?* I asked, rather than insulting her pride by implying she couldn't handle the fight on her own. She was still a dragon, after all. *I can't cross the border like you can. They'll detect me.*

Ocean's snarl rippled through me, threatening to elicit from me a snarl of my own. I bit my lip to keep it down.

We should chance the border. You know who he is now, don't you?

I'd nearly forgotten Ocean asked me to talk to the K'sundii man earlier. Remembering the conversation, I wanted to curl my lip on my own this time. But I avoided making any facial expression except serene sleep.

I know he's creepy, a traitor to K'sundi, but what else is there to know?

Exactly! Ocean said, like that was all I needed to know about him. *However dangerous it may be in enemy territory, it's better than being in his hands.*

This was getting us nowhere. I had no idea why Ocean was so adamant about my not being around some K'sundii-cyborg man she couldn't possibly know, but I needed to calm her down before she did something rash.

Don't do anything. I sent command and order into my mental voice, and her anger subdued slightly in obedience. If there was anything I learned about dealing with dragons, mentally or otherwise, it was that you couldn't let your authority waver. Never let them thrash under your control. *We're going to wait,* I said. I would need Ocean to come in and rescue me. She was right that anywhere was better than here, even if I had to live in hiding for a bit while I came up with a plan. Not like I hadn't done that before.

The past held an answer for me somewhere. Not only on how to leave the country, but now that I was here in the middle of Zendaal, it had me thinking about what exactly the Equalizers were keeping from us by protecting their borders so viciously. Something tugged on the recesses of my mind. There was something here, something that could free us of the Zendaalans for good. It danced just out of reach. I needed to not be drugged to figure it out—and a good meal.

If you rush in without a plan, you will be destroyed, I hissed at Ocean.

She receded further into submission and grudgingly admitted I was right even as she transmitted a surge of anger that meant she didn't like it.

You will come and rescue me, I said, and her spirits lifted a little. *But I'll choose the moment to do so. We only have one shot at this, so we have to choose wisely.*

Ocean grunted in acquiescence. It was as much of an agreement as I was going to get.

CHANGE OF TERMS

At some point, I must have fallen asleep—real sleep, not a drug-induced hammer to the head. When I woke up, it took a bit for the fatigue to leave me. Staying awake but keeping my eyes closed when groggy wasn't the easiest thing in the world. I pitched a thought to Ocean, using her like a tether to the world of the waking.

Ocean, are you there? I said, just to say something. Obviously, she was there. I'd found that even if she was asleep, I could pitch my thoughts like psychic pebbles until she woke up, a fact that further grounded me in the belief that our telepathic connection was very real. I didn't think hallucinations would go so far as to need sleep.

Ocean's mental attention turning to me brought me precious awareness, letting me feel conscious of her surroundings, if I couldn't be completely connected to mine yet. When I sent my thoughts to her, it was like tuning into a private channel between us. I started getting a feed of what she was doing and feeling in this moment—and it made my stomach turn a little. A small animal trapped under her claws meowed. Ocean's teeth snapped closed around its head, bringing it to a swift end. Then she went to work on her meal.

The perspective was hard to describe. I couldn't see what Ocean was seeing, but I was tapped into her other senses, and I was aware of her body. I could hear the snap of bones as she ate, feel her claws become slick with warm liquid, the same substance dripping down her chin. I could feel the small animal in her grasp, as if the dragon's hands were my own.

I bit down the roll of nausea. Finding something to eat in the city must have been hard. Pride replaced my initial disgust as I realized that Ocean, though young, was mature enough not to act out or see humans as a quick meal. It came with her ZST training not to see humans as edible despite the fact that humans *could* make up a dragon's major food group. But the Drake Bond undid that training, and in spite of the freedom to have a much bigger meal than a measly cat, Ocean chose to make do. Here, without dragon riders to keep her in line, without stables to keep her contained. Perhaps fully trained dragons required none of that. Dragons weren't pets. They were our companions. Feeling Ocean's mind revealed so much about their nature to me, on some subconscious level. Her memory was long. Lessons, once learned, weren't easily forgotten. Something told me that even if we'd been separated for years, perhaps even decades, she would still answer to the sound of my voice, recognize it. Drake Bonded or not.

I'm here, Half-Drac, she said as her head snapped up and turned, as if she was looking at me. I knew she trailed the hovercar from a few miles away, following our bond. If I concentrated hard enough, I could sense it too. The invisible tether between us stretched with the distance. If I strained, I could detect the direction the tether led to, right at the lap of the dragon on the other end of it.

Ocean's ears pulled back, and a snarl gurgled from her throat as her thoughts flashed to the K'sundii man. *Has he done something to you?*

I just woke up, I reassured her, finally able to stay awake more easily.

I went still, and Ocean, sensing it, asked, *What is it?*

The hovercar's stopped, I thought, more to myself than Ocean. I woke up because the hovercar stopped. My captors were gone. I felt it under my skin, the lack of human presence here with me, and I risked opening my eyes to confirm it. The two seats to the side of me were empty. Looking up, I saw not a blue sky or a starry night, but a dark gray ceiling and bulkheads overhead.

We'd apparently arrived at our destination.

I turned my attention from Ocean, tuned into my own ears, and held my breath to hear muffled words being spoken outside of the vehicle. It sounded like Zendaalan. Then footsteps.

I shut my eyes a split second before the doors of the car swung open.

"Is she asleep?" asked someone in Zendaalan. Not Attican or Mystery Man.

"Lightly, if she is." This was Mystery Man. Hearing him and Attican talk during the ride here helped me remember the Zendaalan I'd learned in school. I could understand most of what they were saying. "We last sedated her more than a few hours ago. She'll need to be newly sedated before we can move her."

That meant if Ocean was going to come help me break free, it was now or never.

Ocean—

The hovercar leaned, interrupting my train of thought, as someone stepped into the vehicle with me. The doors slid closed again, and rough hands grabbed me...unlocking my handcuffs?

"Deklas?" asked a confused Attican from outside the car.

Someone pounded on the door amidst muttering from some other Zendaalans. This was not supposed to be happening.

I snapped up, my sleeping act abandoned, and faced the man standing over me. He was bending down, his face inches from mine. His red-orange eyes focused on me, eyebrow raised, as though faintly entertained by the shock on my face. The chrome patching his ash-brown skin and whirring in his shoulder—his left arm was completely replaced with machinery, I realized—felt like a lie to his demeanor, smooth and easy. Fluid, with an expression like he saw this whole situation as somewhat funny. The K'sundii man.

I slid away from him, pressing my back against the wall of the car. My breathing came in quick huffs as I braced my fingers against the floor, ready to launch myself away from him. My skin, my entire body, clawed at me with the need, and this time I wasn't sure if it came from me or Ocean. *Away, away, away*, it screamed. Not fear. Aversion. Like two magnets of the same charge, *repulsed*. But why?

The man turned to the door, as if considering the pounding, the Zendaalans demanding his explanation in clipped, cold commands. A strange cybernetic implant on his right bicep caught my attention. It was very precise, an oval, a familiar shape, but I couldn't place where I'd seen it before.

His attention returned to me. "I can't let them have you," he said in K'sundii. So matter-of-factly. No, not matter-of-fact...more like he'd just decided and was realizing it out loud. He moved close, and I flinched, but he only untied my gag, then moved to the driver's seat.

The Zendaalan men looked through the window above my head, barking orders to Mystery Man. What did they call him? Deklas? They demanded that he open the door immediately. I distinctly picked up the words *this was not part of the deal*, muffled as they were through the window. My mind tried to pick apart the situation that was unfolding.

This man, this *Deklas*, was a key player in all of this. Deklas, whom Ocean somehow expected me to recognize from a single conversation, whom Ocean hated with every fiber of her being despite the impossibility of her knowing him. He, who must have aided in my capture, possibly even orchestrated it. He, who had an air about him, one that set him apart from just any ordinary man taking orders. A leader, not a follower to anyone no matter what plan he supposedly agreed to.

Deklas, the cybernetic K'sundii man with a strange Zendaalan name, was saving me. Saving me, not because he'd intended to all along, playing along with the Zendaalans so he could get close, rescue me when I needed it most, but because he simply decided to do so, possibly no more than five minutes ago.

The sound of engines running drowned out the protests of the Zendaalans standing around us. "Brace yourself" was the only warning I got before he threw on the acceleration. The hovercar swerved around in a wide arc, and I was flung against the back door, thanking the Spirits he'd locked it as soon as he came in with me. The car, completing its arc, righted itself.

And then Deklas ran over every Zendaalan standing in his way.

I felt a prickling between my temples. It came in surges until I realized that Ocean was now sending *me* psychic pebbles to get my attention. *Half-Drac, Half Drac,* came Ocean's frantic voice. *What were you going to say? What's happening?*

I wished I knew. As I found my seat beside him and buckled in, where he'd been sitting not more than a few hours ago when I was still gagged and bound, bodies thumped against the vehicle, making it jerk as he plowed through them. Out of the corner of my eye, I saw a few slowly stirring from where they landed on ground, but a couple didn't move at all, blood pooling around them in a sickening red halo. Deklas was killing them like they were flies hitting the glass rather than people. The sight made my stomach turn, seeing their arms and necks bent at wrong angles, crumpled like broken toys. I had no way of knowing if Attican was among the corpses because we were moving too fast. And a shred of guilt nipped at me for hoping he was.

My hands tightened on the seat and my eyes widened as I stared out the windshield. We were inside a massive building, barreling right for the huge doors. The *closed* huge doors. I looked from the doors, to Deklas, then back again. How was he going to get through those solid-looking gates?

He pressed a few buttons and startled me as he leaned over me, no regard for my personal space, his shoulder pressed against my breasts as he fumbled around. Before I could roil with anger, I realized he'd opened a screen. The controls for the laser cannons.

Sliding back over to his place, he said, "If you don't want to die from hitting those steel doors, I suggest you fire."

Half-Drac... Ocean seethed. She knew whom I was with, and once again I ground my teeth with frustration at not knowing who he was. But how did she know?

I didn't have time to think about it. *Stand by,* I told her, and then I obeyed Deklas. The controls weren't hard to understand. With a few taps, the cannons took a second to warm.

And then fired.

The blast recoiled through the vehicle. This thing was meant for battle. The steel doors blew away in a mess of red-hot shrapnel.

And then the sky arched overhead.

We were out.

A shaky breath pushed past my throat. My hands trembled, my mind still reeling. We were driving down a runway, so we'd been inside a hangar. Not where they launched hovercars, but *battle*cars. That's what I'd been traveling in all this time, one of the battlecars the Zendaalans used to navigate cities under their reign and act as law enforcement when they so chose.

I tensed again as a ringing noise pulsed throughout the car. The control screen for the weapons was replaced by a call screen. I moved to swipe it away, like it was a grenade on the screen instead of a call, but as I put my hand forward, Deklas crossed his arm in front of mine, once again uncomfortably close. Horror flashed through me as he answered the call.

"Yes, I gather you're displeased," he responded before they could even start speaking, voice clipped and hard, and I wondered why he bothered answering at all if he was going to treat them with such disdain anyway. I clenched my fists to bite down my annoyance at the way he leaned toward me to speak into the call, his eyes on the road. His invasion of my personal space didn't feel lustful. More like I was a large rag doll annoyingly getting in his way when he needed his controls.

It was Attican's voice, ragged and heated, and that same guilty part of me that hoped he was dead cursed quietly. "What do you think you're doing?"

"I've changed the terms," came his simple answer. He cocked his head to the side, challenging Attican to say otherwise. And then he had the nerve to glance at me like we were sharing some kind of joke.

What the hell was even happening right now?

Attican barked with surprise. "You think this is a game, Deklas? You owe us *everything*. Don't think you can just prance around doing whatever you like and we'll tolerate it. You killed *several* of our men today!"

Deklas chuckled, leaning over to the other side of his seat lazily, looking out at the city that slowly appeared over the long concrete stretch of the runway. Then he glanced down at his prosthetic arm. "Do I seem like a man that cares much about death? You know who I am."

I frowned. Who *was* he?

Attican growled in frustration on the other end, and before he could respond, he was cut off by someone else taking over the call. "Deklas," said the new voice. A woman. "This is Prexa." Prexa's dark hair, streaked with white, contrasted starkly with her pale skin. When she spoke, a metal tongue moved behind her teeth, and the unnaturally bright blue of her eyes told me they were fake, but otherwise, her face was unblemished.

"Finally," said Deklas, driving smoothly into the Zendaalan city. It stretched out and up, incredibly tall buildings clawing at the sky, summing up quite nicely the sensory overload I was feeling at the moment, with flashing images on every turn, screens lighting almost every building with words and characters and people sliding across the displays at a rate impossible to take in all at once.

Prexa, whoever she was, said calmly, "You would like to change the terms. What are they?"

"Have you begun contacting Kahmel Omah?"

I stiffened at Kahmel's name, my head whipping around to face Deklas. That look of amusement was back, and he winked, as though willing me to stay silent a moment longer. *Just wait, I'm getting to the good part*, that look seemed to say.

"Yes," Prexa said, annoyance seeping into her calm intonations. "As that was the arrangement. He's on the line now. He agreed to the terms, as you know."

Bile rose in my throat and my eyes burned. Kahmel. No, no, no.

He couldn't have. He *shouldn't* have. There was only one thing the Zendaalans could have asked for in exchange for my safe return. His surrendering of the throne. Our throne.

His oath to Aithel. I shook my head in denial. He couldn't do it because of his promise to Aithel. The marks on his arms—as much as they hurt him even when he was doing according to his word, they would kill him if he broke his promise.

But then I remembered the kind of man I was married to. Kahmel spent most of his life studying ancient laws; it was in his blood. His parents were scholars. Where they used their position for prestige, Kahmel used his inherited talents to bend the rules just enough to get his way but not break them. It would be just like him to find a loophole in an oath to a Dragon King.

He would give up on K'sundi for me, I realized with sickening horror. He had to know I would be furious. And I knew he was willing to let me hate him to get me back.

I hadn't even recovered from hearing those words before Deklas spoke again. "Tell him whatever you like, but the deal is off."

As he looked at me, a twisted grin on his face, his words from earlier made my blood cold. *I can't let them have you.*

He wasn't talking about the Zendaalans. He was talking about Kahmel and his people. The Zendaalans had been preparing to complete their negotiations with Kahmel. Probably show me alive and well on camera, finish the deal. Deklas didn't want to hand me over.

"He won't be happy about that," warned Prexa. "His people will fight you as long as you have her."

"Let them come." Sick glee lit Deklas's red eyes as he looked at me again. "She's too fascinating to part with. As hard as he'll fight to get her back, I'll fight harder to keep her. Have your people prepare my mansion. We'll be arriving shortly."

I wasn't being saved. Deklas had simply decided to keep me to himself.

THREATS AND ULTIMATUMS

Kahmel Axon Kai of the Omah Clan

I was alone in one of the rooms on the second floor of our latest hideaway—a dilapidated apartment building that smelled of mildew and stifled air. We had commandeered the livable floors, namely, the first, second, and fifth. The fourth had so much water damage in the floor, with enough pressure, it might have created beautiful high ceilings for the third.

The rebels had old punching bags they used to train new recruits, so I had one of those standing in the corner of the room now. Actually, several were lined up on the damaged wood floor, along with a bucket of water. Angry holes rimmed with black burn marks riddled two of the bags already. Besides the one I had hanging up, there were two good ones left, but the one I had hanging was already developing two big black spots where I punched and kicked it. The air stank of burning rubber.

Barefoot, my hands wrapped, I threw punches. I didn't even know how long I'd been here. Clearly, this had gone beyond training. It just felt good to hit something. With every other punch, I lit the end of my knuckles in flames, further scorching the bag upon impact. Calling the flame like that required just the right amount of focus to pull my mind away from my thoughts yet still felt automatic to some degree.

Rand hadn't been talking to me lately. Neither had Arusi, Khes, or Asan. The only ones who dared strike up some conversation with me, the brooding dragon, were the faithful dragon riders. We invited them to join the rebellion shortly after Jashi was taken. For one, if Jashi, being the Faresha, wasn't safe, we didn't think it would take the Zendaalans long to go after the dragon riders that I had been training with for over a year. As a result, the dragon riders were part of my entourage, so to speak, along with Rand, Arusi, Khes, and Asan.

The ones who knew me best didn't bother to ask what my plan was, now that we had stolen our dragons back. Or rather, the dragons we had left, since Ocean had disappeared. Most likely, my friends didn't want to know. But the dragon riders, not having known me as long as the others had, asked. And I told them. They didn't like the answer, but as the others knew and the dragon riders were learning, I had made up my mind and there was no changing it.

We were giving in.

As my leg made furious contact with the punching bag in an arc of fire, the fabric finally burst, and my toes sank into the cotton inside. Stumbling for a moment, I pulled my foot free, then simply switched back to punching, deciding to wear out the bag in other areas entirely before switching to a new one. Sweat dripped from my uncovered arms. The inky black lines snaking along them gently throbbed with pain, serving as a reminder that giving up was almost as risky as not. Aithel, though kind once reasoned with, wouldn't hesitate a moment to use the tattoos of my oath to him to kill me if I didn't seek some other way to protect his dragons, including the Half-Dracs, as we were considered honorary dragons by the Dragon Kings.

Not being Faresh anymore meant I'd have to act fast. There was no saving Jashi if I was dead. First, there were the Half-Dracs. If the K'sundii Court wouldn't protect them, we would have to protect them from the shadows. Make them join the rebellion and squirrel them away like Matrion Taias did for me and Rand. Next, the dragons. Jashi figured out the missing piece in that puzzle. Drake Bonds, the process of using a command word to bond oneself to a dragon, could break the chains of the ZST training, bring their minds back.

If I used the Half-Dracs we rescued and trained them to do that, to find and restore collared dragons while we hid in the underground, my promise to Aithel would be fulfilled, and I didn't need to be Faresh to do either of those things.

Which meant I was free to give in.

The Zendaalans would have only seized Jashi with one objective in mind. I had beat them to the offer, but they were going to give it anyway because they wanted to be sure Jashi and I would stay out of the way. Killing Jashi would have only spurred my wrath, and there was nothing I wouldn't have done to avenge her. They knew that. So the only option they had left was to give her back now that I'd surrendered.

Tending to the Half-Dracs and any dragons we rescued was going to have to suffice for my promise to Aithel to protect the dragons and restore them to their former glory. The Zendaalans wouldn't be defeated, so they would continue to make more ZST dragons, but the rebellion was worldwide. If we continued to spread our techniques on taming and recovering them peacefully, rebels everywhere would be able to use that information to their advantage.

It wasn't what Jashi and I dreamed up at first, but it would have to do. Right now, she was my highest priority. I didn't care if everything else fell away. I would find the farthest, most secluded place I could find. An island somewhere. I'd hide us away and never reemerge. Khes could retake his place as rebel leader. Jashi and I could raise our dragons in our faraway paradise. We could even take some Half-Dracs with us, if they wanted to come, though it would come with the condition that they would never be able to go back to where they came from. I wouldn't take any chances of our discovery.

Rand was disappointed, I knew. So were the others. At the moment, they were upset with me, but soon they'd see there was no other way. The Zendaalans had won, and there was nothing else we could have done. We were no closer to figuring out how to reach

Obellana—the last Dragon Queen we needed to have the Dragon Kings completely on our side to retake what the Zendaalans laid claim on–than we were months ago, when the information would have been relevant. When I still had a throne to promise her that could save her dragons and get rid of the Zendaalans that enslaved them. We were farther still from the promise to make K'sundi see the error in their ways, to convince them that our lives were better off without the Equalizers, if only on the principle of hating them for what they'd stolen from us, the identities we were forced to hide and smother away.

But K'sundi had made it abundantly clear that no matter how much I showed them, no matter how much I loved them, they would always love their false sense of peace more.

Another rip tore open in the punching bag as I sent my fist through weak, blackened fabric. I shook the lint off my hand and stepped around it, picking another angle.

There was a knock at the door.

"Kahmel?" T'shan edged through the door as though I would explode in flames at any minute. The others probably sent him in because they were tired of talking to me. I was getting tired of them, too, so I was glad for it.

"What is it?" I rasped between breaths, chest heaving.

He swallowed, and I knew he was scared. Which meant I knew what this was about. "You were right. The Zendaalans sent word. They want to talk."

It was time.

ATTICAN APPEARED on the screen in front of us despite the fact that he was supposed to be dead, but that wasn't even what I had an issue with. Prexa, an esteemed congresswoman in Zendaal, stood beside him. She worked very close to the president himself. The Zendaaalans were no longer pretending their highest officials weren't involved in the sabotage of K'sundi. At least not here, now. The gloves were off, on both sides.

That wasn't the problem, either. No, the thing I had a problem with was that we'd waited for the good part of an hour before they showed up. Without Jashi.

"Where is she?" I asked in a low voice.

"The terms of our agreement have changed," said Attican, and for a moment, I almost believed he was disgruntled about it. The way he didn't want to look at the camera said even he didn't like the idea of what he was saying.

But I was running on blind fury. Hatred seeped from my pores, and I wasn't willing to listen to anything that didn't go in my favor. The Zendaalans didn't understand who they were speaking to, they couldn't understand, because *I* didn't know who they were talking to either. The man before them wasn't surrendering K'sundi because they were forcing him to. I didn't wait for a call when Jashi was taken. I told Arusi to contact the Zendaalans the second I found out Jashi was in Zendaal. I gave K'sundi up, not because I had to, but because I didn't *want* it anymore. Who would want a country that couldn't even keep its own Faresha in the comfort of her own home? Certainly not me.

So I wasn't interested in any terms. I was never following them to begin with.

"Where is she?" I repeated, and the still calm that was my voice sounded lethal, even to my own ears.

Arusi and Rand, at either side of me, remained silent. They didn't know how to deal with me anymore, but I knew they would back me up in front of the enemy no matter what. Besides, I may have lost my wife, but they'd both lost not only their friend but their Faresha. Perhaps I'd gone off the deep end on behalf of both of them. They wanted to lose it, I knew. But they were still being cautious. By the looks on their faces, though, I wondered how long they would stick to that plan.

Prexa didn't flinch. "You surrendered your country, Omah.

Rather quickly, really." She turned the edge of her lips just slightly, as though she thought I'd be ashamed of that fact. "We don't have t—"

"You can take K'sundi," I cut her off, because I could see where this was going. They thought this conversation was over, and they were going to deny me and end the call. But that wasn't how this was going to go down. "Give it to whatever puppet king will kiss your asses enough to make you happy. I don't care." I stood and moved closer to the camera. Arusi and Rand shifted in their seats as their energy also shifted. Their fear of this new me had been replaced by anger. They were pissed. *We* were pissed.

"There won't be a K'sundi worth inheriting when I'm done with it," I hissed. "In a few short years, I built this country up. You think I can't tear it down?" I meant it. I meant every word. I would *destroy* K'sundi if they didn't give my wife back. And it would be easy. So much easier than getting them on my side, really. Satisfying, even.

"What should we care if you do?" droned Prexa. "The Equalization is for those who want it. We don't need K'sundi." But I heard it. Her voice, just an octave higher than it should be at the end. She was lying through her teeth with that silver tongue.

"No," I challenged. And I dredged up a memory I only went to when it was absolutely necessary. And even then, I'd only ever gone over the entirety of the details once. With my wife. "I remember that day I almost died. When I was discovered as Half-Drac." I pulled up the sleeve of my shirt, showing a scar I'd only shown Rand because he was my brother, and Jashi because I was desperate for her to trust me, and because I loved her. The wrinkled, pink patch of skin the size of a bullet hole where a tube had been driven up and in me, extracting something, before I broke from my binds and ripped it out. "You need K'sundi. Probably more than any other country in the Equalization. Because of the Half-Dracs."

I snarled, and finally Prexa flinched, though whether it was because I was snarling at her with my shirt half-off or because I was finally on to something, I didn't know. "I'll leave K'sundi to burn. But I'll find every Half-Drac in this country and keep them from you.

And maybe I'll finally find out what you've been doing with us—by seeing how well you fare without us."

I had no way of knowing if what I'd said was a true threat to them, and it was contrary to my always carefully planned maneuvers in the past. It seemed I'd picked up some of Jashi's bold and free-spirited thinking that got her *into* as much trouble as it had saved her butt and mine from on multiple occasions. And I finally understood where she was coming from. Because the more I spoke, the more it made sense. The more the pieces we'd been missing all this time were starting to fall together.

The Zendaalans needed us. *Prexa* was the one bluffing. And when she gave her short, clipped, "We're done with this conversation," signaling for someone to end the call, I knew I was right.

The screen shut off, leaving me, Rand, and Arusi alone in a run-down apartment bedroom.

"What's the plan?" Rand asked, and the cold tone in his voice told me all I needed to know.

Arusi nodded, agreeing with Rand.

They were in.

"They're going to give Jashi back," I said. "Or we raise hell."

ENEMY

Jashi Anyua-Omah

I shot from my seat and backed up, pressing my back against the wall behind me, the cramped space too small to get away from the man beside me. The few feet I put between us wasn't far enough.

Deklas tapped a few buttons and allowed the battlecar to cruise, then twisted his chair to face me, hands folded in his lap. He raised an eyebrow, as if waiting to see what I would do.

I curled my hands into fists, ready to fight like hell.

My hands lit up in flames, and Deklas sighed, as though disappointed I didn't come up with anything more creative. But I didn't care about being elegant when trying to kick his ass and take over this whole damn battlecar.

Fire blazing at my fists, I lunged for him. He shot out of his seat and twisted, moving like water. His hand closed around my wrist and he inhaled, my flames flowing off me and into his mouth—like Kahmel had done when we first got married. Except this man's steel grip was painful. He exhaled embers into my face with a jeer. I tried to summon my flames, but it was like Deklas was smothering my *powers*, not just the fire, as he held to my wrist. I jerked my arm, trying to free it from his grip, but he just clenched harder, staring me in the eye, a grin on his face.

A Half-Drac. Deklas wasn't just dragon tribe. He was a Half-Drac.

More pieces to the puzzle as to why Ocean hated him and somehow expected me to know what he was at just a glance. Dragons could certainly tell when someone was a Half-Drac. Did she expect me to be able to do the same? Know that I was being betrayed by one of my own?

But it didn't make sense. My brows drew together as I studied the aged sag around his eyes. He was at least forty. Why would the Zendaalans have preserved this one? Why not kill him at age eighteen like all the others? How could they have known he would choose their side? Was it because they raised him? Allowed him to learn to use his powers on his own, like Kahmel did? Kahmel was only a teenager when he learned to use his fire reliably, and that was without knowing who he really was. He'd only had a few more years of experience since. How much farther ahead would he be if he'd had as much time as Deklas had?

Deklas watched the understanding dawn on my face that he was much better than me with the flames. Even better than Kahmel.

"Pity." He pinned my arms down as I struggled against him. He frowned at me. "I thought you'd be better than this."

He shook his head in disappointment as he pushed me away, watching me. It couldn't be more obvious he didn't see me as a threat, and it made fury push from my nostrils in embers. I swung at him with an angry growl—and he simply stepped to the side, then swiped his leg into mine and sent me sprawling. I sailed head-first into the control panel.

Blinding pain rattled through my head, and I pushed myself up on shaky legs, my vision doubling. Deklas made no move to get me away from the control panel, so I pressed on it, then hissed in frustration as I found it locked. Of course.

No wonder he was calm—there was nothing I could do with the controls locked and the destination set. And I was clearly no match for him. I had no tricks to pull. We were flying stories high; it wasn't like I could jump from here. And even if I could, the doors were locked.

He didn't have to do a damn thing.

I wanted to sink to the floor and cry, but I refused to do that in front of him. Lifting my chin, I seethed, "What the do you want with me?"

Ocean. I still had Ocean. This car would have to stop when we got to his mansion, and that would be my opportunity to have Ocean come and break me away from him. But I still wanted to know.

Deklas tilted his head, considering. "You're a worthy opponent."

As useless as I felt, the comment landed like an insult. "What does that mean?"

Deklas sat back in the driver's seat, turning it to face me. "From what the Zendaalans told me, you've come a long way given how little you had to work with. Both of you, really."

Did he mean me and Kahmel? "Who are you?" I demanded, more confused than ever.

"Dekaar," he answered, entertainment in his eyes. "The Zendaalans call me what they pronounce more easily, but I prefer my K'sundii name."

I clenched my fists. "Who *are* you, *Dekaar*?"

He flinched. But just as quickly, the look was gone. He steepled his fingers over his lap and tilted his head to look down on me. "Now that your husband has stepped down, I will become Faresh. His family is on my side. They will lie and say I am related. Kahmel's brothers won't oppose my rule because I will give them all positions that will keep them content. K'sundi will no longer oppose Zendaal under me, thus the Zendaalans will be content as well." He spread his hands, as though laying the matter plainly out for me. "I am your enemy."

Ocean's snarl buzzed in my head, and I remembered I'd asked her to hold on standby back when I thought *Dekaar* was helping me.

Well, that explained why the Zendaalans seemed to answer to him somehow. They needed him to take over K'sundi. But why go through so much trouble for *him*? Why allow him to make a split-second decision, kill several of their men, and get away? Surely they could have used any K'sundii willing to sell us out. The Court was full of them.

Keep an eye on me, I told Ocean. *We'll be making our escape soon.*

Ocean sent a happy grin, and I focused on biding my time. Figuring this man out. He liked my attitude? I could give him plenty.

My lip curled. "So you'll be the Zendaalans' lapdog for the throne? Let yourself be the only Half-Drac left alive?" I threw away all pretenses, all of the labels that didn't matter here. Because he knew. He knew everything. The Half-Dracs, the fire, everything. There was no need to use the stupid titles the Zendaalans used, Fire Bugs.

Dekaar's face crumpled in confusion, and the expression looked out of place. He gave the impression that he was the one that was always in control, like there was very little he didn't know. And yet, he said, "What nonsense. Why would I kill all the Half-Dracs?"

I didn't know how to respond. How could he be here, way past the cutoff point of other Half-Dracs, seeming to know everything—and yet not know? "No Half-Drac over eighteen survives in K'sundi," I said coldly, then waited. Waited for him to go, *Ah, that's what you meant.* But his face twisted further, and I found myself going on. "Maybe they don't check here in Zendaal, but they check every one of us back at home. If you'd been born a little farther south, you wouldn't be here."

"What do you mean?" His tone demanded an answer.

"Ask your friends," I snarled. "The Zendaalans."

I underestimated how quickly he could change his mind. A moment ago, he was content not to hurt me. Now he grabbed me by the shoulder and pushed me against the window, the control panel biting into my lower back as my shoulders pressed against the glass, forcing my spine into an awkward angle.

"I'm asking *you,*" seethed Deklas, inches from my face. "Why are the Half-Dracs being killed?"

Pain laced through my back where he had me pinned against the hard surface. The taste of blood filled my mouth from where I'd bitten my lip. My breath came in ragged huffs, and as much as I knew I'd better not hold anything back from this lunatic at this point, hesitation held my tongue. This didn't make sense. *He* didn't make sense.

He knew who the Half-Dracs were but didn't know what the Zendaalans were doing to us. Ocean knew him somehow and expected me to know who he was as soon as I laid eyes on him.

Do I seem like a man who cares much about death? You know who I am. It was like he expected me to know as well. The way he had a jeer on his face, sending me knowing looks like I was supposed to be in on some sick joke.. The pieces falling together in my mind were terrifying, but the conclusion was the only thing that made sense.

"You should know—" My words were cut off by his hand flying to my throat and squeezing.

"That sharp tongue of yours is entertaining, but I'm in no mood to be entertained, Faresha," he snarled.

I made a choked sound. I knew he was dangerous, but something urged me to continue. To get to my point. "I'm not being cheeky," I rasped.

He blinked, then loosened his grip, pulling away from me.

Coughing, I rose up and massaged my throat. I turned to him. "You *should* know. They don't let us live. If they could, they would drive us all to extinction." I spoke to him like he'd spent the last thirty-something years of his life in a cave somewhere, like he somehow had no understanding of life outside his walls. But I suspected his case was much worse than that.

He'd been gone much longer than a handful of decades.

"What you're saying is impossible," he growled through clenched teeth, and that was confirmation that my terrible suspicion was correct.

I held his gaze. "I don't know who you are." At his confused look I said it again, more emphatically. "I don't *know* you." I snapped my fingers, lighting a fire over them. "I didn't know I could do *this* until a little more than a year ago. But you did. *We* once did." The K'sundii.

Understanding slowly dawned on Dekaar as his face contorted through multiple expressions. Disbelief. Denial. And then horror.

I went on. "Our history was erased, Dekaar. Killing the Half-Dracs was merely the last step in wiping it out completely." I stalked toward him, and he didn't back down from me as I brought my face close to his. My lips curled in a cruel grin. "No one knows you betrayed them, Dekaar. No one knows you destroyed the Dragon Kings. They don't even know who *they* are." A chuckle rumbled from some dark part of my soul. "Will your victory be as sweet, I wonder, if you're the only one who knows you had to crawl out of hell itself to get it?"

Dekaar's stare was murderous. "Lies," he growled, desperate for his own words to be true.

I backed away, my grin widening. An actual laugh pushed from me, just as cold as before, though I was being as sincere as I'd ever been. Sometimes, the truth was so wicked, it was funny. "The Dragon Kings were angry enough when they described the way you betrayed them. Funny, they didn't even bother mentioning your name, though."

Dekaar. If they had mentioned his name, I might have recognized how similar it was to Deklas, would have pieced together that it was what the Zendaalans called him in lieu of his K'sundii name. But they didn't, and I didn't know Dekaar's face because any record of his existence was gone, along with the rest of our history. If there was any trace of him, it was on an ancient trophy, an urn, a vase, some ancient relic, glazed and mounted in some rich man's house and never truly looked at or examined. And even if they did, with no context, his face was just that, a stranger's face. One no one would recognize or know as the man that made them lose their identity. How could they mourn the loss of an identity they scarcely knew was theirs?

Dekaar didn't reply. I didn't think he could. He turned away from me, his fists clenched so tightly at his sides, they trembled, and we flew on in silence for a few moments. And even when that silence broke, he didn't say anything; it was just the soft clinking of the handcuffs he picked up and locked back into place on my wrists. I didn't even fight him.

A DRAGON'S HEART

The mansion Dekaar took me to was absolutely resplendent—and armed to the teeth. The gate leading to the driveway connected to a forcefield that glimmered in the air around the entire property in the shape of a dome. That would make it difficult for Ocean to get close, I immediately realized with a silent curse. As if the forcefield wasn't bad enough, there were laser guns posted at various levels of the home, on the edges of balconies, off the walls, on the roof, trained on the skies around them, circling in unison when something flew by.

Getting Ocean here was going to be more complicated than I thought.

Dekaar leaned out of his car to tap in a passcode, give a fingerprint, and look into an eye-scanner before the gate opened, the forcefield flickering off in front of us, a space only big enough for the car to get through. A moment after we passed, the forcefield was back up. Exactly the kind of defense system to be expected of a man whose most precious commodity was his own life. He clearly didn't want to lose it again.

Dekaar. A man raised from the dead to take over K'sundi. The story the Dragon Kings told us rang through my head. He gave away the weakness of the Dragon Kings, severing different parts of their bodies and offering them to the Zendaalans in exchange for eternal life. It provided them with the power to give life to the lands they approved of and starve the ones they didn't. At that time, even with all that power, they had no immortal life to give, but had that fact changed over the years? Over the centuries? Was this their way of following through with that ancient promise? But that begged two questions: how did the Zendaalans accomplish it? And now that Dekaar was alive again, did they somehow find a way to keep him that way?

I thought about Attican, who was supposed to be dead and gone. And for the first time, I considered that perhaps he had been. And like Dekaar, he was brought back to finish what he'd started.

This was huge. If this was the technology the Zendaalans had developed, it would be harder than ever to oppose them in an all-out war for the world's freedom.

A pang ran through my heart thinking of what Kahmel gave up for me. Did he even want to save Hemorah anymore? Or K'sundi? I had no idea what he must be thinking, and that scared me. And now, with his sacrifice made in vain, I feared what he was capable of. What else was he willing to lose now that he was enraged?

It hurt to think about him, so I dragged my mind back to the present moment. To escaping. And when I could contact him and demand answers from him...then, I could give him hell.

I centered myself just in time for Dekaar to turn to me and raise an eyebrow. We were parked in his garage. He stared at me long enough that I had to ask. And I hated it because I didn't want to talk to him anymore. I suspected he knew that. "What?" I barked.

"I'm trying to decide what to call you," he said finally. "'Faresha' is outdated now, and I shan't call you by your first name, either. And Mrs. Omah..." he drifted off, and in the silence, I felt all the hatred pouring out of him, not at me, but at Kahmel. *Any* association with Kahmel, I realized with a chill.

"I have a couple names for *you*, wanna hear them?" I murmured.

Dekaar chuckled darkly, and my skin crawled at how quickly his moods changed. But I was starting to see the patterns. He didn't care if I was snippy so long as he wasn't in the middle of strangling me or anything. And he definitely didn't want to be reminded of what he did to the Dragon Kings and to the K'sundii all those millennia ago. That was enough to cause him to slap my cuffs back on and remain silent until we got here. Enough to start strangling. I suspected I could get away with saying anything I liked except about those two things.

"Do you have a dragon name?" His voice came quietly. He had to have been referring to something in K'sundi's past. Something beyond the books we studied for the Dragon Realm entrances, between lines of text. Something we wouldn't know to look for because it wasn't necessary, and we wouldn't know what it meant even if we did find it.

He'd started the topic, but I needed to respond carefully. This was close to the edge. To his dangerous side. "I don't," I said softly. "What is that?"

Beats passed before he answered. "The dragons don't speak our language. They don't respond to it, either. We gave ourselves names they could better understand. Not everyone had one. Mainly soldiers or dragon trainers. Important clan families. And the royalty, certainly."

For a moment, he became something else, a history professor, maybe. Patient, wanting me to learn and know. Telling me because he was...saddened. Saddened by the fact that I had no idea.

I thought about Kahmel, with all his names. Kahmel Axon Kai of the Omah clan. Was one of them his dragon name and he didn't know it? Would having a dragon name make it easier to train the dragons?

"You mean, they're like the command words we use?" I ventured, approaching the subject like I was a cat playing the dangerous game of trying to bat at a balloon without popping it. Drawing the claws back long enough to get what I needed, keep the conversation safe and as comfortable as I could make it.

A muscle worked in his jaw, and for a second I thought maybe the question wasn't as innocent as I thought, but then he said, "Give me an example."

At first I wasn't sure what he meant, then when understanding dawned, I named the one that had rung through my head from the moment I realized what it meant. "*Leh mani stepior.*" The command for the Drake Bond.

Dekaar left the car, and for a moment I thought that was the end of the conversation, that he'd changed his mind again. But then he opened my door, like I was a lady being escorted rather than a prisoner. And if it weren't for the handcuffs and the kidnapping, with the gentle look on his face I might have believed I was. He offered his hand and helped me up, and I had to grind my teeth to keep my nasty side down while we danced around his dangerous side—because I very much resented being handcuffed and kidnapped.

"Come close to me." For a second I thought he was commanding me, then he said, "What you call *command words,*" he closed the door behind him, "is called Butaah, the language of the dragons. What you said means 'come close to me.' It is the most intimate phrase you can utter to the dragons, which is why it triggers such an intense bond when said to the right one."

A language. The command words were nothing but words in the dragons' own *language.*

"But how—"

"We developed the language together." He cut me off—like he didn't want to hear my ignorance again in the form of another question—and I flinched. "The K'sundii and the dragons did. Every K'sundii grew up bilingual; it was customary."

He gripped me by the arm and led me toward the door to the side of us. I glanced around, noticing for the first time the three other cars lined up, all luxury but not a single dragon, ZST or otherwise. I figured the dragons wanted nothing to do with him, just like Ocean didn't, though surely ZST dragons would have no choice. But he didn't have any, for whatever reason.

"So these dragon names..."

"Are names in Butaah," he finished, then stopped at the door leading from the garage to the house. He considered me for a moment. "In a clan family, you received your dragon name on your first birthday. As Faresha, you would have received it in a ceremony just after you were married. In lieu of all that..." He tilted my chin up, and I bit my tongue to force myself to allow it, to keep from jumping at his metal skin touching me as he used his prosthetic hand. "*Eloe*. It means heart. You have a lot of it."

He said it like eh-low-ee, and in spite of myself something in me gave, just the slightest bit, at hearing it. Like it was right.

He opened the door to his house and shoved me inside. "I cannot stay," he said, as if he was apologizing for not being able to keep me company. "And when I am Faresh, I won't be visiting this home often. But I will be present, nonetheless."

I frowned. "How?"

He smiled. "Please. Surely even you know of the phone."

I rolled my eyes and refrained from correcting his use of the archaic word for HoloCaller or telling him that if he called, I certainly would not be answering.

"Farewell, Eloe."

And then he left. He didn't give me any orders or make any demands. Didn't tell me rules I was to follow or punishments for breaking them. He just *renamed me*...and left. The garage door hummed as it opened, and I watched his hovercar pull out, then speed down the driveway before taking to the skies. This situation was starting to feel familiar, only a twisted version of the original because he was *not* my husband, and this was in no way for my protection. This was because he found me *entertaining*, and he decided it best to keep me in a place where I couldn't escape, where he had easy access, but where I was shut away from others. And what better place than his home?

Half-Drac, Ocean's voice came in a sob, and in that moment I realized she always called me that instead of using my name. Was that because I didn't have a dragon name, and she found my name hard to pronounce, even in her head?

I couldn't bear to use the name Dekaar had given me, even though part of me wondered how Ocean would react if I gave it to her to use. I wasn't sure I wanted to answer to it. So I focused on comforting her. She wouldn't be able to help me if she was too emotional. The same went for me. I had to keep calm or I'd miss something—lose an opportunity to leap. I had to stay alert, and so did she.

It's going to be okay, I soothed.

But Half-Drac, I failed you. He has you now. I'm hiding, just as you told me, from a distance. But I can see the manor. His shields and weapons would be too much for me to handle alone.

Now that I knew who he was, I realized how terrified she must be at having me at his mercy. But I needed her to understand that, as bad as this seemed, I was relatively safe, at least for now. Dekaar was volatile, for sure, but I didn't think he wanted to hurt me, not really. He wasn't like the Zendaalans. They were brutal, cold, and heartless. Dekaar was elegant. Erratic and unpredictable, but elegant, nonetheless. The Zendaalans wanted control, a world stripped of anything alien to them. Dekaar simply wanted his way.

The problem was, he couldn't have his way. I had to get back home. And I wasn't sure what Kahmel was capable of doing in order to make that happen. Or what Dekaar was capable of doing to oppose him.

Our chance will come, I told her, and I knew it was hard for her to hear, because I was telling her to stay her hand yet again.

And then it occurred to me: I was in Zendaal. I was in *The Traitor's* home. I didn't imagine he would keep documents on where the Dragon Kings' parts were hidden just lying around the place. He may not even revisit that part of his heart often enough for him to remember. But...he wanted to talk to me. Perhaps I should let him. Learn what I could from him. His knowledge was more valuable than all of our libraries combined. What he knew was better than anything we could obtain in a raid.

And once I was out of here, maybe I could manage to find a way to make it easier for the rebels to get into Zendaal. The problem with getting in had always been that we didn't have a man on the inside. Now I was that man.

I wasn't sure where Kahmel's head was at, but I was sure I could talk him out of it, wherever he was. Get us back on track.

This was like when Kahmel and I first got married, but in reverse. I wasn't a very good spy the first time. Kahmel had known I was spying on him all along. I couldn't let it go the same way with Dekaar. I had to be careful, read his moods, interpret his attitude, and say just enough, never too much. I would give him sass because he expected it —and I needed to let it out every now and then or I'd never last—but know when to shut my mouth before he got dangerous, because even if he didn't want to kill me, that didn't mean he wouldn't do it by accident in a fit of rage. He didn't seem like a fool. Surely, he would have a way to handle me even while he wasn't here, something mechanized he could control remotely. It didn't seem he had any trouble catching up with modern technology, save a few mistakes here and there. He could and would kill me if necessary—even from afar.

And then I noticed Ocean's wording. She couldn't handle Dekaar's weapons and shielding *alone*.

Do as you have been, Ocean, I said. *Hunt, rest, and stay limber.* Then, as gratitude for her swelled in my heart, I added, *You've done well. I will do my best to help you help me. Just keep being patient.* I looked out the window to where the man that brought me here had last been, disappearing into the sky. Traitor to the dragons, to K'sundi, and to the throne. To me. Finally, I'd seen the cause of all that we had been facing. His elaborate plan played out in front of my eyes—separating me and Kahmel, convincing Kahmel to step down as Faresh, and lastly, keeping K'sundi under Zendaalan rule so Dekaar could finally have the throne...and keep it until the end of his immortal life. A plan a thousand years in the making. We were simply the opposition in his way when it all came to fruition.

But we would show him he was just in time to be too late—because we were the wrong ones to pick a fight with.

When it's time, I said to Ocean, *you can tear him apart.* Cruelty dripped from my tone, because maybe cruelty was necessary sometimes. *Limb from limb. Just like he did to your Kings.*

I sensed Ocean's wicked smile. *It would be my honor, Faresha.*

OATHS AND BONDS

Kahmel Axon Kai of the Omah Clan

From what I heard, in my absence K'sundi had become a sea of confusion. People were wondering where I'd gone and *finally* beginning to suspect that perhaps the Zendaalans weren't as honest as they pretended to be. More and more Half-Dracs revealed themselves every day—a problem leaving the Zendaalan officials and Court members scrambling to explain why they weren't making moves to do anything with them.

It was also becoming increasingly apparent that the Half-Dracs were all young. Jashi and I were the only Half-Dracs in the nation over the age of eighteen, I knew. And it seemed like people were realizing that, as well.

I wanted K'sundi to burn, and it looked like the people were going to accomplish it for me. An interesting situation, really. While I was around, it gave the people someone to question and blame for anything they didn't understand or whenever something went wrong. But now that neither Jashi nor I was around, the Court didn't have anyone to interrogate, leaving the people to question *them* for the answers instead and begin to wonder if Jashi and I had been right all along.

People were taking to the streets to protest, asking what happened to me and Jashi, asking what was happening to their Half-

Drac children. Neither the Court nor the Zendaalans had any answers for them.

The new Faresh was supposed to be crowned in just a few weeks, someone the Zendaalans called Deklas, though his K'sundii name was Dekaar. My family was claiming he was a relative—a cousin. It was obviously in order to make his claim to the throne quick and easy. This seemed like a win for them, but truth be told, we were at an impasse. The people were demanding answers I knew they weren't going to get. The Courts and Zendaalans had their new Faresh at last, but how far would he get with the people against him already? A problem I was glad to have caused him before they could get rid of Jashi and me.

I would leave the new Faresh with his problems. People would soon give up trying to get answers from the ones lying to them in the first place. It was time for the K'sundii to turn to the rebels for answers, a resource none of them knew would lead right back to me. Perhaps they'd see irony in that fact once they found out. Regardless, it was a journey for them to navigate on their own. Jashi and I had done as much as we could to lead them to their freedom. The rest was up to them.

The pain pulsing through my arms had worsened ever since I left the palace. It always lessened when I was taking a step in the right direction. A step toward freeing the dragons, freeing K'sundi. The pain let me know how the Dragon Kings felt about my leaving the palace. I had a plan, but the more I thought about it, the more my arms hurt. I was dancing on the edge here. My ideas teetered on blasphemous. But I refused to leave Jashi helpless and alone in Zendaal. She was my Faresha, even if K'sundi wouldn't have her anymore. I was going to save her.

I needed help, and there was only one place with power great enough to get it.

"Are you sure you want to do this?" I asked T'shan through an earpiece connecting us as I rode Huntress, the wind sailing by as we soared through the air. T'shan rode Jashi's dragon, Comet. Comet was wily when Jashi wasn't riding him, but thankfully he was behaving well enough for the dragon rider. T'shan had gotten a lot better as a rider over the past few months, and I suspected there weren't many dragons he couldn't handle. If I had time to think outside of our immediate needs, I'd be proud of him. For now, I was just glad he could keep up. The forest side of K'sundi slipped beneath us as a moving carpet of green. After hiding out for so long, the sharp air made me feel alert. Or perhaps that was the adrenaline. Either way.

T'shan looked at me with an eyebrow raised like he was wondering why I asked. I wasn't sure, either. To say something, maybe. Or to evaluate where his head was. To see whether or not he thought I was going insane. T'shan was the only one I could take with me where we were going. I hadn't even asked Rand, Arusi, or anyone else to come. The other dragon riders were left behind.

Because only Half-Dracs could enter the Dragon Realms.

T'shan looked down at Comet. "We need help," he admitted. Then he looked me in the eye. "And we have to save Jashi. I'll do whatever it takes to get her back, sir."

He'd taken to calling me "sir" in place of his usual "Your Majesty," and I was tired of being called either. "Kahmel," I corrected.

He flinched with discomfort at the familiarity, then nodded. "Kahmel," he said.

I watched the Dragon's Heart River pierce the rows of trees and slide through their ranks like a serpent below us. We'd arrived. "I'm not going to lie to you and say the Dragon Kings are particularly kind," I warned as I signaled for us to start descending. "Especially given the circumstances, I doubt the Dragon King will be too happy to see me. And the last time I pissed him off, he held a claw to Jashi's throat."

I had said it casually, in the same tone one might remind someone to close the door before they leave the house. It only occurred to me at that moment—looking to T'shan as he swallowed hard—that anyone without the burning rage I had running through me right now would probably be afraid. T'shan was afraid, and what I'd said certainly didn't assuage any of his fears. He was right to be scared. I *should* have been afraid. I might have been, if I wasn't...whatever I was at the moment.

I planned to tell the Dragon King that the terms of our agreement were about to change—and in addition to that, make some demands.

The only reason Aithel spared Jashi's life when we first approached him was that I could make him a promise as K'sundi's Faresh. Now that I had lost that position, my oath to protect the dragons and the Half-Dracs meant less.

It meant less. But it was still true. I would protect the dragons, but I was changing strategies. And what Jashi and I had done for the dragons already—adjusting the laws, changing the way the watch towers worked, making people realize the Half-Dracs were being targeted—no matter how quickly they crowned this *Dekaar* as Faresh, he couldn't undo all of that in a day. And in the time it would take him to dismantle all of my hard work, I would operate from the shadows, doing whatever it took to continue upholding my end of the deal with the Dragon Kings.

All of that to say I would cover my ass one way or another. Though that idea might not have been so comforting to T'shan, who was not in the state of mind I was in right now—frighteningly brazen. T'shan didn't lose his wife. He didn't have to be so bold.

"Well, try not to piss him off too much," T'shan said with forced lightness. Our dragons landed, and he slung himself off, taking his earpiece out.

I mirrored him, instructing Huntress and Comet to stay where they were with a command word, and I realized that Aithel may not be the only dragon T'shan was intimidated by. My fists clenched at my sides. *You never let anyone in,* Jashi had scolded me. T'shan's presence was helping me in more ways than one—not just because I needed him to get to the Dragon Realm, but because I was a living hurricane right now, and having someone, *anyone* around, made me feel just a little more grounded. T'shan was making a sacrifice by being here for me. Because he was loyal. And more than that, a good friend.

"Thank you," I said, "for coming with me."

T'shan breathed out, seeming to steel himself. "Well then, I guess now we go chat up a dragon in a magic cave in another universe." He gestured for me to lead.

I chuckled, which surprised me, because I didn't think I had any of those left in me right then. The ground rumbled, signaling that we were close to Aithel's lair, and it sobered the mood. "Let's go."

This wasn't like when Jashi and I visited Aithel the first time. Looking at the craggy rock face surrounding us and watching the dragons dart to and fro, coming back felt strangely familiar—except for the relative silence.

Dragons flocked around us, not so close as to be threatening, but close enough to watch us from afar. Almost like a greeting, or even, dare I say, a welcome.

Dragons weren't puppies. They weren't the kind to greet a familiar face after meeting them once. Khes got the scar on his eye from trying to tame a dragon for use in our army back when this all began. After having fed and housed it for months, it lashed out when he attempted to ride it for the first time.

Yet, as we walked into the heart of a cluster of dragon nests, a place where mere proximity guaranteed the fierce anger of the ferocious creatures, we were met with stillness. I marveled at the shift in behavior from when Jashi and I first came here. We'd almost been ravaged by the freshly hatched dragons just for coming near the opening of the cave that granted entrance to the Dragon Realm. Dragons hatched seasonally, and these were slightly bigger than the hatchlings from the year before, but were most likely the same ones. And they were acting downright peaceful.

Odd, but not reason enough to turn back. If the dragons were content not to attack us, I would just take it that from the downpour of misfortunes the Great Spirits had bestowed upon me, a dredge of luck had slipped through for today's outing.

Which reminded me, T'shan needed to be prepared.

"How well can you manage your fire?"

"Okay enough," said T'shan, to my surprise. "It slips out when I get scared or sometimes when I have nightmares, but for the most part I can keep it under control."

"Can you summon it at will?" I asked, impressed. He was farther along than Jashi had been when I found her. But then again, his parents knew about his abilities, so he could practice if he liked. Not like Jashi, who grew up with orphans she had to keep her secret from most of her life. "If not, I have a lighter. You'll need it to activate the entrance to the Dragon Realm."

T'shan laughed. "You waited until now to mention that?"

We arrived at the mouth of the cave, and I breathed deeply.

"I—er—" I *had* gone insane. I was usually more prepared than this. But I wasn't myself right then. Perhaps it was an indication that this wasn't as good an idea as my pulsing anger made it seem. But I didn't see any other way.

T'shan opened his fist, and what I saw distracted me from any other thought. Instead of fire, *sparks* flew. They hopped from his palm and flitted around him like mini-fireworks popping from his hand. "This is as much as I can manage. Will it do?"

I couldn't focus on anything other than his fire. Or rather, his version of it. The thought had never occurred to me that our fires could differ from each other, that we could all have different styles, different approaches to the ways we used our abilities.

"Yeah, that should work," I managed, returning my attention to the matter at hand. "As long as you can light something with it." I moved to step inside, then stopped. "Things have been..." I drifted off, because he knew how things had been. "But I'll try to make time to train you, like I did Jashi. You should know how to do more than this. It's impressive you know as much as you do, though. I thought I might have to teach you on the spot."

T'shan smiled. "Nice to have you offer to teach me something without my having to twist your arm."

I scowled at him despite knowing he was right, and T'shan moved ahead of me, into the cave.

It was time to meet Aithel and tell him our deal, as it stood, was off.

TO DANCE WITH A DRAGON

I entered the cave behind T'shan and was brought back to the moment I'd done this with Jashi. The craggy cave walls swallowed us whole, and we trod the lightly etched path in between the cave's jagged teeth. The ground shook again, this time with more force. We were close. Jashi had trusted me for the first time, then. We had united to gamble on this wild quest I set us on. I'd taken a risk and come out on top that time. I'd been right about the existence of the Dragon Kings. All we'd had to go on were some relics and a gut feeling. And Jashi put her trust in that. In *me*.

I ignited my hand in a ball of flames to light our way, and a stab of pain laced through my arms, reminding me the circumstances had been different the first time. This time I knew full and well I may be pushing the Dragon King too far. I was going anyway.

"Are you all right?" asked T'shan, concern in his voice.

"Fine," I said through a clenched jaw. "The shrine isn't too far from here."

We moved in silence, me grinding my teeth with every step, feeling the pain fresh and new, which, I was sure, was Aithel warning me not to come. But we moved on. We came to the pedestals, two short pillars topped with brass bowls flanking an old K'sundii flag. The dragon and the shield. Our life, our protection, our allies. The ones we betrayed over a thousand years ago. The ones we needed today if we were ever going to get our freedom back. The one I was going to confront because I needed his help to get my wife back.

And then fear wormed its way in as I considered what failure would mean—that I would lose Jashi. And that fear, strange as it was, forced me to be brave—because nothing, no matter what the Dragon King had to throw at me, was worse than that.

"Let's get started." I stepped up to one of the pedestals, the same side I'd taken last time. I held my burning fist aloft, and with a toss, the fire arched from my hand into the brass bowl waiting for it. When it landed, it erupted into a pillar that shot toward the ceiling, heat pouring into the room as it blazed.

T'shan watched, jaw slack.

I gestured to him. "Now you do the same over there."

"Yeah, I'll just do that," he muttered, his low voice reverberating through the cave walls, even over the roar of the fire. He walked over to the pedestal, took a breath to steady himself, and then opened his hand. For a moment, nothing happened. And then the sparks flew. They jolted from his palm and scattered to the rock floor. He held his palm over the bowl and tipped it like he was pouring a handful of water rather than sparks. With a sputtering flash, a few of them fell into the bowl. It was enough. Fire burst from the bowl as soon as they touched it, arching toward the ceiling.

The rumbling rose to a crescendo, shaking the cave hard enough for chunks of the ceiling to come loose, clattering to the ground. A streak of white flashed in the darkness beyond us, reaching us in an instant. Its grip closed around me and then T'shan.

The world whipped away around us. We were off.

T'SHAN GAPED at our surroundings while the dragon of in-between whisked us away through the liquid black that was the Dragon Realm.

I wasn't sure if "used to it" was a phrase that could ever apply to coming here. It would always be a miracle—a shot of wondrous relief that this was all *real,* that I hadn't dreamed up the pain of being burned alive when Aithel put these marks on my arms.

The shock of wonder dulled as we neared our destination, because rather than waiting inside his glistening onyx castle, Aithel stood outside, staring right at me.

The dragon of in-between dropped us off at his feet, and when T'shan tumbled to the ground at my side, it was the first time Aithel's eyes broke contact with mine.

"And who might this be?" he asked. Every question the Dragon Kings asked was a secret test because they never asked a question they didn't know the answer to. Aithel had been the one who revealed to me and Jashi that T'shan was a Half-Drac in the first place. All of the Dragon Kings could keep an eye on the Half-Dracs. No matter what we'd done, whether we deserved it or not, we were still connected.

I knew better than to answer for T'shan, though I wanted to, to protect him from the challenge that flashed in Aithel's eyes. It was a test to see if T'shan would rise to it or cower away.

T'shan's fists clenched, and I remembered he was a dragon rider; hopefully he remembered as well. He pushed his chest out and his voice came out surprisingly steady. "T'shan. I'm here to accompany Kahmel."

"Why?" Aithel leaned his massive face down to meet T'shan's gaze, his head easily the size of the Half-Drac's body. *"He's not your Faresh anymore, from what I hear. Are you clinging to some hope he'll reclaim his pathetic throne?"*

Pathetic throne. If I wasn't sure we were on hostile terms before, that confirmed it. Aithel was angry.

"I don't care who's on the throne." T'shan didn't back down. "I'm loyal to *him.* He's the only one looking out for us."

Aithel rumbled out a chuckle, and his gaze returned to me. *"Why are you here?"*

It didn't sound like a question. "Things have changed," I dared to say. "I can't fulfill the terms of our agreement as it—"

Paralyzing pain cut off the world around me. It was beyond just my arms. Everything hurt. My lungs constricted. It was worse than when he'd branded me. I writhed in agony, and it took me a moment to realize the screaming echoing off the walls of the castle was mine.

"Kahmel!" I heard, distantly.

T'shan's voice was drowned out when Aithel's words penetrated through the pain, into my mind. "*I am not your Court system, Kahmel,*" he growled, his tone lethal. "*You cannot dance around an oath to me. I'm insulted by the attempt.*"

"What do you expect?" T'shan shot back.

The grip of pain loosened, not because I was forgiven, but because Aithel's attention had turned to my friend. The Dragon King's pause was not an invitation for T'shan to go on. It was more like a break in proceedings while he considered how truly stupid the human specimen in front of him was. Even in my blinding world of agony, I had some wherewithal to gape at the audacity in T'shan's tone. When had he gone from scared to blasphemous?

T'shan went on. "If you know Kahmel was deposed, you know why. The odds are stacked against us. And what have you given us to help? Nothing but useless riddles and tricks. How can we uphold our end of the deal when you withhold the ability for us to do so?"

"*Kahmel left. He didn—*" Aithel snarled.

T'shan cut him off, and I said a prayer to the Spirits that he wouldn't be struck down where he stood. "Averton *knew* Jashi would be taken," T'shan snapped back. "He knew, and all he did was give her a vague warning that didn't do anything. She was still taken. And then everything fell apart."

T'shan had been filled in on the details of what happened when Jashi and I were in Vahdel. I didn't realize how much it had affected him. The ferocious passion in his eyes bore witness that he held Jashi in high regard. The fury at her being taken made him bold.

Aithel didn't respond immediately, shocking me. "*True,*" he admitted. "*We're not completely open with you, no.*" He laid the fact plainly, though I detected some admiration in his tone. "*I told you full cooperation would come when all the Dragon Kings had agreed. And as of yet, they have not."*

In other words, in spite of it all, they still held us at a distance. Dragons didn't take trust lightly, and I would be foolish to believe Aithel would give it to us freely—not after they'd all been betrayed, no matter how long ago it had been.

"That's going to have to change," I said, finally able to breathe.

Aithel narrowed his eyes, danger flickering in them, but the pain didn't return. He growled the words slowly, *"What does that mean?"*

Straightening, I said, "I can still fulfill my promise—"

Aithel laughed, cutting me off. *"You couldn't turn the people's hearts when you were their Faresh, and you expect to do so as a commoner?"*

"My promise was that I would protect your dragons, along with the Half-Dracs. I'll do that. From the shadows. I don't have to convince people. I'm still the leader of the rebels, and they obey me. They'll protect the dragons and the Half-Dracs because I'll tell them to."

Aithel paused, considering.

T'shan exhaled, relaxing slightly. I admired him for still looking mad about it.

"On one condition," I added.

Pain racked my body once more, and Aithel laughed as I doubled over, twisting in agony. *"You test what little patience I have left for you. You left here so humble last we spoke. What has boldened you so?"*

"Because I was cheated," I growled through the pain, and the pain slackened. Not because Aithel was distracted this time, but because I'd gotten his attention. I looked him in the eye. "I had everything in place to fulfill my word to you, and I had every intention of doing so. It's as T'shan says: We were warned by Averton that the Zendaalans would try to sabotage our progress, so we took every precaution. Yet we were outmaneuvered, not because we hadn't won the people over—the people have been protesting my absence, as you already know, I'm sure."

Aithel didn't react, but I knew he knew. He always knew.

I went on. "We were bested because those in power snared us. A snare that could have been avoided had Averton been honest from the beginning. If we had known Jashi would be targeted, we would have never brought her back to the palace. We'd have hidden her with the rebels, in spite of Zendaal's threats." My lip raised in a snarl. "I would have allowed K'sundi to become a rebel country to fulfill my word to you and remain as Faresh."

"*Why do you think he didn't tell you?*" Aithel's voice was quiet, so quiet it made me pause.

"You tell me."

Aithel made a rumbling sound, and it took a moment to decipher it as a sigh. "*Because it wouldn't have made a difference. Your enemy was too cunning, too quick, and too prepared. You may have hidden your wife away, but they would have found her again. The best way to warn you was to keep you from knowing what he knew, so you would stay calm and rational enough to realize that your wife can handle herself. And she will. Now it's time for you to make sure you catch up to her.*" He walked away, toward the castle, the ground rumbling beneath him as he did. It was as much of an invitation to follow him as we were going to get.

We trailed behind him.

RAGE

ithel led us into the onyx castle, and I was reminded once again that this was an ethereal creature that didn't have to make any logical sense. The enormity of the castle stretched on and on, the ceilings so high they disappeared into nothing. Around us, the black floors reflected starry light spilling in from the windows in a milky glow. It was like the galaxies themselves surrounded us.

Aithel didn't stop once we were inside, and T'shan and I took that to mean we were supposed to walk with him.

The Dragon King's voice came burdened, and I was surprised because he'd been threatening to kill me not a few moments ago. But dragons were temperamental, and it shouldn't have surprised me that their Kings were no different. *"There's more to this battle than you know."*

"Why didn't you tell us?" asked T'shan, still mad.

"Because time and fate are cruel," said Aithel. *"Kahmel and Jashi arise at the same time as our greatest adversary—one who had eyes and ears throughout their palace. And we wouldn't risk his hearing our plans."*

I was confused. When had this gone from death threats to divulging secrets?

"Averton could only tell you that Jashi was in danger," Aithel explained, *"because any attempts to protect her would have resulted in the same. Whether she be with your rebels or in the palace, your*

adversary knew the best way to take the throne would be to take her from you, and he wouldn't have stopped until he succeeded."

I thought about the attempts on Jashi's life that happened soon after the Zendaalans realized she was on my side. The attempts on mine all but stopped. Was she the target all along? Or had the enemy shifted focus when she came into the picture?

"Why?" T'shan asked, voicing the question for the both of us. "Why not Kahmel? Wouldn't the result be the same?"

Aithel stopped and gazed out the starry window. *"At first, he might have been content with that. But the more Kahmel and Jashi pushed against him, the more he became fascinated by their attempt. He'd assumed taking the throne would have been instantaneous. Meeting resistance frustrated him, then intrigued him. Now he's infatuated with it."*

Heat churned in my chest as my need to get Jashi away from whoever this was burned hotter. "Who the hell is this guy? Someone that wanted the throne after Adisoh and his clan were assassinated?"

Aithel shook his head, still not looking at us. *"He was the reason Adisoh's clan was assassinated."*

Understanding dawned on me, and I realized where Aithel was going with this.

Aithel started walking again and T'shan and I followed. We stepped into a courtyard, stars hanging above us. The grass in the middle grew plush and green; potted, leafy plants were arranged all around.

"What are your conditions, Kahmel?" Aithel asked finally.

"We work together."

Aithel stopped, and I realized that all this moving through the castle was him pacing. What I now recognized as concern in his eyes faded when he looked at me. Aithel had to be sure I wasn't going to back out of our agreement completely. I got that. He'd been burned before, and he had to be careful, a sentiment I could relate to. He wasn't mad at me. Not really. He was a dragon. And so was I. I remembered how he had tested me by making me protect Jashi when we first encountered him, and I realized that he had done so to make sure she was my top priority. Because he loved *all* of his dragons, Half-Dracs included. The Dragon Kings acknowledged K'sundi's Fareshes and Fareshas. Just because K'sundi had chosen a new Faresh didn't mean the Dragon Kings accepted him. Aithel wanted his Faresha back too. And he wanted me to show enough determination to fight anyone, even him, to save her.

I liked Aithel, I decided in that moment. I liked him a lot. "We need the dragons to help us get Jashi back. We know how to free them from the ZST with the Drake Bonds."

The enormous dragon's lips peeled back into a frighteningly toothy grin. *"Finally."*

I held back complaints about how he could have simply told us from the beginning. I was starting to understand how the Dragon Kings worked. They were older than dirt. If things didn't go well with Jashi and me, they would wait until someone else came along, even if it took another thousand years. Maybe two. They would rather wait than deal with someone who wasn't worth it or someone who would either betray them or was too incompetent to rise against the numerous challenges they would have to face. And I understood that. Even now, facing the Zendaalans was hard. But it was even harder dealing with the people now convinced the Zendaalans were heroes. Those that would sell everyone else out to please them.

I bowed, to Aithel's amusement. I continued anyway. "I know the entrances to the Dragon Realms are sacred, the most guarded secret. But you're going to have to tell us how to get to Obellana." I raised my head to look at him. "I'll make it worth your while."

"Oh?" There was genuine curiosity in his voice.

"I no longer want war with the Zendaalans."

It was a thought I'd kept to myself, and T'shan stiffened at my side. I hadn't even been sure I was going to mention it until the words left my mouth.

"Then what do you want?"

"Once we have Jashi back, we can collect ourselves...then strike against Zendaal."

"*And that isn't a war?*"

"Only to get your parts back," I continued. "I would have gone to war to free K'sundi and the rest of the world from the Zendaalans. But I no longer care about them."

Hunger flashed in Aithel's eyes, and he became every bit the predator his nature made him, one that was thousands of years old and starving for blood. "*Who do you care about, then?*"

The Kings never asked a question they didn't already know the answer to. He knew. He wanted me to know. "The dragons," I answered. "And just the dragons. The Half-Dracs are dragons too. But not the others. K'sundi doesn't want freedom. I'm tired of fighting them for it. But to fulfill our agreement, I'll save the dragons, as I promised. For that, all I need are your parts back, and then you can help me save the dragons. Then you can do whatever you like to whoever you like. Whatever accomplishes our common goal."

"*There's no telling what will happen to the rest of the world if you topple the balance of power and leave them to pick up the pieces on their own.*" His tongue lashed out and flicked across his lips. Hungry. Starving. "*No telling what we'll do.*" He and the other Dragon Kings.

"That's what I'm counting on."

Aithel's laugh was a roar that rumbled through the whole castle. He stood on his hind legs to reel back further, making him a skyscraper as he did. He landed back on all fours, and the earth rattled hard enough to nearly knock us lowly humans to the ground. "*Stay here for a day,*" Aithel implored. "*We have much to discuss, Faresh. The snappy one too. I like him.*"

Faresh. So I was right. The dragons lived by a different code. Politics were a ridiculous notion to them. Trust and leadership were merits earned by grit and fealty, by honor and justice. K'sundi may not want to admit it, but this was where they came from. The dragons chose us because we were most like them.

Not anymore, though. But perhaps that was why Aithel liked me —because I was the dead spirit of K'sundi brought back to life.

Aithel sobered. *"I have much to tell you about the man who has your wife, as well. We have held back much from you, but I believe you're ready to understand everything."* He turned his back to us, this time toward a hallway lined with doors.

Bedrooms, I realized.

This was it. There was no going back.

I worried T'shan would look at me in silent fear from now on, maybe even ask to leave the rebels after hearing all the things I'd just said. Knowing that this was no ruse or clever choice of words—that I was as serious as I'd ever been.

But I was met with a nod of approval, maybe even admiration. And I reasoned that the rebels were perhaps a league of revived dragons, and I counted myself lucky to be leading them into the biggest battle we'd ever fight.

Against our own. Against the world. Against humanity itself.

Casting our lots with the dragons of the world instead.

Dekaar, the previously unknown K'sundii who would be crowned Faresh, was the Traitor. And he had Jashi.

The information left me reeling despite the fact that Aithel told me hours ago. T'shan and I sat in our room, T'shan eating and me just staring at my plate. It turned out that there was food here in the dragon realm—fruit trees and root plants and vegetables. Odd, seeing as dragons ate none of those things. But then again, I didn't understand anything in the Dragon Realm, so that was fine.

The dragon of in-between was a servant of sorts in this realm, and there were other dragons like him at Aithel's beck and call. He gave a short growl, and glowing, snaky dragons of pinks, blues, and yellows slipped through the air and did whatever he asked. In this case, to serve us in our rooms and keep us comfortable.

One of them, the blue one, took T'shan's plate as he finished it and shimmered away. My plate, topped with juicy and neatly sliced fruit, was still untouched. The pink dragon hovered in the air above it, waiting to see if I would give it up.

I gestured for the dragon to take it, and T'shan and I were left to our room, alone.

My wife was taken by the very same man who betrayed the Dragon Kings and took something from each of them so the Zendaalans would have enough power to make him Faresh and grant him immortality. And they fulfilled their promise. A thousand years late, but hey, what hurry was he in?

When I asked how it was accomplished, Aithel confessed even the dragons didn't know. But they knew their power was being used to do it. A combination of magic and technology, I surmised. The former being the thing the Dragon Kings could feel at all times like a tether to their being, the latter being man's personal magic. A magic the dragons didn't feel like the wind under their wings or the flame in their breath. They were just as confused as I was as to how The Traitor was miraculously revived, all of his memories intact. He knew who he was. He knew what he wanted.

He wanted my throne. And he wanted my wife.

That was why the Zendaalans had to go back on their word. Aithel warned that Dekaar's moods were like storms on the coastline —fickle, intense, and raging one moment, calm and clear the next. Likely, the Zendaalans hadn't even known Dekaar would be keeping Jashi until he suddenly decided it. And they wouldn't go back on their word to make him Faresh no matter how much he put them in jeopardy. If it weren't for the fact that he was the aim of my resentment, I might admire him for being a K'sundii man with Zendaalans under his thumb.

If it was true that Dekaar was now somehow immortal, he was the answer to all of their problems. They had a Faresh who would never turn against them. They would never have to rely on K'sundi's system to select a leader who would favor their rule. Dekaar got to live forever. They got to keep K'sundi forever. Everybody won.

Aithel told me, ironic though it may be, Jashi was probably safe, at least for now. Dekaar would treat her better than the Zendaalans might have under the same circumstances, as long as she kept her wits about her. He saw her like a collector might, with awed admiration and possessiveness. It was how he saw K'sundi. He would keep both intact, as best as his tumultuous moods allowed.

K'sundi, he could keep. But I was at least glad Jashi wouldn't be starved, sick, or tortured.

I was playing a game that'd started long before I was even born, which was why I was always a step behind. This was beyond me. Dekaar had much, much more time to prepare for this. But...he wouldn't feel the need to push so hard if I wasn't nipping at his heels. And with my target narrowed, my goals were much simpler, harder to foil.

I left the cave yesterday, after Aithel and I talked, to send a message to Rand. T'shan and I agreed—we'd be staying with the Dragon King a bit longer than the one day he offered. He had a lot to tell me, it seemed. And I had much to discuss with him.

Dekaar wanted to play? Fine.

Let the games begin.

LONG LIVE THE FARESH

Jashi *Eloe* Anyua-Omah

Dekaar left me with the handcuffs on, but it turned out he'd simply done so to show he was upset with me for bringing up his past. I found keys to the handcuffs lying in plain sight in the mansion's kitchen, a kitchen stocked with all the food I'd need for a while. It meant however he intended to keep me fed, he wouldn't have to worry about it for quite some time. Despite my being left unfettered and with no rules to follow, leaving Dekaar's mansion was, unsurprisingly, not as simple as walking out the door.

I assumed the forcefield outside was configured to allow him in but keep everyone else out. But all the doors and windows were sealed shut. Had his spontaneous decision been more planned than I thought, or was his house capable of a complete lockdown all along? I was more inclined to believe the latter. From the heavy defensive systems surrounding his home, saying he was paranoid was an understatement. The system was likely to keep anyone else *out*. Though in this case, it served just as well to keep someone in.

A thorough search of every corner, drawer, and surface revealed no way to control the defense system. My thoughts were all over the place. How was he controlling such a complicated system? Could he have been carrying the controls with him somehow? Maybe they weren't even in the house. I stopped as an idea surfaced above the other whirling thoughts. Dekaar was a cyborg. His body could be the control.

With a frustrated sigh, I gave up looking for a way to manipulate the home. I picked one of the many bedrooms the mansion had to offer and crawled under the covers of the plush bed. I didn't even say anything to Ocean. All of the exhaustion building up from the past few days—from being kidnapped, tied up, drugged and then sleep-deprived, and then kidnapped *again*—caught up with me all at once, and I passed out.

When I woke up, it felt late in the day. The clock on the wall—a traditional clock, of all things, with two spokes that spun slowly while a third ticked with every second—proved I was right. It was well into the afternoon.

The Traitor has not returned since he left you here, Ocean reported.

I wiped the sleep from my eyes and forced myself to sit up because if I sank back into the sheets, I would sleep until it was night again. I mentally reached for Ocean, and I felt her tensed and poised. Had she been like that all night? I wasn't sure where she was, but I knew she wouldn't be close enough to be spotted or targeted by the security system. *How do you know? Do you...* The words were hard to say, because I knew she'd been wounded because of Dekaar. They all had. And I didn't want to push too hard. *Do you feel him somehow? Sense his whereabouts?*

We all do, said Ocean. Her ears pulled back against her head. *I thought you Half-Dracs did as well. But I suppose you've forgotten. We cannot.*

The hurt in her voice stung. I got out of bed and went to the window. I knew what would happen, but I tried pressing on it anyway. The pane didn't budge. Dekaar's mansion was fully furnished and decorated, complete with violent abstract paintings on the walls and little statuettes on the side tables in the hallways, figures of women carrying urns propped on wide hips. I'd tried throwing one of those statuettes at a window yesterday, but the only thing that chipped was the arm of the statue as it landed. Now it lay on my nightstand, holding up the urn with one hand.

What do you call him? I wondered, thinking of my conversation with Dekaar yesterday. Half wondering, almost hoping, he wasn't telling the truth. Not that it made any difference if he was, it just felt wrong somehow, learning something so intimate from him.

We stripped him of his name, Ocean said, icy. *He is only The Traitor. As I said.*

At first I didn't know what she meant, and then I remembered our exchange:

I know he's creepy, a traitor to K'sundi, but what else is there to know?

Exactly!

I'd just been describing him, not realizing that I was using his new dragon name. Not a word in the dragons' language, in Butaah, but in our own. The Traitor. Ocean had thought I understood.

The sky was bright blue as I gazed out the window. It'd been cold yesterday when I was brought here, but the sun was warming the air up. The sun was so cheery above this metal city, warming the half-metal people. I wondered if it could burn them. I hoped it could.

The hate that burned in me for Zendaal paled in comparison to the hate I had for Dekaar. And as much as I despised him, I wondered who I should despise more, him...or the people who had abandoned the dragons after he'd stripped their Kings. They hadn't come to their rescue, hadn't come to avenge their other half. Half-Dracs were exactly that: Half Dragons. Aithel and the rest were *our* Kings as much as they were the dragons'. The K'sundii abandoned the dragons, then they embraced a people who made them reject everything they once were. And now it was all forgotten.

Should I have a dragon name? I asked, small.

Ocean straightened, stiffening. I could tell she was mad. Maybe not at me, directly, but certainly at what I represented. A long lost connection that she remembered, but I had forgotten. *It would deepen our connection, yes.*

Our connection could be even deeper than it already was?

Though I hadn't intentionally conveyed the thought, Ocean must have sensed it. *To all dragons...Half-Drac.*

Her irritation grated against me. She wanted to use the name Dekaar had given me. She hated that I didn't know I was supposed to have a dragon name to begin with and was desperate for me to give her anything other than a *title* to call me by. She didn't care that it came from Dekaar, she wanted to be able to call me *something.*

I decided it didn't matter that it came from Dekaar. As much as I hated to admit, if it wasn't for him, I wouldn't have known I needed one in the first place. I wondered how many other things the dragons silently ground their teeth at, frustrated that we didn't know. The Drake Bonds would help, as it did with Ocean and me. But how could they know what to tell us? Ocean thought I knew who The Traitor was. We'd been apart, spiritually, for over a thousand years. A few conversations wouldn't get us all caught up.

Then call me Eloe.

Thank you, said Ocean, relieved.

Before I could wonder how that simple exchange would deepen my connection with the dragons, the sound of ringing made me jump. It rang throughout the house, loud enough to make me clamp my hands over my ears. The bedrooms were on the second floor of the mansion. The ringing was coming from the first floor.

As I made my way down the steps the noise got louder, hurting my ears. At the bottom of the steps I could see that the wall above the fireplace, which had previously been vacant, now had a glowing screen on it. A HoloCaller.

I frowned and raised an incredulous eyebrow as though Dekaar could see my reaction through the screen that wasn't even turned on. Did he really think that if he called, I would answer?

But it turned out the choice was never really mine because the call opened, and rather than the screen showing Dekaar's face, it turned off and a projector shot bluish light from the ceiling, erecting an image on the floor, stacking it piece by piece, until the man was standing before me.

So this was what he thought a phone call was.

"Hello, Eloe. I'd apologize for being late," his projection said, giving me an appraising look, "but it looks like you've only just woken up."

I put a hand through my hair, feeling the coils matted and flat against my head where I'd slept on it last night without a silk cap to keep the curls bouncy. Not like it mattered. Since I'd immediately crashed after assessing the house and what it had available, I hadn't showered or changed out of the clothes I was wearing when I'd been taken—a bright orange robe that mocked the position I no longer held, according to Dekaar. He was probably on his way to K'sundi right now.

From my searching, I knew there were clothes in the drawers, none of them feminine. But I would make do with what he had available.

I rolled my eyes. I had no reason to respond to him, so I turned to leave.

I took a step then jumped back as I hit something solid, a forcefield. Whipping around, I found Dekaar with his face placid.

"I didn't have time to make my home comfortable for you," he went on, as though nothing happened. "But I hope what the Zendaalans prepared for me suits you well enough."

So it was the Zendaalans who stocked the fridge. Perhaps not to keep a prisoner, but so Dekaar would be provided for while avoiding contact with people. Dekaar was the one being given all the freedom, but his home seemed like it was already a prison, even before I was brought here.

I gritted my teeth. "Just fine, thank you."

He pursed his lips into a smile, and it was then that I noticed the way he lightly swayed as he stood. Not drunk. I didn't think he would fall for such vices. No, he was stabilizing himself. Like you would when standing in a plane.

"I'm coming home," he said.

At first I thought he meant this house, but then my skin crawled when I realized what he was talking about. K'sundi.

"What's left of it, anyway." I crossed my arms. I didn't have an explanation for why Kahmel gave it up, but if he just dropped K'sundi all of a sudden, it would be a mess. It was already a mess before he gave it up—especially after Kahmel and I revealed that we were Half-Dracs. I didn't get to really know how that turned out because we had to go to Vahdel almost immediately afterward. And after that, I was kidnapped.

Dekaar only shrugged. "I came back; so can they."

I ground my teeth. "What do you want?"

"The K'sundi Court has officially pronounced me the new Faresh." His chest swelled with pride. He paused, and I realized he was waiting for my reaction, wanting to see the pain in my eyes.

But the news didn't sting as much as I'd expected it to. I knew what his aim was now. And Kahmel wasn't resisting. Some part of me, the hurt part that hadn't understood why Kahmel would sacrifice his country, was starting to understand why he did it. Kahmel couldn't have been too happy with the people surrounding him in the palace. The Court would have found a way to blame him, me, or both of us for my sudden disappearance and the disaster that would result from that. No one would believe him if he said the Zendaalans were behind my kidnapping. Maybe Dekaar didn't have to steal K'sundi from Kahmel. Maybe Kahmel didn't want it anymore.

And maybe, as much as it hurt, I couldn't blame him.

The K'sundi I wanted to save was different from the one it was now. I was trying to save what K'sundi could be. I wanted to get back K'sundi's past—good, bad, and ugly—because it was still part of us and so K'sundi could have a future worth preserving. But I didn't want it as it was now. The K'sundi of today created my parents, who found out about my fire and, instead of protecting me, left me to die. It created the people who would never give me a chance, even as a *child*, because my eyes weren't the right color. Because they didn't want a daughter with attitude. The K'sundi of today left me with nothing until Kahmel came along, willing to let me hate him to save me, and they fought us both every step of the way.

I thought I'd have questions for Kahmel when I talked to him next, but that hurt part of my heart was scabbing over now. Kahmel saw all of this and did what he could to keep his promises to me, to keep me safe, even if everything else had failed. And now, the first words I might say to him were, *I understand.*

Dekaar wanted me to be hurt. If anything, I was relieved. Let him chase his own tail pleasing the Equalizers and the Court system they set up. If he thought dealing with *me* was loathsome because of what I didn't know, just wait until he was among his own people.

I cocked my head at him and then I bowed. "Long live the great Faresh of K'sundi," I said sincerely.

Dekaar didn't say anything. The screen shut off, and the shield grid around me powered down.

DENS AND TUNNELS

Kahmel Axon Kai of the Omah Clan

Aithel decided to change the terms of our agreement. I thought he may have to brand me again, but it turned out simply changing his mind was enough. I marveled at how little we really knew about the dragons. Aithel always knew when I was doing something he didn't approve of, or even thinking about it. What exactly did my oath allow him to do to me? Read my thoughts? Have a clearer picture of what I was doing at all times? Or could he do that all along? I wasn't sure. And it wasn't the time to ask. We had bigger issues to address.

Aithel was finally being open with us. In his own way.

"There's a way to save your wife," Aithel explained, leading me through the halls of his castle. He didn't ask T'shan to come, and I didn't think T'shan minded. He butted heads with the Dragon King and was getting tired of the fact that Aithel enjoyed it. *"But there's much you need to know. Much you're behind on. You will have to learn by my side as quickly as you can."*

I nodded, and Aithel gestured with a claw for me to go inside a massive room with a doorway big enough for him to walk through. All of the rooms were intimidatingly massive except for the bedrooms. I stepped inside and gasped.

It was a library.

Books upon books upon books, rows of them, aisles of them, walls brimming with them, stretching up to the ceilings. Books were stacked in piles on the floor, in the corners, against the walls. The room was tall enough for Aithel to stand in, but the aisles were spaced for humans. This room was only for humans. Worthy humans.

Aithel saw me as worthy.

The Dragon King nodded toward an aisle at random. *"You could probably spend the rest of your life just studying that shelf."* He growled, and a glowing dragon appeared at his side. *"So ask for the books you need. Read about realms and the different breeds of dragons. You may peruse whatever else you'd like, but those are the topics that will help you save your wife."*

He left, and I had the entire library to myself.

So I got to work.

My head swam with information. I wouldn't have known the whole day had gone by if it wasn't for the glowing dragons that brought me breakfast, then lunch, then dinner. I didn't leave the library. I barely noticed the meals.

I read the topics Aithel told me to, and so much of it was beyond me I had to ask for more books just to understand the ones I had. By the time the next glowing dragon brought me dinner, I was sitting on the floor, surrounded by at least a dozen books, all of them just to understand the first one I picked up.

I was going to complain to Aithel that this wasn't going to work, but every time I came close, I found something else that caught my interest.

Butaah. I kept seeing that word, and I thought it was the name of an ancient race of people. But then I realized only the language was being referred to, not the people. So then I thought it may be a language the K'sundii used to speak. And then I recognized a word or two as I scanned over the text that appeared to be in Butaah.

Like *k'mhet, hos vihenal,* and *ned rial.* Fire, to land, and to come. The command words.

This bit of progress helped me forget about complaining.

The books about the realms referenced even more terms I didn't understand. Dens, the Realm of Not, Tunnels... Each word was mentioned as though the term was self-explanatory, and then I was knee-deep into another line of research.

Hours must have passed after I was served dinner, because the next dragon that came tried to drag me off to bed. I shook it off and got back to reading. I knew I should sleep, but I couldn't pull myself away from what I was learning.

I didn't even look up when footsteps came my way.

"I was starting to think Aithel ate you or something," T'shan muttered, setting a plate in front of me before plopping down on the floor beside me.

"Is it morning already?" I asked, noticing only then how tired my eyes were.

"Yes, you've been here all night. It's breakfast time. What are you reading about?"

"Everything." I pressed my palms against my eyes, seeing lines of text appear in rows behind my eyelids.

T'shan picked up a book and started flipping through the pages. "Let me guess. You're going to stay here a bit longer than the few days you originally agreed to."

I sighed, opening my eyes and waiting for them to refocus. "If I have to, yes."

T'shan frowned at whatever page he was reading. I recognized the cover. It was one I tried getting through earlier, but I couldn't remember what I was using it for. To help me understand one of the terms I was researching? But it was more confusing than the book I was trying to interpret.

"What are Dens?" T'shan asked.

Ah, right. That was what that book was about. "No idea." I set my book aside and took a bite out of the biscuit T'shan had brought me, savoring the soft texture. When I took a sip of the tea, I wished I hadn't because it made me realize how heavy my eyelids felt.

"Realm of Not," T'shan read from the page. "Butaah, *Mufi eltep—*"

"Wait," I said, shaking off the drowsiness from the tea. "What was that last thing?"

"I'm just reading some of this ridiculous jargon," T'shan said, tossing the book to me. "That last one looked like a foreign word. It just kept repeating."

Butaah. It was a word in Butaah. That was the real name for the command words. I read the passage T'shan had opened. That was right, this book was confusing because I didn't know what Butaah meant, and I, too, dismissed it for all the words I didn't understand. Now I saw them in a new light.

"Was that important?" T'shan asked, scooting closer to look over my shoulder.

"Maybe," I muttered, scouring the page. T'shan was right. The text did repeat that phrase throughout the passages. A phrase to speak to a dragon, I now knew, because it was the language the dragons understood, the bridge we'd used to communicate with once. The other passages started to make more sense. That phrase *Mufi eltep* was used to open Dens, whatever they were. Dragon nest caves?

I tossed the book aside. When I shut my eyes, I was tempted to keep them closed and go to sleep right there.

"Whelp," T'shan said, standing. "Glad to be of help."

"*I see you haven't left,*" said Aithel.

I looked up to see him standing in the doorway. I must have been exhausted if I didn't hear him coming.

T'shan started for the entrance, then stopped as the massive Dragon King blocked his way out. "He'll probably be here for months, at this rate."

Aithel cocked his head at me. "*Come, now, Half-Drac. It's only been a day.*"

"You know," I said, standing. "You could just tell me what it is you want me to know. There's too much I don't understand in these books. T'shan's right, it would take me months to get even a basic understanding."

"*True,*" Aithel said, coming into the library, still blocking the exit.

T'shan, seeing that, found a seat by a shelf and picked up the book nearest to him, scanning it.

"*If you didn't have the oldest dragon alive as a tutor.*"

I perked up at that, and so did T'shan.

"*Tell me what confuses you,*" Aithel offered.

"What are the Dens?" I asked first, since that was the wall I'd slammed against when he came in.

"*What have you read about them so far?*"

I shrugged. "Nothing I can understand. I just read something that mentioned activating one with a command word—er, I mean, in Butaah."

Aithel grinned. "*So you finally know of our language.*"

T'shan raised an eyebrow. "That's what that word meant?"

"*What else?*" asked Aithel.

"That's it." I picked up the book I'd tossed aside. "It goes into more detail, but I have no idea what it means to activate a Den. Is it a dragon nest cave? Why would it need to be activated?"

Aithel laughed, like one did when a child said something particularly ignorant and had no idea. He swept a foreleg around the room. "*This is a Den. The greatest and most sacred Den there is, but a Den nonetheless.*"

The Dragon Realm. That was why Dens were mentioned in every book the glowing dragons brought when I asked them to bring me books about realms. "There are more realms than just the Dragon Realm?"

"*Not more realms,*" Aithel explained. "*It is the same realm. The Realm of Not.*"

"I saw that," T'shan mentioned. Then he flipped through the book he'd picked up. "It's here too. Is that what you call...all of this?"

Aithel nodded. "*You will not find the stars in this sky at night in your own realm. They belong to a realm all to themselves. The realm of Not."*

"Why is it called that?" I asked.

"It is not here, nor there. Therefore, it is Not. It's where they come from." He glanced at the glowing dragons floating about the library.

"The dragon of in-between," I muttered.

Aithel nodded. *"Precisely."*

"So what does all this mean?" T'shan asked. "How does any of this help Jashi?"

"We can keep her safe here," I said, realizing it as I was saying it.

Aithel didn't say anything, just watched. But approval gleamed in his eye. This was why he wanted me to research it on my own—to see me come up with the same solution he did, to both of our problems.

I sat up straighter. "We can keep *everyone* safe here."

"But only Half-Dracs can come here." T'shan raised his eyebrows.

"To *this* Den," I said, looking to Aithel for confirmation. "Because, like you said, this one is sacred. But the other ones can be reached by anyone. Anyone with a dragon and a command word."

Aithel nodded again.

THE DRAGON KING took us to another room of the castle, where a map etched in dark metal stood in the middle of a large dais. On the map, dots glowed at various points, white lines connecting the dots.

"What is this room?" T'shan asked.

"It's where I keep a map of Dens," Aithel said, gesturing with his head for us to approach the map.

As I watched, the lines connecting the dots faded and then reappeared somewhere else, connecting other dots. "The Dens connect...but the connections don't last?" I asked.

"Very good." Aithel walked the length of the dais, pacing like a professor rather than an ancient creature older than Hemorah itself.

"Dens have openings at various points on your planet, and even on other planets."

That was when I realized some lines were going way off, away from the continents in the center of the map and pointing at dots on other sections. Off the planet. I snapped my fingers. "That was how the K'sundii reached Obellana."

Aithel nodded again. *"Precisely. They waited for the Dens on Hemorah's moon to form Tunnels between each other—"*

"Tunnels?" T'shan asked.

"The connections between Dens," Aithel said, gesturing to the ever-changing map.

That explained one of the other references I didn't understand.

"Each Den will connect at least once with each other every year. The Tunnels only hold open for a few minutes."

"Then we can use the Dens to get to Jashi!" T'shan exclaimed.

I looked at the map. It didn't take long to find Zendaal. Jashi had her tracking device on still. I had the location memorized. "She's here, near the capital." I pointed, then found a Den close to there. I watched as the map's lines glowed and faded. That Den was connected to somewhere in Med Mali right now. "But we could take any Den in Zendaal to get out. The biggest problem is getting into the country."

"But your men would be scattered," argued Aithel, pacing the podium once more. *"Each Den is open only a few minutes, as I said. You would need significant resources to retake your wife, and adding more chaos to an already delicate situation would be unwise, at best."*

Foolish, but Aithel didn't say it.

"You have another idea."

"In your world today," Aithel said, lying down and crossing his forearms, *"there are borders. It has been your biggest obstacle thus far and has slowed you down significantly, which allowed your enemy to catch up with you."*

I hadn't thought about it that way, but he was right. It was the reason I had to keep up the war with Omani, the reason Jashi and I had to sneak away to Vahdel, and the reason we couldn't get to Jashi now.

"*But there is an event,*" Aithel said. "*One that occurs once every four years. The Convergence. All of the Dens will be connected for three days, during the annual Fire Festival.*"

The one K'sundi celebrated with the fiery icon that ascended the Dharia mountains and brought back knowledge.

"That's perfect," I said, standing. "We'll get Jashi back and—"

"*Not just Jashi,*" Aithel interrupted, his eyes glimmering with mischief. "*This is my request for you, Kahmel. The next Convergence is this year.*" He paused to let it sink in.

The Fire Festival. It was in a little over a week. "We don't have much time, then."

So fast. Everything was happening so fast.

"*Before the Convergence, you will gather up as many of your people as will join you. And take as many Half-Dracs with you who will come as well. You will take them all to stay in the Dens with you. Along with Jashi.*"

"In a week?" He wanted me to plan some kind of...grand exodus or something, in a little over a week?

"Wait," T'shan said. "Stay in the Dens? For how long? Didn't you say each of them only connect for a little while? We'd be able to get them in easily enough, with a three-day window to work with, but with little five-minute windows, it'd be impossible to get them back home if they wanted to go."

"They wouldn't be going home," I realized out loud.

Aithel grinned. "*They would stay in the Dens until the next Convergence. The Half-Dracs, as most of them are children, would be protected from the new Faresh. And we would have our Half-Dracs back.*" Him, the other Dragon Kings, and the dragons, themselves. Aithel looked back out at the stars. "*For four years, we will have them back.*"

"And then what?" asked T'shan "We just sit around for four years and then...?"

"*We battle for our parts back*" was Aithel's answer as he looked back at T'shan. Then he held my gaze, those reptilian eyes seeming to glow against the starlit skies. "*Over the course of three days.*"

Not four years to hide. Four years to build an army, and then fight for three days with no borders. Aithel was asking for a lot. I was asking for a lot. But for what we both wanted to achieve, we had to be willing. I had to be willing to toss everything I thought I knew to the side, embrace whatever madness awaited me next, and do whatever it took to protect my own—and get my wife back.

I had to be fast, and there was no time to make sense of anything. But none of that mattered. Because the things I was fighting for were too important to stop and try to make sense of anything. Aithel was on my side. We had a solution, along with a near-impossible problem. But when had that ever stopped us before?

ANOTHER BROADCAST

When T'shan and I left the Dragon King's realm—or his Den, rather—I called Rand on the HoloCaller. Before I could say I had a lot to tell him, he quickly explained, urgency in his voice and in the lines of his face, that in the few days since I'd been gone, everything in K'sundi had gone to hell.

The new Faresh presented the Zendaalans a peace offering. He would allow them to take the Half-Dracs, whom they still called Fire Bugs, and bring them to Zendaal to be examined by the scientists there, on the grounds of their having the most advanced medical expertise in the world.

Parents quickly realized what that meant: The new Faresh would take their children away and have them experimented on by the Zendaalans. And they didn't even know what I knew, which was that in all likelihood, those children wouldn't be coming back home.

This whole time, I was beginning to realize, Jashi and I had been building up tension. We'd been pushing and pushing, and it felt like we were getting nowhere. But all the while, we were making it harder and harder for people to go back to thinking like they always had because we'd given them so many reasons to question what they were taught to accept.

If the dragons could be trained without collars, why keep pushing for collars?

If Jashi and I hadn't done anything wrong, why had the Zendaalans harassed us?

If Jashi and I revealing our powers made others do the same, why were the Zendaalans threatened by that?

The pressure had built up, and the people were on the brink. I'd left, and Jashi had disappeared. The new Faresh who had taken my place was about to take their children and present them to the enemy as a peace offering.

And what had resulted from that was an explosion.

Dekaar announced his decision shortly after I entered Aithel's Den with T'shan. Every day since, the K'sundii had been in an outrage. Rand sent me videos of people demanding answers from the Council at the House of Legislation. Hundreds of them protested, refusing to be turned down. They gathered at the Zendaalan embassy in K'sundi, demanding to know why I'd left and asking what happened to Jashi. Zendaalan officials and K'sundi officers combined were sent to deal with the problem, but the people weren't taking it sitting down. The more the government tried to suppress them, the louder and bigger their protests became.

It was quickly becoming global news. News didn't circulate much from rebel countries to Equalized ones, but people were tapping into illegal networks and broadcasting people holding up signs in support of the K'sundii.

"WHERE'S JASHI?"

"CHILDREN ARE NOT EXPERIMENTS!"

"SAVE THE FIRE BUGS!"

The rebel countries, more than anyone, knew this was different. Every time the people had come against the Zendaalans in the past, it had resulted in that nation being labeled a rebel country. But now the world was watching. Even Equalized nations were asking about Jashi and me, especially Daoliu and Cirssa Kun. Videos of them were circulating everywhere.

"Zendaal and the officials of K'sundi cannot allow these questions to go on unanswered," said Cirssa, staring at the camera—without her contact lenses on. Her bright orange eyes glared with fierce intensity. "Where are Jashi and Kahmel? And what do the Zendaalans want with the Fire Bugs?"

The world, in just a few days, had devolved into chaos.

And I had a week to get as many people as I could find to save Jashi and then wait for four years for a chance to strike.

Those two events could go very well together.

By the time Rand was done catching me up, I decided there was too much to be done to waste time explaining to him what my plans were, so I just told him to gather the others and meet me at our latest base. I considered what Jashi said about showing the people who I was. Who I *really* was. If it wasn't for that advice, we might not be where we were today. Zendaal struck back, but not without consequences.

Now it was time to take off another mask and see how the people reacted.

WE SET up recording equipment at an abandoned warehouse. Asan worked to get things ready, and Rand bumped fists with me, nodding in approval. "Nice to see you come up with a plan that doesn't terrify me, for once."

Funny, because this plan, out of all of them, terrified me the most. "Thanks," I said, wondering why every time I peeled off another layer of armor, it felt like I was fighting by becoming vulnerable. Attacking with openness. A deed that felt contradictory to its very purpose, and yet, here I was, doing it again.

"Ready, Asan?" I asked.

He gave a thumb's up and pushed record.

"I've been hearing a lot of people asking where I am. Well, here I am. And I'm a little irritated, to be honest. Jashi's missing. I might have mentioned that before. Anyway, I noticed a lot of you have started protesting against the Zendaalans and the new Faresh with their stance on the Fire Bugs—because the Half-Dracs are mostly children. Ever wonder about that, by the way? Actually, let me not get ahead of myself.

"The main reason I'm here is because of the protests—a valiant effort, truly, but one that will be short-lived if you don't protect yourselves." I stepped closer to the camera. "I'm offering you a solution to that problem. You're going to have to trust me, though, because it's a wild idea. But it will keep you safe—and your Fire Bug children, who I believe are the ones we're all most concerned for."

I backed away and crossed my arms over my chest. "You have a week. If you're ready to fight for your lives, our freedom, and your fire-hearted children, it's time. Join the rebellion. Find members near you; they'll tell you everything you need to know. When you come, try to keep in mind—not a few months ago, you didn't know the Fire Bugs existed. Be prepared to have your scope of what's possible expanded again. That's all I can tell you for now. I'll tell you the rest when we meet. Face to face."

I signaled to Asan to stop the recording, and the red recording light blinked off.

"Rand may like the idea," Khes said, crossing his arms and staring at me dubiously, "but I'm still not convinced. You're revealing your ties to the rebellion, openly inviting K'sundii to find a chapter close to them and join, and expecting K'sundii officials not to use the offer to find our people and sabotage us from within."

"I know there will be K'sundii officials after us," I said, slipping on a jacket as Asan handed it to me. "Especially with Dekaar in office."

"Right," said Rand. "When are you going to explain all that? What you have against the new Faresh—besides the obvious, I mean."

I was still mostly silent on everything Aithel had told T'shan and me. One week. We had one lousy week to make sure everything was in place. I was determined to make this work. It was the only shot I had at saving Jashi. And even though it didn't affect me one way or another if Aithel got what he wanted and had the Half-Dracs hidden in the Dens, he and I had come to an understanding. If this was what he wanted, I would do a damn good job of executing it. What Aithel wanted with them after that was his business, but I would get the Half-Dracs and the dragons back together for him. Time was a commodity I didn't have right now, so explanations would have to come later. Right now, I had to act.

"When the time comes," I said by way of explanation, then looked to Asan. "Are we ready to head out?"

"The van's waiting for us now."

I nodded, then looked to Khes, Rand, and Arusi in turn. We would all be going our separate ways here. They didn't know it yet, but if they agreed and everything went according to plan, this would be our last time alone together like this. Because we were short on time, we would need to split up to each lead a group of rebels and new members into initiation and filtering and working overtime on background checks for new initiates as fast as we could run them. But Khes was right. Once Dekaar saw that video, he'd do everything in his power to stop the rebels from getting anywhere, both from within and without. We were in a hurry, and we'd surely miss something, and someone would slip past our notice undercover.

But wolf or sheep, they were all going in for four years with no contact with the rest of the world. Not much good they could do as an informant in that position.

"We don't have much time," I said to all of them because I was sure they all agreed with Khes. He had relinquished his title of rebel leader to me when I became Faresh. These people, his people, were in my hands, and I didn't take his faith in me lightly. "I'm going to need you to trust me now more than ever, because we don't have time to get everyone on the same page until just before this all goes down. But trust me, it's not going to matter one way or another if a few rats get past us."

Arusi shrugged, like this was nothing. "We'll always trust you, K. No need to worry there. I mean, nothing you tell us ever makes sense until it all falls into place, anyway."

Khes and Asan laughed, nodding in agreement.

"All right," Khes said, still chuckling. "If you're fine with it, I'm fine with it. Let's get ready to welcome the new recruits." Then he turned to leave in his own vehicle.

"We have a week," Rand said pensively. "And after that Aithel will help us get Jashi back, right?"

That was what I'd told them, and I nodded to confirm.

"Then whatever it takes. Let's get your wife back."

I smiled, and he turned to leave too.

"See you when it's time," Arusi said simply, then went on her way.

Asan nodded to the van parked outside, where T'shan was waiting for me. He'd be taking us right back to the entrance to Aithel's Den, where we'd wait until the week was up. The rest would be up to the rebels.

And to K'sundi.

A CHANGED NAME

Jashi *Eloe* Anyua-Omah

After I talked to Dekaar, I intended to scour his clothes for something gender-neutral enough, wondering if my curvy hips would even fit into the narrow trousers I saw him wearing earlier. But I soon found I didn't need to. When I'd searched the first time, I was looking for a way out of the house, not really paying attention to how the clothes looked. Looking closer, I realized the clothes were of Zendaalan make, made of fiber that could stretch to just about any size once you squeezed into them. The gray pants and white shirt I chose were as androgynous as anything. Plain, but the clothes would do. The sandals I'd worn here were too bare, leaving my feet freezing, so I slipped on some house shoes I found lying around.

The kitchen had food, and I was hungry, so I found some bread, a little sliced poultry, and lettuce, figuring I may as well use the leafy greens while they were still good—they would be the first to wilt, after all. I ate my sandwich, barely tasting it.

I mentally reached out to Ocean, finding our connection quickly. If I didn't know any better, I'd say she hadn't moved since I last spoke to her. And then I considered that maybe she hadn't. Curious, I stretched deeper into the bond, like casting a line in water. And then I felt her hunger and cursed under my breath.

Damn it, Ocean, you have to get something to eat, I scolded. Her hunger was gaping and vast. Dragons had huge stomachs, and hers was practically empty. A cat was a snack, and I didn't think she'd had anything since that.

Ocean hesitated, and I was ready to unleash a slew of curses if she objected. I couldn't let her waste away watching over me like this. She was poised to protect me, but I was still her master. I had to protect her too.

Before I needed to utter any profanities, however, she seemed to understand what I needed. *Very well...Eloe.*

I softened. Hearing Ocean call me that made the name special. It took the sting I felt from Dekaar and replaced it with warmth. Familiarity. I didn't mind that I got it from Dekaar. He may be my enemy, but that didn't mean he wasn't right. *Eloe* felt right. It felt... like mine.

Ocean's attention pulled away from me then, the connection ebbing. She flew off to find something to eat and needed to concentrate. So I held off on the questions I wanted to ask her about dragon names and what it meant for me to have one.

The space in my mind she had occupied turned cold, and for the first time, I realized how lonely I was. And perhaps that was the other reason Ocean had neglected herself, feeling that loneliness in me and trying to fill it. Ocean was a sounding-board whenever I was alone. She gave me somewhere to go, if only in my mind. And without it, the fear that I'd been keeping just ahead of, moving too fast to let it close, caught up with me. For myself, and for Ocean, I had to push it back. I could be scared later. At least for now, I was relatively safe. Attican wasn't here, nor any of his companions. That was good. And there was no one around to tell them what I was doing here, though I wasn't foolish enough to believe Dekaar wouldn't have hidden cameras around. Even Kahmel had those throughout the palace for safety measures. And it saved my life, once. Dekaar most likely had a way to keep an eye on me from wherever he was, somehow.

I stared at my empty plate, pushing around crumbs the bread left behind with my finger, not sure what to do with my time. All I could think about was escape, but, truth be told, I had no idea how to go about that. *What would Kahmel do?* I wondered. He would look for a way to exploit Dekaar's weaknesses, wait for an opportunity. Catch him off guard.

Dekaar's mansion was immaculate and gorgeous, but it didn't carry anything personal about it. The place may as well have been a hotel room.

Picking up the dishes, I supposed I may as well busy myself, so I washed them.

The kitchen had knives, but with no one around, the only person they would have served to harm was myself. I wasn't even sure if Dekaar ever planned to return here.

I didn't think Dekaar wanted me dead, so he would have to keep me fed. At the very least, a few months from now when the food finally ran out, he would have to send someone to restock the stores. But I didn't want to wait a few months only to find out he had some way of detaining me—like those forcefields he threw up when it suited him.

I scowled, putting away the plate and wishing I had something else to clean, something to keep my hands busy. I looked down at them, wet and covered in suds.

There was always fire practice, I mused.

I snapped my fingers, allowing the fire to burst from my fingertips and grow into a flame as wide as my palm with a roar. The fire licked up the water from my hand, steam curling from my fingers.

A forcefield dropped around me, an alarm blaring. Pain flared everywhere, and it took me a moment to realize that it was not a forcefield, but a *containment* field. The kind used to trap unruly animals or dragons and give them a shock when they got out of control. And like a pet, I was being reprimanded. The smell of scorched flesh filled my nostrils, and when the field dissipated, a shower of water came down.

Damn him. A Half-Drac himself, Dekaar's house had every precaution against Half-Drac intruders.

I stumbled forward, leaning over the sink, breathing. And then the call came in. It rang briefly this time before the holographic projection activated.

"I see you've tried using your fire," mused Dekaar from behind me.

I spun to face him, fuming. I huffed, pushing my hair out of my face, angling my head back and stealing a quick downward glance at him that I hoped didn't seem too interested. He was sitting this time, and the projector included the chair he was in. Not from the palace, I noticed. Not our chairs. But it didn't look like it was from someone's home, either. It had one of those nondescript patterns hotels always used, which was likely where he was staying.

Not that any of these little details helped me much. They only told me how close he was to taking my throne. But at least it made me feel oriented. Gave me some idea of what was going on.

I crossed my arms. "Didn't expect me to just sit around on my ass, did you?"

"I suggest you behave," he said simply, and I realized he was in no mood to be taunted.

Was it because of what I'd said before? "Long live the great Faresh of K'sundi"? I'd essentially shown him I would turn my back on K'sundi and leave it to him. The way he glared at me, it almost seemed like he resented me for saying it. The hypocrite.

Dekaar didn't give me time to respond before the hologram disappeared and I was left grinding my teeth in frustration. I wanted to throw something. See something shatter. There was nothing to do, nothing to glean from. There weren't even any systems to hack, from what I could tell. Even the holographic projector retracted into the ceiling once its job was done. Not that I knew how to hack.

For a moment, I let myself taste the futility of all of this. Allowed myself to think there was no point in trying to leave, that Dekaar made no move to restrain or inhibit me in any real way because I simply wasn't a threat.

But for every moment thinking about pointlessness, I forced myself to see Dekaar. See the way he needed to watch me crumble. I filled myself with the defiance that refused to let him have what he wanted.

He wanted me to hold onto K'sundi, so I would let it go.

He wanted me to go crazy with nothingness, alone in this prison of a mansion, so I would keep myself busy. Doodle sketches on the wall every minute of the day if I had to. Tell myself stories. Reorganize the furniture. Do whatever it took to keep my mind busy.

If my mind was busy, I was alert, aware—ready to see an opportunity and leap for it—and make good on my promise to Ocean to let her have at Dekaar.

So I changed again to get out of my wet clothes, and I set to work—occupying myself. I found a pen, and luckily for Dekaar's walls, I found paper. Then I set myself down in the mansion's library—one full of Zendaalan philosophy and nonfiction I wasn't interested in—and started doodling. I was shit at drawing, so I just drew little details, starting from the corner and expanding out, making little swirls and dots and lines and angles. I didn't make wide strokes; that would take up too much of the paper all at once. I just needed to keep my hands busy doing something methodical. And even though I wasn't trying to improve, I noticed that by the time I finished filling out a page, the lines didn't look as wobbly, and the opposite end of the page was a good deal neater than my starting point.

Perhaps I'd make it out of here an artist.

I pulled out another piece of paper, glancing at the Zendaalan books on the wall and wondering how long it'd take me to get bored enough to get started on them, and a thought crept in, unnoticed until I sat down to draw again and my hair, still wet, dripped onto the paper. I started thinking about how Dekaar popped in to taunt, and it made me question how he could put up a forcefield wherever he wanted in the house.

How was he controlling the house from wherever he wanted, anyway? I wondered again. The rebels talked about stuff like this around me, and I didn't always understand, but it started to make sense now. They talked about private networks a lot. It wasn't easy setting those things up.

So how did he have this place set up so there wasn't a piece of equipment inside the house, but obviously there was a complicated control system outside of it? Surely all of that couldn't fit in his cybernetic implants. There had to be something else, somewhere else, maintaining the house's system. Someplace I could send Ocean.

I'm back, said Ocean, and I reached for her, felt her fullness to make sure. Thankfully, I was met with satisfaction. She licked the blood from her teeth as she flew, probably back to the spot she'd left when I sent her to go eat. *I found a dairy plant.* She announced gleefully, and I made a noise in disgust. Zendaalan dairy plants were as friendly as they sounded. If she snatched a few cows from there, I was sure sitting in her stomach was a better fate than those metal grates they lived between. *Don't worry, I made sure not to get caught,* she added. *I waited until they were transferring the animals between stalls and snatched a few quickly.*

Great job, I said, stifling a chuckle. I wasn't sure how closely Dekaar was watching me, and if he caught me blatantly reacting to what Ocean said, he might piece together I was talking to a dragon. He would know more about the Drake Bond than I did, of course, so he would know what talking through one looked like.

And I found something else, Ocean announced, and I felt her land with a great swoop of her wings. *Dragons.*

At that, I couldn't help my eyebrows shooting up, and for fear of making any more facial expressions, I fixed my gaze on my half-finished page, going back to doodling, though absentmindedly. *Here? How?*

Collared ones, Ocean clarified, and I sank. But she either didn't care or didn't notice, she was so excited. *There were many animal factories near the dairy plant, and a training plant was one of them.*

What good does that do us? They're as mindless as you were before we bonded. I leaned onto the arm of my chair, less enthused than I was a moment ago. My drawings weren't looking too shabby, despite the fact I was barely focusing. It just showed how much improvement one could make on something one they had absolutely nothing else to do. I decided to try my hand at simple drawings, starting with leaves and flowers. Since my hand was steadier, the shapes didn't look completely terrible. And if I didn't think about it too hard, I might have been enjoying myself.

But you have a name now, Ocean said, as though the matter was simple. *It'll make it easier to convince the dragons to help you.*

I had to force myself not to stop drawing. With every sentence, I had another dozen questions. *A dragon name can help you rally up dragons to my side?* I decided to start with.

Yes, that's what it's for. She spun around, her tail trailing her as she did. *We're not so different from humans, Eloe. We talk when our minds are intact.* There was a tinge of sadness in her voice as she added that. *They may be hard to reach, but the dragons can hear my voice. Dragons...we don't see things as you do. We feel.*

I stopped at that, momentarily, then continued drawing, making vines that connected from one end of the page to the other, like a train of thought. Wasn't that how our bond worked? I felt Ocean, though I couldn't exactly see through her eyes. Dragons weren't literally blind, no, but perhaps there was a part of them, on another plane of existence, where this was what they experienced. This sensory state, devoid of light, made of something else.

With a dragon name, Ocean went on, *you become more palpable to me. More real. Not just a Half-Drac, you're Eloe. When dragons communicate with each other, we don't use words. We use feelings. Now I can tell them what you feel like, and they'll be able to find you.*

I was slowly beginning to understand. I could tell Kahmel everything that was happening to me here when I got back, describe what sensations felt like, or what things looked like. But Ocean was saying that dragons *only* communicated with feelings. They transferred sentiments, rather than verbal exchanges. Having a dragon name made me easier to *understand,* as well as describe to other dragons. It hurt seeing how important this was and how I might have never known if Dekaar hadn't told me, frustrated, much like Ocean, at all that I didn't know.

It also explained how all of the dragons felt the same hurt as their Kings when it came to The Traitor.

But even if you got a few dragons to wander over here, I reasoned, still not quite sure how she'd even manage that, *what would you do once they're here? You can't break their collars or free their minds. Only the bond can do that.*

You'll bond with them, Ocean said, as though it were the simplest thing in the world, as though I hadn't gone through half a dozen dragons before I got to her back in Vahdel. And from what I read, at least based upon the books Kahmel and I had available back at the palace, that was standard, not just because I didn't have a dragon name.

How am I supposed to bond with a dragon you drag over here, I said, tired of all these concepts I still didn't understand, *without getting close to them?*

They just have to hear you speak the words, Ocean said, and I felt her lips pulling back into that toothy grin dragons gave when they smiled. *All that will bond to you will follow. I will bring enough to guarantee success.*

I drew desert flowers now, like the one still hidden in the curls of my hair. With enough dragons standing around, at least some could bond to me. And dragons fought most viciously in groups. Ocean could get me out if she had the support. Kahmel could testify to how quickly a group of determined dragons could get through a shield generator when given the chance. That was why they had to be tamed or electrocuted before shields were even useful against them.

This could work. But...

I can't open the windows, I said, making frustrated little swirls. Then I decided they looked somewhat like leaves of a tree, so I modified them a bit, then started making the lines of a trunk under them. *Your dragons won't be able to hear me.*

Won't they? answered Ocean coyly. She was using the holes in my knowledge about dragons against me.

I frowned at the page as though I could see her there, and I felt her grin in response. As if now was the time to be teasing.

This will be risky, she explained. *I will not be able to get the dragons out of the training facility discreetly.* Ocean looked to the side, as though seeing the dragons she spoke of even now. *I'll break through their defenses, bring the dragons with me, and come here. Their authorities will be following me, and we'll have to escape.*

So we'd be going from the frying pan and into the fire. As soon as I was out, I would have to find someplace to hide with a bunch of dragons and stay hidden until I could find a way to contact Kahmel and we could figure out a way to rendezvous. All providing Ocean had a way for me to speak to the dragons outside without being able to make so much as a crack in these windows. They may as well be made of steel. Not to mention, I had no idea what it was going to be like to be drake-bonded to several dragons at once. I barely understood Ocean's and my relationship as it was.

But I noticed I was drawing desert flowers again now, filling the last empty parts of the page with more desert flowers than I could count, making the last corner look like an oasis. Hope, in the middle of depravity.

Let's do it.

ZOO ANIMAL

Though Ocean and I had a plan in place, or the semblance of one, I decided to bide my time, both to work out the logistics and prepare for my escape and to continue to carefully observe my captor. After all, he'd given me the single most important bit of information I'd need to make an escape when he'd told me about my dragon name. It felt foolish not to get as much information as possible out of the situation.

I sat on the floor doodling, my back supported by pillows, as I thought. The fact that Dekaar had answered any of my questions was a mystery in and of itself. He wasn't like the Zendaalans with their simple, straightforward—albeit malicious—goals. Dekaar was more complex. He hated Kahmel, yet he was intrigued by me. He hated the dragons, and his actions had brought about this future, but he also...regretted it. He was appalled by the future he'd created. I could see it in his eyes when he was faced with my ignorance.

If he hated the dragons so much, why did he even care that we'd lost so much knowledge about them? About ourselves? He was probably plagued with opposing feelings. He hated the dragons. He loved the dragons. He hated me. He loved me. He hated the Dragon Kings. He worshiped the Dragon Kings. Contradictions could exist within him at the same time. It was why, as nonsensical as it was, I could mock and tease Dekaar as much as I liked and he wouldn't hurt me because he liked me. But if I made him remember—made him think too hard about how he came to be and what it took to get here—he would kill me.

And as disturbing as it was, he would probably even mourn me afterward.

If I was going to get any more information from Dekaar, I would have to walk a thin line. In the meantime, I doodled. I didn't like exercise much, but being cooped up with nowhere to go, I got antsy. So I did jumping jacks, jogged in place. My stamina wasn't the best, and I got winded, but it felt good to move.

And after a few days, Dekaar called again.

The ringing vibrated through the house and reached me all the way in the mansion's basement—a mostly empty space, but one I was considering using as a jogging track. The noise startled me, and that startled Ocean. Being surrounded by silence for days made noises stand out all the more. But once I realized what it was, I calmed. I soothed Ocean with a mental image of me stroking her behind the ear. Imaginations were as useful a communication method as words when using the Drake Bond. The image of her leaning into the touch and nudging me with her snout came as a response. But in the image, her ears were still pressed back, still alert, though she allowed herself to be soothed into calm. A fitting reflection for how I was feeling too, really.

I came up the stairs and made my way to the living room, pressing my hands to my ears as I drew closer. The ringing finally stopped as I sat on the sofa, leaning back and crossing my legs as Dekaar appeared before me. He wore Kahmel's sash, the mark of the Faresh, across his shoulder and down to his opposite hip.

I refused to let him rattle me, no matter how jarring it was to see that sash on anyone besides Kahmel or me. "You know," I said, cocking my head to the side, keeping my tone even, "you could send me an eWatch so you don't have to rupture my eardrums every time you call."

Dekaar raised an eyebrow in surprise. Surprise at my composure, I guessed. The last time he called, I was mad, tense, afraid but determined not to show it. Now I was reclined, relaxed, but deceptively so. Elegantly coiled, like a snake ready to strike.

Dekaar read this quickly. His thoughts flashed across his face as clearly as if he'd said them out loud. He wondered if I had discovered some weakness he was not aware of. Had I come in contact with someone? What secret did I have? For I must have one, if I no longer feared him.

But he was wrong about that. I did fear him. I feared him greatly. Though I had some semblance of a plan, I had no guarantee it would work. No rebels to support me, come to my rescue if something went wrong. And I had nowhere to go, even if I did make it out.

The difference, however, between me *now* and me a week ago was that I had decided. Whether I was here or in K'sundi, a Faresha or a peasant living in the streets of Zendaal, I could be comfortable in duplicity too. I wanted to save K'sundi, but not as it was. It had to change to be valuable to me again. Today, he could have it.

Soon, he would discover he didn't want K'sundi either. His plan had worked too well. His victory was too complete. He was a king with no one to rule. K'sundi was a shadow of itself, from his ancient perspective. No dragons, no Half-Dracs, no Dragon Kings. What did he have left? Politics? I almost felt sorry I wouldn't get to see him dance around the rules and regulations and make ones of his own only to have the entire Council each have a different reason for opposing him. I was sure that wasn't the kingdom he was planning on inheriting.

What he didn't know was that whether I succeeded or failed in my escape attempt, I would still laugh whenever I pictured him slowly realizing just what his victory really meant.

And so I reclined.

Dekaar straightened, then strode to my side, seating himself next to me on the armchair, his holographic image shimmering for a moment as he sat. It was like sitting by a ghost.

And in a way, I was.

"Gotten used to your new situation, have you, Eloe?" Dekaar said, nodding to me.

I hated hearing him call me that, as though he'd branded me for himself.

The slight scowl on his face made him look sick. My calmness bothered him. He was as paranoid as I once thought Kahmel was. Only now I knew Kahmel was only cautious, knowing that his enemies were waiting to trip him up at any given time. But Dekaar was a thief, waiting for someone to usurp what he'd stolen, just as he had.

I laughed. "What do you expect from me, Traitor? I'm the princess you've locked away in your impressive tower. Should I cry when you call? Or bang against bullet-proof windows every night?" I crossed my arms, huffing. "I don't have the energy. Now was there a point to your call?"

"Don't expect your husband to come for you," he snapped. "He's as powerless as you are now."

My stomach clenched because I wasn't sure how Kahmel was doing. For all I knew, Dekaar could have *him* locked away somewhere as well. Or Kahmel was running for his life every day. Though, at the very least, "powerless" still meant alive.

Something was off here, though, something about the way Dekaar scanned the room, as though making sure everything was as it should be. Like he half-expected there to be a huge tunnel in the floor under the bed. Like he was questioning the security of his home. Why? He'd been so sure of its impregnability thus far, why become paranoid now?

"All you ever do is gloat," I said, turning my lip up at him. "You're only telling me what I already know. Why call at all?" I was baiting him, hoping to get something from him I could use.

Dekaar didn't answer right away. He examined his metallic hand. "Zendaalan technology is amazing," he said, changing the subject completely. "Everything they believed I needed to know about the modern world was given to me in an instant from a device half the size of a man's thumb. A chip, apparently."

I raised an eyebrow. I wasn't expecting to learn about how Dekaar came into the world. Or, came *back* into the world, more accurately put. So that was how they brought him up to speed on the progression of society. They installed it into him. Not even common Zendaalans could afford such luxuries. That required a brain transplant, which was one of the most dangerous procedures. I supposed Dekaar had an implant for every major organ, coming back from the dead and all. But then, what exactly about him was flesh? This wasn't a Dekaar-robot, this was still the man who lived and breathed a thousand years ago. So how did they preserve his body for so long? And what brought it back to life?

"It included information about the world's many technological advances," Dekaar went on. "Not to mention famous names and faces, current laws and political opinions—even modern colloquialisms in K'unsdii—along with a dozen languages. I am *more* than a man now, if anything. And yet, for all of their genius, the Zendaalans tend to be quite crude."

"Crude?" I tried to imagine what could possibly seem crude from his ancient perspective. I thought everything would fascinate him.

Dekaar nodded. "As I said, I am more of a man now, and yet," he gestured to his face, half of it covered in chrome, glowing lights, and seams. "Ugly, hm? Their machines lack finesse, spirit. *Humanity*, literally and figuratively. Out of all of the information they could deliver in an instant, they didn't think it necessary to give me anything beautiful. I had no idea what modern music sounded like. They told me what comedy shows on the HoloScreens were, but I had to actually see it for myself to laugh at them"—he chuckled, as though remembering some particularly funny line—"hard enough to bring tears to my eyes." He huffed, glancing away. "When I saw how many gaps were left in their training, I insisted on spending a few months getting to know the world for myself. I didn't trust them to show me the good parts, and I was right."

I nodded, knowing precisely what he meant. That was what they'd done to culture all over the world, really. Stripped it down to what they saw as necessary, but taking the true heart out of it all. K'sundi was lucky enough to retain a few holidays, but our traditions themselves were long gone, labeled as barbaric and done away with. It explained why they hadn't bothered making Dekaar aware of how the Half-Dracs were being handled. They thought it was good enough to know they were handled, not how it was done. Crude was a good word for it. It wasn't that their machinations didn't work. They just had no elegance.

"Of the things I discovered," Dekaar said, "the most enthralling of them all, to me, were the zoos."

I frowned, losing his point completely. "What's so special about zoos?"

His eyes glinted with something that made me press my back farther into the cushion behind it. The look of a wild man.

"They're absolutely incredible," he said, his voice teetering on the edge of mania. "Every spare moment, I went to any zoo or aquarium I could find. I even found pet stores fascinating. The Zendaalans knew dragons and Half-Dracs could be problematic to their reign if ever allowed to be fully empowered." He waved a hand dismissively. "Their solutions were barbaric. Electric leashes and," he shuddered, "obliteration." Then he looked back at me, grinning. "They should have put you all in zoos. Beautiful creatures should be admired, not eradicated. And what better place than behind a glass wall? Completely contained, but still able to be appreciated from up close." He cocked his head. "You asked why I call. It's because I intend for this home to be your zoo. And what's the point if I don't get to admire you for myself from time to time?"

My stomach turned. I had learned nothing except how truly appalling Dekaar really was.

And then he shouted, the noise breaking through his chest like the roar of a beast, "You are *never* leaving, you understand? So you can wipe that *smug look* off your face, because you aren't getting out.

I've. Won. There is nothing left for you to do. Not you or your ridiculous husband. So why don't you both just give up?"

He realized what he'd let slip at the same time I did, and he scowled. "I have nothing to be afraid of," he said, more to himself than me, and the holograph flicked off.

But I'd heard all I needed to hear. I knew what was bothering him. Kahmel. Kahmel was doing something. Something that made Dekaar nervous.

That confirmed it. It was time to get out of here. Kahmel was waiting for me.

Though even if Kahmel wasn't getting ready to do something on his end, I wasn't about to stay long after that little speech. I didn't want to be Dekaar's little zoo animal any longer.

SHOUT

The next morning, I woke up with a purpose. It was time to get out of this hell-hole.

Are you ready? Ocean conveyed.

Let's get this over with was my wearied response. I couldn't be sure how closely Dekaar was watching me, so I went about my typical morning routine—or at least the one I'd built since being brought here. Namely, eating breakfast and heading right to the library to draw. I'd accumulated a small collection of drawings, and I pondered whether or not to take them with me. On one hand, I was actually kind of proud of a few of them. They weren't amazing or anything, but they were kind of cute. On the other hand, they represented the one thing I could do here, besides exercising and messing around in the kitchen, and I felt like if I had to look at these drawings one day in the future, I would scream.

I was still weighing the options when Ocean reached out again.

I'm at the dragon training plant. After I break inside to free the dragons, I'll be pursued, so there will be cars chasing us when it's time to get out.

I nodded to myself as I added details to the crude sketches of Comet and Ocean standing beside each other. Drawing dragons was intimidating, but so was my mission today, so I decided it was a good day to be brave.

Do it, I said.

I squinted at the drawing on the page, realizing what was

bothering me about it. Ocean's head was far too big, and the paws on Comet were much too small. I sighed. It was a lost cause. I crumpled up the drawing and threw it aside, hoping it wasn't a bad omen for the next few hours.

I reached out to Ocean, and I felt her roar. She charged, and though I didn't know exactly what she was pushing through, I could tell she was ripping and shredding something. A fence, a cage, something like that. Her claws made sweeping, tearing motions, and then heat pulsated from her mouth as she breathed flames at whoever had come to stop her.

She leaped into the air briefly before landing somewhere else and doing something similar. She said she'd collect enough dragons to ensure the Drake Bond would work. She must have meant it, because I counted three more times she hopped into the air, landed, and ripped to shreds whatever containment was being used to keep the dragons inside. She was struck briefly by low-powered lasers. It wasn't like in K'sundi, where the dragons were seen as a nuisance and attacked without mercy. The dragons here were a product, and the Zendaalans wanted to avoid damaging their goods as much as possible. I was sure the surrounding Zendaalans were strategizing a way to capture Ocean and get a free dragon.

But they were out of time. She jumped into the air and took off.

I have the dragons, Eloe, she said. *They'll be sending capture vehicles soon, so we don't have much time.*

So how do I establish the bond? I asked, calmly going into the kitchen and pouring another cup of coffee. I suppressed the raging storm of anxiety inside that was questioning every part of this plan. Afraid there was something about the mansion I hadn't taken into consideration. Terrified Ocean and the other dragons were going to get hurt by the laser defense system. And having no idea how we were going to sustain ourselves once we were out.

I'll tell you when the time is right.

I frowned. *I think the time is right now, Ocean. What the heck are you talking about?*

Just trust me, Eloe, she said, and at the begging tone in her voice, I decided to just shut up and listen. She wasn't just being coy. There was a reason she wasn't filling me in on everything. Maybe she was a little nervous about whatever she had in mind? I could only wait to find out.

Like I'd done every morning, I opened drawers as if looking for something and slipped several items from each one into the sleeve of the hoodie I'd chosen to wear today. A small knife, some scissors, a can opener. I pretended to find what I was looking for, a toothpick, and started using it. I'd done the same thing with food over the past few days—mostly packets of oatmeal and energy bars, small things that wouldn't spoil and were easy to hide in the clothes drawer when I went upstairs to change.

We're almost there. Get ready, said Ocean.

I jogged up the stairs, careful not to jostle the sharp objects in my sleeves too much. *How close is almost?*

I can see the mansion.

It was time. I went into my room and opened the drawer where I kept all my smuggled things in a long sleeved shirt with the arms and bottom tied at the ends. I'd torn a few holes in the collar of the shirt and slipped a drawstring from a hoodie through the holes so it would draw closed like a backpack. I wrapped my newly acquired sharp objects in underwear and slipped them in before drawing the top closed and slinging the sleeves around my shoulders and tying them behind my back.

"Suspicious activity detected. Contacting Deklas," said a system alert in Zendaalan. A forcefield dropped around me.

Dekaar's voice came over the house's intercom almost immediately. "Going somewhere?"

"As much as I've enjoyed being your little exhibit," I said, looking up at the unsuspecting black dot in the ceiling Kahmel trained me to recognize as a camera, "my husband is waiting for me."

I saluted him with two fingers and reached out to Ocean.

The dragons are here. Fall into the bond, Ocean urged me. *And speak the words.*

I had to contain the urge to strangle my own dragon. This was what she thought I would be able to figure out in the split second I had before Dekaar did something about this pathetic escape attempt? *Fall* into the bond? What did that mean?

You have to go farther than you've gone thus far. It's a little dangerous, she confessed. *But you're going to have to trust me.* She swerved as she flew through the air, dodging laser fire.

"I don't understand, Eloe," said Dekaar, chuckling, pulling me away from my thoughts with Ocean. "How exactly are you planning on..." His voice drifted off. He knew what a Drake Bond could do better than I did.

I needed to act now, before he made the connection between my silence and the dragons his outside cameras would pick up on soon.

I closed my eyes and threw myself. I threw my focus at Ocean with everything I had and quickly realized what Ocean meant when she said it was dangerous. The bond sucked me in like quicksand. I lost myself. I could no longer hear Dekaar or feel the shirt tied around my arms.

I was inside Ocean. Her vision opened up to me. I gaped at the dragons she brought with her, and her mouth followed the expression with me. There were dozens.

I looked back, and Ocean's head followed me. The Zendaalan squad cars were close on our tail, but Ocean had conveyed a thought that registered as a command to the ZST-trained dragons to protect themselves, and they launched pillars of fire toward the offending hovercars, holding them off.

Ocean looked back toward the mansion, and my vision was forced to follow. They were coming up on it now.

Use me, Eloe, Ocean said. *Say the words.*

And suddenly I understood. We were bonded in this moment. Deeper than anything any human could ever experience.

It was time for Dekaar to realize he could have anything *but* a dragon in a zoo. Because no collar, wall, glass, or forcefield could ever truly contain us. And the walls of this zoo were about to come crumbling down.

I opened my mouth, and Ocean's opened with me. I reached for her vocal cords, and my words rumbled through her throat in a voice that mimed my own, like a parrot's.

Leh mani stupior!

Ocean's roar rippled through the air, probably heard miles from here. Then she shoved me out. I fell out of the connection, suddenly aware of my body. My head throbbed. I had crumpled to the ground. And alarms were blaring.

"Threat detected," the system said, and the lasers outside whirred to life. "Contacting reinforcements."

Then my concentration split, like a kaleidoscope. Four, five, six dragons fell into sync with me.

I had *seven* dragons under my command.

I sent my mental voice like a broadcast, using everything I'd learned from Ocean and Dekaar to ensure this worked.

I'm Eloe, I introduced myself, shakily getting to my feet, and I felt recognition ripple through all of them. Ocean had conveyed as much to them, and they knew who to expect when they arrived, even if she'd conveyed it to them while their minds were under the control of their ZST training. *I'm going to need your help to get out of here.*

I tensed as pain rippled through them all at the same time. Their collars.

But before I could despair, Ocean moved. She grasped one of the dragons, closed her powerful jaw around the collar, and snapped it off like it was made of aluminum. She shot off to do the same to another dragon, while the one she freed mirrored her actions. Within seconds, all the dragons were freed.

The house shook as they landed and pummeled into it.

The blasts of laser fire rang through the air, but they struck the house more than the dragons. There were too many of them for the lasers to keep up. From where I stood, I could see them out the window, and even the dragons that hadn't bonded with me were fighting against the Zendaalans. Just like in Vahdel.

Dekaar appeared beside me.

His holographic form flickered as the dragons raged on. They were getting to his main control system, I surmised, because the shield erected around me was starting to flicker too.

"Well played, Eloe," he admitted.

My fists clenched at my sides. I was tired of his creepy fascination.

"You learned how to Drake Bond. I hadn't expected you to come so far in such a short period of time. I forget the meaning of time, sometimes. I won't be so ill-prepared next time we clash. I expect you to prepare yourself likewise." And with that, his hologram vanished and the shield came down.

Two red blurs streaked outside the window. *Brace yourself!* came to me through the bond.

I darted to crouch behind the door of the room. Half a second later, I heard the wall collapsing and two dragons hissing in victory. Not roaring, I realized, because they were conscious the noise might rupture my eardrums. I thanked the Spirits the dragons restrained themselves.

When the cool air brushed against my skin, the reality sank in. I was free. The Traitor had lost this battle, but he knew this wouldn't be the last time we met. And he expected me to keep my wits about me because otherwise it wouldn't be interesting to him.

With a shiver, I slung my legs around the dragon nearest me. Both of these dragons were Wingless, their serpentine forms taking up most of the room even though they were roughly a fourth of Huntress's size. The one I rode now was dark red, like blood. The other was bright crimson.

Ready to go, Eloe? asked the blood-red dragon. He was male. The other was a female, and she hissed a snicker beside him. They were enjoying their rampage.

Let's get out of here, I said, and we launched into the air without another word. I grinned at the damage the dragons had managed on my behalf. The mansion was quickly being reduced to rubble and charred plaster. Sirens sounded in the distance, but the hovercars that had been pursuing Ocean were crumpled on the ground, all twisted metal and broken glass. The Zendaalans inside were either barely moving or not moving at all.

Among the damage, something caught my eye.

Wait, bring me down, just in front of that building.

The dragon I rode landed, muttering complaints on a frequency I couldn't quite catch, but I understood he wasn't happy about being prevented from taking to the sky with his newfound freedom. I felt similarly. But this was more important.

This small building just outside the mansion had all kinds of high tech systems glowing inside. This was probably the control room for the house's systems—which meant it could hold some valuable information.

The room had collapsed into itself, most of the systems popping sparks and showing flickering screens, pieces of the ceiling embedded into the hardware. I wished I had tech from the rebels, something to download information with, because some of the systems, especially the ones closer to the door, were intact.

Then I remembered what Dekaar said, and I realized there may be a device with information on it already. If Dekaar ever needed to download new information, he might use something here.

My heart leaped as I spotted a chip that had fallen to the ground just below a broken forcefield case. He kept it secure, but the security system was destroyed by the rampaging dragons. I picked up the chip with shaking hands. I didn't dare hope.

Dekaar's memory chip.

Hurry, Eloe, urged Ocean. She was looking up at the sky, watching more Zendaalan hovercars coming right for us.

I slipped the chip into my pocket and saddled the dark red dragon. We rocketed into the air, and I quickly discovered this dragon was much faster than my other ones. He ripped through the sky like a dart, wind pushing against my face with almost suffocating force. I just tucked my head, not daring to tell him to slow down.

Rocket would be a good name for this dragon.

A roar shot through the air, and the sky in front of me shimmered with blinding light. I squinted as something dark and long emerge from the light. A Wingless black dragon? No...not just *any* Wingless black dragon.

Huntress—Kahmel astride her lithe form.

He wasted no time. Kahmel swung Huntress around to fly at my side, then she rose in altitude until they were above me.

"Watch out!" was all the warning I got before he dropped down, rocking me and my new dragon, Rocket hissing in protest. Kahmel leaned forward, one hand around my waist, the other pressed against my dragon's neck with a guiding grip. "Hope you don't mind me commandeering your dragon for a minute."

I laughed deliriously. "How are you here? What—"

"I'm sure you have a lot to explain too," he interrupted. "I thought I was going to have to fight my way in and rescue you. Turns out I'm just your getaway car. We'll catch up in a minute." He pressed his head into my hair from behind, pushing his cheek against the hairpin I hadn't taken out since I left K'sundi. "You did a fantastic job." He moved his hand down to mine and squeezed. "Now I'm going to need you to trust me again."

With that, he swerved Rocket around, throwing his weight from side to side to avoid laser fire as the Zendaalans closed in on us from behind.

Then I realized where we were headed. Kahmel was driving us directly into the face of a building.

"Kahmel...?"

"Just trust me." He squeezed my hand again. And then he shouted, "*Mufi eltep!*"

Huntress roared, and the air shimmered in front of us again.

And we disappeared.

PART II:

FANGS

WHEN THINGS CHANGE

The world exploded in a flash of light. When the light faded, I was surrounded by swirling colors, stars that blinked and flashed in the distance, and *dragons*.

Flocks of dragons, more than I'd ever seen before, soared overhead, arcing through the endless sky. Thin, craggy mountains with more dragons perched on top of them reached up toward pinked skies speckled with stars and a faded crescent moon hooked in the heavens. Rocket landed on ground patched with grass and tall wildflowers that swayed with the gentle breeze.

We'd emerged from a glowing tear in the world, and soon Huntress followed, then Ocean, then the other five dragons I'd bonded with. And it hit me for the first time that I was bonded to *seven* dragons. I felt them all bubbling within me, fighting for attention. They were all excited, and the result was dizzying.

I dismounted Rocket and stumbled.

Kahmel reached to steady me. "Are you all right?"

I blinked, reconnecting to him, to here. Grounding myself made the dragons in my head fade to the background a little.

Instead of answering, I seized him in a hug, squeezing hard, still convincing myself he was real. He wrapped his arms around me and squeezed, too, resting his head on mine, and we stayed like that until I was content to let him go.

"What is this place?" I said, finally managing to release him and look around.

The answer came from eight mouths, and it made me sway again.

"It's called a Den..." Kahmel started to explain, not knowing that dragon voices were overlapping him and drowning out whatever else he said.

You finally figured out how to access the Dens! rejoiced one of them, another Wingless. Her coloring was a deep violet, and I pegged her as an Elemental immediately. Though what purple Elementals did, I wasn't sure.

About time, commented Rocket.

Are you going to draw Den maps again? asked the other red Wingless I decided was Rocket's twin sister. They looked about the same age and had similar coloring, so I didn't think I was wrong. Which reminded me, the rest of them needed names too. *You should draw Den maps again! It will be so much easier to travel that way!*

Do you even know how to draw Den maps? asked a Draconian dragon dubiously. His scales were a hypnotizing swirl of brown colors, glinting with an orangish sheen like copper. Some instinctive part of me thought he might be an Elemental too, even though his coloring wasn't as vibrant as Elementals typically were. The orange sheen gave him an otherworldly vibe that made me suspect he was something more.

She can learn! replied Rocket's sister.

Wait, I think her mate is saying something, said a black Draconian. He hopped into the air and circled us lazily. *He seems a bit worried.*

What's his name, anyway, Ocean? asked the youngest of the group, a pink Draconian female barely the size of an adult dog, most likely a freshly hatched dragon.

Calm down, all of you, Ocean reprimanded. *You're making her dizzy.*

Finally a thought I agreed with.

"Jashi!" Kahmel was grasping me by the shoulders and looking at me with terrible concern in his tangerine eyes.

I needed to explain.

"I'm sorry, are you hurt? You seem disoriented. What did he do to you?"

"One question at a time," I said as he helped me sit down. Before he could say something else, I held up a finger to hold him off, took a deep breath, and tried to center my attention again. I gestured to the dragons surrounding us and looking on with what might have been concern, if dragons could manage it. "I sorta drake-bonded with them all to get out."

Kahmel noticed for the first time that Ocean was among the dragons surrounding us. "Ocean! So she left on her own..." He looked back at me. "To save you."

"Yeah, she did." Pride swelled in my chest. "She's the only reason I was able to get out at all."

Ocean stomped excitedly, clearly enjoying the praise.

Kahmel looked around at the rest of the dragons. "All of these..."

"Are mine, now, yes." I sighed, rubbing my temples. "And they're all trying not to speak all at once because they're giving me a headache."

"Wait, what?"

I forgot that just a week ago it was weird that a dragon was talking in my head. And now I had seven.

"Let's get to that later," I said, waving the topic aside as my headache worsened. "Let's talk about where we are now." I looked up at the rose-colored skies and glittering stars, then back at him. "Want to explain?"

"Right." Kahmel brushed a hand through his curly hair. "Basically, it's like the realms we go to for the Dragon Kings, but you don't need to be a Half-Drac to enter. You just need to be riding a dragon when you say the words '*mufi eltep*'. They're dragon command words. Or Butaah, but that's another—"

"You know what Butaah is?"

He frowned. "How do *you* know what Butaah is?"

Rather than answer, I sighed and stood. "We're going to have to compare notes later. Right now I'd like to get to wherever you're living these days now that we aren't royalty, because I have a feeling we're going to spend a lot of time going back and forth with shocking revelations to share."

Kahmel stood and dusted himself off. "You mean like the fact that Dekaar is The Traitor? Yeah, I know that too. Aithel told me. He's the one who told me about the Dens."

Well, I supposed that caught us up.

"But you're right," Kahmel admitted. "You must be exhausted. The dragons have a place for us to stay. You rest, and tomorrow we'll get each other caught up."

The way he turned then, avoiding eye contact, I was reminded that in the time I'd been gone, he'd stepped away from the throne, voluntarily from what I could tell. And I didn't know where he stood on our original mission anymore. Where we stood.

But I didn't say anything. He slung himself onto Huntress's back, and I followed after, gripping him from behind and thinking about the promises we'd made to each other. I promised to stand by him. He promised to evolve with me. I'd only been gone a few weeks, but so much had happened, I wondered if it was enough to make us both break our promises, make Kahmel go down a path I couldn't follow him on. Or make me change to the point Kahmel couldn't relate anymore.

My dragons followed behind us as Kahmel launched Huntress into the air, and I was so lost in my thoughts, I couldn't even hear whatever they were saying in my head.

"*Mufi eltep!*" Kahmel called, and the world ripped open again, light blinding for a moment until we passed through. And then we were out in the open air again, this time flying above a stretch of forest.

"There's a Den the rebels and I are staying in," he explained. "The Half-Dracs in particular, to be specific. I'll explain why later, but they're essentially trainees. The rebellion has a lot of new members."

"That sounds like good news," I said drowsily. I'd slept well the night before, and the sun was still high in the sky, but I suddenly felt like I could sleep for days.

Kahmel nodded, and the way he hesitated a little made me dread whatever he was going to tell me in the morning. "Anyway, we're going to have to Den-hop for a little while before we reach it."

I barely understood what all this meant, but I nodded, then remembered he couldn't see me and muttered something just to show I heard him.

Are you all right, Eloe? asked Ocean as Kahmel shouted and took us through another glowing tear in the sky. This time, we emerged in a Den blanketed with night. The stars shone brightly against grass that whispered against the wind.

Eloe. Something else I had to tell Kahmel, another way I'd changed since we'd been apart. Here he was shouting spirits-knew-what and hopping through space and time like it was nothing, and I still didn't know what led to his stepping down from the throne. Was I going to be upset with him about it? That was the reason I'd been taken, to force his hand against something we both saw as important. And he gave it up. I knew he had to be worried about me, but did that mean he should just give up on everything we fought for? I loved being K'sundi's Faresha now, and I didn't want to be anything else, but he was the one who brought me in on this journey. And he just... gave it all up?

I was sure he didn't know whether I'd be mad at him or not, either, which was why we were both silent as he opened another rip between realms and we emerged in a desert with blazing heat that felt familiar against my skin.

Were we already in K'sundi, or close?

More than a little overwhelmed by everything that was happening around me, I focused on Ocean, doing my best to shut out the voices of the other dragons. To my surprise, when I intentionally blocked them out, their voices died down rather quickly. Was it out of courtesy to me? Or had my decision to listen to one dragon in particular shut the rest out automatically?

I wasn't in a good state of mind to come to any more conclusions for the day.

I'm just hoping everything is the way I left it, I answered Ocean's question honestly, talking mostly about me and Kahmel.

Ocean grumbled defensively, and I chuckled. *No need to kill Kahmel, I don't think. I'll let you know if I change my mind, though.*

Ocean hissed a chuckle back, but I wasn't sure if she was playing or not.

All thoughts vanished from my mind when Kahmel made another jump and we emerged in a Den with a sky fixed on twilight, pink on one end, dipped in deep blue on the other, stars sprayed like freckles all across. The gap opened a few yards away from an island floating in the middle of it all, where a huge mansion stood in sparkling marble and alabaster glory. It reminded me of the old parts of the palace, where it looked like we'd stepped into a century of the past. The old K'sundii flag, the one with the dragon and a shield on its face, flanked a grand entrance to the manor. We landed, and I realized the mansion wasn't the only building in this Den. There were little islands off in the distance, each with old houses built on them, people milling about, some on dragons, some just staring at everything, like they were getting used to it too.

"This is where I'm training the new rebel Half-Dracs," Kahmel explained, and I gaped at him. Because of course I had nothing to worry about.

Things had changed. But our drive stayed the same. It was the same mission with a different coat of paint on it, and a lot of new traumatic experiences, but mostly the same. And I loved that Kahmel and I were both going to be able to keep our promises.

A FOUR-YEAR PLAN

Kahmel Axon Kai of the Omah Clan

I had about a day of experience with the Dens, and so far I found they each had a different sense of time, and the skies came in all kinds of colors. In this one, night turned the sky purple on one end and dark blue on the other. The stars never faded here, but they became even brighter at night. Morning brought a pastel color pallet with it. No sun carried the light here, it just...happened. The days seemed to follow the same twenty-four hour schedule we were used to, and despite the fact we didn't see a sun, the moon came to hang over the night all the same.

Jashi and I had slept in separate rooms the night before. When we arrived at the Den we were staying in, she ate, found a room, and slept hard. I didn't want to disturb her. I also...wasn't sure where we stood. So much had changed since we'd been apart. I'd changed the plan. Would she want to stick around for this new idea? A lot about the plan was similar to the old one. We were still planning to restore the Dragon Kings, we still had to meet with Obellana. The only difference was we wouldn't be looking to transform K'sundi anymore. I hadn't known my parents were working with the Zendaalans to set up Dekaar as Faresh, but in a way, it was fitting.

Dekaar betrayed the Dragon Kings, but the K'sundii people did nothing to protect the dragons in the aftermath. They chose Dekaar without choosing him at that time. He represented a resentment for the dragons that all the K'sundii at the time were feeling. He was just the only one to act upon it.

And now Dekaar was back, this time chosen by K'sundii officials themselves. They didn't know who he was, of course, but once again, he represented everything they supported in spirit. Part of them would choose anyone over Jashi and me just to get rid of their immediate problem rather than allow themselves to see the one we were forcing them to see.

They let Jashi get taken from me, they picked Dekaar, and I was inclined to let them live with their choices.

Here in the mansion, the dragons provided food like they did in Aithel's Den. Aithel told me the slinky, glowing dragons' official title —spirit dragons. They were non-sentient spirits that did the bidding of the dragons and Dragon Kings that resided here. Apparently the Dens were where the dragons originally came from, before they roamed over and began to occupy Hemorah. And here, the spirit dragons served them all and kept them happy. The dragons then lived between Hemorah and the Dens, preferring to live in both. That was, until the Dragon Kings were imprisoned and the ZST took the dragons' minds from them and they forgot how to come here.

I looked out the window of my bedroom, out at the dozens and dozens of dragons flying around the floating island. Knowing how the Dens worked, I realized how the dragons probably showed up in Gheres when Jashi and I went. They were starting to travel through the Dens again and ended up there.

A knock at the door pulled me out of my thoughts. I turned and stood when I realized it was Jashi at the door.

"You weren't lying when you said there were a lot of new people here. The only ones I recognize are the dragon riders. I'm glad you brought them, too, by the way. I can't imagine how that conversation went. How did you get them all to come?"

"Uh..." I muttered,because my mind immediately drew a blank. *It wasn't easy,* I could have said. *I made a broadcast making people choose between me and their new Faresh and was swept away by how many people joined the rebellion after that.*

At a certain point I wasn't sure if we could even contain them all, but Aithel assured me the Dens were as plentiful as they were spacious.

Those would have been articulate thoughts. But my thoughts were overlapping each other. How was she? What happened with her and Dekaar? Did he hurt her? I wanted to tell her I was so, *so* sorry all of this happened at all. And she was asking me a question that had nothing to do with any of that. So all I could say was, "I asked them to come."

She waited for me to expound, and when I didn't, because I couldn't come up with words that made sense after that, she frowned. "What?"

I shook my head, as if that would make the thoughts fall into something coherent. "I'm sorry, I'm distracted. It's a long story." And then I realized why I was so confused. "I was going to explain it all when we talked with the others."

I couldn't mention much to her yesterday, but I managed to let her know we were going to be talking with Rand and the others at noon. We couldn't connect to any networks from inside the Dens, but we synced our watches before separating to make sure we could meet at the right time, while the Convergence was still happening. The new rebels started coming in on the first day. I went to get Jashi yesterday. Today was the last day. The Convergence would end this evening. We had to make every minute count.

Jashi nodded in understanding. "Oh, right, that makes sense. I just...wanted to talk before we brought everyone else in."

"Oh," I said stupidly. Because all I could think was she was upset. She was upset about this entire change of direction I decided on without her, and she was disappointed in me. This wasn't what she wanted. *Sure, let's talk,* that would have been an appropriate way to begin the conversation, but I didn't manage that and instead just pulled up a chair in front of her and stared at my hands for a few seconds, not knowing what to do with them. And then I realized that the silence was because she hadn't started speaking yet. That she was the one who came in here, so she must have had something to say, only she hadn't started saying it yet.

"I know you're going to tell me about it later, when we're with the group," she said, breaking the silence at last. "But that's going to be... the game plan. The mission. I want to know about...us."

"Us?"

"I mean, we can't go back to living at the palace. We can't live here in this magic mansion forever. Where are we going to go?"

Us. We. This wasn't about our relationship. It was about our living arrangements. I wanted to slap myself for not realizing it sooner. There were plans for the rebels, but she needed to know what my plans were for us to live. Especially growing up as she had. She had to know I wasn't planning on our being *homeless*.

"Right, of course," I said, feeling like an idiot. "The thing is, we can stay here. The only problem is, we'll have to stay here for a while. Years. I was only able to come and get you the way I did because right now the openings are aligned to stay open for three days. But today's the last day of that. After this, we'll have to either leave and find somewhere to hide—which I don't want to do—or stay here until the next time the portals align and stay open. I want to keep us safe. The dragons will take care of us here. I arranged it with Aithel. All we have to do is meet up with the last Dragon Queen, Obellana, and get her approval. After that, we have four years until we have to leave."

Jashi's eyebrows shot up, and I could tell this was a lot to take in. Just yesterday she didn't know there were any other openings into... somewhere else other than the Dragon King's realms, and now I was asking her to live in one for four entire years.

"It's not like we couldn't leave at all," I continued explaining, hoping she wouldn't feel too closed in with this arrangement. "Once we learn the pattern of the portals and when they open, we'll be able to frequently leave and come back here if the need arises. Nana's not here right now because she's helping Arusi with the new members on their end, but when we meet up, she'll be coming with us to live here. I convinced Lora to stay too."

I didn't mention Talad because he and Jashi had a nasty falling out and I didn't think it was my place to invite him back here, especially since he most likely wouldn't be in any danger staying in K'sundi. Not like the Half-Dracs, or Lora, who would eventually be found out as a close friend of Jashi's. All they'd find from looking into Talad were ties to the Zendaalans that would worry no one. So, I thought it best to leave the subject of her ex-friend alone.

"Lora's here?" Jashi said, and a smile lit up her face that made me relax some. Everything else had been forgotten for a moment. "How did you convince her to stay in some magic portal to nowhere? And don't say 'I asked,'" she added, making a face.

I laughed. "Well, I can get into that when we talk with the rest. Like I said—"

"It's a long story," she finished for me, then leaned back into the bed, resting on her arms. She looked up at the ceiling. "Four years... That's a long time."

I folded my hands together. It was a long time. It was a lot to ask of her. But it was the only way I could think of to keep us safe. To keep us all safe.

"What about after that?" was her next question, and I grimaced.

"Harder to say. I...I don't know about getting K'sundi back from Dekaar. The Courts—"

"Let him have it."

Taken aback, I just stared at her for a moment. For one, because I was surprised, for another, because I was impressed.

"I think part of K'sundi wants us," she said, cocking her head. "But not enough of it." An eyebrow arched. "I assume you struck some kind of deal with Aithel to prevent him from killing you. Since you're still standing here, ex-Faresh and all."

I spread my arms, a gesture meaning, *I'm still here, aren't I?*

She nodded. "Good." She turned to look out the window, out at the dragons soaring high in the dichromatic skies. "I think I could stand living here for a while. Maybe beyond the four years, if it came to it. Hell, I like not having to worry about rent." She angled her head back to look at me. "Don't you?"

I loved her.

And I decided to show her just that, coming over to her side at the edge of the bed and moving over her reclined form, slipping my arm around her waist and pulling her into a kiss. Not a long one. She was still tired. Just enough to show her how I felt. How grateful I was. How much I missed her. How scared I was while she was gone.

I pulled away, and her arms trailed up my chest before looping around my neck, and for a moment we hung in that precarious space, close, tired, and remembering how much we missed each other.

Then she pulled herself up until she was hugging me, her legs moving across my lap to give me a better angle. I straightened, then squeezed her tighter.

And we sat like that for a good while.

The Beginning of a Long Journey

Everyone was called to meet in the Den where Jashi and I were staying. To make things simpler, since it was the Den the Half-Dracs were staying in, we called it the Fire Den. Seemed as good a name as any. The Fire Den had connecting Tunnels, or portals, that connected to three cities in K'sundi, it looked like. Once the Convergence was over, they would open and close at intervals we had yet to observe, so learning how they worked would be valuable in the future.

In the meantime, we all gathered while we still had nine hours and some change before the Convergence ended.

We were in the manor's living room. All of us: Rand, Khes, Arusi, and Asan, along with the dragon riders, Lora, and even Nana.

"Lora!"

Jashi's childhood friend embraced her.

"I'm so glad you're here," Jashi said.

"Yeah, things were getting kinda crazy in K'sundi," said Lora, pulling away. "Living in some kind of alternate dimension is a weird solution, but hey, I guess you get what you get."

Jashi laughed, and even I chuckled, because that pretty much summed up the situation. The others greeted her and exchanged as many hugs as they could get. T'shan was first in line after Lora. I gave them a few moments before breaking it up and asking everyone to get back to their seats so Jashi wouldn't get too overwhelmed, and so we could get started.

Jashi and Lora sat down together on the couch, and from my position leaning against the mantle of the fireplace, I decided to begin. "All right, so, Jashi, I think you know most of what's been happening with us at this point now, but I'm going to try to quickly summarize it all. I left the throne because you were taken, and I knew that would be the condition for the Zendaalans giving you back. But when Dekaar changed all that, I went to Aithel for help. He explained who Dekaar was as well as a plan to get you back that both allowed us somewhere safe to stay and allowed the dragons to reunite with the Half-Dracs by offering them protection here."

"So that's how you're keeping up your end of the deal with Aithel," Jashi said, pursing her lips.

I nodded. "Aithel has an additional condition for allowing our oath to continue—after the four years are up, we're going to emerge in Zendaal from the open Dens and attack, find the parts they stole from the Dragon Kings, and bring them back."

Jashi glanced at Lora, as though waiting for her shocked reaction to all of the crazy shit.

"I've already heard this," Lora explained, though she still shook her head after hearing the whole explanation again. "Nana was the one who asked me to answer Kahmel's call and join the rebellion. Well, *told me to*, to be accurate."

Nana shrugged.

"Kahmel's call?" Jashi questioned.

Asan spoke up. "We had to gather as many Half-Dracs as we could, so Kahmel recorded a video and broadcasted it all over K'sundi.

He told them about the rebellion and that if anyone wanted to choose you and him over Dekaar, they should join and be protected."

"And that worked?" Jashi said, raising her eyebrows.

I was as shocked as she was now when it happened. People came in by the droves. Our hard work hadn't been for nothing, after all.

Rand leaned against the arm of his chair. "We have more people than we know what to do with, honestly. We explained the whole thing. Having people understand the Half-Dracs were real and in danger helped them cope with the other absurdities they had to understand, but it was still a shocker to everyone involved when we took them through the Tunnels into the Dens."

"It still is. I mean, look at that." Lora pointed out the window at the pink and blue sky blinking with stars. "But we can't go back to the new Faresh. That man will ruin K'sundi. Anyone with any sense can feel it. We're better off here."

I knew it, but hearing someone else say it threw me off for a moment. Lora trusted me. She and everyone else who decided to leave everything and come here. To protect their children. To stand up for Jashi and me.

I cleared my throat, collecting my thoughts. "Right. So. There's one downside to this four-year plan."

Jashi frowned, cocking her head. "What would that be?"

Rand, Arusi, Khes, and Asan all glanced at each other because this was the part they dreaded the most too.

Arusi said it first. "We're going to be splitting up."

Those words hung in the air for a few moments. My friends had been my team for so long now. The idea of being away from them for four years was painful, and that held doubly true for my twin. We hadn't been apart since we were forced to leave our parents' house.

"Wait, why?" Jashi objected.

"We have to," I explained. "We're dealing with thousands of people who aren't used to any of this. Traveling between realms, fire powers, Drake Bonds—it's all a bit much. We're splitting everyone up in groups, and each of us will be in charge of one. You and I are the only ones who will stay together, Jashi."

She looked at them all, obviously sad that this was the last time we would see each other for a while. She just got back.

"After four years are up," I went on, hoping to help her see the bright side, "we'll be able to pool our notes on the patterns of when the Tunnels open. Then we'll be able to see each other as much as we like, since we'll know how to time when we leave and how to visit someone else."

Jashi seemed to visibly relax at that. "All right, I suppose. At least it's not forever."

That sentiment settled on all of us. Because she was right. It wasn't forever. We were building connections between us and the people we were watching over. We would come out stronger and more connected than ever. Away from Zendaal. Away from the Equalization as a whole. We could surface when we wanted after this. Find dragons to tame, trade with rebel countries as much as we liked. The dragons would no longer be providing us food after the four years were up. That was a limited privilege the Dragon Kings were offering us, but once the Dragon Kings had their parts back, rebel nations would be able to replenish their resources, and our trades with them would be even more fruitful. I was sure they would love to receive dragons and training on how to ride them in exchange for any supplies we needed. It would help them defend against the Zendaalans, who would surely come after them in retaliation in the aftermath.

This was feasible.

No, this was *hope*. We had hope. One neither the Zendaalans nor the corrupted K'sundi Courts could take away from us.

"I have something to share," said Jashi. "Give me a sec." She got up, jogged into the hall and came back after a few moments with a... shirt? The arms were tied together and the bottom was tied into a knot. It was bulky, like there was stuff inside it, and I realized she'd had that around her back when I came to rescue her yesterday. A rudimentary backpack.

She opened up the top, because it was pulled together with a drawstring, and I had to admire her ingenuity for a moment. I gasped when she pulled out a chip.

"I stole this from Dekaar's mansion. It has all of his...memories on it, I guess?"

I was slack-jawed. Because every time—*every time*—Jashi exceeded my expectations. Even kidnapped, stolen away from home, and in another country where I couldn't protect her, she managed to achieve above and beyond anything I could expect.

That was my girl.

Khes erupted with laughter. "I don't know how you manage to do it, girl, but you're always full of surprises. The damn cyborg's memories! You managed to pilfer a copy of his brain!"

Jashi smiled then went on to explain, "Pretty much. He explained how when he...came back...he had to be given information on how the world had progressed since he died. I don't know what all is on here. I grabbed it just as I was leaving, which was in the middle of dragons breaking a mansion apart, Zendaalan officers on their way, and shortly before I was escorted through a portal into another realm. Suffice it to say, I haven't had time to look too much into it. Could be useless. But..." Jashi turned it over between her fingers. "I was thinking. He couldn't have known where the Dragon Kings' parts were taken after he died, right? He gave them to the Zendaalans and died of old age, as far as we know. That kind of thing would be important for him to know now."

"That chip might have the location of the Dragon Kings' parts." Rand took the chip from her. "If everyone is okay with it, I'm about to jet. We're going to need the proper equipment to examine this thoroughly, and I'd like to go get it before the Convergence ends."

I nodded to him. "Do it."

And Rand was out.

Jashi smiled, but the look faltered for a moment, and she looked down at her hands in her lap. "Anyway, there's more. I learned a lot while I was with Dekaar. He insisted on it, almost. It was weird." She looked up, glancing at the faces around the room before finally resting her gaze on mine. "He hates the world he's created. One where we know nothing about our past, who we once were, and ultimately, what he's done to get to where he is. But this is the world the Zendaalans had to create to keep up their end of the deal and ensure K'sundi had him as Faresh forever. He's really confusing to be around, to say the least."

"He was there with you?" Arusi asked, frowning in confusion.

Jashi shook her head. "No, only in the beginning. He took me to his mansion, then left. After that, he checked up on me regularly with a holographic projection of himself."

That made sense. And it gave me an immense sense of relief. He wasn't around to do anything to her, it looked like. She was okay, at least physically.

Jashi continued. "He told me interesting things about us, as a people. Like we used to have dragon names. Royal clan families especially, or those who rode a lot of dragons essentially. He didn't want to call me Jashi or Faresha, so he gave me a dragon name."

Confusion twisted my face and disgust rose in my gut. What kind of psychopath just *renames* someone?

But Jashi held my gaze. "It was weird, but I was glad he did it. You see, since Ocean followed me, I was able to feel our connection through the Drake Bond. The Drake Bond does more than just help us form a deeper connection to a dragon, it allows us to talk. In our heads."

"Telepathy?" Arusi asked, astounded.

A vigorous nod from Jashi. "Exactly. But it's a lot deeper than just sharing thoughts. We share feelings. It's hard to explain, but...in the same way dragons understand us better when we use command words, or *Butaah*, they understand dragon names better than our K'sundii ones." She looked at T'shan, who had been listening intently this whole time. "If I asked Ocean, right now, to go to you, she wouldn't really know who I'm talking about. But because I have a dragon name I can use, you could tell a dragon you were Drake Bonded with not only who I am, but they would be able to find me on their own after that. Because a name isn't just a title to them. You convey what that person *feels* like in a single word. That's what dragon names are. And why they're important." She looked over us all. "We're going to all need one, especially for the fight four years from now. If we can get some from the Dragon Kings, that would be fine. I know I got mine from Dekaar, but... I don't know. I still feel like it fits me." There was fire in her eyes then. Pride. One that overcame any obstacle, even when she had to learn from her enemy. "I'm Eloe, to the dragons. Dekaar said it means heart, and you know, I kind of like it."

I smiled at her, because she was incredibly strong, and she was right. Eloe suited her.

Jemmorah shyly raised her hand. "I have a question."

I gestured for the young dragon rider to continue.

"Those other dragons that followed you are Drake Bonded to you, right? Does that... I mean, they aren't *all* talking in your head or anything...are they?"

"They...are." Jashi bit her lip, looking off to the side. "I still have to learn how this all works, honestly. Based upon what I read before I was captured, other K'sundii warriors had multiple Drake Bonds too. But I don't know how they kept all the dragons out of their heads when they didn't want them there. I'm pretty sure the connection weakens at a certain distance, which is why Ocean followed me. But she didn't follow too closely, and I could still feel her when she flew miles away to hunt or get more dragons to help me escape. I think meditation helps, though." She looked to me and smiled. "It helped yesterday when you brought me to the Den."

She'd mentioned having a headache because they were all trying to talk at once, but it was now clear that was also why she'd been woozy. I thought it was just the shock of being taken into a Den after being chased by the Zendaalans.

I still wasn't sure what to do with the news that Jashi had…how many dragons had she brought with her? I counted seven, including Ocean. Seven dragons in her head.

Jashi continued, "I'm going to have to train myself on how to deal with this, like you did, Kahmel, with your fire. I have four years to get used to it, after all. I think I can do it. And the more I learn, the more I can help the trainees understand too."

Arusi nodded. "That makes sense. Just to be safe, we should warn the dragon riders against using the technique until we understand it better."

"I agree," Jashi said.

Worry gnawed at my gut because I wasn't sure what all that meant, but Jashi was right. This has been done before; we just didn't remember. And at the very least, she had four years without having to look over her shoulder to perfect the technique. Neither of us knew what that was like. There was no telling what we'd learn in these four years away.

The more I thought about it, the more I liked the idea. We were becoming more. We were evolving. And when we emerged on the other side after these four years were over, the Zendaalans wouldn't know what they were dealing with anymore.

I didn't know who we'd be in four years.

But I knew we would be formidable.

THE ALL-SEEING DRAGON QUEEN

We split into five groups. Jashi's and mine was composed of mostly Half-Dracs and their parents, so ours was called the Fire Den group.

Then there was Rand's. Jashi and I would be training the Half-Dracs to dragon ride, but Rand was in charge of teaching everyone else, so anyone who wanted to learn was to go with him. So his was dubbed the Rider Den group.

Arusi managed the more timid group, older people and the disabled and anyone who didn't want to fight when the four years were over. Hers was the Shield Den group.

Khes's group was made up of those who were already part of the rebellion or those who had just joined and still wanted to fight, but who weren't quite comfortable with the idea of riding a dragon. His was named the Iron Den group.

Asan took anyone who still had doubts about the whole thing, mostly those who had been against my campaign before they realized Dekaar was blatantly selling them out to the Zendaalans. They were the most wishy-washy of the group, and Asan predicted some may leave the Den early. We'd already decided not to go after anyone who deserted. We called theirs the Water Den group.

Jashi and I had one more item of business to attend to before we could retreat into the Fire Den. We had to visit Obellana.

There wasn't much ceremony to it, even though this was the moment we'd been anticipating since we first found out we had to gain the alliance of all the Dragon Kings. The moment when we would officially have all of them on our side. From what Aithel told me, Obellana's agreement was all but guaranteed, but though the Dragon Kings could convey their sentiments to one another—perhaps similar to that shared sensory experience Jashi described—they couldn't converse. And if Obellana had any objections or opinions, she would have to tell us herself. So we still had to go see her.

We decided to ride Comet to Obellana's Den.

"Are you ready?" I asked Jashi.

She took a deep breath. "I've been ready since you first asked me to help you, Kahmel. Let's do this."

I nodded, and we climbed onto Comet's back. I hugged Jashi from behind, and she took hold of her dragon with the grip of someone who'd been riding her whole life rather than just for the past year.

Just as Aithel had explained it to me, I told Jashi how the Dens worked. It had been the first time I'd needed to speak a *sentence* in Butaah, to make the dragon aware that we were looking for a Tunnel. They weren't visible to humans, but dragons could *sense* them and knew precisely where they were when flying. Thankfully, Aithel showed me where I could study the words I needed to speak to the dragons.

"*Bel cantish cherem,*" Jashi said. *We look for entrance.* And though Comet didn't react right away, after Jashi kicked at his sides and we flew into the air, he started to emit a quiet growl—an indication he was looking for a Tunnel to slip through.

I pointed Jashi in the right direction, and the closer we got, the louder Comet's growl grew. Once we were at the Tunnel, the growl became a quick howl that let us know we could proceed. I was still in awe of how much time had passed since anyone had done this with a dragon, yet they still reacted automatically to the signals we established with them eons ago.

"*Mufi eltep,*" Jashi shouted. A phrase that meant *open the door* in Butaah. Comet roared, opening a rift in the sky ahead of us. In a dazzle of light, we slipped through. We emerged over one of K'sundi's deserts, far from the cities. The sand appeared red from the evening sunlight. The dunes rolled in waves as far as I could see.

I pulled up a compass on my eWatch to get my bearings. I pointed left. "That way toward the next Tunnel."

Jashi veered Comet in that direction, and before long, we reached the point that would connect us to the next Den. The rebels had marked it with a wooden stake in the ground, using coordinates from Aithel's maps that translated well to our own maps.

Jashi urged Comet toward the stake, and the dragon howled as soon as we flew over it. She shouted again, *"Mufi eltep!"*

We jumped through more Dens and Tunnels and stretches of desert before we finally reached the last one—a Tunnel just off the jungle half of K'sundi that led to a Den shrouded in night. When we jumped through the next Tunnel we emerged not in K'sundi, not even on Hemorah, but on Hemorah's moon.

Hemorah now hung in the sky above us, a big blue orb no bigger than my thumb in the far, far-off distance. Hemorah's moon had its own breathable atmosphere, provided by the lush greenery that covered its surface. Some called it the celestial garden because of how many varieties of exotic flora grew here. The creatures that lived here, animals, by all intents and purposes, couldn't live back on Hemorah. They could only eat the plants that grew here, and the minerals in the soil the plants needed were unique to the moon.

Looking around, I could say with absolute certainty that the celestial garden had rightfully earned its title.

The world was bright, almost neon tones of green. Jashi and I dismounted Comet, almost floating to the ground in the lighter gravitational pull. The leaves of the plants swayed around us lazily, in tune with their own rhythm and the whispering breeze that drifted through the air. Flowers bloomed in saturated colors of pinks, blues, reds, and yellows. The air tasted pungently sweet, the grass infinitely soft, and for a moment, it felt like we had stepped into a dream.

"Look." Jashi pointed.

I followed her gaze to where a building stood in the distance. The International Research Center. A building with a domed ceiling had hovercars buzzing around it like bees around a hive—a reminder that this wasn't a dream, and we had to lie low.

"Let's hurry," I said in a hushed tone as though whoever worked in that building would somehow hear us from here.

Jashi must have felt the same way. She whispered to Comet to stay, and we moved silently through the dense wood. According to Aithel, the entrance to Obellana's Den was not far from here.

As if in confirmation, the ground began to shake as the entrance felt our presence.

Checking in with Jashi, I asked, "I take it you can't hear your dragons from here?" Which sounded a lot dumber out loud than it had in my head.

Jashi chuckled. "Nope, not a thing. Couldn't hear them anymore after the first jump. I'm starting to get used to it, actually. I'm learning how to tune them out when I'm not interested in listening. Works for most of them, but Lily is still hard to—"

"Lily?"

She blinked, as though remembering I was not privy to her internal conversations with her dragons. "Sorry, that's the littlest. That's what I decided to name her. Cute, right?"

"Very." I shook my head at how much had changed in the little time we'd spent away from each other. But I'd promised to change with her before she was taken from me, and I was going to learn to roll with this new development. "So have you decided on names for the rest?"

Her face lit up, but we were interrupted before she could tell me what names she'd chosen.

We had arrived.

The forest opened up into the clearing without warning. Pillars stood around the caved-in ceiling they used to prop up, leaving the two pedestals in the center of the devastated building uncovered. The forest had claimed the rubble and rock, moss and vines dangling over them, covering them in fuzzy green. Jashi and I carefully made our way to the center of the ruins, stepping over the fallen rocks, and reached the pedestals.

Jashi nodded to indicate her readiness, and I launched a ball of fire into the first dusty bowl, watching the flame arc toward the sky as Jashi mirrored my movements across from me.

The rumbling intensified, and a flash of white snaked through the trees in a bee-line toward us. A spirit dragon—the dragon of in-between.

The dragon gripped me in its claws, and then Jashi, and we were off. One moment we were soaring above the trees of Hemorah's moon, the next, we were floating through the stars.

Shards of crystals erupted at the foot of Obellana's floating castle in clusters. The towers of the castle itself were a hard, translucent material that glinted with starlight and fragmented the light into rainbow colors thrown all over its surface. The only thing that rivaled the castle's awe-striking beauty was Obellana herself.

The deep purple of her head and shoulders grew darker down her body until it turned pitch black. Her scales glistened in the light like they were slicked with oil. She watched us with pink irises. No... pink *iris*. She had one eye, but not like Aithel's one eye because the other had been stolen from him. Obellana's one eye, positioned in the center of her head, looked to us with eagerness.

She stomped the ground with excitement like Huntress did when she hadn't been ridden in a while. The crystal palace rumbled behind her and whined with a high pitched resonance. Obellana roared, a sound I'd never heard come from a Dragon Queen or King. The noise shot through the atmosphere with an ethereal quality, like it could surpass time and space, less like a roar and more like a single note, sung in harmony like a tuning fork.

"It took you Half-Dracs long enough. How dare you visit me last when I was the one that looked forward to seeing you the most?"

She stepped back from the edge of the floating island to make room for the dragon of in-between to drop us. We landed before her, confused as hell.

"You...have one eye," Jashi said.

Obellana erupted into a fit of laughter. The castle sang with her as it hummed with a higher-pitched version of her voice. "*Yes, yes, I do,*" said Obellana, still chuckling. "*And you have bright orange ones. What of it?*"

"Sorry to keep you waiting," I said. "But we're here now. And we need your help."

"*Oh, don't I know it,*" she purred, lying down and cocking her head coyly. "*I've been watching you two for a while. I thought you'd never get together! And when the Zendaalans took Eloe! I was furious. Just when you two were getting cozy!*"

I didn't know what we were talking about anymore.

"Just what kind of help do you think we're asking for?" Jashi put her hands on her hips, tilted her head, and raised an eyebrow like she wondered if The Traitor had taken the Dragon Queen's mind.

And frankly, I was beginning to wonder the same. Was she... '*shipping*' me and Jashi?

"*Oh, fine, you want to get right to business, then let's get right to business. I will aid you in your mission; you have my full support. Happy?*"

"Y-yes?" I stammered, unsure what else to say.

"*Good!*" she said, then turned away.

One of her jet-black wings was missing, and an ache settled in my chest—that's what Dekaar had taken from her, her wing.

I didn't have much time to think about it though, because Obellana looked back at us. "*Well, aren't you coming?*"

"Okay, wait." Jashi crossed her arms and literally put her foot down as she swayed over to the other hip, pursing her lips. "I don't mean to be offensive or anything, but...what else is there to talk about? I'm not sure what else we have to say. We do have to get back before—"

"Yes, yes, yes, the Convergence. I'm well aware. And perhaps I have something I'd like to discuss with you, hm?"

She continued striding toward her crystal castle, and Jashi and I were left with nothing else but to follow her.

She led us not inside but around the castle, to an outer court. The crystal walls surrounded us, the space beyond it warping as we walked by. We stood at the foot of the castle in a plaza lined with white tiles laid in a circular pattern on the floor. The Dragon Queen made a hissing sound, and spirit dragons slithered in, bringing one massive cushion for her and two regular-sized ones for me and Jashi.

"Sit, you'll be much more comfortable," she said as she settled in, curling her tail around her body as she rested on the cushion.

We sat, and Obellana let out a long exhale, one with the burden of a thousand years. *"What a rare opportunity,"* she mused.

I wasn't sure if she was speaking to us or not and decided to keep quiet as she went on.

"You're trying to hurry and get back because what you have right now is a rare opportunity. The Convergence, a chance to connect the world in a single moment, in a single instance, and do what needs to be done."

She looked at us both, with that single eye, as though we were children and she was waxing on about something we were still too young to understand. *"Right now, you're learning the power of predicting a rare opportunity,"* she continued, *"of knowing just the right pieces to put in place so that they turn out in your favor, when the time is right. Planting seeds to sprout when the season is ready. You know what I'm saying, don't you?"*

Not really, but I was beginning to think her words meant more than they appeared to on the surface, like she was talking about something currently beyond us. "I think so," I said, trying to keep up.

She let out a growl of satisfaction that told me I answered correctly. *"Have you ever thought about how rare it is that you married your wife, Faresh?"*

I blinked, not prepared for the conversation to go back in that direction. But if there was anything I'd learned about dealing with the Dragon Kings, it was that they didn't ask questions lightly.

"It's not something I take for granted." I looked at Jashi, thinking of everything we'd endured together. "I'm very lucky." That was an understatement. Jashi and I shared something that had survived through being enemies, friends, in love, stripped of the throne, a kidnapping, and ultimately brought back together. I would never take that for granted. I didn't think either of us ever would.

"*You shouldn't,*" said Obellana. "*A journey sprinkled with little miracles to bring you where you are now. It's extraordinary.*"

Jashi turned back to the Dragon Queen and sighed, leaning back and propping herself up on her arms. "All right, I get that. But what does that have to do with anything happening now?"

Obellana tilted her head so she looked down at us with her one, large eye. "*I, too, see opportunities. And I've been preparing for one for a very long time, now.*"

She stood and looked between me and Jashi. "*I must ask you both a question. It's very important, so please consider it before you answer.*"

Nothing Obellana had said thus far was making much sense, but a gut instinct told me there was something more here. Something crucially important. And I nodded.

Jashi must have done the same, because Obellana nodded with satisfaction. "*Are you afraid of change?*"

Like everything else she'd said, the question was a surprise. An important one. Wasn't that what everything boiled down to? I asked Jashi to stand by me as I tried to change K'sundi. Jashi asked me to always evolve with her. To change as she changed. And even now, the plan had changed. We were still saving K'sundi, really, only in a different way. Starting with a different group of people.

I didn't think I was afraid of change. I fought for it every day. "No," I answered confidently.

"Yes," was Jashi's meek answer. She sat up, avoiding eye contact with me.

"Interesting," Obellana remarked. *"Well, I did ask you to answer honestly. Why are you afraid of change, Eloe?"*

I was surprised at Jashi's answer as well. To me, she was the epitome of change. She'd changed so much since I first asked her to marry me. She'd changed since I first met her, all those years ago when we were young. Jashi used to be afraid of dragons. Now she had eight, with seven of them able to talk to her in her head. And evidently, even her name had changed. She was Jashi, but also *Eloe* now. How was she someone afraid of change?

"Change is unpredictable," said Jashi, still not looking up. "You can't tell what's going to be left on the other side of it. Who's all going to be there with you. You may not even recognize yourself by the end of it. Change terrifies me."

That explanation left me with a brand-new sense of admiration for Jashi. Because she *was* the epitome of change, and what I thought was easy for her terrified her every time. But she did it anyway.

"Oh, too true, dear Eloe," agreed Obellana. *"Now, on to my next question. Will you help me usher change into this world?"*

The world began to *sink.* Her words, they were doing something. I felt like I was descending deep into...something, beyond the physical or literal. Her words, the descent, they extended across multiple levels.

Understanding.

I was sinking into understanding, somehow. Her words nestled their meaning into my mind as it plunged deeper. What she was asking was no light-hearted question. The world fell away, and there was nothing *but* this question I was meant to answer. And as bad as this was, what she would ask for next would be much worse if I wasn't prepared.

I had to think hard about how to answer. She was being vague, yes, yet she was telling me everything I needed to know. What was my answer?

My being, my mind, swam back to the surface, understanding in tow. I understood. And my answer was still the same.

"Yes," I said once my mouth started working again and the world came back into focus.

"Yes," Jashi responded, as well. The disoriented look on her face told me she'd gone through a similar experience. And knowing what she said before, I was even prouder of her answer.

Obellana seemed just as proud, and grinned widely. "*Good. That's all I needed to know.*" She leaned forward and blew on me, then Jashi. Her breath was cool, like that slight chill you felt when you opened up the freezer.

My eyelids became very heavy, shutting on their own, and all thoughts vanished: the Convergence ending in a few hours, Half-Drac trainees waiting for us, wondering how Jashi would deal with all the dragons in her head—it was all gone. All I wanted was to sleep.

My body sank down into the cushion beneath me, and the last thing I heard was Obellana, first speaking to a spirit dragon. "*Let them rest with me until the very last minute before the Convergence ends. Then take them to their dragon and have him carry them back home.*"

Then, to us, "*You'll stay with me while your bodies recover. I am the all-seeing dragon, but my presence also heals, restores. You'll need it, believe me. Let us hope the seeds of opportunity we've planted will reap as abundantly as we planned, hm?*"

And then the world went black.

JUST US

I awoke in the Fire Den manor, lying in bed, with Jashi asleep next to me. I was confused, but I felt like I had just gotten the best sleep in my life. I had energy and focus...but confusion as well.

I slid out of bed and started for the hall, only to realize I was in a pair of loose shorts and a t-shirt. Did someone help me get undressed?

Jashi rolled over and opened her eyes. She rose out of bed with her hair askew, curls stretched across her face in a way that made me chuckle. She yawned, got her hair out her face, and looked around. "We're back home?" She glanced down at the pajamas she wore. "How long have we been asleep?"

I shook my head. "I'm not sure." I opened the door in hopes someone was around. "T'shan? Kent! Is anyone here?"

Ashed's head popped out from the end of the hall. He smiled. "You guys are finally awake!"

Jashi came up behind me. "How did we get here? How long were we asleep?"

He shook his head, eyes wide. "It was crazy. Comet brought you guys back right before the Convergence ended. You were out. You slept through the whole ride and didn't even wake when we moved you. We figured you couldn't sleep in your dragon riding gear and mission clothes, so we changed you into something more comfortable. Hope you don't mind. Jemmorah changed Jashi, just so you know."

I wasn't as concerned with who changed who, but it was good to know, nonetheless. "So wait, the Convergence..."

"Yeah, it's over." He grinned, like he was excited about it. "We're all stuck here together."

THE FIRST FEW weeks after the Convergence were the hardest. The dragon riders, oddly enough, were the most excited about the whole ordeal. Everyone else, mostly adolescents and their parents, were freaked out the entire time. The spirit dragons brought us food, though, and rather than let everyone deal with this strange new situation on their own, I thought it best we dined together as often as possible. The mansion Jashi and I stayed in had a huge outdoor dining area, and after gathering up as many dining tables as we could find in this little pocket universe, we invited people to eat with us at dinner every night.

After that, things started to settle down. People laughed easier. We all felt more connected to each other, to this shared experience.

Then there was the training with the Half-Dracs. Jashi's method of teaching Half-Dracs how to control their fire, it turned out, was even worse than mine. She didn't like meditating herself, so I wasn't sure why I thought she could teach it to others. In the end, we decided to leave me in charge of the fire training. I taught the Half-Dracs every day, which was a challenge, because children liked meditating even less than Jashi did. But we improved, day by day. And it was nice to see so much progress, to see them enjoy what Jashi and I couldn't have at their age. Here with us, they were free to show how scared they were of their powers. And the more they learned, the less afraid they became.

Though the meditation thing wasn't her forte, Jashi was really good at training people to ride the dragons. In addition to those we'd brought with us, dragons drifted into the Fire Den from time to time, and Jashi put her newfound skills to work catching them with the dragon riders and bringing them to our little community as means of transport. The floating islands had no other way to connect other than by dragon, so it was a necessity. And Jashi managed to get even the most fearful of our community members to learn to ride. Maybe it had to do with that fear she confessed to Obellana. She had been just as afraid as they were. And if she could do it, so could they.

And they did.

Within a few months, things started to normalize. I was really proud of what we'd built here. It was like a small pocket of what I dreamed could happen in K'sundi. I was surrounded by K'sundii people who would have never let Jashi be taken, I knew that for sure. And they were reconnecting to the dragons, like Aithel had wanted all along.

Perhaps oaths, bonds, dreams, and promises were all relative. At the end of the day, it was a feeling. And you knew what it was when it enveloped you.

This was it. This was what I'd been dreaming of for us all this time. And it felt good. It felt really good. We had four years to enjoy this. Four years. And if our community was willing to stay, even longer. I couldn't complain.

Jashi and I sat on the balcony outside our bedroom, watching as dragons flew through the skies above us. Below us was our community. Children practiced the routines I'd taught them. Small bursts of flames shot out from little fists as they learned to rein in their powers, to accept them rather than be afraid. Their parents stood close by, watching, monitoring—even coaching, reciting the advice I gave the children during practice.

Jashi leaned against me, resting her head on my chest, and I stroked her hair.

"Were your parents afraid of you?" she asked, her eyes on the children. Her thoughts seemed far away, and it didn't seem to have anything to do with the dragons in her head. When she was distracted like this, their thoughts didn't reach her.

The idea of my parents fearing me had never occurred to me. I shook my head slowly. No, my parents never seemed afraid of me. Confused, yes. Somewhat distressed, maybe inconvenienced. They were afraid in the sense that they had no idea what my gifts were or where they came from, and they were afraid of discovery. But never of me. "No," I answered. "They wanted to keep me safe, to a certain extent, even if just for their reputation. It served as motive enough to want to shelter me until a solution came to take me off their hands. I suppose some part of them might have been afraid, since they were so willing to give me up when the time came. But I never felt it, growing up," I confessed.

Jashi nodded, looking on at the children in silence for a moment. "I'm glad not all parents were like mine. I mean, even Nana would have raised me like you're raising these kids if she hadn't had the other children in the orphanage to protect. I don't know what might have happened if I'd ever been adopted. But I'm kinda glad I stayed with Nana. I don't know if anyone else would have understood how to raise me. To raise us. We're not just training the kids to love themselves, you know." She squeezed my hand. "We're helping the parents learn to embrace their kids too."

I kissed her head, because I couldn't reply to that. I wanted to protect her and keep her safe, but I couldn't protect her from her past. From the trauma she experienced before we were involved. My parents were terrible, but I couldn't imagine going through what she had. Being a child and being so afraid of her own self. Being made to feel, by all the adults in her world except for Nana, that she was unworthy. Knowing her powers scared her own parents out of loving her.

She looked off into the distance with glazed-over eyes. Now it was the dragons speaking with her.

"I got them all worried," she said, chuckling. She removed her hand from mine and rubbed circles on her temples. "Where the hell is the off switch on this thing?"

"There are times they can't reach you," I reasoned. "What makes that happen?"

She refocused on me, and I could see how difficult it was for her. The way she blinked a few times before she answered. "When I'm concentrating too hard for their thoughts to come through. Like in an emergency. Or when something catches my attention enough to pull me from their voices."

"Can you tell them to quiet down?" I tried.

She shook her head. "They're not doing it on purpose. I just hear them communicating with each other. I can't ask them to stay quiet on my behalf all the time. They do sometimes, though, when I'm really struggling."

But it wasn't a permanent solution, in other words.

Jashi looked off to the side, probably listening to one of her dragons. Then she groaned. "Meditation, again?"

"What are they saying?" I asked, ignoring her complaints.

She rolled her eyes. "They're saying I should practice shutting them out and focusing on my own headspace. It sounds a lot like meditation to me."

Something like a grounding exercise, it sounded like. "I think I have an idea," I said.

She sighed. "Of course you do. Fine, fine," she conceded, then pulled away from me and went inside, coming out a few moments later with two large cushions. She placed them on the ground and sat cross-legged on one of them. "I know the drill." She gestured to the one she'd placed across from her.

"How about a mantra?" I offered. "That's a good grounding exercise. Especially since your issue is being able to hear your own thoughts over the dragons'."

Getting serious, she sat up straight and nodded. "So what do I do, repeat something over and over?"

"Essentially," I agreed. "But it's a little more than that. You'll need to choose a mantra that will help pull you out of your head and ground you to your surroundings. Something easy to say under your breath. Short and to the point."

She pursed her lips in thought. "Leave me alone?"

Of course she couldn't be trusted to do this on her own.

I kneaded the space between my eyes. "Repeat after me."

Smiling, she nodded, and we both closed our eyes.

"I am safe," I said, and she echoed me. "I am present. I am loved."

She paused on the last one, and I opened my eyes to see she had opened hers too. "I am loved," she finally said, looking me in the eye. "I really feel that one. Especially lately." She averted her gaze, rubbing her arm. "It took me a while to realize it was true. When I was little, I was afraid to think about it because anyone I got attached to could be taken from me at any time. Even Nana, if I was adopted." She shrugged. "I guess I got used to that cautioun. It's just how I am now. I'm not quick to trust. I don't think I ever will be. I don't really like relationships that don't last. I think I'm so cautious about loving someone because of how hard I can love, when given the chance."

I laughed, and she stared at me with an eyebrow raised until I calmed down. "*You're* slow to trust?" I said between chuckles. "T'shan had to tell me off just to get me to allow the dragon riders to train under me. You were the one who told me I had to get closer to the people. That's the only reason I revealed myself as the rebel leader."

She chuckled. "I think you can thank your parents for that particular character flaw. Royal clans are so closed off from everyone."

"Yeah," I agreed. "Though it's helped me in some areas, like keeping enemies at bay and protecting us from threats on the inside, as much as possible. But on the other side of that, it keeps people from ever really understanding how much they mean to me. I spend so much time in my own head...I forget I don't actually say what I've been feeling all along."

I realized we'd deviated from our original meditation exercise, but when had lessons with Jashi ever been linear?

When Jashi and I had been together in the past, I always had to hold a part of myself back. At first it was because she didn't trust me, and then because I could tell she was afraid, and she just articulated how I'd felt beneath the surface all along. Now those barriers were gone. We'd been torn apart, brought back together, and we'd been through completely different experiences in our time away from each other—yet our trust in each other was as strong as ever.

I looked down at my lap, clenched my fists. "I'm so glad you're okay." I slid over beside her and pulled her into an embrace, and she stiffened against me for a moment before she relaxed and hugged me back. She squeezed hard because I think it dawned on the both of us how scared we really were when we were apart. I couldn't—wouldn't—think about what I would have done if something had happened to her. "I wanted to save K'sundi," I whispered into her hair. "But now... I only want you. Your fire and your tenacity and your willingness to learn *anything*. Between us and the rebels, as long as there's somewhere we can be happy and free... I'm content. And I know that's selfish. I *know* it's selfish. But I don't care anymore. I can't be without you, Jashi. I don't care about anyone outside of us."

"If that's selfish," Jashi said, pulling away, tears in her eyes, "then let's be selfish together." She laced her fingers with mine, smiling mischievously. "Dragons look after their own and set the rest of the world ablaze. That's just who we are. It's no use trying to fight it."

I smiled back at her and kissed her nose. "Then let's fight for us," I said against her neck. "Now, and when these four years are up."

"Just us dragons."

I tilted her chin up and kissed her, holding nothing back for the first time. Leaning into her touch as her hands warmed my chest, I pulled her closer, and she curled against me, our bodies melding together in perfect sync. She slid her arms around my neck, and I cupped the back of her head, pressing her lips deeper against mine. I drew her warm breath into my lungs as the kiss intensified—my need to get ever closer, to kiss ever deeper, filling me with desperation, like I was parched and dying and between her lips I'd find the water of life.

I gently laid her back on the cushion, not breaking the contact between us, my heart pounding so hard I knew she could feel it against her chest. I ran my fingers down her side, where the heat from her skin seeped through the silky material of her shirt. Jashi moaned and arched into me...and I pulled away, embers flying between our lips. Jumbled thoughts crashed through my brain as fast as the heated panting of my breaths. "*She might not know... There are ways to...to be safe.*" Feeling cold without her pressed to me, I nuzzled against her neck. "There are other married couples here," I explained awkwardly between breaths. "They...uhh...they found out they could ask the spirit dragons for a special tea..."

"Oh." She bristled slightly.

I pulled away fully this time, sitting up beside her. Maybe she wasn't ready. "Are you okay? Because—"

"No, no," she said quickly. She closed her eyes and bit at her lip, then sighed and looked at me. "It's just my first time, is all."

"Mine too."

Her breath hitched and her mouth fell open, and I laughed at the incredulous glaze in her narrowed eyes.

I tried but failed to keep the smirk off my face as I pulled her in close again and whispered against her ear, "You ever think about the things that initiate our fire? Anger, fear, sadness. *Passionate* emotions."

The realization dawned on her as I trailed kisses down the side of her face. "Oh."

"Makes it a bit difficult to keep my fire secret, wouldn't you say?" I slid my hand up her thigh and tensed when she gasped slightly.

"Let's just figure it out together," I said as I paused from kissing her neck. I stood and took her by the hand, helped her up, and then led her into the bedroom, closing the curtains to the balcony once inside.

CHANGE

Jashi *Eloe* Anyua-Omah

I was glad to find out the contraceptive tea the spirit-dragons provided worked for me and Kahmel, as well as the other couples in the Fire Den.

Our first time was...interesting, a little awkward. We had to help each other figure things out. The next time was better. After that,we kind of got the hang of it.

And like Kahmel said, the intimacy triggered our fire. It was possible to hold it back, but it was hard to concentrate on both "tasks" at the same time. Of course, both of us being fire-proof, it didn't bother us any. But if one of us hadn't been a Half-Drac, it would be a lot harder. Not impossible, I was sure, but an interesting thing to think about.

It reminded me of what Obellana mentioned—about how Kahmel and I were the first Half-Drac couple in a long time. A depressingly long time. We were in a new era, and the thought was thrilling.

Over the next few months, I was able to master the dragons in my mind, and it had been a lot easier than I'd feared. Saying my affirmations a couple times under my breath helped bring me back into the moment anytime the dragons were getting loud.

I am safe. I am present. I am loved.

I loved my affirmations, actually. It had become my new favorite form of meditation.

I had, officially, named all my dragons. Besides Ocean and Comet, there were Rocket and Royal, the twin red Wingless—Rocket, because he was the quickest dragon I had, and Royal because she was *definitely* the proudest. And sometimes a royal pain in the ass.

Oak, the brown draconian with swirling colors, was confirmed to be an elemental. An earth elemental, to be exact, meaning that, rather than breathe fire, he could raise the earth with his voice. A talent I wasn't sure what to make of.

Legacy, a black Draconian, was the only one in the group besides Ocean that ever showed any sort of restraint in my head. He was a very calm presence, often attempting to quiet the others on my behalf, and I appreciated his patience with me as I learned how not to go insane with all these dragons in my head space.

Dream and Lily were wild cards. Dream was a purple Wingless elemental—we still weren't sure what she could do, and she wasn't keen on telling us, either. Dream was only a little older than Lily, who was the youngest, a hatchling.

Dream was the quietest, other than Legacy, but that wasn't a good thing. She was often off causing trouble when she went missing for too long, either with other dragons or the poor citizens of the Fire Den. She liked to prank them, stealing clothes that were set out to dry, knocking over boxes of food the spirit-dragons brought. Anything to get on everyone's nerves. And I was left to apologize in her wake.

Lily, the baby of the group, was full of energy and always asking questions. She was a pink draconian that let out fire in burps and often flew into things because she was so distracted with our frequently one-sided conversations, she would forget to look where she was flying.

All in all, we were just a collective mess. But I liked it. I loved who we were, all of us. The only thing I wanted now was to learn the patterns of how the Tunnels opened so we could be with Rand,

Arusi, Khes, and Asan again. Otherwise, I agreed with Kahmel; I didn't mind being selfish.

There was one other thing I worried about, though; neither Kahmel nor I knew why Obellana had acted so strangely before she sent us away. All her prattling about change gave me the impression she had something up her sleeve, and the anticipation of what that might be crept up on me every so often. I wondered if she was meaning to surprise us when these four yearswere up, or if she intended to drop something unexpected before that.

But after a few months, everything seemed fine. Kahmel and I had space to truly relax for the first time—a sensation that was foreign to both of us. Even before everything with Kahmel started, I lived from paycheck to paycheck, never able to let my guard down. Letting go was nice. Overdue.

As these thoughts buzzed around in my head, I resisted climbing out of bed, even though it was late morning. I just wanted to lie there for a few more blessed minutes. Kahmel didn't help my sudden bout of laziness any, as he rolled over and pulled me against his bare chest, nuzzling against my neck.

This man. I shook my head and smiled. He acted like I was his teddy bear or something.

"Excuse me," I mumbled, still half asleep. "I need to drink my tea, remember?"

"Oh, right." He released his hold around my waist. He was the teddy bear, really. "That's important."

"Exactly," I reprimanded, squirming free. "Unless you want little hot-heads driving us crazy for almost four years."

I reached for the tea cup, and as my fingers closed around it a sharp pain shot through my chest. I dropped the cup and it shattered on the floor.

"Jashi?" Kahmel's worried voice seemed far away.

I couldn't concentrate on him. The pain spread until it pulsed through my whole body. My vision blurred, and the room spun around me.

Kahmel gripped my waist and sucked air through his teeth. "You're burning up."

The pain in my chest came in waves. The wave would settle for a moment but then rise up again, stealing my breath. I couldn't even tell Kahmel what was wrong.

"We have a doctor with us." Kahmel scrambled off the bed. "I'm going to go get him."

A shadow eclipsed our bedroom, and Ocean landed on the balcony with a thud, my other dragons circling in the sky behind her. *It's no use. What I sense coming from you...* Her nostrils flared as she sniffed the air. *It smells like Obellana. She must have done something.*

"Obellana," I seethed through clenched teeth. I *knew* she had something planned.

Kahmel looked back and forth between us, confused. I couldn't catch my breath enough to tell him what Ocean had said.

Ocean nudged the door. Kahmel shot from the bed and tore it open. The cool air was like ice to my blazing-hot skin.

"What is it? Do you know what to do?" Kahmel asked the dragon, desperation in his voice.

Ocean dipped her head as she came into the bedroom and loomed over my writhing form, then nudged me gently with her muzzle. *We need to get you to Obellana. She's the only one who will know how to heal you.*

How? I asked.

Kahmel's oath.

What was she talking about? Another burst of pain ripped through my body, blinding my senses.

"What do I need to do?" Kahmel's voice. Distant, like an echo.

The pain subsided slightly, and I blinked away the blurriness in my eyes as I panted shallow breaths. Kahmel held Ocean's head, looking into her eyes, trying to communicate with her. Ocean wriggled from his hold and nudged at the marks on his arms.

Kahmel looked down at them. "My promise? What about my promise?"

A memory of falling into the bond with Ocean back in Zendaal flashed through my tortured mind. I yanked on our bond, pushing thoughts and impressions of my need into her, and she understood. She fell into *me* this time, and my mouth moved with the words that needed to be said.

"You've fulfilled your oath," I said, a growl to my voice as Ocean spoke through me. Kahmel's eyes widened, but Ocean continued, *"The Dragon Kings will grant you a favor because of that. Ask Aithel to make an exception for Eloe. To take her through the Dens and straight to Obellana."*

I looked Kahmel in the eye with Obellana's intensity. *"Obellana has done something, I'm not sure what. But it will bring about the change she craved. Gather people who will go with her. She'll have to stay with Obellana. But you only have one favor. You'll be able to send her to Obellana, but she won't be able to come back until the next Convergence."*

"What? Why can't I come with her?" Kahmel asked, eyes wild.

Ocean was saying Kahmel and I would be separated again.

"Do you really think it wise to abandon the people here?" Ocean reasoned. *"The Half-Dracs need training. And should they abandon the dragons in your absence, the very favor you seek to ask would fall on deaf ears in absence of the fulfillment of your oath."*

Kahmel paused, biting his lip with hesitation. "How do I contact Aithel?"

"It's time to remove your marks," Ocean said.

Her presence withdrew from me, pulled back into her own body. The sapphire dragon loomed over Kahmel, drew back her claws, and raked them across his arm.

His flesh remained intact, but the black marks that had inked his skin for the past year squirmed from his arm and wriggled into the air like black snakes. They hovered there, squirming through the air as I writhed in the bed.

Kahmel looked up at them, confused, but quickly gathered his wits about him. "Aithel? I'm calling in my favor."

The inky marks shuddered, freezing in place where they hung. Then they started to glow.

Kahmel continued, a touch of panic in his voice, "I need you to use your powers to tear an opening through the Dens and take Jashi to Obellana. Jashi needs to go now, and whoever will keep her company will go as soon as I can gather them."

"*Your favor has been acknowledged,*" Aithel's voice rang through the room.

A streak of white light, the dragon of in-between, glided into our bedroom and stopped just short of me.

What was happening? Was I being taken away from Kahmel again already? I clutched my chest, shaking my head, tears sizzling into steam as soon as they touched my burning cheeks.

Kahmel eased me onto the glowing dragon. He stroked my hair gently, looking me in the eye while I tried to untwist my voice from where it was tangled in my chest.

"I love you." The panic left his voice as he soothed me. "Everything is going to be okay. We'll be together again when this is all over."

I could only whimper and groan in response, the air once again stolen from my lungs by the agony. What was happening to me? Why now?

Kahmel squeezed my hand, pressing strength into it. He held my gaze as he continued to stroke my hair. "It's not like last time," he said. "You're still safe. You're still loved. And we know when we'll be together again. I'm going to miss you, but you have to get over this...*change.* It's going to be all right."

My body throbbed with pain, but his words seemed to soothe it, if only a little.

"I love you too," I managed to whisper.

He kissed my hand and let me go.

The dragon of in-between launched through the balcony doors, my dragons trailing behind us. The world ripped open and swallowed us whole. We emerged on the other side in a world of twinkling starlight and crystal towers. Finally, the blinding pain subsided. The closer we got to Obellana's castle, the more the pain faded.

When we landed, I marched straight to Obellana, who perked up and grinned. I crossed my arms and scowled, trembling as I fought to keep my vicious anger in check, because as mad as I was, she was still an infinitely powerful and immortal dragon—albeit one that had pissed me off.

"What did you do to me?" I said through clenched teeth.

"*I apologize, Eloe,*" said Obellana, surprising me with a look of sympathy in her single eye. "*Truthfully, however, I did very little.*"

I frowned, confused.

Ocean, who had landed only seconds behind the dragon of in-between, said, "*But I sense Her Lady's power on her.*"

"Yes," answered Obellana. "*My protection. I've seen the future of the Half-Dracs for quite some time now. It's simply taken a very long time for it to come about.*"

"What are you talking about?" My patience was wearing thin, and I didn't have Kahmel around to keep me from saying things I shouldn't around the Dragon Queen. So I pursed my lips to remind me to keep them closed.

Obellana noticed, an amused glint in her eye. "*Well, you and the Faresh are married, Half-Drac, and you were to spend four years together, unbothered by anyone. You were bound to have children at some point.*"

What? "Wait, back up."

"*The dragons change and evolve. They always have. The dragons have gone beyond simply breathing fire, haven't they? There are elementals now because they evolved. That's what happens when you live long enough. But unfortunately, the Half-Dracs haven't.*"

The change she'd mentioned before. "You're saying...Half-Dracs may be able to do more than just use fire?"

"*Not this generation, most likely,*" she said. "*But the next...*"

There she went with that implication again. I shook my head.

Words stumbled out of my mouth, "I don't—Kahmel and I—I'm not pregnant."

"*The time is right for you now.*" Obellana whistled, and a spirit-dragon appeared with a cup of tea, reminding me I never did drink my tea this morning. "*You can drink from this cup, and the change will be postponed if you feel unready for it now. I will leave the choice up to you. But the Half-Dracs have been meant to change for centuries. The pain you felt was the evolution of your species. Your body is preparing to initiate that evolution with your child. That is why I granted you the gift of my healing power. I gave it to both you and your husband when you were here. In my presence, your pregnancy will be easy.*"

She lowered her massive head so her eye was level with mine. "*In the coming years, when it's time to face the world, you will need your child as much as your child will need you. You can drink the tea if you wish, but I recommend that you don't.*"

I realized that Obellana was in no way mocking or ridiculing me. She, as strange as she was, cared for me and the Half-Dracs. Cared for our future. She worked in strange ways because the past, present, and future were all blurred lines to her. I wondered if she really knew the difference.

Kahmel and I had come back from our visit here feeling better than ever when we woke up in the Fire Den because she'd prepared our bodies for the change in the Half-Dracs she knew would come from us—the first time Half-Dracs would reproduce in centuries. Whenever it happened, whoever it happened to, the results would have been devastating without the Dragon Kings. Particularly, Obellana.

"Are all of our pregnancies going to be like this?" I asked, my mind spinning with the immense decision I had to make.

"*Not at all,*" Obellana said. "*Dragons and Half-Dracs are connected. You've come to understand, to some extent, how that connection works. Telepathically.*" Obellana looked up to the heavens, as if gazing at something beyond the both of us. "*We *communicate on purpose, of course. But there is always a thread. An accidental transmission of information that occurs at all times, subconsciously. Invisibly. The network of threads that connect us together has many names. She was once known as the Tree of Life; later, the Dragon's Tree. Among the dragons, we call her The Mother; even we Dragon Kings call her as such."*

The Mother. Such a beautiful name. The dragons attributed their persistent connection to one another to The Mother.

Obellana gave me that toothy dragon grin, as if she could feel my admiration and approved of it. *"This pregnancy will be the hardest because it is the first,"* she went on to explain. *"But by my side, it will be much easier. After you and your child have changed, the change will be easier for the rest. The Mother will connect your experience with the other Half-Dracs, and their bodies will learn the lessons that yours have. The Mother will always teach her children whatsoever will keep them alive and healthy, as she always has."*

That was such an indescribably beautiful way to explain how the dragons and Half-Dracs evolved. A mother taught her children whatever was necessary to allow them to survive. I wanted to know more, and I realized that this connection, *The Mother*, needed my contribution to establish a foundation for the rest of her children.

I wasn't sure if Kahmel had thought about having kids any time soon, but it looked like, as usual, I'd be surprising him by making the decision ahead of him and letting him find out later. But the idea of being a mother scared me. It wasn't that I didn't like kids, but I was terrified of letting them down. I never had a mother. How was I supposed to know how to be one?

"It looks like your entourage has arrived," noted Obellana.

I turned to see the dragon of in-between. No, *several* dragons of in-between, carrying dozens of people. Many of them were those I'd trained to ride dragons in the Fire Den. Some of them were parents with their Half-Drac children.

I spotted Nana, Lora, and T'shan, all of their faces twisted with concern. All were coming to make sure I was all right. They'd dropped everything to follow Kahmel to the Dens. And now they'd done it again to take care of me.

Our people. Kahmel and I declared to each other that this was all that mattered to us anymore. And as long as these people would still have me, no matter who sat on K'sundi's throne, I was their Faresha. I didn't *have* to be the one to pave the way for their Half-Drac children to have children. If they stayed under our protection long enough, I was sure they'd have the chance to offer their contribution to The Mother. But it would be my honor to pave the way on their behalf. Kahmel had made me Faresha, but this decision really made me feel that more than ever before. I was doing this for me and Kahmel. For our children and their children. I didn't have to be the first. But this little community Kahmel and I created together in the midst of chaos made me want to.

"You can take the tea back," I said to Obellana.

I turned back to her, and she actually seemed relieved. "*I will take good care of you and your child, Faresha.*" A wicked grin spread across her face. "*The world won't know what to do with themselves when we reemerge.*"

PART III:

TEETH

FOUR YEARS LATER

Kahmel Axon Kai of the Omah Clan

The Convergence would start soon, today. We waited at the outside dining hall of the Fire Den. I sat at the head of the table with Jemmorah, Kent, and Ashed. As they knew me best and were the most experienced of all the dragon riders, they had taken on leadership roles. They were—collectively—my second in command.

I was having trouble sitting still; over the past twenty minutes I'd stood, paced, and sat back down multiple times. Now I tapped my fingers on the table, staring at the place I expected the Tunnels to appear.

Jemmorah laid her hand over mine. "You're nervous."

I shrugged and pulled my hand out from under hers, rubbing the back of my neck.

"Of course he's nervous," Ashed said. "He hasn't seen or heard from his wife in four years."

Glancing down at the table, I sighed and verbalized the thoughts looping through my head. "Jashi was twenty when she left, which means she's twenty-four now." I looked up at my friends. "We've spent more time apart from each other in our marriage than together." I was almost thirty now. We'd missed so much time together.

As if reading my mind, Kent nodded and said, "It's a long time to be separated, for sure. But you'll pick right up where you left off, I'm sure."

That was my hope. But Obellana had asked if we were open to change—what if part of that change was in the way Jashi felt about me? Why had I ever told the Dragon Queen I was open to change? I'd asked myself that question many times in the past four years, all the while thinking that Jashi was the smart one to be afraid of change. I should have answered like her—maybe if we'd answered no, none of this would have happened.

I stood and looked again to where the Tunnels would appear soon, my thoughts consumed with Jashi. *Is she okay? Was Obellana able to heal her or had she been suffering in pain this whole time? Would whatever had happened to cause her pain come back when she returned here?*

Four years of questions and only vast nothingness in response.

I shook my head to clear it. I wasn't the only one feeling the tension in the air. We were all ready to fight for the Dragon Kings. The Half-Dracs had grown incredibly talented in their abilities these four years, and all the members of our community knew how to ride dragons.

They knew the story now. They understood the history that kept us bound under the Zendaalans. They mourned how long the dragons had spent under their abuse. And more so, how the Zendaalans were allowed to slaughter their children right under their noses.

They'd listened. They'd cried. Now they were angry.

I watched four young children chasing a group of chickens over by the pens. After my Den had almost unanimously agreed they wanted to continue living in the Dens when all this was over, we'd begun preparing for the time when the spirit-dragons would no longer be bringing us food. We'd recorded the patterns of the Tunnels and now had accurate calendars for our Den, as the Tunnel appearances cycled back every year. We'd been able to make short trips back to K'sundi to buy necessities when the need arose, and we'd started buying meat about six months in. We bought cattle and chickens after the first year, supplying our own meat ever since then.

A murmur of excitement came from the crowd, and I turned away from watching the children just as several Tunnels opened in the sky.

Rand, Arusi, Khes, and Asan flew in on their dragons through different Tunnels in the pink and blue sky. I took an anxious step toward them, searching the sky for Jashi. My stomach fluttered as several Wingless dragons poured in through a fifth Tunnel—carrying the people who had gone with Jashi to Obellana's Den. Each Wingless dragon carried several people at a time, dropped them off, then returned to the Tunnel to retrieve another group.

Rand dismounted his dragon and came to my side. I spared him a quick glance, noting that my twin...looked different. We'd looked alike most of our lives, having similar tastes in clothing and hairstyles.

The locks of hair running down his back shifted as he turned to watch the people returning from Obellana's Den. "Where are all of them coming from?"

Arusi, Khes, and Asan joined us while I pondered this change in my brother.

"Kahmel!" Lora yelled from astride a dragon she shared with Nana. She helped the older woman dismount, then said, "There's so much to tell you."

"Where's Jashi?" I rushed up to her.

"What do you mean, 'where's Jashi'?" asked Arusi.

I brushed her off. Everyone would get their explanations in a minute.

"She's coming," said Lora. "She wanted to make sure everyone left Obellana's realm safely. She'll be the last one through."

Questions came at me from my friends who had just arrived from their own Dens. I held up a hand to silence them and said, "I'll explain later," then turned back to Lora. "Is she okay? What happened?"

"I...think it's best you discuss that with your wife. But she's fine."

I scowled. That answer told me nothing.

Lora turned to the people beside me. "Jashi got sick while we were here in the Fire Den. Obellana took her in so she could recover."

My four friends frowned in unison.

"She's fine; she—oh, look, there she is."

Jashi rode one of her Wingless dragons, Royal or Rocket; I couldn't tell the difference. The rest of her dragons flew behind her like a small pack, all bigger than when they left. She rode with what must have been the last of the people who had gone with her, most of them parents with their Half-Drac children. She even cradled one of those children in her arms as she rode her red Wingless through the air.

I pushed through the various reunions happening all around me to get to her as she landed, dragons lined up at her sides. She helped the child down—a little boy, it looked like—and then she grinned at me.

I pulled her into my arms, hugging her tight against me. "I missed you so much," I said, though the words were insufficient. I pulled away and took in her form, shocked at how different she was. Her hair was cut short now, haloing her head in a short afro that brought out her features. Her middle was softer than before, her chest fuller, and her hips wider. But she was also the same Jashi that had left. The same wide, orange eyes that sparkled with mischief. The same beautiful smile that promised trouble. And thankfully, she was no longer writhing in agony. She was intact.

"I missed you too." She kissed me lightly.

Questions I'd been wanting answered for almost four years bubbled out of my mouth. "What happened when Obellana took you in? Are you okay?"

"I—"

Rand cleared his throat. "Sorry to interrupt. I'm sure there's a long story behind what exactly happened here, but we do have other matters to attend to, and the Convergence only lasts so long. The chip Jashi brought back *was* one of Dekaar's memory chips...and it did have the location of the Dragon Kings' parts on it."

Jashi's eyes widened, and she looked at me. The child she'd arrived with squirmed, hiding behind her legs. His eyes were such a light orange, they were almost yellow. "We'll talk later," she promised as one of the people who rode with her picked the little boy up and cooed at him as she walked away.

We gathered at the dining table, and since Rand had the most pertinent information, he began. "It's been a long four years, and I know we'd all like to get caught up on everything we missed while we were apart."

I knew then that my brother had changed drastically. He held our gazes as he spoke. No teasing or joking in his tone. He'd spent most of our childhood letting me take the lead. It seemed that four years of being the leader of the Rider Den had brought out a side of him he'd never allowed to surface, the intelligence he'd smothered with humor all this time.

"But first things first," he continued. "When Jashi was captured by the Zendaalans four years ago, she managed to steal this chip from Dekaar, the resurrected traitor of the dragons from a thousand years ago."

He tossed the chip on the table as mutterings went out. "From it, we gained the following information—" He pulled out his eWatch, then enlarged and flipped the holographic display so we could all see it. "However the Zendaalans managed to bring Dekaar back, he came back with very little memory of the past and no knowledge of the present. On this chip we found not only data on current world events, but also a detailed account of Dekaar's past. We're still poring through the information for important details, but the part that's most relevant to us now is this—they uploaded into his memory the location of the Dragon Kings' parts." He pointed at a section of the holograph. "They're being stored in an underwater bunker off Zendaal's east coast.

"Water Elemental dragons would help us immensely. They can

swim, so all we'll need are suits. Our plan is simple. We arrive in Zendaal through the open Tunnels and escape the same way. We may not have several countries on our side like we initially planned, but we have the element of surprise—and we have Jashi to thank for it."

The table applauded, myself included, and Jashi averted her gaze, smiling bashfully.

"We're leaving tomorrow," Rand said once everyone settled down. "Today we'll prepare. The suits won't be hard to obtain from the rebel factions that stayed in K'sundi."

I had a feeling Dekaar wouldn't take the offense sitting down. He knew more about the dragons and Dragon Kings than we did. He could come to the Dens. The only thing that might slow him down was the world's ignorance about how to properly ride the dragons to mount an attack against us, once he figured out how we were appearing where we liked without a trace.

But we would cross that bridge when we got to it.

"Ah," Rand said, stroking his chin. "Kahmel, Jashi, did you have anything to add?"

I chuckled, along with several people at the table. "No, I think you covered everything well enough." I glanced at Jashi. She still had something to tell me, and the others still didn't know we spent most of the last four years apart. But none of that was relevant to the task at hand, and whatever we had to discuss wasn't important enough to ignore everything we needed to prepare for the raid tomorrow.

"I have something to say." Jashi drew every gaze in the vicinity. "What we're doing isn't to be taken lightly." She looked everyone around the table in the eye. "We're going to change the world tomorrow. With the power of the Dragon Kings' parts taken from the Zendaalans, they won't be able to control who wins and loses anymore. We're all wanted in K'sundi, and every other Equalized nation, but if we succeed, we'll be able to go anywhere and come back here as we like. We're selfishly changing the world in our favor. The people here with us—the rebels, the Half-Dracs, the dragons—that's all that matters now. We weren't given a chance to have a place in this world. It's time to carve one."

They applauded her again, and I was once again proud of the woman Jashi had become. She really grew into her role as their leader quickly. I was impressed.

We all dispersed. Rand decided he and the men from the Rider Den would be in charge of finding Water Elementals. Apparently, their trips exploring outside of their Den revealed good spots to find Elementals along a coastline in K'sundi. Khes and the Shield Den went off to create a definitive plan to ensure the raid would go smoothly. Arusi, Asan, Jashi, and I were going to be on the raid, and I approved the decision to leave the dragon riders I trained in charge of the Water, Shield, and Iron Dens.

I looked for Jashi as soon as talks were over, but she'd vanished. It took me a minute to spot her with the same kids and parents she'd come here with, along with Lora and Nana.

"Are you sure you want to go on the raid with them?" Nana was asking.

"I'm fine, Nana," Jashi said, hugging herself. "It's not like when I was—Oh, Kahmel."

The people clustered around her like a small posse in a defensive position. What was going on? "What do you mean, 'Oh, Kahmel?'" I asked. "We have to talk. What happened to you?"

Jashi hesitated, and Lora filled in, "There's still a lot you have to do for the raid tomorrow, right? It might be best to talk after that."

I glanced at Lora, wondering why she was acting as an intermediate. Why didn't Jashi want to tell me whatever was going on? It was like this *was* her defense team, protecting her from questioning.

"You don't need to be distracted," Jashi finally said. "And I'm fine."

"You keep saying that..." Worry trickled down my throat. What were they all keeping from me?

"I'm the only one who can talk to the dragons," she said, her stance firm. "You need me tomorrow. I promise to tell you everything afterward." She leaned forward, breaking free of her lady-gang, and kissed me. This one was more lingering than the last. It said everything she wanted to say but had to hold back. It asked me to trust her, and I responded that I would. I always would.

She pulled away, then said, "I'll be staying in another one of the manors for the night. I'll see you in the morning."

And with that, she and her small group peeled away, leaving me with even more questions than I had before she arrived.

DESERT OUTLAWS

Jashi *Eloe* Anyua-Omah

I brushed a finger along my son's cheek as he slept next to Nana. Kai. A three-letter name borrowed from his father. Kahmel Axon *Kai* of the Omah Clan. Kai was a Butaan name, apparently. Kahmel's parents probably never knew, but it seemed a lot of clan families unknowingly used Butaan for their children's second and third names, I'd learned from the libraries in Obellana's Den. Obellana told me *Kai* meant bold. It described Kahmel, definitely, and it was a quality our son would need if he was going to survive in our world of fire and dragons. So that was what I named him.

I kissed Kai on his head, watched his little chest rise and fall. Three years old. Still squishy and small. I had set my house on fire as an infant, and it made my parents leave me with Nana. Looking down at Kai, I would happily burn down the world to keep him safe, and I was glad to know I was nothing like the people who brought me into this world.

Nana stirred, turning to look at me. She squeezed my hand. "You've grown so much," she whispered, pride glimmering in her eyes, the smell of cinnamon gently wafting with her movement. She stroked Kai's hair. "I'll look after this one. You do what needs to be done."

She was right. There was so much that needed to be done. A long-awaited conversation with my husband, for one. But that would have to come later. After. Right now, it was time to go. And my son couldn't be in better hands.

Today's the day, said Oak.

Yes, and you're staying here, I conveyed as I strode outside. The main mansion out here in the Fire Den was just a few floating islands away. My dragons were scattered, flying through the air or lying around one of the many floating islands. I caught a streak of yellow in the sky above me, and in a moment, Comet landed in front of me, shaking the ground as he did. I couldn't talk to him in my head like I could the others, but I still got to know him better over the last four years. Ocean was agile, but Comet was powerful. Not only was the draconian more feral in his flight patterns and attack movements, but he was an Elemental with electric abilities.

Everything Kahmel and I had worked toward depended on how today went. Today, we'd be reclaiming the power of the Dragon Kings. Restoring prosperity to all of Hemorah. I'd never taken a life on purpose before. At first, the idea gave me hesitation. But Kai changed all that. If his future depended on it, the decision was easy. Fire was great, but it only deterred enemies rather than taking them down quickly. Comet's lightning would eliminate any opposition that came against us today.

I sighed as I felt Oak's mounting disappointment. But I would need all of my concentration today. I'd gotten used to being connected to all of my dragons, but the connection could still be distracting at times, and I couldn't afford to be distracted. I would, however, need at least one dragon I could connect to mentally. As we approached the Dragon Kings' parts, I felt it would be important to have a dragon I could communicate with directly. And despite Dream being one of the youngest, I'd learned her elemental power while I was with Obellana, and I was sure she would come in handy today as well.

A red Wingless landed beside Comet as I climbed on his back. Royal. *Are you sure you don't need more backup, Eloe?*

If she didn't ask us for help, she's probably fine, countered her almost-identical counterpart, Rocket, who was darker than his more crimson sister.

Before I could answer any of them, as usual, Legacy came to my rescue. The black dragon landed and growled challengingly. *Eloe needs to concentrate. Leave her alone.*

Thanks, Legacy, I said. Then I addressed the rest of them. *We're not sure how long this will take, so if I'm not back by tonight, I'm going to need you all here with Kai.*

The dragons called Kahmel "the Faresh" because he didn't have a dragon name, but because Kai was already a name in Butaan, the dragons understood it as well as they understood mine.

At that, all of the dragons sobered, their priorities suddenly changed. From the moment he was born, they treated Kai like royalty. It sort of scared me a little. Kahmel and I *were* royalty for all intents and purposes, but the way the dragons treated Kai was different. They regarded Kahmel and I as leaders of an ally country, like I might treat Cirssa and Daoliu. But they treated Kai like he was *their* royalty. While they treated the Dragon Kings with sovereign respect, in some strange way...it was like they saw Kai on a level just below that, which made no sense to me, but I never asked the dragons about it. Obellana said Kai was the beginning of a change for the Half-Dracs. I wasn't sure what that meant, but I knew she was telling the truth. I sighed. There was a lot I needed to tell Kahmel, when there was time.

Kai started teething when he was three months old. At a year old, he could use his fire. Not only use it, but control it in little bursts fired at anything that startled or annoyed him. He took his first steps when he saw the dragons outside his window flying around, and he started walking toward them. And if I, or Nana, or Lora didn't stop him whenever he ran outside the manor, it seemed like he would take off into the air and join them.

He'd never been afraid of the dragons, not even when he was an infant, and if I didn't know any better, I'd say that whenever I caught him staring off into space, not paying attention to a single thing around him, he was talking to them, the same way I did.

Lily darted through the air in a clumsy, drunk-looking pattern, interrupting my thoughts. *We'll take good care of Kai!* she giggled, ignoring Legacy as he warned her to fly carefully.

The other dragons grumbled their agreement, knowing full and well what I was doing by asking them to look after my son but unable to help the fact that it was working.

Ocean came from where she'd been sleeping behind the manor. *I'll look after the dragons,* she said, sensing what I was going to ask her before I could even ask. Out of all of the dragons, our bond was still the strongest. Just like, despite the mental connection I shared with all the rest of my dragons, Comet would always have a special place in my heart. There was something about firsts, I supposed.

I nodded to her, then flicked Comet's whiskers. "Let's go." The dragon shot into the air as Dream trailed behind us.

Sneaky move, Faresha, Dream admonished, earning an eye roll from me in response. The second-youngest dragon, yet she was the one with the most opinions. *But I suppose there's nothing to be done about it! Every dragon on Hemorah would want to be with you today. It's no exaggeration to say this might be the most important day in history for us. You should be glad the others gave in as easily as they did.*

I shook my head and sighed. No pressure.

Comet landed in front of the manor where Kahmel and I stayed before I had to be taken to Obellana's Den. Kahmel stood with Huntress, dressed from head to toe in a protective fly suit and helmet, holding out a similar suit for me.

Reading dragon minds for four years left me with the ability to tell what they were thinking even when they weren't sharing their thoughts. My husband, sometimes more dragon than man, was no different. He watched me as I dismounted, dragging his thoughts away from what he wished we were doing right now, after four years apart from each other. But there were ten-thousand-year-old dragons to avenge, a nation to upheave, and a future to decide in a day. I knew he understood that, and I watched as he put his thoughts aside and looked at me with determination in his eyes. "Are you ready?"

There was a lot that could go wrong. Dekaar had proved to be an adversary to take seriously. I didn't think he'd be sitting around for four years just waiting for us to do something, knowing Kahmel was missing, knowing I was alive. But even so, I grinned at Kahmel, because as scared and anxious as I was, I also knew that this day had been centuries in the making, and thus, long overdue.

"More than that," I said, taking the communicator and gear from him as he handed them to me. "I'm excited."

Today was the last day of the Convergence, but even without it we could have navigated here, near a small town in K'sundi. Each Den group had learned the rotating patterns of their Tunnels. Kahmel informed me on our way over that the Fire Den had four Tunnels, two of which opened every month, whereas the other two opened yearly on two different dates.

While we waited a little ways away from the Tunnel, I worried silently about any countermeasures Dekaar might have prepared in advance. He'd waited over a thousand years to have his chance at K'sundi. There was no way he was just going to sit on his hands and let the two biggest threats to his reign run around free where he couldn't find us. He knew more about the dragons, Half-Dracs, and Dragon Kings than we did. It was possible that when he found no trace of us in K'sundi, he figured out that we'd escaped to the Dens. He wouldn't be able to come after us, though. Opening a Tunnel required a command to a dragon in Butaan, and there was no way he would teach his soldiers Butaan just to find us—not after everything he'd done to erase K'sundi's past.

I turned my thoughts to the mission at hand. It had three stages. The Dragon parts were being held in a bunker off the coast of

Zendaal, underwater. The rebels would go ahead of us and hit the bunker first with the water Elementals Rand and the Rider Den crew found. Once they'd broken in, Kahmel and I would go in for the second stage of the mission—retrieval. We'd go get the Dragon parts ourselves, and then we'd all work together for the last stage of the raid —retreat.

Our dragons lay nearby on the sand dunes. It had been a long time since I'd seen K'sundi's desert and felt the kiss of K'sundi's sun on my skin. It felt strange being here now, knowing we were outcasts. I wondered what the people thought of us now. Did they think of us at all? Kahmel's reign had been so short, mine even shorter. Our efforts were worth it in my eyes, if only for the small group of people who supported us now. But once all the Half-Dracs and their parents had departed K'sundi, was there anyone left who believed in us?

Dekaar is paranoid, I thought as Kahmel and I, wearing camouflage gear, watched drones fly overhead. They were part of the latest line of surveillance technology Dekaar had imposed on K'sundi. He'd been watching for any hint of movement from Kahmel or me. The K'sundii were constantly being questioned, monitored, perhaps even spied on, if the rumors our people heard were true. There was talk of citizens having their homes raided in the middle of the night, parents and children separated for questioning. No one was spared from Dekaar's severity.

The most disturbing of all of the rumors was the one claiming Dekaar was on the lookout for any and all Half-Drac children—and when his people discovered a Half-Drac using their powers, those children went missing.

From what we heard, even the Courts didn't know what to do with Dekaar, but because of his Zendaalan supporters, they couldn't object to anything he wanted. The Court got what they asked for—a Faresh the Zendaalans approved of, but the cost of their wishes was heftier than they anticipated. Dekaar was a tyrant. He didn't show himself to the public unless he was threatening supporters of the rebels left in K'sundi or demanding that Kahmel and I show ourselves. He sanctioned violence against civilians he suspected of supporting the rebellion, and the people were terrified.

When the rebels gave their report, I could scarcely believe it was K'sundi they were talking about. It sounded like a foreign country, surely not the place I left only a few years ago. Not the place I'd watched from the palace as the dragons flew over the horizon and the city lights flickered in the distance.

But it was what they'd asked for. They were only just beginning to understand what that meant.

One way or another, though, all of that would be coming to an end. Once the Equalizers were gone, there'd be no one to sustain Dekaar. If K'sundi had changed so drastically in only a few years with a new Faresh, I wasn't sure I'd recognize Hemorah with the Equalizers gone.

But whichever way Hemorah went was not my concern. Our people, the Half-Dracs, the people who decided to follow us to the Dens and had stayed faithful to us this whole time, my son, my husband, and my dragons were the only things that mattered to me anymore. My world. It was only a coincidence those two worlds would coincide today.

The silence was broken by a sharp alarm. The signal.

Kahmel and I scrambled to our dragons and held our breaths as we waited for the coded message.

Two short beeps and a long one: the rebels had broken through the Zendaalans' defense.

Then two long beeps, a pause, and a short one: They were ready for us.

Kahmel looked to me and nodded. Then, to Huntress, he shouted, "*Mufi eltep!*"

The world ripped open, and we led our dragons through the tear and into a world of chaos and laser fire.

CHOPPY WATERS

Jashi *Eloe* Anyua-Omah

Before us lay the ocean. The underwater bunker was hidden just off the Zendaalan coast in an unremarkable area. Zendaal could be seen in the distance, lining the horizon in the east. No one was supposed to know this was here. *We* weren't supposed to know this was here.

Zendaalan ships swarmed in the air to defend their territory. But we had the element of surprise on our side, and they had no idea where our rebels were coming from. So they were late to the game.

Two dragons hovered in the air, side by side, just above where the bunker was presumably located.

Rand appeared at our side. "Ready?"

Kahmel and I nodded, and he led us to where the other two rebels waited for us atop dragons that were a rich cerulean blue, complemented by the blue skies above and crystalline water beneath them. Water elementals. It was time to see what they were capable of.

Hehehe, Dream chuckled deviously in my head. *I'll get my chance soon enough, though.*

I rolled my eyes.

Rand's dragon riders turned their dragons upward, flying high into the sky, their silhouettes turning black against the sun. Then they arched downward, spiraling toward the water.

"*K'meht achnir!*" the riders shouted.

The dragons roared, their pitch going higher and higher until I couldn't hear it anymore. The water churned and gurgled until it finally exploded. I threw up my arms to shield myself from the spray, but soon realized there was no need. The water blew up and around us, spiraling up into the air in a watery funnel. The funnel descended as the dragons flew past us and into the hole they were tunneling out. The water had split open for the dragons, and if I didn't want to get wet, or perhaps drown, I realized I'd better stick close to them. I yanked at Comet's whiskers and made him follow them, Kahmel close at my side as we dove.

More dragon riders appeared behind us, another set of two with blue elementals, carving the hole again as Rand and a few others flew into it with us. Our small squadron was formed, piping an opening through the water that went deeper and deeper. Soon, the water closed above the last riders, making us into a long moving bubble going farther into the depths of the sea. In the swirling walls of water around us, I spotted fish being tossed around in the spiral.

We finally arrived at the seafloor. All of our dragons landed, the water elementals with their mouths open as they continued their high-pitched roar, maintaining the bubble around us. The blue dragons marched forward until their bubble enveloped a metallic orb-like structure that jutted from the ground—the entrance to the facility holding the Dragon Kings' parts. The rest of the facility was beneath us. Underground.

The Zendaalan ships that saw us go under had probably figured out by now what we were after, which meant we would have submarines on our tail soon. We had to act fast.

"*Fez kara!*" I shouted to Comet, echoed by Kahmel, Rand, and the other dragon riders. Dream didn't need a command word. She knew what I was thinking. Our dragons leaped up in response, slamming down against the metal walls of the facility's entrance and twisting the steel in the grip of their claws. Even a dragon as small as Dream could do damage when she put her mind to it. They tore and raked at the structure while sirens blared from inside the building. A group of Zendaalans rose from the lower levels of the building just as our dragons ripped an opening for us.

Kahmel, Rand, and I led our dragons into the underwater structure, and our dragons made quick work of the ill-prepared Zendaalan soldiers. With no airships or submarines to aid them, they weren't much of a match for us.

The small structure barely fit two dragons inside, but that wasn't much of a problem with the roof and walls torn open. There was an elevator that was no doubt about to send more soldiers our way.

The three of us secured special harnesses around our waists, and Rand urged his dragon forward to rip the doors open as the elevator descended, and they dived down the elevator shaft after it. Kahmel and I followed, my stomach sinking as we fell.

The elevator now rose toward us, and Rand's dragon landed on it with a deciding smash. The elevator was knocked back and the cords snapped. The sound of people screaming resounded through the small tunnel as they plummeted to the ground.

It was odd knowing those men probably didn't survive, but it didn't bother me. All I had to do was think of Kai and imagine how they wouldn't hesitate to insert a needle in his arm and kill him like they'd tried to kill Kahmel. When the elevator crashed, I simply nodded. They were dead because they chose to be complicit in the killing of children like my son.

We continued to dive, Dream close at my side. Two, three, four flights down. I counted the doors as we fell.

Rand directed his dragon against the wall of the elevator shaft just short of the door to the seventh sub-level. His dragon scraped its claws against the concrete and came to a screeching halt. Rand's harness prevented him from lurching forward or losing his grip. I bit my lip and braced myself to do the same. I jerked when Comet's claws clutched the cement, and I was grateful for the harness when we came to a stop just above Rand.

Rand moved forward, his dragon prying open the doors ahead of us. He led us as his dragon crawled forward and into the opening like a lizard.

We entered a hall and were immediately surrounded by Zendaalans with lasers, and despite the gunfire, I was just glad to be right side up again. I pulled back, letting Rand and Kahmel stride forward. With a single command, their dragons unleashed pillars of fire that licked at the walls and blasted the enemy backward. I brought up the rear because Comet's ability was so volatile, and I didn't want to hurt the others. Besides, Kahmel and Rand were doing plenty of damage themselves.

Everything was going according to plan.

Until Dream spoke up.

Where are the Dragon Kings' parts?

I stopped Comet dead in his tracks as Kahmel and Rand moved further ahead. *What do you mean 'where are they'?*

Dream came around to flap in the air in front of me. Panic poured off of her and into me, and I had to bolster myself, my mind, to prevent her emotions from affecting my own.

Aren't the Dragon Kings' parts supposed to be near here?

Are you saying you can't feel them? I asked, keeping the rising urgency creeping inside of me in a far corner of my mind so she wouldn't feel it, even by accident.

They're not here, Dream insisted frantically. *We should be close enough for me to feel them, but I haven't felt anything.*

"Jashi!" Kahmel said over my earpiece. He and Rand had cleared a path, and they were about to move on to the next room. The one that was supposed to hold the Dragon Kings' parts.

But Dream was telling me they weren't there.

Could the parts be farther down? I asked. But realization crawled up my chest, and the fear that I'd pushed to the back of my mind came rushing forward. I knew Dekaar wouldn't just sit around and do nothing while we planned. If he'd discovered I stole the chip from him, he probably knew we'd come for the Dragon Kings' parts.

They're not here, she emphasized, confirming my fears.

"Jashi, what's going on?" Rand asked. He and Kahmel had reached the end of the hall.

Instead of answering, I moved forward on Comet and pushed ahead of them both. "*Fez kara!*" I yelled, and Comet slammed into the door, tearing his claws across the metal until it bent and tore under his grasp, pulling them aside. I slung off Comet's back and strode inside.

The large room was empty.

Clearly, it *used* to house the Dragon Kings' parts. There were podiums topped with thick glass cases as tall as my body. Empty.

"Did you really think," jeered Dekaar's voice, "I wouldn't notice you took my memory chip?"

His holograph appeared in the center of the room, and seeing him again after four years of being in hiding was still too soon. My blood boiled, and when I roared, fire poured from my lips. Dream echoed my scream, our voices bouncing off the steel walls as the alarms continued to blare. I barely noticed Kahmel grabbing me, holding onto my raised arm I was about to swing at a man that wasn't even there.

"Let's just get out of here," Kahmel soothed, and I loved him even more in that moment, because I knew what it must have taken for him to simmer his boiling rage down to such a gentle whisper on my behalf.

"Coward," I spat at Dekaar, knowing he could hear me and knowing I shouldn't let him get to me. But my and Dream's rage were pooling together, and I couldn't tell who I was speaking for anymore, but our sentiments were one. "Look at you. Appearing in illusions and tricks of light. You're The Traitor, the Dragon-Slayer, ruler of K'sundi and servant to the Zendaalans, but you're nothing but a face."

"And you're nothing but a penniless queen with nothing to rule," Dekaar countered.

"*I* have nothing to rule?" I laughed, moving away from Kahmel, and this time he didn't stop me. "You think you control K'sundi, but really, they control you. They always have. They used you to free themselves from their loyalty to the Dragon Kings, and then they let you die. And even worse, they made themselves into a nation unfit to be ruled, not even by you. What do you have left to rule, Dekaar? A foolish nation without dragons, strength, or fire? You don't even have that; the Zendaalans do. So what do you really have left, Dekaar? Tell me, were the thousand years you waited for this moment worth it? Was it all that you hoped it would be?"

Dekaar roared and whipped his head around as fire crackled through the air in an arc around him, revealing the true Dekaar: a dark dragon with scars a thousand years old. "You're wasting your time. The longer you spend here with me, the longer the Zendaalans have to catch up with you. You have nothing. You are nothing. Eventually you'll realize that."

"That's where you're wrong," I said, holding my head up. "I am *everything*. I am a nation, and fire, and dragons. I am everything you will never have but wish to rule. And for all of your scheming and planning and plotting, you will never rule me. *You* are the Faresh of Nothing."

Dekaar's hologram rushed forward, his hand moving to something at his side—a dagger. He plunged it in my chest, where it simply phased through. I stared him down, and he glowered at me, real fury in his almost-red eyes. "Come do it yourself, Traitor," I jeered.

"It's time to go, Jashi," Kahmel pushed. "Our people are upstairs."

I clenched my fists and pulled away from Dekaar, turning to run after Kahmel. I remounted my dragon and looked back before we started climbing back up the elevator shaft. Dekaar's hologram hadn't moved. He still held the dagger.

And he was glaring at me.

SNAKES IN THE GRASS

Kahmel Axon Kai of the Omah Clan

Dekaar.

I'd seen what he looked like from news articles and such, but seeing him in person, hologram or not, was something different. The way he looked at Jashi—he saw her as more than just an opponent. He was obsessed with her, and Jashi could feel it.

Our dragons started the ascent up the elevator shaft, and all I could think about was getting to our people before the submarines arrived.

That, and the fact that Jashi had provoked Dekaar mere moments ago.

"He's planning something," Jashi said through our earpiece, the first thing she'd said since we came down here.

"I think that's apparent," came Rand's voice. The frustration in his tone told me he was just as upset as we were.

"No," Jashi pressed, "not just moving the Dragon Kings' parts. He was ready for us. He was too calm."

"Calm?" I asked. Watching him mimic stabbing her almost brought me to the edge. If it wasn't for the way Jashi held her composure and faced him, I would have dragged her out the moment he'd started talking. But I refused to smother her voice. I trusted Jashi's instincts. Despite her impulsive nature, her instincts were usually spot on. Even so, saying Dekaar was acting calm seemed a bit much.

Jashi chuckled. "That's because I ticked him off. His temper's even worse than yours, Kahm."

I wasn't sure what to react to first, the fact that she knew our enemy so intimately, to the point she was comparing his personality to mine, or her calling me *Kahm.*

"What you saw is pretty much how he is," she went on. "If he was upset by our coming, you would have been able to tell."

"But he knew we were coming," objected Rand. "What would he be upset about?"

"He wasn't even surprised," Jashi insisted. "Even if he knew we would come, he shouldn't have known *when.* He's easily perturbed. If how livid he got after I pissed him off should tell you anything, it's how he should have reacted when he found us there, at all. He has something up his sleeve. Stay alert."

"Understood." A sinking feeling crawled into my gut as her words sunk in. She was right. Knowing we were coming was one thing. Knowing *when* was another. Knowing *when* could only mean one thing—there was a traitor in our midst.It meant this entire operation was in jeopardy.

Our dragons arrived at the top floor, the incessant wail of alarms still sounding in the background. But the operatives who manned the water Elemental dragons were still there, waiting as they should be. The water Elementals maintained a pocket of air for them, and the connection to the underground facility pumped fresh air into the opening, so they were fine.

And Jashi's warning started to make sense. The submarines should have been there by now.

Something was wrong.

"Let's go!" Rand shouted to the operatives.

They needed no further encouragement. With a word, they and their dragons shot into the air, and me, Jashi, and Rand followed close after them. We flew through the depths of the ocean as the

Elementals maintained our bubble of air, having no way to tell if one of the enemy's submarines was on top of us.

We emerged from the water into the middle of a swarm of Zendaalan airships.

"Kahmel Axon Kai," called a voice I recognized over a speaker. Prexa. "You've been found guilty of a multitude of crimes against the Equalization, as well as crimes of treachery against the throne of K'sundi. Surrender. You're completely surrounded."

Jashi narrowed her eyes, and Dream sprang into action. Jashi must have given her dragon a silent command. Dream flew in front of us and screeched, and the air around us shimmered, then solidified. Jashi had told me what her Elemental was capable of before we came here, but seeing it in person was another thing altogether.

Dream had created a forcefield around us all. The Zendaalans started firing, but they couldn't penetrate Dream's field.

"Let's go," Jashi called, leading us all from astride Comet.

We followed. Dream shook with the strain of sustaining the forcefield against the Zendaalans' continual barrage. She was powerful, but she was still only an infant. She wouldn't be able to sustain her shields much longer. But it didn't matter; we were close to the Tunnel that would take us to a Den where we could hide away and get back to base.

"*Mufi eltep!*" Rand shouted, opening the Tunnel and allowing us to phase through.

Light dazzled and sparkled around us, and then we arrived in a colorful Den speckled with floating islands and small manors that was starting to become endearingly familiar.

"*Ulpesh eltep!*" called Rand, and the Tunnel sealed shut, preventing more fire from raining on us through it, and keeping the Zendaalans from pursuing.

We all made it through.

But we'd failed. Dekaar had moved the Dragon Kings' parts, and we were back to square one. How would we figure out where Dekaar had moved them? I cursed under my breath. Even if we figured it out, how would we navigate to the location, given that the Convergence would be ending in a few hours?

We'd waited four years for this opportunity, and Dekaar had used that time to humiliate us completely. We'd understood that Dekaar would likely figure out a way to oppose us, but that didn't make the humiliation any less crushing.

More than that, though, was what this might do to our people. Would they be discouraged? Would it make them want to go back to K'sundi? We'd continue to take care of them as long as they were willing to stay. We'd carved out a way of life for us in the Dens now. We had food, shelter, even medical care thanks to the doctors who had joined us. But would this loss make them want to give all that up and go back to K'sundi, back to what they were used to?

My thoughts were disrupted by a shimmer in the air some distance from us. Khes and his men came out of the Tunnel soon afterward.

"I take it things didn't go well," Khes said, dismounting his dragon as we dismounted ours.

Jashi glanced back the way we came, as if expecting Dekaar to come flying out of it on a dragon any minute. "He knew. They expected us to be there." She stroked Dream comfortingly, the dragon arching her back into the motion. Dream seemed to need it. Her demeanor, usually perky and somewhat sassy, was now deflated, defeated, even. "I want to hold a meeting with everyone, before the Convergence ends."

"What for?" asked Khes. "You don't think—"

"I do," she interrupted, holding his gaze for several heartbeats Then she leveled her intense gaze on everyone else.

Gone was the girl I knew who hesitated to fill the shoes of the leader I needed her to be for K'sundi. Not only was she ready to lead now, but she was ready to weed out anything and everything that threatened her rule. Even if that threat turned out to be a close friend. A swell of pride filled my chest to see how tenacious she'd become.

Jashi's voice held an edge of iciness. "Dekaar's hologram was waiting for us. He didn't just know we were coming, he knew *when*."

That sentiment settled in the air, and everyone understood what was at stake here. She was sniffing out a traitor, and it didn't matter if it was one of them—she was willing to deal with it the same way I dealt with traitors in the palace. Only this time, I knew she wouldn't cry about it like she had for Tasneem.

"When Kahmel took in the Half-Dracs and their relatives," Jashi continued, "it's possible the Zendaalans snuck in a rat. Kahmel and I talked about that risk before we were separated. He told me he knew it was a risk because of how little time he had to vet members and that we would address the concern if the risk became real. That reality is here, now."

A man stepped up. "I don't know about everyone else," he said, crossing his arms. "But as far as I'm concerned, the Zendaalans were ready to kill our children on a massive scale, and you were the only ones with the ability to save them. You're the ones who took a risk on behalf of us. If someone took advantage of that and snuck in as a result, they deserve what's coming to them. Do what you have to, Your Majesty."

Your Majesty. It wasn't just the dragons that still considered Jashi and me as Faresh and Faresha, so did our people. Knowing that made this failure a little less detrimental, in my eyes.

We would be okay.

"Well said." Khes crossed his arms over his wide chest. "I'll get my people together, and we'll meet in the Fire Den." As he spoke, his men started mounting their dragons. It was unsurprising that Khes's men followed so fluidly to his demeanor. He'd been the leader of the rebels in K'sundi before me for a reason. In fact, it was hard to tell which members had been there before the onslaught of new additions. They all fell into line behind him smoothly.

I hated to imagine any of them betraying us. But Jashi was right. There was a reason Dekaar was so sure of himself—and we had to find out why.

Khes cringed, glancing at Jashi with a lopsided smile. "And here I was, all ready to surprise you."

Jashi slung herself back onto Comet. "Surprise me?"

"Well," he said as he mounted his own dragon. "I figured you must be worried sick about your other friend in K'sundi. We never got the opportunity to swap stories or talk about anything other than the essentials when we all met up again. He wanted to meet with you earlier, but we had this mission to complete first." He smiled again. "Your friend Talad joined my Den; he's waiting for you in the Fire Den now—"

Jashi took off.

Talad.

Talad had been in the Dens all this time.

Talad. He'd joined the rebels, got into the Dens—waited four whole years for his moment to strike. We'd briefed everyone on our mission for today because we couldn't afford not to. And he fed everything over to the Zendaalans.

Jashi was gone before any explanation could be given, leaving a confused Khes in her wake. I went after her, still reeling.

Jashi told me about Talad's involvement in her kidnapping while we were in the Den. No one else knew about him. Neither did we know when we were recruiting new rebels before Jashi rejoined us. *I* wouldn't have trusted Talad to join us after his little temper tantrum when Jashi invited him to the palace. The way he was comfortable with casually disrespecting her didn't sit right with me. He refused to acknowledge her as Faresha, even then. He couldn't see her as anything more than his childhood friend. That would have been dangerous to bring into the fold, even based upon that alone. But I didn't think to tell the rebels. Even if I had, we were in such a rush, there was no guarantee anyone would even get the message in time. He slipped in at the perfect moment.

Jashi moved between Tunnels at break-neck speeds. I was barely able to catch up to her and Comet. She called out *"Mufi eltep!"* and was off into the next Tunnel, the next Den, and then through another Tunnel to make her way back to the Fire Den.

"Jashi!" I called to her over the comm, swearing under my breath as she moved into another Tunnel just ahead of me. Our communication signals didn't carry over between Tunnels, as they were pockets of another dimension, as far as we could tell. Not quite within radio range.

The blinding lights were still leaving afterimages in my vision as I chased Jashi into a Den, following as close as I could as she darted for another Tunnel.

"He's prepared for this!" I shouted, only to be ignored as she leaped into another Tunnel.

"Jashi!" I yelled as we flew over a city in Zendaal. The Tunnel in K'sundi leading to the Fire Den was only a few jumps away. "We know who the rat is." I tried to reason with her, confounded by her reaction. I knew she was angry at Talad, but to run head-first into danger like this, when she had all of the support she needed with Khes, Rand, and the others? "Slow down, let's wait for the others."

"There's no time," she spat before leaping through another Tunnel.

What was with her?

"What do you mean, no time?" I asked as we emerged into another Den. The distance between this Tunnel and the next was larger, thankfully. It gave us more time to talk before she could jump again. But why wasn't she listening? She wouldn't even slow down to talk to me. "Jashi, we can use this to our advantage. He's waiting for you; that means we can—"

"I was pregnant when I left, Kahmel."

And just like that, the world disappeared. Realms, dimensions, space and time, it all faded to nothing. Jashi and I were flying through the tri-colored sky of a Den, and I couldn't see any of it. I couldn't hear the wind that sailed past me as Huntress raced to keep up with Comet. I couldn't feel the reins that kept me in control of her between my hands.

Jashi was gone for four years. Her body looked different. The boy...the one that clung to her when she returned.

"Talad is alone with your son," she said, choking back a sob. She shouted to open another Tunnel.

Except I moved ahead of her and went through first.

I'd been waiting to learn more about bonding before letting anyone try it, myself included. But none of that mattered now.

"*Leh mani stupior,*" I called to Huntress. Even before I felt the connection, I knew it would work.

I felt Huntress's awareness, felt her reaching out and exploring mine. She tugged on the invisible tether that had stretched between us as the connection was made, felt my urgency. And she synchronized herself with it. She flew faster than I'd ever known she could fly. Heat radiated from her chest, ready to blow. Even though I'd only glimpsed him once, even though I didn't even know his name yet, she understood my rage, my furious need to protect my son, and she mirrored it.

Talad had already touched my wife and helped my enemies steal her from me.

But he would not live to touch my son.

Combustion

Huntress landed at the Fire Den, skidding to a stop. I didn't dismount. All I could think of was finding Talad and my son.

My son.

Lora ran toward me, Taias following close behind and—my breath caught—she was holding him. He looked at me with his orange-yellow eyes, his little fists clutching Nana's shirt as he watched me. My son. I didn't know he existed ten minutes ago. I didn't even know his name. But at that moment, I knew love at first sight was real. Because I loved him.

And I hated Talad, and the Zendaalans, and the world for putting him in danger in his own country. I was mad at the dragons for keeping Jashi from me while she was raising him. I saw his face, and I knew that if any harm came to him, the world would have hell to pay.

"Where's Jashi?" Lora asked, looking behind me.

I'd flown far ahead of her, it would take time for her to catch up.

I ignored her question. Lora was a loyal friend to Jashi, and besides Taias, there was no one else here to take charge. "Get everyone out of here. Talad is here; he's—"

"It was pretty dumb of you to open your gates to every shmuck that showed up," said a voice behind me.

Dread slid down into my stomach when I turned to look at him.

Talad was riding a dragon of his own—Khes and his men must have trained him. In his hand he held a small, square device. A digital clock on its face was set at thirty seconds. A little red light flashed at intervals, and Talad's thumb hovered over a button in the center of it.

A bomb.

Jashi swept through the tunnel opening, followed by a shocked and confused Khes and the rest of his men.

"Stop!" shouted Talad.

Everyone froze. Jashi glanced between us all, her eyes widening when she saw what Talad was holding. Fear darkened her eyes when her gaze moved to Taias holding our son.

"If anyone moves or tries to run away," Talad announced, "I blow this whole island away."

The scar over Khes's eye crumpled as a furious, deep scowl set in. "What the hell is this? You were supposed to be her friend!"

"She was never my friend, apparently!" Talad shouted, a manic tone to his voice. He sniffed, rubbing his free arm across his face. "You know Jashi was like a little sister to me? And then you people had to go spouting in her ears, make her think she's somebody all of a sudden. Things were great when she knew exactly what she was: a bottom-feeding bitch who deserved what she got."

I hated how a look of betrayal eclipsed Jashi's face. My heart ached for her.

"Only you dumbass rebel people would ever see anything in these demon-eyed savages," Talad went on, adding a final insult to what was once his and Jashi's friendship. "Now I know just how much of a freak she is. I could have woken up in flames the whole time we lived together! No wonder the Zendaalans are determined to get rid of you." His wild eyes returned to Jashi. "Now you don't get to be the only one bought off by the life of luxury, Jashi. Zendaalans are paying a pretty penny for all the info I've given them over the years. And clearly"—he gestured to the world around him—"there was a lot to tell."

"Foolish boy," Nana barked from behind me. "You good-for-nothing, *foolish* child."

"Nana," I said firmly, making silence roll over everyone around me. My message was clear. Our raid was a failure. My son, along with everyone I cared about, was being threatened by this useless childhood friend of Jashi's. Talad was *mine*. "What do you want?" I asked evenly.

Talad sniffed again, smudging snot all over his sleeve, waving the bomb around like it was a toy in the other hand. "Here's how this is going to go. Nobody but you and that bitch has to die today. Surrender. There are Zendaalans waiting on the other end of that Tunnel." He pointed to one of the exits of the Fire Den. He danced his thumb around the trigger. "Come with us peacefully, and I won't set this off."

I analyzed the options. Dream might have been able to throw up a force field if it weren't for all the firepower she'd protected us from earlier. She was still a young dragon, and her stamina wasn't comparable to a fully-grown dragon. If she could have been useful, Jashi would have silently used her already.

But something wasn't right. Talad had all this time to himself. If it were me, I'd be holding a switch that could detonate a litany of explosives littered all over the base. But he held the bomb in his hand. Was it the only charge he had? If so, there had to be a reason.

Then I realized Talad had been with the Iron Den. Khes trusted our people, but he'd also been the rebel leader before me for a reason.

Likely, Talad couldn't get away with stowing too much without getting caught, either by Khes or his men. They were loyal and vigilant. It couldn't have been easy getting anything past them, fellow rebel or not. Khes ran a tight ship. Everyone was aware of each other and what they were doing. Anything out of the ordinary would have stood out.

The bomb was set to go off thirty seconds after it was initiated. That was barely enough time for *Talad* to get away. I almost wanted to laugh. The Zendaalans saw him as disposable. They were prepared to let Talad die to fulfill his mission today.

And then I did laugh, making Talad flinch and look at me incredulously—along with everyone else. And somehow, that just made the situation even funnier.

"Come on, Talad. I know you're an idiot, but you can't be that stupid, can you?" I chuckled, and Huntress stalked forward, our thoughts and intentions in perfect sync.

"Don't move!" he yelled, pulling his dragon back as he shook the bomb for emphasis. But I saw the look of comprehension in his eye. He knew what I was laughing at. He realized his role in this whole mess. He was just a pawn. An easily manipulated pawn who couldn't think of anything better to do with the money he'd been rewarded than to waste it on his addictions, all because he couldn't think past a wad of cash. He was so easy. So damn easy.

"You know you're going to die today," I said, ignoring his command as Huntress and I advanced. She snarled, and I stared Talad in the eye, watching as understanding dawned on him. I was *not* okay. He was dealing with a madman who was really, *really,* good at pretending to be sane. "If the Zendaalans aren't here with you now, it means they still don't know how to come through the Tunnels, and you couldn't sneak away and let them in. We're all too close to one another for you to be able to get away with that. You're a *failure.* And you know you're going to have to set that bomb off if you want any chance of doing what the Zendaalans told you to do. And you have to do what they told you to do, because if you don't, they'll kill you. If you *do* set that bomb off, you'll die with us. And if you *don't* set that bomb off, *I'll* kill you anyway."

"W-will you really risk everyone else just to—"

"Take me in, Talad," I jeered, and Huntress towered over him and his dragon. "Turn your back to me. Lead me to the Zendaalans. But you won't do that, because you know what I'll do. You're just scrambling for any other solution than what you know you have to do. You have to set that bomb off, and you won't be able to get away in time, and you're going to die. And if I get to you first, you still die. And that's just hella funny."

He sniffed, switching strategies. His reddened eyes were pleading. "Please..."

"Don't be pathetic," I snarled, Huntress echoing the sentiment from beneath me. "Read y..."

Talad growled in frustration.

"Go."

Talad pressed the button and tossed the explosive, speaking a word to get his dragon to start flying.

Huntress—The black dragon lurched into the air before I could complete the thought, catching the bomb in her claws before it hit the ground, and streaking after Talad. I leaned over and grabbed the explosive from Huntress's claws, straightening as she caught up with Talad, flying above him. She slammed down on him, her claws digging into his dragon, holding him with a deadly grip.

I glanced at the bomb. Twenty-five seconds.

You know what we have to do, don't you? I thought, and felt Huntress's resolution even before she answered back.

We are of one mind, came her solemn reply.

The Drake Bond connection was powerful. She could feel my desperate urgency and how fast she needed to be for us to have a chance. We just might make it through the Tunnel where the Zendaalans were waiting on the other end—and close it behind us.

My thoughts raced faster than Huntress and I flew.

Jashi and the others would follow through with the plan. We

were so close, and I would sacrifice anything to get them to the finish line.

Even if I couldn't join them.

I hoped my son would know how much his father loved him. I hoped Jashi would tell him.

At least I'd be taking Talad with me.

"*Leh mani stupior!*" a voice shouted from close behind me.

And the world tilted.

Khes's dragon slammed into mine, tearing Talad and his dragon from Huntress's claws. As Huntress and I careened to the side, Khes lurched forward and snatched the device from my hand.

"This was my mistake, Kahmel," he said over the intercom. "I'll be the one to correct it."

The bomb had fifteen seconds left. Huntress struggled to stabilize herself as Khes and his dragon launched ahead of us, dragging Talad with them.

"*Mufi eltep!*" Khes shouted, and the Tunnel flashed open.

"Khes!" I yelled.

He turned back and winked his scarred eye, saluting before he shouted again, closing the entrance. The blast of the explosion rang out, and a tendril of fire escaped into the Tunnel an instant before it snapped shut. The sharp noise rattled the air, silencing every other sound, and left in its wake a single-toned ringing in my ears.

One moment, the world on the other side was ending, that terror and mayhem seeping through the entrance like a dragon slinking through a cave to lash out at the air. The next moment, the dragon was leashed, forced back into the opening it peeked through. The small glimpse we got into the hell on the other side was enough to know that whatever or whoever was there would not survive the onslaught. Khes had trapped himself, Talad, and our would-be ambushers with the combustible dragon that was the explosion to save us all.

He'd robbed me of my sacrifice and offered himself instead.

The silence the closing portal left us with did no justice to the shock that rippled through us all. If anything, the quiet was louder than the explosion. It contained all the screams and cries left trapped in our chests as the portal's closure left us too shocked to breathe.

Huntress hovered in the air for a few moments where Khes's dragon had shoved her. Her thoughts seeped over to mine. She was the dragon most familiar with Khes other than his own because of her experiences in K'sundi's war with Omani from a year ago.

So she was the first to break the silence with a long howl.

And the rest of our dragons soon joined in the heart-breaking chorus.

DAWN OF HEAVEN AND HELL

Jashi *Eloe* Anyua-Omah

S hock.

It rolled through the air and settled over us all like a chill. We were frozen, disbelief holding us in an icy grip. The only sound that could be heard was the wailing of the dragons, each cry amplifying the other, a solemn orchestra.

The way the Tunnel closed was so resolute. The Dens really were self-contained worlds, and the Tunnels folded space and time to make the distances feel closer than they really were. But when they closed, you really understood how far apart each point was. Here, right now, it was calm. Treacherously peaceful. The only indication that hell lay on the other end of the Tunnel Khes disappeared down was that brief flash of heat and red-hot light. The sound that exploded through the entrance a split second before the Tunnel closed, sucking up all the light, heat, and sound inside of it, smoothing out the wrinkle that brought heaven and hell together, revealing the Tunnels as the miracles they were, a miracle that portrayed peace and stillness, while our hearts cried out with the dragons for the hell our friend sacrificed himself to, sealing the door to heaven behind him, so the two would remain apart.

For a while no one moved. Especially Kahmel. Huntress brought him back to the ground, and he dismounted, but his eyes stayed trained on the space in the air where hell was unleashed for a moment before Khes reeled it back in.

Khes had been the leader of the rebels before Kahmel, and I realized that made Khes the closest person in Kahmel's life besides Rand, after he was abandoned by his parents. I never did get the chance to know Khes as well as I wanted to. We were working so hard, trying to get laws passed, missions accomplished, dragons tamed—I always thought there would be time. My mind had a portrait with five people in it, a constant I didn't realize I relied on while I was with Obellana: Kahmel, Rand, Arusi, Asan, and Khes, teasing, laughing, yet able to get serious and do what was necessary for their people. It felt like a piece of my heart had been cut out to imagine part of that perfect picture being ripped away. It felt wrong.

Kahmel stared out at the sky for a while, and it occurred to me that in the same way Nana was that person I needed, that guiding pillar of wisdom they don't tell you you need after you're legally called an adult, Khes had been that person for Kahmel.

I always wondered how Khes came to give Kahmel his position as rebel leader. Nana *had* to take me in when I was dropped at her doorstep, regardless of the strange abilities I came with. But what about Khes? What pushed him to embrace my husband, a teenager with fire spewing from his hands that he could barely control, and take him in? Take Kahmel under his wing and even use his expertise to the point that he resigned when Kahmel found a way to secure a position on the throne? I wished I'd asked him that. Thanked him for taking care of Kahmel when no one else would. If it weren't for Khes, Kahmel and I would have never gotten this far.

Kahmel, as though he'd been thawed, turned around. He moved like a corpse, with stilted steps. At first I wasn't sure where he was going until I realized Nana was there, with a terrified-looking Kai at her side.

I muttered a curse, looking to the heavens as though an answer would halo above me. This wasn't how I wanted them to meet. This wasn't how this day was supposed to end, darkened with failure, betrayal, and the death of one of our closest friends, combined with the love and joy of Kahmel and my little family coming together for the first time since we separated four years ago.

I went to Kai, Nana stepping away and letting us have our moment as Kahmel kneeled in front of us both, eyes distant, yet unmoving from his son.

Kahmel reached out a hand, and Kai looked up at me, questioning with his eyes. I bit my lip to keep from crying. I had planned this moment for years, but now that it was here, my heart thrummed with anxiety. Kai was all of three years old. How could he possibly understand? How could I possibly explain?

Throat dry, I said, "This is your father." I pushed Kai's hands into Kahmel's. "Kahmel, this is Kai. He's three years old and a Half-Drac, just like us."

Kahmel's eyes met mine, and my heart ached when I saw what was holding him hostage—guilt. Kahmel was devastated to lose his mentor, his friend—but he was grateful. It dawned on me in that moment what really happened—Khes sacrificed himself so Kahmel wouldn't have to. If it weren't for Khes, it would be Kahmel on the other side of that portal between heaven and hell, doomed to never see the fruit of his labor, the future of his people, or, unbeknownst to Khes, to find out that his only son was named after him. Kai.

Khes died to save Kahmel, to save his future with the rebels and the Half-Dracs. With his family.

I wasn't sure if Kai completely understood what I was telling him or what was going on, but he didn't resist when Kahmel pulled him in and wrapped his arms around that tiny little body, dwarfed by Kahmel's bulky frame. Kahmel reached out and pulled me in next, and it was enough to release me from the spell of paralysis. I leaned into his embrace, held the two men in my life, and buried myself in Kahmel's neck. I didn't even realize I was crying until I felt the moisture between Kahmel's skin and mine.

And Kahmel, always so strong. For his people. For us. I didn't hear him cry, but I felt him shuddering as he held me and Kai closer.

THE NEXT FEW hours passed in a blur. Rand took a group of people with some dragons to do what, I didn't quite know. Nana shepherded Kahmel, Kai, and me inside the Fire Den's main manor like confused lambs, and we didn't protest. She and Lora took over, commanding people this way and that. The next thing I knew, I was being corralled into bed, Kahmel just behind me, holding a confused-looking Kai in his arms. We all lay down, and at first I thought I wouldn't be able to sleep a wink, but the collective events of the day crashed down on me all at once, and I was out.

When I woke up, the sky was that early morning, milky color. Except here, that milky white was mixed with a pastel pink that swirled together like strawberries and cream.

Khes was dead. Talad was dead. One I only knew for a few years, the other I spent a good part of my life with. But it was the former my heart wept for, and the latter...I didn't. The lack of emotion over the death of someone I'd called a friend felt strange. The hole in my heart Talad left didn't get wider. It was like he was cut out long ago, and his death simply made that fact more pertinent, but no more damaging.

The sheets bunched up in my tightened fists, and I gritted my teeth. When I'd reached out to Talad for help the first time, it was what sent me into the hands of the Zendaalans to begin with. A fact I forgave him for because I didn't imagine he knew any better than I did. But the next time we saw each other, he turned against me, and it only got worse. He was there when I was kidnapped. He helped my assailants. And the very next time I saw him, he almost destroyed my family, the little corner of the universe where I finally felt safe, so long as I had my people. He would have taken that from me, and Khes had to make the decision to limit the damage to just himself, thwarting Talad's efforts.

The only emotion I could find for Talad was a weak flame, one that burned against him for making me glad he was dead, because it didn't have to be this way. He could have been like Lora, here with me, part of my family. But he made himself like the bodies of the Zendaalans piled on the other side of the Tunnel along with his own —meaningless. Simply the removal of a problem. I didn't regret the coldness I held toward him. My regret was instead for a friend I would never have the chance to love like I might have loved Talad. And I hated Talad for taking that friend from me, glad he couldn't steal my friend away without ending his own life in the process, and unapologetic about being glad.

I turned over, startled when my eyes fell on Kahmel, who was wide awake, looking at Kai. The pink in his eyes told me he hadn't slept at all. And the amount of time it took for him to notice I was looking at him made me think he'd spent the whole night just like that, staring at his son.

When his eyes met mine, he glanced at the door to the balcony behind me, nodding his head toward it. He wanted to talk.

Now for the conversations that were long overdue, along with about a dozen new ones.

I eased out of bed, careful not to stir the toddler who was snoring lightly. He snorted when Kahmel moved from his side, and I froze as he shifted and curled into himself in the absence of his father, then drifted off again.

I stepped out onto the balcony and watched Kahmel as he followed behind me. His eyes lingered on Kai until he couldn't see him anymore, then he closed the door and sat across from me.

Kahmel buried his face in his hands and sighed, not speaking for a while. I waited patiently. Everything was...a lot.

He finally removed his hands from his face, sucking in a breath as he entwined his fingers in his lap and leaned forward. "When did you find out?" he asked, nodding toward the bedroom. Toward Kai.

I chuckled. I wasn't sure where to start. Rather than try to organize my thoughts, I just gave him the facts as they were. The fact that Obellana predicted Kai's conception, that she came to save me from a dangerous pregnancy and to inform me that his birth was paramount, though the details on what exactly made him important was as difficult to understand as anything else the dragons told us. When I finished, Kahmel wagged his head, looking off in the distance as he leaned his elbow on the arm of his chair, hand covering his mouth.

He stayed silent for a few more minutes before he looked at me again. "I..." he started, uncharacteristically furtive, antsy even. "I wish...I'm sorry. I'm sorry I couldn't be there with you."

"You couldn't have known," I said, sighing as I thought about the events of that day. Every time I wished there was a way Kahmel could have come with me, the rational part of me kicked in, knowing there was no way he could have. I was with Obellana, and it must have taken all of the willpower he was capable of to leave me with her, knowing he wouldn't see me for another four years, to make sure I was safe. To make sure I was okay. He had no idea he was doing it for the sake of me *and* his son.

Kahmel drew in a long breath, again looking away from me. "I had a fleeting thought about you being pregnant," he admitted, surprising me. "After you were gone, I realized you'd dropped your tea beside the bed before drinking it. At first, I was worried, but I figured that if we could get the dragons to bring the tea here, you could simply ask for it once you arrived with Obellana."

I got up and slid into his lap, forcing him to lean back and look up at me as I pushed my fingers deep enough into this hair to touch his scalp and dragged my hand back, stroking his head. His eyes turned glassy, like my touch was enough to defeat the restlessness he'd spent all night battling.

"Obellana gave me the option." My voice was low, surprising him away from the clutches of sleep starting to make his eyes droop. But I sent him back as I rubbed a thumb against the side of his forehead before pulling my fingers through his gorgeous curls again. "I chose not to take it."

Understanding dawned drowsily on his face. He drew his fingers through my hair, too, and pulled me into a deep, ferocious kiss. His hand bunched in my hair, pulling just enough for me to feel the desperation in his touch. He thanked me in his kiss, apologized into it, mourned into it. And I made sure he got as much as he gave.

When he finally pulled away, he pressed his head against my chest, and I tangled my fingers back into his soft curls.

"I'm not sure where to go from here," he admitted, and I realized this was a sacred place he was letting me into. The place where he was unsure. It was a side of him he didn't show to anyone but Rand, most likely. I imagined it was a side he wasn't allowed to show to his parents. He picked up my hand and kissed my knuckles. "We can go on living in the Dens, as long as the rebels—"

"Our people," I corrected him, and he looked at me in confusion. "They're more than just rebels now," I said, rubbing his knuckles with my thumb. "Or are you going to send Kai and the other kids on missions too?"

Mention of our son gave me an automatic victory. He shook his head quickly, then amended his statement. "As long as *our people* want to stay..." I nodded my head in approval. "We can keep living in the Dens. But we're back to square one when it comes to finding the Dragon Kings' parts, and we have to keep up our end of the deal with them."

I grimaced, considering his wording again. I remembered something from when I was with Obellana. "I don't think this is about our deal anymore."

Kahmel paused, then gestured for me to continue, clearly not following but wanting to hear this new perspective.

"Aithel told you he would grant you a favor in return for fulfilling your promise to them. But your promise was to bring the K'sundii back to the dragons and to protect the dragons themselves as well as to get the Dragon Kings their parts back. You brought *some* of the K'sundii back to the dragons," I said, looking out at our little community. "We learned about the Drake Bonds, and we can use the Dens now, but back in K'sundi, all of the laws you established protecting the dragons have been undone. The only dragons that remain protected are the ones that are hiding out with us or have retreated into the Dens on their own."

Kahmel nodded grimly. He likely heard the same reports I did from our people who left the Dens to collect information and resources.

"The Dragon Kings trust you," I concluded, realizing it as I spoke. "This isn't about some deal anymore. That was what we needed to get started, but our hearts are connected to the Dragon Kings, and theirs to ours. They consider your promise fulfilled because they know that you won't stop until it is. And by working together, you and the Dragon Kings have managed to form a smaller version of your dream until we have what it takes to get it all—to have everything. We need the Dragon Kings to be whole because until they're complete, we aren't complete. It's not because we made a deal, it's that we need them to be restored to their former glory because that's the way it should be."

Kahmel nodded slowly, eyes distant, but he rubbed small circles into the back of my hand, telling me that he was more here now. And that it was a lot for him to feel this way. To feel trusted.

He shook his head. "That still doesn't change the fact that we have no idea where to start."

I considered the conundrum, then a small spark started in my mind. "Four years is a long time," I pondered. "But it also isn't."

Kahmel tilted his head, confused. He placed a soft kiss on my lips. "You've lost me," he murmured, face hovering below mine.

I kissed his cheek, and he brought my hand to his lips again. "The Dragon Kings' parts *were* in that bunker. Dekaar had to move them to keep us from getting them. But what could he do? Build another bunker?"

"Not in only four years," Kahmel realized, and my work was done. The cunning in him had been reignited, and I resigned to nestling my head in the crook of his neck to let him work. "Wherever he has the Dragon Kings' parts now, it can't be nearly as secure as the bunker was."

"We don't even know when he moved the parts," I murmured. "He had to get something ready, then transport the parts. If the move was recent enough, the trail could still be fresh."

"Four years isn't that long at all," Kahmel agreed, intertwining his fingers with mine and kissing them while nestling my head further into his neck.

"We won't let Khes's death be in vain," I swore to him, and he clutched my hand firmer.

"No. We won't."

FUNERAL ARRANGEMENTS

The rest of the morning went on as a strange melody between grief and blissful comfort. Kahmel and I stayed out on the balcony with each other until Kai woke up, and even then, Kai just got in my lap—while I stayed in Kahmel's—and we remained like that, stacked up on top of each other, until the sky got bright with afternoon light. Kai was quieter than I'd ever known him to be. I thought he might be overwhelmed, but when I heard him start to snore again, I decided that maybe he could sense that odd mix of grief and bliss and respected the silence it demanded as much as we did.

When we became too hungry to stay there any longer, we left our place of solitude. We went down to be with everyone and found that life was going on, despite the fact that we hadn't moved since we woke up. Lora had taken over for Nana and had the place running like the orphanage, way back in the day. Everyone took their full plates to the dining area outside, and when Lora noticed us, after a few words to some of the people leaving, we were served with new heaping plates of a freshly cooked late breakfast. The Fire Den, as well as all the others, was flourishing with development. The eggs and bacon came from animals *our people* raised right here in the Den. As Kahmel and I had already planned before we were forced to separate, the Fire Den learned to cultivate their own food in preparation for when the spirit dragons could no longer serve them, and the results were impressive. Everyone walked away looking perfectly satisfied. They lacked for nothing.

Part of me had feared they would hesitate to live so differently from they were used to. We were asking them to live independently of everything they grew up with. Live on the run. But then again, perhaps when Dekaar declared open season on their children, they knew nothing would be the same again, anyway. Not if they wanted to protect them.

Perhaps that love for their children made them capable of whatever it took to save them.

Seeing the bravery my own parents refused to have infused some measure of strength into me. I was heartbroken Khes wasn't here to appreciate it all with us, but he'd been willing to die for this community for a reason. It was a community worth saving.

Eggs and bacon never tasted richer.

"Lora told us we'd find you here," Arusi said, Asan trailing behind her.

My mind drew an outline where Khes's hulking form should be standing next to them, the scar over his eye shining in the bright afternoon light. Then, like a ghost, the outline faded.

Kahmel set his plate aside. He hadn't eaten much. I didn't think he had much of an appetite. "Where's Rand?"

Kai tugged on my nightgown after demolishing his breakfast. "Can I go play?"

I breathed, trying to settle the nerves that rose on end for some reason. I wasn't used to parenting and managing business at the same time. "Just wait a little, Kai." Lora and Nana had informed the rest of the community about Kai, so I turned him to Arusi and Asan, who, despite the grieving they must have been going through, managed a smile for him. "These are my friends, Kai. That means they're your friends too."

Kai didn't seem convinced. He flinched when Arusi crouched to his level and tried to shake his hand. Rather than take it, Kai did his best to scramble into my lap.

I slid my chair back to give him better access and shrugged to the others.

As Arusi rose to her feet, Asan nodded to Kahmel, addressing his initial inquiry. "Rand is getting ready."

Kahmel frowned. "For what?"

"You don't remember?" Arusi took a seat across from us.

Asan mirrored her, and Kai eyed the two warily. I inwardly groaned, hoping it wouldn't take long for him to get used to them. It occurred to me that after having nothing but the same people around him for his entire life, he wasn't used to seeing people he didn't know.

At least it showed that he and Kahmel were off to a good start. Kai didn't flinch around him, though I wasn't sure if he was necessarily comfortable yet.

Asan folded his hands over the table. "Rand took some of the rebels—"

"Our people," I corrected, like I had to Kahmel earlier.

When Asan looked confused, Kahmel motioned for him not to object and just move on, and I smirked at my unopposed victory. Sometimes it was nice when your husband was the boss.

"Rand took some of *our people*," Asan corrected himself, following Kahmel's lead, "and went to the other side of the Tunnel last night. You might not have noticed, though, he went around getting everyone rallied together not too long after you went into the manor. He was determined; we couldn't keep up with him."

I barely remembered that. I knew Rand left with some people, but I didn't know they were going to the other end of the Tunnel. My stomach twisted, knowing what they'd find on the other side. "Why did they do that?" I asked, ignoring Kai as he hummed and rocked from side to side in my lap, trying to bring my attention to his boredom, not understanding how dangerous the situation had been yesterday.

"He went to collect the body," Kahmel answered for Asan, leaning against the table and putting his face in his hand.

Collect the *pieces* of the body, Kahmel didn't clarify. And the thought turned the twist in my stomach to nausea. The determination in Rand's eyes when he left... He didn't want the

Zendaalans to get to Khes first. He had to be just as close to Khes as Kahmel was, but he didn't even ask Kahmel to go with him. No, he was *saving* Kahmel from even having to think about it, I realized. He saw Kahmel and Kai and me. Saw our little family. He left Kahmel to be with his family and faced the matter of Khes's body on his own.

Kahmel came to the same conclusion. I knew by the heavy breath that followed, his face still in his hand. I knew he felt guilty. But I wished he wouldn't let himself feel that way. Khes made the choice to sacrifice himself. Kahmel didn't ask him to. Kahmel had to learn to let people help him, even if it hurt them, if they chose to do so. To rob them of their sacrifice would be to rob from them the love they were offering.

At that moment, I knew I couldn't ask for a better brother than Rand, and I was grateful to know he was mine.

"So where is he now?" I asked, setting Kai down and whispering that he could go play now. I initially wanted to wait until Rand joined us so he could meet his uncle, but clearly that was no longer an option.

Kai ran off to Lora, who was standing on the sidelines behind me. Arusi watched him leave before she said, "Preparing for the funeral."

RAND and the people he brought with him carried a long chest with a black mantle covering it. The rest of us followed in a line through a series of Tunnels and Dens to reach the Shield Den. We decided to bury him in the Den where he trained his people to be so close, where even Talad, living among them, could only accomplish so much. A vengeful part of me rejoiced in the fact that Khes received the honor of being buried here, among his people, and that Talad would be collected and put away like garbage with the rest of the Zendaalans whom their own government didn't really care for.

Every time Kahmel tried to make some contribution, say a few words, help Rand and the others with the body, he was shoved back in his place, forced to let everyone else handle things for once. Rand shoved him the most. More than just the locks that hung from his head now, Rand had changed in the last four years, and he wanted Kahmel to see that. No, he was *forcing* Kahmel to acknowledge it.

Rand gave Khes's eulogy. I cried for the stories I knew about and even harder for the ones I didn't because I would never get to hear Khes tell me about them himself.

Kai was so patient through it all, though he had no idea who anyone around him was, his own father included. But he, seeing my reaction, stayed solemn the whole time. He even patted my back when he saw me crying, mimicking Kahmel at my other side, making me chuckle in spite of myself.

When it was over and we came back to the Fire Den, Kahmel addressed the people gathered around, the only responsibility Rand allowed him to carry thus far. Kahmel briefly described what he and I had discussed earlier, reinforced the gratitude we had for everyone here with us, and officially introduced his son, Kai. Kai looked uncomfortable being introduced to so many people, but it was important that they knew who he was.

There remained another uncomfortable discussion to be had. Kahmel hadn't been able to take all of the rebels to the Dens with him four years ago, obviously. So when they decided who was going to come, those closest to him took priority, as well as the new members with children. The rest of the rebels in K'sundi were instructed to lie low under the leadership of the new Faresh. Their only mission from then on was to protect their own and any who sought their help.

After the four years apart from them, we needed to strategize with the rebels in K'sundi again. But I feared Kahmel's paranoia after what happened with Talad. I didn't want him to have to question his own people's loyalty. It was as I'd said, the rebels weren't just rebels anymore. They were part of us. We were a community. And we couldn't function with distrust. It was Kahmel's honesty, not his secret-keeping, that had brought the people who were loyal to us now.

Our new plan wouldn't work without the rebels in K'sundi. Before now, we'd always made raids on the homes of rich clan families, maybe museums with artifacts containing clues. Now things were much more serious. We needed information from the Zendaaalans themselves. We needed government secrets. We needed private correspondences. We needed to be more coordinated than ever, and that meant things were going to be more dangerous than ever.

Kahmel and I were the most wanted people in the country, possibly in all of Hemorrah, and if anyone found out we had a son, he would be targeted. Our people needed to know who Kai was so they could help us protect him.

When Kahmel finished introducing Kai, the people started a chant, quietly at first, then louder and louder. *"Long live the Fareshiki."*

Long live the little king.

THE NEXT FEW days found Kahmel and me in Aithel's Den, making use of his library. It was the most extensive resource for mapping Den locations and how often they opened. As we originally agreed, the Fire, Shield, Iron, Water, and Rider Dens all made note of the Tunnels within their own Dens, as well as any Tunnels found nearby. Kahmel and I compiled the data while Kai messed around underfoot. All the drawing I'd done when I was with Dekaar, and again with Kai and Obellana, made me more accustomed to using pen and paper than my eWatch's typewriting tools. I jotted down notes to record later in our shared map files instead of using my eWatch. Kai, seeing me scribbling away, lay at my feet, making doodles on a few pieces of paper of his own.

Kahmel worked beside me, raising his eyebrow at my pen and paper but making no comment as he typed away, cross-referencing documents titled "Observed Tunnel Opening Schedules" that hovered in front of him.

Frankly, we were just keeping ourselves busy. There was little we could do to contribute to what needed to be done right now.

As I suspected, Kahmel was hesitant to open communications with the rebels in K'sundi, but as he had no other choice, he made little complaint. His fear, which, granted, was valid, was that Dekaar was preparing to mobilize the Zendaalans into the Dens. I agreed with him on that end, at least. Talad had been with us because he spoke K'sundii fluently, without an accent. Butaan utilized a lot of the same diphthongs and similar vowel pronunciation as K'sundii. And even so, I struggled pronouncing what I used to call dragon command words. The word structure was familiar, but the almost-vicious pronunciation befuddled me every time. Butaan demanded a very clipped tone and execution of sentences I wasn't quite used to. For Zendaalans, who already struggled to keep up with K'sundii, seeing as most of us spoke enough Zendaalan to understand them anyway, it would take a while to have enough command of Butaan to start launching attacks to our Den, and that was providing they could locate us to begin with.

Still, four years was both a short amount of time and plenty of time. It wouldn't be too far-fetched to imagine the Zendaalans getting close to being able to use the Tunnels, especially if Dekaar insisted.

But in private, I gave Kahmel a little comfort. While the Zendaalans might be forced to learn Butaan from Dekaar to keep up with us, even *with* the language of the dragons, they had to be willing to *use* the dragons themselves. The laws Kahmel had established to keep wild dragons safe were all but eliminated. Meaning Zendaalans would have to use their own dragons for traveling between Dens, and I didn't think their ZST dragons were capable of understanding Butaan. That would slow their progress significantly, not just for any Zendaalans that would come looking for us, but for any spies who might be hiding among the rebels in K'sundi. Only the very rich in K'sundi could afford to purchase a dragon, and the very rich rarely joined the rebellion. The only way even our own rebels could come with us to the Dens would be if we landed them some of the dragons we found and trained from here. And we could easily limit access to dragon-riding to only those we vetted and trusted.

That made Kahmel a lot more comfortable.

So now it was just a waiting game again. I didn't feel right sitting around in the Fire Den manor, not knowing what was happening on the outside, and Rand noticed Kahmel wasn't doing any better either, so he suggested this task to the both of us, and we were all too eager to agree. Besides, it gave Kahmel some time alone with Kai.

Regardless of my antiquated methods, it was clear I was a lot more productive than Kahmel was at the moment. He kept glancing at Kai on the floor beside me, some measure of jealousy in his eyes. While Kai wasn't straight-up afraid of Kahmel like he was of the others—even Rand, it turned out—Kai still wasn't particularly interested in Kahmel, either. Kai was perfectly content staying by my side, and leaving Kai with Kahmel only resulted in tears. So our little mapping task gave us a good chance to let Kai be around Kahmel and myself without giving him the alternative of running to someone he was more familiar with instead of Kahmel, like Lora or Nana, or the young Half-Drac children that came with their parents to Obellana's.

As Kahmel kept eyeing Kai, looking out of place, the screen hovering in front of him had the same paragraph written and rewritten each time he went back to work, and I didn't think he was going to get much done today.

As if realizing this, Kahmel sighed, set his documents and eWatch aside, and turned to Kai. Our son looked up at him from the wild scribbles beneath him.

"What are you drawing?" Kahmel asked.

I tried to focus on the maps in front of me, comparing them to the maps Aithel had here, trying to concentrate on that rather than be nervous about Kai opening up to his father. I knew it would happen eventually. Three years wasn't that long in comparison to the rest of his life. When Kai was older, he probably wouldn't even remember the years he didn't know his father. But a knot still tied itself in my stomach, and I realized how much my sense of time had changed since having a child.

When it was just Kahmel and me, I could worry about each day as it came, face problems as they arrived. But being responsible for a whole other person forced me to look at ten years from now, twenty. Wondering if he would have everything he needed to not have the same problems I did. Hoping I could avoid letting him experience the traumas I had. Knowing I couldn't possibly protect him from everything. It was enough to make me walk on pins and needles all day, if I let those fears consume me.

But I took comfort in the fact that Kahmel was always living a decade ahead of him, and that despite not knowing his son existed, he'd been preparing for his future unknowingly, just by his obvious dedication to his people.

I wasn't alone, and I admired anyone that had to be. It took having a dedicated group of friends and the Queen of the Dragons to keep Kai from hurting himself all the time, and he'd still gone missing every now and then, always found later, chasing some infant dragon around like they were playmates rather than the actual *humans* in his life. But Kai's affinity for dragons was another issue altogether. One I blamed entirely on his father.

Kai looked down at his drawing, then back up to Kahmel like the answer should have been obvious.

"Day-gones."

Kahmel, not as fluent in *Kai-ese* as I'd become, frowned in confusion. "A what?"

"Dragons," I translated for him, chuckling. "I was proud when his first word was 'mama', but 'day-gone' was the second, and I don't know what that says about his priorities."

Kahmel creeped closer to see Kai's drawings better, Kai gnawing on the end of his pen and watching Kahmel cautiously. I tried to ignore the way that made my stomach twist and got back to writing notes about the maps I was looking at.

"Ooh, I see it now," Kahmel said, and I tried not to smile. "That's a very nice dragon. You like dragons?"

I practically heard Kai's eager nod. "I like day-gones."

"You like your mom?"

At that, I whipped my head around, and I wasn't sure why my cheeks burned when I saw Kai nodding just as eagerly. "I like mama," he confirmed.

"I like your mama too. She's pretty."

Kai smiled as though he was glad to hear someone admiring his mother like that, and I found myself unable to relate to whatever he might have been feeling. I never had a mother in my life, or a father, for that matter. I didn't know what exactly he wanted to hear or know about me other than what I presented to him, or how hearing Kahmel complimenting me made him so happy, but it made me strangely shy and proud at the same time.

Kahmel nodded in agreement. "That's why I married her."

"Oh really?" I challenged him, raising an eyebrow. His *how I met your mother* story wasn't exactly that straightforward.

But Kai's eyes widened with interest. "Really?"

To both our surprise, Kai put his pen down and climbed into Kahmel's lap, despite the fact that Kahmel was only crouching and there wasn't much of a lap to sit in. Kahmel corrected the problem and rose to sit back in his chair, carrying Kai with him. Kahmel flashed me a smile that made my heart warm. He really was in love with his son, and I didn't realize how much I needed to see that.

"Well, that's not the only reason, of course," Kahmel went on, leaning back into his seat.

And it occurred to me that I never really tried to tell Kai our story. First off, I just wanted Kai to know who Kahmel was, tried to describe what he was like. But without parents to base my experiences off of, I didn't think knowing how Kahmel and I met would be all that interesting to a toddler. Apparently I was wrong.

Kai was enthralled, looking up to Kahmel with those orange-yellow disks that had his father smitten.

"She's also smart," Kahmel said.

I resisted the urge to object. I wasn't sure if impulsive-and-sometimes-right qualified as being smart.

"She's funny, really funny. And she's the only person I know who can surprise me as much as she does," Kahmel added, laughing, making Kai laugh with him, and I laughed because Kai had no idea he was precisely one of the surprises Kahmel was referring to.

"Mama surprise?" Kai asked, still laughing. "What surprise?"

"Oh, tons," Kahmel said, still looking at me.

I hoped he wouldn't go into too many details about how I surprised him. Kai didn't have to know his mother didn't always have everything together.

Asan burst into the room. "Kahmel, Jashi." Upon seeing us laughing, he grimaced. "Sorry to interrupt, but this is important."

"What is it?" Kahmel asked, sobering up.

And I might have been imagining it, but Kai seemed to come to attention, mirroring his father already.

"The rebels in K'sundi need to talk to you. There's been...a strange development."

I frowned. "What does that mean?"

Asan shook his head. "It's best you see for yourselves. There are more Half-Dracs in K'sundi now."

"You mean babies? More Half-Dracs have been born?"

"That's the thing," he said, looking between Kahmel and me and Kai, looking at our eyes. "The rebels in K'sundi have been running overtime trying to keep up. But it's looking like anyone dragon tribe, like you three, has *developed* Half-Drac abilities. They're...mutating somehow. They'll have to give you the details themselves, because I don't completely understand what they're saying. And Dekaar just passed a law to allow the Zendaalans to hunt and capture all of them."

Dread slid down my gut, and I glanced at Kahmel, at Kai. Their bright orange eyes. Dekaar, the heavens-forsaken hypocrite. He just declared open season on anyone who looked like us.

THE NEO-DRACS

Kahmel Axon Kai of the Omah Clan

I didn't want to leave Kai just as I was starting to make progress with him, but the situation left me with no choice.

Those of the dragon tribe were few and far between. We all had the glowing orange eyes that set us apart from our fellow K'sundii. Nowadays, we were stigmatized with being as savage as the dragons we were once known for taming. Only, we hadn't known that was somewhat close to the truth. And personally, I didn't mind being known as a savage. It was what I needed to be if I was going to save my people from our opposition. With the Equalization, it was us against the world. Being a little savage wasn't necessarily a bad thing in order to survive against that.

All Half-Dracs were dragon tribe, but not all dragon tribe were Half-Dracs. At least up until now. It sounded like that was changing.

Jashi and I rode Huntress back to K'sundi. Ever since Huntress and I established a connection, I found that my experience wasn't nearly as verbal as Jashi described hers. Huntress and I didn't use our connection to talk much. Rather, we shared an understanding, most of the time. I could tell when she was hungry, I knew when she fed herself. I discerned when she was wondering what I was thinking and when she sensed the gist of it and became satisfied.

But in this case, I reached out to get some kind of grounding, and I needed words, for once.

Do you know anything about this? I asked tentatively, still not quite used to speaking in my mind and being met with an answer that didn't come from my own head.

Huntress hesitated, surprising me. *I have felt a change, yes. But it would be best to hear the explanation from one of your own. It will help you understand what is happening. And why.*

That vague answer was all I got, and it was clear the conversation was over as Huntress sealed herself off—something I didn't even know she could do.

I had no idea what to expect as we were taken to a warehouse I'd hid out in when I left the throne of K'sundi. Conveniently, it was next to a Tunnel.

I'd prepared myself by asking Asan for as many details as he could give me. Rand was already at the warehouse, we were meeting him there. But ever since Asan told us the Half-Dracs were changing, Jashi had been silent, and something told me she wasn't as surprised as I was.

She'd been hiding out with the Dragon Queen of Prophecy for four years, not to mention she had half a dozen dragons with the ability to talk to her anytime they liked. Perhaps she knew something about what Huntress was referring to, or she'd heard something from Obellana some time ago. I knew from experience that sometimes the things the Dragon Kings said only made sense in hindsight. But when I asked her what she was thinking, she said she wanted to wait until we met with the K'sundii rebels, and I was forced to be alone in my confusion, much like my conversation with Huntress had left me.

Inside the warehouse, we were met by a dozen rebels or so. Rand stood with a group of people that never seemed to leave his side. They'd become something of a posse for him. Perhaps Rand was more charismatic with dreadlocks.

He had his arms crossed, and he raised his eyebrows when he saw Jashi and me approaching. "This is...interesting."

One of the rebels, a woman with bright orange eyes and her curly hair in a bun, stepped forward. "I lead the rebels stationed near the capitol in Hashir."

I nodded, remembering her. I'd worked with her indirectly and knew her mainly by reputation. "Sachinn, right?"

Sachinn nodded back, offering a small smile at the acknowledgement. "When you disappeared years ago, I think I speak for most of the rebels in K'sundi when I say I understood your reasoning for doing it. Though none of us ever knew how you were able to disappear so completely, it wasn't long before we were glad you did." Her gaze turned serious. "Dekaar is a tyrant. His search for your whereabouts has been relentless, and Half-Dracs who didn't disappear with you were captured under suspicion of working with you. Dragon tribe too. Most of the people brought in for questioning never came back, and we still can't figure out what happened to them or where they were taken."

Anger pulsed through me and heat rose in my chest. It was worse than I thought.

Sachinn went on. "We did as you instructed, and most of the rebels' efforts here in K'sundi have been dedicated to protecting those being targeted, not that we had to go looking for them. The numbers of people joining the rebels because of you and Jashi sky-rocketed after you abdicated the throne. We started to establish a stronger underground system in order to protect the vulnerable, even smuggling K'sundii citizens to other countries where Dekaar's influence wasn't as strong." She frowned and shook her head. "But we eventually started having to smuggle K'sundii citizens to rebel countries instead. Dekaar and the Zendaalans are too close. The Zendaalans have been equally brutal in their search for rebel members and anyone we attempt to stow away. Equalized nations are no longer safe for us. So we've established a stronger base in Vahdel and taken many dragon tribe and Half-Dracs there for protecting."

Jashi sucked air through her teeth by my side, and I knew she was thinking back to how bad Vahdel was when we went there over four years ago. If it was the better of all the options, things really were looking bleak here.

Sachinn took a breath. "Things never calmed down, but we established a sort of norm. All of that changed a few years ago." She reached out a hand, and Jashi and I jumped when a flame sparked in the center of her palm. She looked at us through the fire. "That didn't used to happen before you disappeared." She closed her fist and the flames along with it. "The only explanation we can offer is that the dragon tribe has mutated somehow. At this point, we have not encountered a dragon tribe member who has not changed in some way."

Jashi frowned. "In some way?"

Sachinn pursed her lips. "I'll get to that in a minute. First"—she looked between us—"Rand and some of the others who disappeared with you held a meeting explaining what happened to you all. He also explained that you were subject to an attack, and I know your biggest concern is going to be security, as a result."

Damn straight, I thought.

"But we need help holding down the fort over here," Sachinn insisted.

I clenched and unclenched my fists. I'd known this time would come eventually. I'd need to sift through the rebels here in K'sundi and decide who to allow access to the Dens, not only for their sakes, but also for ours. Connecting to the rebels in K'sundi was an important step toward discovering where Dekaar hid the Dragon Kings' parts.

"We have someone willing to help us, but it comes with a condition," Sachinn said.

My nostrils flared, and Huntress curled behind me aggressively. "Who would expect to make demands *of me*?"

"Not a demand," said a familiar voice. "A request."

Cirssa Kun stepped out from the shadows of the warehouse dressed in a dark shawl that hid her features until she pulled the hood back. She wasn't wearing her contacts anymore, revealing her bright orange eyes in their full glory, and I cursed myself for not thinking of it earlier. I'd completely forgotten she was part dragon tribe.

The Empress of Gheres looked Jashi and me in the eye. "Daoliu has told our citizens that I've fallen gravely ill to explain my disappearance. But I have joined your rebellion. And he's asking you to protect me in exchange for his complete support. He's willing to hide as many rebels as you need." She had a sparkle of mischief in her eyes as she added, "And provide firepower, should you decide you need it."

My eyes widened. He was willing to help me wage war against Zendaal, if we protected his wife.

Sachinn looked to me and Jashi again. "Now, I said that the dragon tribe has been changing. Some of us have developed the same abilities as you and Jashi. Others..." She motioned for Cirssa to demonstrate.

Cirssa nodded and spread her fingers. Rather than fire, arcs of *electricity* danced and stretched between her fingertips, drawing a gasp from Jashi. My mouth fell open.

"You're...you're like Comet," Jashi remarked.

The dots connected in my mind. There were dragons, and then there were Elemental dragons.

Now there were Half-Dracs. And Elemental Half-Dracs.

"They're calling us the Neo-Dracs," Cirssa said with a warm smile as the electricity receded and she folded her arms. "The changed dragon tribe members, I mean."

"And that's why," Sachinn concluded, "though I know you're concerned about security and allowing access to the Dens, I believe it would be the best course of action to protect the Empress. And by doing that, you will have all of the resources Gheres has to offer. She has nowhere else to go, and I don't think she'll pose a threat."

Jashi looked at me with pleading eyes.

I chuckled, and it seemed to surprise everyone in the room. I turned to Cirssa. "Well, it looks like you're going to get that dragon you wanted after all. You're going to have to work on your K'sundii pronunciation, though."

It was my turn to be surprised when Cirssa pulled me into a tight hug, clutching me like her life depended on it. "Thank you," she said in a shuddering voice, and I realized that her life *did* depend on this.

Sachinn and I talked over a few more minor details before we left. Jashi had pulled Cirssa aside to talk. After I finished with Sachinn, I joined the two engaged in a heated conversation.

Jashi looked at me with anger flashing in her eyes. "Dekaar's turned K'sundi into a circus!"

That was a reality I accepted the day I decided to step down from the throne. The way the Court was running things, whoever was to become Faresh after me could only be even more foolish than the court members. I figured the technical term for a group of clowns was a circus, anyhow.

Jashi went on, "The people haven't stopped protesting. They really want us back. It's the Court that won't back down. They're being blatant about it now. Elections for those that sit as Court members are being overturned in favor of those who kiss up to Dekaar. Even royal family clans are turning against the way the government is running things. And because Daoliu stood by us when the Zendaalans were accusing us, Zendaal is threatening Gheres with rebel status."

Cirssa looked exhausted. Dark circles framed her orange eyes, and her usually full cheeks looked uncharacteristically sunken in. The situation was leaving more than just K'sundi in shambles, but with Zendaal being overtly aggressive even toward their own, surely the leaders of the world were seeing just how meaningless their titles really were when Zendaal didn't get their way.

Cirssa bowed her head slightly. "Daoliu would be here to thank you himself if he could. But it is as Jashi says, and he's already under suspicion for claiming I'm sick. He can't afford to go missing as well. But I am truly grateful. I know you are carrying your own world on your shoulders." A hard look entered her tired eyes. "But I mean it when I say that my husband will do anything you ask for doing me this favor. All of this talk of rebel country or not—it's time to put an end to it once and for all."

"Let's make one thing clear," I said, helping Jashi onto Huntress, earning daggers because she didn't understand why I was treating her friend like this.

Cirssa, however, folded her hands neatly in front of her, listening with humility.

"I'm not interested in saving the world anymore." I climbed onto Huntress as she growled in satisfaction with what I'd said. Even without turning, I knew Jashi was silently agreeing. She knew where we were at this point, and as much as she loved her friend, we had a son at home that reaffirmed where our priorities lay. "The moment I stepped down from the throne, the world lost its only hope."

Looking up at me, uncertainty flashed through Cirssa's features for the first time since we'd started speaking.

"I'm only interested in saving my own people," I said, borrowing Jashi's term and truly feeling like it applied. "As far as I'm concerned, it's us against the world. What I plan to do will weaken the Zendaalans because it benefits my people. If the rest of the world benefits from that, that's a byproduct, not the intention. We don't help outsiders anymore."

She looked confused, fussing with the tips of her fingers. "Then...?"

"Then if you want our help, what does that make you?" I challenged.

Understanding lit up her features, and she held her head up. "You're right, it is us against the world. I will be your people, Kahmel. I'll make sure the rest of Gheres is too."

I nodded, then offered my hand to help her onto Huntress, and we flew off.

WHEN WE GOT BACK to the Fire Den, Jashi announced she had to talk to me, and Cirssa and pulled us away from the rest to the smaller manor where she'd stayed when she first came back from Obellana's.

She took us to the dining area, then took a deep breath as Cirssa and I looked at her in confusion.

She kept glancing out the window, and I realized her dragons had followed us.

She was talking to them, I realized.

"Well, I didn't know *this* was what she meant!" she exclaimed out loud, sighing and shaking her head, face in her hand. Legacy, the black dragon, made a sympathetic trill that sounded like a reply, and Jashi waved the dragon away.

The rebels in K'sundi weren't quite as familiar with the concept of Drake Bonding as we were. Cirssa frowned in confusion. My confusion, on the other hand, had less to do with Jashi's internal conversation with the dragons and more to do with the fact that Jashi hadn't looked nearly as surprised as she should have been after seeing Cirssa had developed the same abilities as Jashi's electric Elemental.

Cirssa remained silent while Jashi conducted her inner dialogue. I knew Jashi had some explaining to do, and I wasn't leaving until I got an answer, so I waited as well.

Finally, Jashi turned her attention back to us, or more specifically, to Cirssa. "Is it true? Anyone who belongs to the dragon tribe has become—what do you call it? A *Neo-Drac*?"

Cirssa considered the question, leaning her head on her hand. "Well, to be more specific, as long as the dragon tribe eye color shows, that individual will develop abilities." She glanced at me. "You have a twin, but you're the only one with the orange eyes. In theory, you both have the dragon tribe blood in you, but you're the only one who developed the eye color."

I nodded, realizing that we didn't have any dragon tribe here in the Dens that weren't *already* Half-Drac. So we wouldn't have noticed the change like the dragon tribe that were left back in K'sundi.

"How many people have developed different abilities?" I asked. "Other than fire, that is."

"No small number," Cirssa said, straightening. "Some developed fire along with another ability, including, but not limited to, telekinesis, levitation, unusual strength. Though, interestingly, only those who were not already Half-Dracs manifested abilities other than fire. For example," she gestured to Jashi and myself. "I don't imagine you will show the same mutations as the Neo-Dracs have been experiencing. At least, not based upon what we've seen so far."

Then where does that leave Kai? I wondered all of a sudden. Jashi said he was Half-Drac. We never discussed when, exactly, she found that out. Could he develop these strange new powers as well?

Jashi looked at me, seriousness in her eyes. "Obellana told me this would happen."

I frowned. Cirssa, as I imagined the conversation was now beyond her, said nothing about the mention of the Dragon Queen. But I knew that was why Jashi had been quiet all this time. "She predicted this too?"

Jashi started to pace. "I didn't know what she was talking about. She said the Half-Dracs were evolving. If what she said is true...then all of this has to do with Kai."

"That's ridiculous!" I snapped without thinking. Finding out I was a father generated all kinds of feelings inside me I didn't know I was capable of. And as I realized that the Half-Dracs were changing, I found myself suddenly hoping, *wishing* that it had nothing to do with Kai. I didn't even have a good reason for wanting it. I just *knew* I didn't want this, whatever the dragons had planned for him.

He's my son, I wanted to shout at the dragons outside. *Leave him out of all of this destiny nonsense. Leave us all alone.*

But the anger that flashed in Jashi's eyes made me realize the one I was snapping at was her, not the dragons. And the fact that Kai was her son as much as he was mine, and that she was the one who had been brave enough to have him on her own, without any support from me, just so she could do her part in this grand scheme she didn't even know about at the time, put me in my place, quickly.

"Everything else Obellana said has come true, Kahmel," she said, glowering. "We're the first Half-Dracs in centuries to survive long enough to have children. The Half-Dracs were meant to evolve with the dragons a long time ago. These *Neo-Dracs*, that's the future we're meant to be fighting for."

No, I screamed inside. There was no sense to the sentiment. I was simply denying everything presented to me right now as soon as it had to do with Kai. I wanted to snatch him away and hide him somewhere, as if that would change anything, as if him existing in an entire other world already wasn't enough to stop the change he was somehow initiating. As if that would stop whatever he might eventually develop.

I looked at Jashi, wanting to tell her to stop. To realize what she was asking of me.

There was no Drake Bond between us, but Jashi tilted her head up in challenge. Her eyes reflected all the promises I made to her, all the discussions we had about *our people*, our future together. She saw the question in my gaze, and rather than answer, she shot it back at me. "Well? What are you going to do?"

I wanted to rage at everything. At the dragons for making me, my family, my emotions, nothing but pawns in a massive game much larger than anything I could have imagined. At everything that went beyond anything I could plan or prepare for. At myself, for falling so completely and utterly in love with Jashi over nothing more than a gut feeling that my entire future lay in her hands. And at myself again, for being right, for finding myself in this same situation time and time again—when facing Aithel as he threatened to hurt Jashi, when Jashi doubted my love for her, and now—forced to buckle, to *bow*.

And here I was, buckling again.

I was happy with the people we kept to ourselves here in the Den. We had a small circle, and that was good enough.

But that circle was about to get bigger.

You see why I chose to let your wife tell you, Huntress said, not bothering to hide the sass in her tone.

Is there anything you dragons don't know before I do?

Very little.

I sighed, both to Huntress and Jashi. "If Dekaar stays on the throne, the Half-Dracs...and the Neo-Dracs will always be in danger."

Jashi cocked her head, eyes still challenging. Waiting for me to buckle.

I bit my lip, tired of dragons, Half-Dracs, *Neo-Dracs*, all of them. No wonder Jashi wanted to move to some small town somewhere and disappear. I should have followed her lead.

"I'm going to take our throne back," I said. Buckling. I looked to Cirssa. "I hope you were serious when you said Daoliu has firepower."

Cirssa smirked devilishly. "Very."

I nodded, sinking into my own mind to decide the best way to go about what was already creeping into my thoughts. Huntress growled in satisfaction, and I groaned at her to go back to whatever she'd done before to seal herself off from me. I was ignored.

"Well," Cirssa spoke up, finally. "What's this I hear about you two having a baby?"

DEN OF COUNCIL

A few days later, I was walking around some fields in the Rider Den with Kai. The development Rand and his Den had accomplished was impressive. They dedicated a group of islands to the west for farming. The one Kai and I were roaming was home to acres and acres of wheat, fenced around the edges with forcefield technology. It was a mix of ancient technique with modern advancement that made me proud of *our people*.

I held Kai's hand, reveling in the fact that he hadn't even noticed we'd left his mother back on the main island. Jashi and I silently coordinated this attempt at getting Kai to be comfortable alone with me.

I looked at his little hand in mine, wondering what it would be capable of in the future, about the kind of future we were creating for him. When it was just about us and him and the Half-Dracs, these Dens were more than enough until we brought power back to the Dragon Kings and left the world to make what they would with the results. But the world we'd left behind was changing drastically. All because he existed. Because Jashi and I survived long enough to make him; the first Half-Dracs to have a child in centuries.

We still didn't know what Kai was capable of, really. His eyes perked up anytime someone mentioned dragons, a fact that made me proud, but also made me wonder. Was his interest because of his upbringing or some instinct? Some part of the change that was happening to our people? Was he a Half-Drac? Or a *Neo*-Drac that had yet to show his other abilities?

Jashi and I decided I would take Kai out here to the fields for a few minutes, see how he reacted. It was going well so far; I hoped she wouldn't mind my taking longer. I figured Cirssa would keep her plenty busy, anyway. She and Lora were becoming fast friends as well, and the three were covering the three years of stories about Kai Cirssa had missed out on. Part of me wanted to be in on that conversation. I missed out on those three years too. But I couldn't make up for three years just by hearing about it. I needed time with Kai.

Kai yelped, pointing at something while he hid behind my leg. "*Spi-yer!*"

Following his finger, I realized what he meant. *Spider.* "It's just a bug, Kai." I chuckled and moved to pick it up.

But Kai moved faster than I did, his little palm lighting up in flames. He darted from behind me, launching his fire at the ill-fated spider and setting the grass aflame in the process.

"Kai!" I exclaimed, leaping to pull the fire from the grass before it could spread, grunting as the heat escaped into me and pricked my skin like fire ants. Dragons he had no problem with, but *spiders* scared him?

My sudden change in attitude turned me into the bad guy again. Kai looked terrified, backing away and closing his fist, extinguishing his flames. Then came the tears.

"Shh..." I tried to comfort him, crouching and approaching cautiously. "Everything is okay now. The spider is gone, okay? You got him, you definitely got him."

"Daddy mad..." he cried, with an innocent look that betrayed the incredible abilities he displayed mere moments ago.

I chuckled. "Daddy's not mad," I said, wondering what about parenting made you talk in the third person on impulse. "Look." I opened my palm and let a little fire dance in the middle of it, and instantly, the tears stopped.

Kai wiped the streaks from his cheeks, looking at my hand with awe.

"I'm just like you," I said as warmth blossomed in my chest at the way he looked at me. I loved the fact that our abilities were something we had in common and he would never have to grow up like I did, thinking he was something to be hidden away and feared for who he was. Kai would grow up loving himself, his powers, and his community.

My son reached his hand forward, shocking me as my possession over the flame was revoked, Kai's will taking over as he eased the flame into his hand and examined the fire like he was, for the first time, truly understanding who I was to him. He looked back up at me and grinned, and the look on his face made my eyes prickle.

Kai closed his fist and launched himself into my arms, giving me the tightest hug his little body could manage. I wrapped my arms around him and picked him up. I ruffled his hair, wondering at how much it felt just like Jashi's curls. Our little boy really was a miracle. He deserved the world.

And I was determined to give it to him.

Kai pulled away, an inquisitive look on his face. "Daddy like day-gone?"

"Yes, I already told you," I said, chuckling.

Kai grinned and fished something out of his pocket, and when I saw what it was, I knew Jashi would kill me if she knew he had it. "I find day-gone tooth!" he announced enthusiastically.

My first instinct was to snatch it from him, but I remembered how off-put Kai was when he saw me panic, so I put on a smile. "Oh wow," I said, trying to look as impressed as Kai obviously wanted me to be. "Can I see that?"

Thankfully, Kai offered it with pride, as though I, too, should see how accomplished he was for his incredible find.

The tooth was the size of my thumb and razor-sharp at the tip. It was a wonder it didn't cut a hole in his pocket, or worse, his thigh.

"Where did you get it?" I said, trying to slip the tooth into my own pocket unnoticed.

Kai wasn't so easily fooled. "It's mine," he protested, reaching an open hand out, waiting for his treasure to be returned.

I sighed, taking the tooth back out. Maybe I should turn this into a lesson. "Well, Kai, dragon teeth are dangerous." I showed him the sharp end. "You see that? Little kids shouldn't play with that."

The tears threatened to come back. His lip poked out, and I knew my reputation was on the line here. "How about this? I'll hold onto it for now. I'll give it back," I added quickly when his lip started quivering. "I promise I'll give it back." I made a mental note to try to find something to file the end down with and ask Jashi if she wouldn't mind letting this slide. Then I thought of a good way to keep this sort of thing from happening again *and* find more ways to spend time with Kai. "How about this? Me and you can go looking for dragon teeth together sometime. Then we can bring them all back home, I can make the teeth safe for you, and we can start a collection together."

That won him over. He grinned, wiping tears for the second time. "Okay!"

I sighed in relief and slipped the tooth in my pocket again. "Where did you find this?" I asked again, looking around, wondering when he had the chance to pick up the tooth when I wasn't looking.

"Not here." Kai shook his head. And I was glad at least Jashi wouldn't be upset with *me* over his little discovery. He must have slipped away when no one was looking and found it on his own.

"Oh," I said. "Where was it, near the stables?" I looked over at where Rand had his dragons corralled, wondering if maybe it was a good idea to go now, while we were already together and having fun.

"Day-gone," Kai explained, as though the answer were obvious.

I laughed. "I know it's a dragon's tooth, Kai. Where did you get it from?"

"Day-gone!" he insisted, and at first I thought he misunderstood me, until he started mumbling in what Jashi called *Kai-ese*. But I understood clearly when he mentioned a *day-gone*, mimed opening a wide mouth with his arms like kids motioned the opening of a crocodile's mouth, and then mimed picking something off the tongue, demonstrating with his own mouth.

Dragons regrew their teeth often. Once a year, at least. Their new teeth grew under the old ones, and when they fell loose the dragon either spit them out or swallowed them whole. I assumed Kai found his little treasure on the ground somewhere. But he'd *reached into a dragon's mouth* and plucked the tooth off *its tongue*.

And then I knew two things. One, Jashi and I were going to have a talk. And two, perhaps I should get Kai a little tracking device of his own.

When Kai and I got back to Jashi, Cirssa, and Lora, they were all getting their dragon-riding gear on. Thankfully, Jashi wasn't at all worried when Kai and I took a little longer than expected. Finding out about his little fire accident and dragon tooth-finding habits, however, she was less than enthused. After I survived the barrage of questions on what I did when I discovered the tooth, what Kai said, what I said, and what we did afterward, Jashi finally calmed down enough for me to get in a few questions of my own.

"Why didn't you tell me Kai was that good at controlling his fire?" I asked, and when Jashi looked up at me, I realized that perhaps I was a little more excited than I wanted to admit about that fact, rather than worried. But it was one thing to launch his fire at the spider because it bothered him. It was another thing completely to be able to take my fire from me and admire it on his own.

She spread her hands to either side. "I didn't know!" She slapped my arm. "And why are you smiling?"

"Am I?" I was more than a little proud that our son had accomplished so much in such a small amount of time, and I couldn't keep the grin from creeping up my face.

Jashi didn't look nearly as excited as I was, so I wiped my face and donned a more serious expression, which only seemed to aggravate her further. She rolled her eyes. Then she looked over my shoulder at where Kai had the two women infatuated, cooing to him and offering him little trinkets to fiddle with.

Things were changing. And we were the ones heralding the changes on our horizon.

"What have we done, Kahmel?" she asked, leaning on my arm.

"We've done good." I stroked her hair.

"What do we do with a child who might end up more powerful than we ever were?"

She was right. If this was how powerful Kai was already, who knew what he would be capable of when he was older? We still couldn't be sure he wasn't a *Neo-Drac*.

"We give him the world," I answered.

Jashi rose on her toes and placed a kiss on my lips. "You'd better get to work, then."

WE NEEDED to know where Dekaar had moved the Dragon Kings' parts. But I also wanted the throne back now. For Kai. Because he and all the Neo-Dracs needed each other as much as Jashi and I needed the Half-Dracs with us now. And we couldn't protect them all by slipping away to the Dens. One day Dekaar was going to catch up with us. As a smaller group, we could evade him, but if we included all of the people Cirssa described, we wouldn't be able to keep running away from him forever. It was time we took our palace back.

Over the next few days we dedicated all of our attention to coordinating with the rebels in K'sundi to figure out where Dekaar was hiding the Dragon Kings' parts.

He kept all information about the movements of the Zendaalans in K'sundi confidential. And the Zendaalan officers in K'sundi were very armed. They had upped their security measures, not just in K'sundi, but worldwide. They had turned their pursuit for Jashi and me into a witch hunt. They were ruthless in their search for any and all information as to our whereabouts or the movements of the rebels.

Thankfully, though, the people and the government weren't on the same page anymore.

The rebels in K'sundi weren't hiding out in abandoned warehouses and in the desert plains as much anymore. Common people took them into their houses. Some small businesses, motels, restaurants, and stores allowed rebels to use their services for free.

Jashi was right. She was always right. The people in K'sundi remembered us. They remembered the way we fought for them when I allowed them to see what I was doing for them behind the scenes. How Jashi and I were being treated. They hadn't forgotten our sacrifices. And now that more of them were evolving into Neo-Dracs, they knew who to turn to.

So, as far as I was concerned, the two problems could be combined. Taking the throne and getting the Dragon Kings' parts didn't have to be independent tasks.

I came up with a new plan—gather the people who would side with me, utilize Daoliu's support, and retake the throne by force.

Then drag the answers out of Dekaar himself. He was a cyborg now. He could either offer up the information, or we could extract whichever parts held the information by our own means. Either option was fine by me.

We needed a meeting point for the Den leaders and any of their newly assigned chief officers. I would have had T'shan as my chief officer, but he'd filled Khes's role as leader of the Iron Den. Jashi ended up picking for the both of us, selecting Cirssa and Lora. T'shan made all of his friends, Kent, Ashed, and Jemmorah, into his chief officers. We found a Den that was convenient to travel to from each of our territories that we dubbed the Den of Council. There, we found a dilapidated building and combined several dining tables from floating manors into the center of the building. And thus we constructed the first Council I actually was comfortable in. No, a Council I felt I belonged to and felt a duty to satisfy.

I looked to either side of me, seeing that I had all of their attention, and I got straight to the point. "You know about the Neo-Dracs. If there's as many as Cirssa is saying, we're going to need more than just the Dens to protect them. They're Half-Dracs just as much as the people we protect today, and I promised the Dragon Kings I would protect all of their dragons, Half-Dracs included." I drew in a breath and blew it out through my nose. "So we're going to take the palace back. But I refuse to take K'sundi as it was. When we take our country back, everything is going to change." I gestured to everyone at the table. "You will be the new Council members. Selected rebels in K'sundi will become the new members of the Court, which means we're going to be kicking out the existing Council and Court. And Faresh, of course."

Asan scoffed, wiping away an imaginary mote of dust from the table. "I think as far as anyone's concerned, you and Jashi never stopped being Faresh and Faresha."

Jashi smiled, and I nodded in acknowledgement. "Thank you, Asan. And I admit, the only reason I'm entertaining the idea is because the people in K'sundi seem to feel the same way."

"Yeah," Jashi muttered. "All it took was revealing our fire, me getting kidnapped, and Kahmel resigning from the throne."

I sighed. Summing up the last several years was a depressing exercise, but she was right. It took a lot to get here. And a baby, apparently.

"I can't speak for K'sundi," Cirssa spoke up. "But I believe even the rest of the world didn't realize how much power they had given over until you and Jashi resisted the Zendaalans. And when we watched what Dekaar did to K'sundi..." A shadow passed over her face.

One I knew well. It came with understanding the weight of an entire people rested upon your shoulders, and whatever happened to them, even if there was nothing you could do about it, you wished whatever gods may exist would act on your behalf. Because knowing they were doomed to suffer...it was the reason I could never rule

K'sundi as it was when I left. I wouldn't rule a people choosing their own suffering, but I would do what I could for a people who didn't, yet suffered in spite of that.

Cirssa looked up at me with steel in her eyes. "We knew that all it took was a strong enough opposition, and we, too, could be revoked of our thrones. That no matter what laws we had in place, no matter what structure we adhered to as a culture, the Zendaalans would overrule it all and enforce their rule. And as long as they retain that right, none of us truly rule. I believe the K'sundii have come to this conclusion after seeing the alternative when you and Jashi were removed. I believe your people call it a 'wakeup call.'"

"Wisely put," Rand remarked. "But this is all just something nice to think about without a plan to make it work. So the people support you now. Maybe that gets rid of the Court. Maybe even the Council. But Dekaar? The Zendaalans will fight tooth and nail to keep him. He represents their permanent control over K'sundi, the country that threatens their rule the most. They won't let us take him out without a fight."

I laced my fingers together, leaning over the table. "I don't expect them to. So let's talk about what we have to fight with." I nodded to Cirssa.

"Gheres is prepared to support you, no matter what you choose to do," said Cirssa plainly. "However, it will take time for our troops to arrive in K'sundi. Whatever your plans are, it will have to take into account the time it takes the Gheresans to arrive."

"That could be days," Jashi said. "And all we have are rebels to fight against armed Zendaalan soldiers, not to mention K'sundi officers still fighting on the government's side."

"Rebels...and dragons," I added. "And the ability to create Drake Bonds."

DEKAAR'S SECRET

Jashi *Eloe* Anyua-Omah

The building we conducted our Council in was worn down, to the point the ceiling had crumbled over most of the room. We had to carry the chunks out and sweep up the rubble just to put the tables and chairs in. I watched as my dragons circled in the air above us, listening, through me, to the conversation.

I wasn't sure if just using dragons was the answer to the problem this time. But I was glad I was here, surrounded by friends, to discuss ideas.

Arusi raised an eyebrow. "Are we ready to incorporate the technique in our training with dragon riders?"

That was a good question. "I suppose we don't have any other choice," I said honestly. "I mean, while I was away, I got used to having different dragons in my head." I smiled at Kahmel, grateful for all the training he did with me, though I resisted at first. I definitely relied on that training while I was pregnant and alone with the dragons in Obellana's realm. "Certain meditation techniques helped me, you know, not go insane with multiple dragons in my head." I turned to look at the rest of the table. "But I don't know if I'd recommend getting rebel members to Drake Bond with more than one or two. I bonded with several in an emergency." And I definitely wouldn't recommend doing that kind of thing just for the hell of it.

"I read about army generals in K'sundi," I continued. "When they used Drake Bonding, they had stables spread throughout the country for better positions in battle. But I also think it helped manage having so many bonds at once. The connection weakens when you're farther from the dragon you're bonded to, but the connection stays strong for some distance. I'd estimate at least a few miles."

Kahmel nodded. I kept forgetting he now shared that experience with me. He'd bonded with Huntress, a connection I was happy for him to have. Comet couldn't bond to me; I'd tried before. But that was fine. Each relationship with each dragon was different, and not every relationship had to be as deep as a Drake Bond. It was telling of Kahmel's personality that he only had one dragon, and he was able to establish a bond with her. Kahmel just naturally gravitated to the kind of friends who created connections that lasted a lifetime.

"I agree," Kahmel said, crossing his arms. "And it's not enough to make up for rebels who aren't trained soldiers, but it's something. Here's what I'm thinking: the Zendaalans are more heavily armed, and there's no chance for us to infiltrate their ranks, whereas with K'Sundi, if the people are on our side, we could *possibly* get a plant into the palace guard. So we need to address the Zendaalans first."

So he wasn't expecting the dragons to be the only solution this time, either.

What he'd said about dealing with the Zendaalans caused memories of my time in Zendaal to flicker in my mind. Ocean, who was flying around outside the building, came to attention when she perceived my thoughts going back to that experience we shared. She'd been in my mind the whole time then and could help me remember certain details.

"Dekaar has a strange mansion," I said, starting with what I could recall first. My outburst garnered everyone's attention, but I didn't pay them much mind as I focused on remembering. "It wasn't like he said something to someone and they pressed a button for him to make things happen there when he wasn't present," I went on, clarifying my thoughts out loud. "We would have HoloCalls, and he'd control different parts of the house, at will. He erected forcefields in different parts of the house to keep me in line."

Kahmel stiffened, his chest swelling with anger. He took a slow breath to tamp it down, likely reminding himself he couldn't change the past and that I was here now, not with Dekaar.

As for me, I took some comfort in the fact that I wrecked that pretty mansion of Dekaar's before I left. I made a note to remind Kahmel about that later.

Lora raised her finger to get everyone's attention. She, too, looked pained to hear about my terrible experiences but, like Kahmel, recognized we had to stay on topic and move on. "Am I missing something, or is that completely separate from what we're talking about?"

"Just what are you getting at, Jashi?" asked Arusi. I was grateful for her always-calming presence. No matter how absurd my ideas or how ridiculous I acted, she always believed in me, no matter what. It was nice to see that our time apart hadn't lessened her faith in me.

"The original plan wasn't for Dekaar to take me," I started, communicating both to those at the table and my dragon flying above us. "Why did he have that kind of technology already installed in his home? I always wondered about that."

Kahmel rubbed his chin. "So the Zendaalans already had some kind of system installed in Dekaar's home so he could control it remotely—"

I shook my head as I remembered why that fact was significant to me. "He called me from all the way in K'sundi, and he was able to manipulate anything in his house from there."

Asan's eyebrows shot up. "All the way from *K'sundi*?"

"Maybe I'm missing the point," Lora admitted beside me, "but I still don't know what any of this means."

Rand did. He pursed his lips. "The Zendaalans already had the technology needed to carry a signal from K'sundi to Zendaal. Dekaar is one of the deepest government secrets there is. They must have a *private* network, likely in *every* Equalized nation, connecting back to Zendaal."

Lora frowned, the idea clearly making her uncomfortable. I didn't blame her. The Zendaalans clearly had the power to walk all over the nations under their Equalization, do whatever they liked without being questioned. And they have always had the luxury of having their doors closed to every other nation, never allowing outsiders in who could testify to how they actually lived in their own country. But I observed them first-hand. And I was determined to recall every detail that could be of use.

Lora shook her head. "But why would they even need something like that?"

T'shan leaned forward on the table, propping his chin up with a fist. "Communication is the obvious answer. Either with each other, or more likely, with systems. If they can access their remote devices from all the way in K'sundi, that means data, information, or signals can be sent from Zendaal directly to any Zendaalan at any time as well. Just like how we used the Dragon Watch Towers for the rebels."

Kahmel nodded as he considered the implications out loud. "We used the Dragon Watch Towers to hide signal-boosting towers for the rebels. The Zendaalans are doing the same thing. Private networks connected through their signal boosting towers and hidden, most likely, in all of the territories under the Equalization." He leaned forward, understanding lighting up his eyes. "They had to already have them in place if Dekaar could control his house from so far away."

I didn't suspect they dedicated such precise and expensive technology just to make glorified smart homes. Discovering what else they used those signal boosters for could be key—could reveal a weakness.

"How did the Zendaalans bring Dekaar back from the dead?" I

asked, making the conversation take another sharp turn with a question I was sure everyone had been wondering about.

"Even the dragons don't know," Kahmel said. "Aithel said as much when he told me who Dekaar really was. All he knew was that the Dragon Kings' power was being used to accomplish it."

My eyes widened.

Ocean, did you know that?

The azure dragon emitted a low growl that reverberated through me as a rush of anger seeped through her. *Yes. He bears the scent of our Kings. Even after all this time, the smell of their blood is still strong on his hands.*

"But what if it's more than just *their* blood on his hands?" I said, and I only realized after a moment that I'd said it out loud. But I wasn't concerned about keeping both conversations separate. "What do the Zendaalans do when they kidnap Half-Dracs? It wasn't enough for them to try to kill Kahmel. They were trying to get something out of him."

I saw Kahmel shifting out of the corner of my eye, likely rubbing the scar their devices left in him. But I kept my eyes trained on one spot, determined to follow my thoughts through. I was on the verge of something.

"Kahmel, you're an expert in history," I said desperately. "Before the Equalization, when the Zendaalans were dying from the Withering, was that around the same time the dragon tribe began to dissolve?"

Kahmel frowned, like I was making him remember a subject in school he hated studying. "I'm more well-versed in K'sundii history," he admitted, scratching his head. But he wasn't giving up. He stared beyond me, like he was searching a library in his mind for the information I was asking for, and I thanked the Spirits for such an intelligent husband who remembered details much better than I did. "I know what most do. Like how the Withering was the catalyst for the development of Zendaalan cybernetic technology," he recalled. "How their advancement made them revered around the world for their technological savvy and ability to resolve their differences to solve their common problem."

"Right," I encouraged him, and everyone else at the table remained silent, as if our deliberations were some delicate construction they didn't want to disrupt lest it come crumbling down. "And when was that? In comparison to one of K'sundi's eras?"

He placed his hands on the table like he was going to push off any moment. "The decline of the dragon tribe was around the same time, yes." He shook his head. "History before the Equalization isn't as detailed, but in the Age of Knowledge, which was just before the Equalization, the dragon tribe was already on the decline. So it can be assumed that the dragon tribe was facing trouble around the same time the Zendaalans were facing the Withering."

Rand nodded, joining the historical examination. "We don't have a lot of information about K'sundi's history before the Equalization, which is why we had no idea about Butaah, dragon riding, and Drake Bonds."

"Or when *Dekaar* was alive," I added. I watched as realization dawned on the faces of those sitting around the table. They knew what I was getting at. It was sinking in. And they were seeing how big this was, if I was right. "We didn't even know he existed."

"How old is Dekaar?" I asked Ocean aloud so the others could be included in my half of our conversation.

Ocean's ears flattened against her head, her eyes narrowing as a snarl emitted from somewhere deep in her chest. She gave me a number that made me dizzy, but I wasn't sure when the Equalization began in comparison, so I typed the number out in my eWatch and slid the screen over to Kahmel.

"Kahm, this is important," I said as he looked at the number I passed him. "Is he *older* than the Equalization?"

"Well, that's a lot easier to answer." He highlighted and copied the number and then tapped and swiped through different screens. "There were varying opinions about when the Equalization became official." He ran a series of searches and typed the results into a calculator. "The Zendaalans wanted to make it seem like the world wasn't worth thinking about before they came around. But K'sundi named their eras, as you know," he said, as though anyone other than Rand could actually follow him. "The K'sundii noted the time each era began and ended, specifically. Figuring out when the Equalization began is simply a matter of adding all the eras together and subtracting the number from the current year. The sum is the age of the Equalization." He slid the results on his screen over to me.

My mouth fell open. "Dekaar was born eighty years before the Equalization was established." No one needed me to tell them what that meant. We didn't know when he died, but assuming he lived to see his forties, he was alive when the Zendaalans were developing the cure to the Withering.

"What if..." I looked to everyone at the table and could tell that even Lora had caught on to my meaning, but I finished anyway. "... the Zendaalans are somehow using the Dragon Kings' parts to power their cybernetic technology? What if the Dragon Kings' parts help their technology bring the withered areas of their body to 'life'? The same way they use it to bring life to Equalized nations? And it's only recently that they developed a way to use it to even regenerate the dead—which is how they brought Dekaar back and why the Dragon Kings can sense their power being used to animate him."

"That would mean"—Rand put a hand over his mouth as his mind wrapped around the concept—"that there's more to Dekaar needing to keep us away from the Dragon Kings' parts than just to spite the Dragon Kings. Because if we make the Dragon Kings whole again, they'll take their power back...and he'd be gone for good this time."

"More than that." Kahmel tightened his hands into fists and the corners of his mouth twitched into a brief grin. "If we can get the parts to back to the Dragon Kings, the Zendaalans would lose more than just their influence over the world."

"They'd go back to dying from the Withering," I concluded. The silence in the room pronounced just how huge it would be if this were true.

Cirssa placed her delicate hands on the table, examining them nonchalantly as she said, "Then our plan should be split into two." She moved her right hand away from the left. "On one hand, we need to get Jashi and Kahmel the throne back." She slid her left hand farther to the left. "And on the other hand, attack Zendaal—not a direct attack, but an ambush." She raised the left hand. "So if one group can find the Dragon Kings' parts and deliver them to the Dragon Kings"—she raised the right hand—"Dekaar and all of his Zendaalan supporters will be crippled, leaving the throne open for the taking."

"We need to be able to position ourselves for a proper ambush," Arusi agreed, T'shan nodding at her side.

"But we know Zendaalans use some kind of network to communicate," said T'shan. "We've all seen it. We just didn't realize they had a private network in addition to their common ones."

He was right. When Kahmel and I were detained during our speech, the Zendaalans all moved at once, as if they received the order at the same time. I thought there might be some Zendaalan official in the crowd who gave the signal. But now I knew it was possible the order came from all the way in Zendaal.

Jemmorah cocked her head, a sly grin spreading on her face. "So what you're saying is, first we disrupt their communications network so they can't organize when we strike."

I nodded. "Then we can get our people into position while they're disorganized."

"In that case," Kahmel said, thinking out loud, "like you said, Cirssa, this isn't a direct attack. We could arrange for our people to sneak a much smaller troop of Gheresans into K'sundi."

Cirssa's eyes lit up. "That's true." She bobbed her head once. "Then we have a plan."

One of the women that stayed with me in Obellana's Den rushed into the room. Concern crumpled her features as she looked at Lora. "Lora, what are you doing here?"

Lora frowned. "I came to join the meeting, didn't you know?"

The woman shook her head, face turning to ash. "Nana thought Kai was with you." She looked at me, and my gut sank. "I came to ask if you'd left Kai with Lora. But if she's here, we have no idea where he is."

THE BOY-LIKE DRAGON

Kahmel Axon Kai of the Omah Clan

With a thought from me, Huntress descended in front of the Council building. I slung onto her back with a single movement. Jashi was already on Ocean, and the woman who'd come for her jumped onto a dragon of her own. We all rocketed into the air as the woman communicated over an earpiece.

"The last any of us saw Kai, he was in the Fire Den," she said as I shouted to open the Tunnel and we raced over a small town in K'sundi. "We looked in all the places he's usually playing with the other children, but none of us found him. The other children haven't even seen him in a while."

I shouted to reach another Tunnel, another Den, another Tunnel, another Den.

All I could think of was the last time this happened: when Jashi was taken from me.

What if Dekaar figured out how to access the Dens? What if he found out about Kai?

Aching dread spread through my chest. I couldn't imagine anything happening to my little boy. I'd barely had the chance to get to know him. Rage flooded my mind, anger that could set a city ablaze, but also fear, the crippling kind that could bring this grown man to his knees.

Upon our arrival at the Fire Den, we found that an organized search was already being conducted, and for the briefest moment, my chest felt a little lighter because this wasn't the same as when Jashi was abducted and there had been no one but my closest friends dedicated to keeping her safe.

The people called Kai their Fareshiki. Their little king. Though I'd lost my throne in K'sundi, the people here never stopped seeing me and Jashi as their Faresh and Faresha. And they didn't take it lightly when their Fareshiki went missing.

People called Kai's name from every direction. Even the younger children walked beside their parents, looking around in their favorite playing spots. Their little heads poked out from the tunnels and hidey holes, calling Kai's name repeatedly.

Dekaar would not easily sneak someone into this community and spirit my son away like they did my wife.

"I'll check the main manor again," said Jashi over our earpieces. "Just in case he went back home."

"Good idea," I agreed. "I'll check the—"

Huntress took a sharp turn I didn't ask her for, flying toward a group of dragons hovering in the air a good ways away from the main island of the Fire Den.

What are you doing? I asked, but Huntress wasn't focused on me. Her attention was directed toward the dragons flying in circles. They were young dragons, about the size of large dogs. They must have been hatched early on, perhaps when we first entered the Dens. They couldn't have been older than a few years.

Huntress acted like a patient mother, snarling to get the attention of the younger dragons, and they finally stopped playing to focus on her. The group was larger than when I first noticed them. There had been three dragons here a moment ago. Now there were five?

The air shimmered, and another two slipped in through a Tunnel we hadn't discovered before.

A few moments of silence passed, and I realized the dragons were communicating. Then Huntress's attention was on me again. *They've seen Kai,* she announced.

My heart leaped in my chest. *Where?* I asked, frantic.

Another few moments of silence, and then the air shone again as all of the dragons disappeared through the opening...and came back with Kai, riding one of the younger dragons. Grinning.

They were playing a game, Huntress supplied, a measure of relief and exhaustion in her voice that reflected my own.

What...how did—? I started.

Huntress went silent again, her attention back on the dragons. I could feel the rebuke in her attitude. The dragons seemed dejected, like they weren't sure where they went wrong.

I turned to Kai and nearly choked on my own spit—his attention was focused on Huntress as well, and his face fell along with those of the dragons around him.

He mumbled something in Kai-ese and flew with his little dragon back to where Jashi waited atop Ocean, landing on the ground next to her. Jashi scooped him up, announcing to the rest of the searchers that Kai had been found.

I was still reeling when Huntress rumbled a chuckle in my mind. *The children didn't realize they were to contain their play to only this Den. I apologize. I will inform Kai's other playmates not to escort him beyond this realm in the future.*

I almost didn't want to ask the question, but knew I had to. *Were you...*

Huntress waited, confused at my hesitation.

The feeling that something was very wrong rooted itself deeper in my stomach.

What is it, Faresh? asked Huntress.

Were you talking to Kai? I made myself ask.

He was talking to both of us, Huntress stated, as though the fact was simple. *He apologized and then asked his friends to take him down to Eloe. Didn't you hear him?*

My mind was spiraling. Kai *was* a Neo-Drac. That was why he wasn't afraid of dragons. That was why he reached into a dragon's mouth, unafraid. He could communicate with them the same way dragons communicated with each other, with feelings and sentiments, with experiences and names that meant more than just a word. He didn't *have* to speak clear words to the dragons like he did with Jashi and me. He just conveyed how he felt, and they understood.

And what was more, the dragons didn't know we *couldn't* hear him in that way. Because the dragons couldn't quite comprehend what we didn't understand. They thought our being half dragon made us nearly the same as them. Only in Kai's case...that was true.

He had no fear of the dragon he simply plucked a tooth from. He probably asked for permission and everything, as simple as asking his mother for a cookie.

I rubbed my face, and then I laughed, because I couldn't think of anything else to do. And then, rather than answer Huntress, I directed her down to where Jashi was clutching onto Kai with a death grip. Because it was time to talk about our son again.

Jashi and I sat in the living room of the manor, Kai and a few baby dragons playing on the floor with his blocks.

Huntress and Ocean couldn't fit in the room, but it had a set of floor-to-ceiling windows that gave the dragons the ability to see inside, and vice versa, so we could talk like adults.

Because of course we were co-parenting with dragons.

"I believe," Jashi started aloud, looking to me for confirmation, then back to the dragons outside the window, "the best way to conduct this discussion is for Kahmel and myself to speak verbally, understanding that the dragons we're bonded to will understand us best. But we will have to pause after each of you speak to inform the other what that dragon has said. Likewise, as only one dragon will understand one of us, you will have to do the same to the dragon beside you. All right?"

She paused, heard an answer, then nodded to me.

"All right." I pinched the skin between my eyes. "So, just to make sure we're all on the same page. Both of you can...talk to Kai?"

Huntress frowned in confusion, as if the answer were obvious. She wasn't nearly as verbal as Jashi's dragons, at least from what Jashi told me, and I knew that was all the answer I was going to get. I nodded to Jashi, and my poor wife sighed, leaning on the arm of her chair and shaking her head as she watched Kai play with his blocks and hand them to the dragons beside him like they were human children rather than potentially dangerous dragons. But of course, to Kai, they weren't dangerous at all. They were playmates.

Jashi held up a finger to hold me off from asking another question. "Ocean didn't know we didn't know, and she thinks all the other dragons likely feel the same way."

Kai looked up at us. He got that same distant look in his eye Jashi got when she was talking to her dragons, and I couldn't believe I hadn't noticed it sooner. I just thought he was easily distracted. But what did this mean? He could talk to dragons without a Drake Bond. Did that mean the dragons disrupted his thoughts as often as they could Jashi's? Jashi used meditation to ground herself when they became overwhelming. What would our three-year-old do? Or rather, what was he already doing? He didn't seem to be as foggy-minded as Jashi was when she first initiated bonds with her dragons. He directed his attention to anyone speaking to him easily. Was it somehow different for him?

Kai tilted his head and scrunched up his face, confused, and I looked to Jashi, wondering if I was missing something.

"Did he"—Jashi turned to Ocean—"say something to either of you?" Jashi frowned, then sighed, kneading the space between her eyes, and I hoped she was beginning to understand what she'd put me through throughout our entire marriage. "She's confused. She says... Kai was talking to *us*." She held up a finger when I opened my mouth to speak, then translated, "Apparently, Kai was asking if he'd done anything wrong."

I looked at my son's inquiring eyes—eyes that couldn't fathom why *we* were confused. I took a deep breath, glancing at his mother. I realized at that moment that, really, I knew we would create something special together. I knew we would change the world. We had a baby. And the rest of the Half-Dracs were changing as a result. The *Neo-Dracs*. It was quite possible Kai was the very first one. He'd been close to dragons since infancy.

I knew Jashi and I would change the world. Did the fact that I didn't know *how* we would change the world really matter? The moment we started crossing over into worlds unknown, speaking to Dragon Kings, riding dragons and winning wars, we signed off on the world as we knew it.

Kai was bound to be unique. But he wasn't alone. There were Neo-Dracs like him all over K'sundi that needed protection, both from the forces against them and from themselves. Because anyone Kai's age wouldn't even know that they were doing anything wrong. Kai and the others deserved more than just the Dens to discover themselves in, together with their family and community. They deserved a world dedicated to understanding them better, dedicated to making the world safer for them to live in. Kai wasn't in much danger here because he was surrounded by people that loved and cherished him. But the Neo-Dracs were vulnerable out there. Even parents with the best intentions would be like Nana, who was forced to make Jashi hide herself, traumatize herself, internalizing her powerlessness to control abilities she didn't understand.

As I crouched down beside my son, the dragons playing by his side scattered, picking up the sentiment in the air, no doubt. I scooped Kai up in my arms and stroked his hair for a few moments. Jashi crouched beside us, giving me a small, grateful smile. Sitting on the floor, I opened an arm and pulled her in as she leaned forward.

Kai put his little hand in mine, and I marveled at how small it was for a moment, then clutched it. I told Kai how much I loved him. I told Jashi how much I loved her. And then we spent some time explaining to Kai that we weren't the same as he was, but that we loved him no matter what. It ended up being fortunate to have the dragons nearby, able to better explain to him sentiments we couldn't, and let us know what Kai was feeling when he, quite literally, didn't have the words.

I had missed an entire three years of Kai's life. I missed seeing Jashi carry him, missed watching him come into the world. I'd lost one of my closest friends, and there were thousands of Neo-Dracs on the other side of these Tunnels living on the run for simply existing.

But when my son looked up at me, a man who should have been a perfect stranger to him, I realized that his abilities made me something more than that to him. He understood things without being told, and now that he knew we didn't share that ability, he knew how to navigate our relationship better. He smiled, exposing all his little teeth, and then he hugged me. "I love you, Daddy."

That was all it took to convince me that Jashi was right when she said we wouldn't let Khes's death be in vain afterall that we'd gone through to get here. I told Jashi we were the only ones who could dance in the flames and not get burned.

The world as we knew it was burning. But we were half dragons. Flames only encouraged us.

I hugged my son tighter, and I was glad to know he could understand how I felt without words. Because I was crying too hard to say anything.

THE LECRECIUS BOT

We coordinated with the rebels in K'sundi and informed them of what needed to be done and what we were planning to do. T'shan and his friends volunteered to be in charge of that relationship. It seemed that they were all too glad to imagine Jashi and me taking the throne back, and more than happy to get started.

But despite T'shan's enthusiasm, there was very little those of us who resided in the Dens could do other than keep up communication with the rebels in K'sundi.

All of the people that followed us into the Dens were now wanted criminals. Even the children. Our faces were plastered everywhere: on screens, displayed on buildings, in the news, and on the internet.

We could no longer use certain Tunnels that opened in K'sundii cities because of Zendaalan battleships waiting nearby. So now, in order to meet with the rebels, we left the Den through Tunnels that led to K'sundi's desert or jungle and arranged for a rebel to pick us up and drive us to the city to stay with one of the rebel supporters, hiding in their homes.

A few months had passed since we last spoke to Sachinn. During that time we'd celebrated Kai's fourth birthday, which was a few days before mine, so our people surprised me by celebrating both of us on the same day. It seemed strange to have such happy moments right now—after Khes's death, after years of being separated from Jashi and my friends, and then coming back to K'sundi and seeing the citizens hiding away in their houses, afraid to go out in the streets for too long.

Seeing K'sundi like this, yet knowing the people were more determined to help the rebels and me, instilled in me a strange sense of hope that thrived in the middle of this turmoil in a way that I didn't understand.

Jashi, Jemmorah, and I traveled through a Tunnel that exited in the K'sundi jungle where a rebel met us and drove us to the home of one of our supporters to meet with Sachinn. She wanted to show us something she and the rebels had discovered while investigating the private network the Zendaalans used to communicate. T'shan and his friends had excitedly told us it was incredible but wouldn't give us any more information. Even as we rode to the meeting, Jemmorah would tell us nothing more than, "You have to see it to understand," all the while trying to suppress an excited grin.

Sachinn met us at the back door and ushered us into the living room, gesturing for us to sit on the couch. On the coffee table in front of us sat a robot unlike any I'd ever seen. It was a simple box, with so many wires coming out of the back connected to little devices scattered behind it that it looked like the robot was sitting in spaghetti. The only way I knew it was meant to be a robot was because someone had taken a marker and drawn crude features to represent a stereotypical robot's face, complete with eyes and a square grid for a mouth.

I looked to Jemmorah and then back at the sad robot sitting in its own mess. "What am I looking at?"

Sachinn crossed her arms with a smug smile on her face. "Meet Lecrecius Awlen."

Jemmorah chipped in. "I'm the one who gave him a face."

Jashi crouched in front of it, frowning at poor Mr. Awlen. "If you can call it that."

As Jemmorah crossed her arms, ready to object, I cut her off, wanting to get to the point. "What exactly *is* Lecrecius Awlen, Sachinn?"

Sachinn chuckled and tapped the head of the robot as the older man who was kind enough to let us stay in his home brought us all piping hot cups of coffee. "That's the name of the Zendaalan officer who donated his parts to our little research project."

Jashi grimaced and backed away as though it was a body in front of her instead of a sad robot with a poorly drawn face on it. "Wait, what do you mean, 'donated his parts'?"

"Sachinn's just being dramatic," the old man remarked, surprising me as he sat down in his armchair to join the conversation. I knew he wasn't a rebel; I'd been informed ahead of time. He was simply a supporter. But it was refreshing to see him so familiar with the rebellion, comfortable with its members in his home, knowing them well enough to tease them and know about their tasks because he genuinely wanted to help. This wasn't the K'sundi I left four years ago, but it was the K'sundi I'd left all of the materials for them to build themselves. I was glad to see they put in the work to bring this idea to reality while I was gone.

The man leaned over the arm of his chair as he stroked his chin in thought. "We've done whatever we can to protect the Neo-Dracs. We just had a group of kids and their parents staying here a few days ago."

Sachinn nodded in acknowledgement.

The old man continued, features sobering. "The Zendaalan officers and those traitorous K'sundii authorities have become more and more violent. So we do what's necessary to protect our own." He nodded with a grimness in his expression that cemented exactly what he meant by that.

Sachinn shrugged, holding the cup of coffee the man had offered her as she leaned against the wall beside him. "Death has been happening on both sides for a while. It's just more frequent now. But ever since you told us about how the Zendaalans have been communicating on some secret channel, we've been paying closer attention to the Zendaalan bodies left after a skirmish."

I raised an eyebrow, and Jashi looked like she was going to be sick. "What have you found?"

Sachinn's eyes lit up with mischievousness. "It took a lot of work. We had to enlist the help of volunteers, doctors, and engineers working together just to understand how things work. Turns out, you're right, most Zendaalans we've had the chance to examine had access to a communications network we couldn't access. At first."

Now even Jashi was impressed. "You have access to the network?"

Jemmorah gestured to the robot. "Lecrecius Awlen does." She patted the little thing on the "head."

"And he's happy to cooperate, unlike the Zendaalan officer he came from, may he rest in peace."

"Wait…" Jashi looked at Lecrecius like he might jump up and ask for her ID at any time. "So he was an actual *officer*?"

Sachinn sipped her coffee. "He has the parts from an actual officer. And he's the result of a lot of experimentation with Zendaalan cybernetic components."

I had to admit, the tenacity of the rebels and K'sundii citizens alike was admirable, if a little unnerving.

"So what have you found?" I asked, reaching for the two cups of coffee on the table. I offered one to Jashi, but she grimaced and shook her head. Lecrecius had deprived her of her appetite. I put the second cup back and sipped on mine.

"First off," said Jemmorah, gesturing to the multitude of cords behind the robot head. The devices connected to those cords didn't look like typical K'sundi technology, they had much more chrome. "Cyborg technology is complex."

Sachinn scoffed. "The understatement of the century."

Jemmorah nodded. "The way it was explained to me, apparently not all Zendaalans have access to that private network Jashi found out about. Not even all officers have access. The rebels examined several bodies, it seems. It does look like more officers have been granted access lately, probably because they need information about the Half-Dracs, the Dens, and all that in order to look for those of us who live beyond their dragon-less reach."

Jashi chuckled, and I shook my head. When had my people become so nonchalant about living on the run?

Sachinn continued, "Even if an officer has access to the network, his cybernetic system is programmed to check him for signs of life every few hours. You see, the technology often outlives its user. Apparently, it's very common for the cybernetic components of a dead Zendaalan to be donated. They last a long time. So, the cybernetics are designed to check its host for a heartbeat and brain signals every few hours. Otherwise, they shut off and, as far as we can tell, can't be turned on again unless authorized by a Zendaalan doctor."

"This is all very fascinating," Jashi said, leaning on the edge of the couch and clearly trying not to look at Lecrecius over on the coffee table. "But what does this have to do with connecting to the private network?"

"Quite a bit," said Jemmorah. "If the cybernetic parts go offline, there goes any chance of connecting to the private network."

Sachinn nodded. "So we needed a Zendaalan official's body, and it needed to be pretty fresh. After about three hours, his cybernetic parts shut down for good. Mr. Awlen was our lucky break. After a chase with some rebels that were forced to defend themselves, we got a call about Mr. Awlen and were able to get to the scene fast enough to prevent the systems from shutting down."

"Because of this guy!" announced Jemmorah happily, gesturing to the robot. "He can emulate brainwaves and a heartbeat to keep the cybernetic parts we got from Lecrecius active."

"That's how," Sachinn added, "we were able to study the network itself. It's pretty complex and heavily encrypted." She gestured to the parts scattered behind Mr. Awlen. "Any officer granted access to the network has an encryption key installed that not even he himself has access to. It's just automatically activated whenever he accesses the network or receives data from it."

Jashi looked at the results of our lucky break with a little less disgust. "So how did you guys get access?"

The old man leaned back, crossing his arms behind his head. "My nephew always has been good with all these highfalutin' technology thingamajigs. I volunteered him to help the rebels out when I heard about Sachi's problem."

I tried not to chuckle at Sachinn's nickname as she narrowed her eyes, daring anyone to laugh.

Jemmorah, clearly trying not to smile, said, "Yes, his nephew was a lot of help. He's the one who figured out what we needed to make our Lecrecius robot work better. Essentially, we didn't need to crack the encryption code, we just needed Lecrecius to pretend to be a Zendaalan."

Jashi shook her head. "You've lost me."

"It's simple," Sachinn said, strolling over to the robot head. "If you were a Zendaalan officer, you'd barely even be aware of the encryption code you're using to read and send information. You just know it's there, and it's working. So as long as Lecrecius is here making the network believe their officer is still alive and well—"

"They're still sending him information," I concluded, realizing just how powerful our little friend really was.

Sachinn nodded with a grin. "Normally, the information is translated into a form that imitates brainwaves, and the Zendaalan would understand it as if it came from their own mind. Images, sounds, texts—anything."

The older man took out a little screen and handed it to me, saying, "I don't understand any of that, but according to my nephew, this screen will show you all that stuff Sachi just mentioned."

I admired the little device in my hand. A machine that could unscramble the brainwaves Lecrecius received and translate them onto a screen. This man's nephew was impressive.

Jashi leaned closer and looked at the screen with me. It showed mostly directions to different locations. It looked like the positions

Zendaalans were taking to look for the rebels. I laughed. This was brilliant.

Jashi took the device from me and pursed her lips. "This is great for following the Zendaalans' movements, but it doesn't tell us what else they're using the private network for. I'm having trouble believing they need such a complicated network connecting all the way to Zendaal just to communicate raid locations."

She was right.

Sachinn was prepared for the question, though. She leaned on the robot, a lopsided smile on her face. "Lecrecius doesn't just receive information. He can ask for it too.'" She gave us a chip, smaller than a coin. "This is a collection of what we've found." Then she frowned. "It's some pretty heavy stuff. I'd wait until you're back in the Dens with the rest to read it all. If you need anything else just let us know, and we'll see what we can do with Lecrecius."

"There is a catch, though," Jemmorah noted, and Sachinn pursed her lips.

"Yes...it looks like we can only use Lecrecius for another three months," said Sachinn. "After that, his encryption key expires. Apparently, the key gets refreshed when Mr. Awlen reports at a Zendaalan office, something he'd do often enough not for it to matter to him. But for us, it means we only have so long to use Lecrecius before we'll need to get hold of another freshly dead Zendaalan officer—a miracle we were lucky to come across once and can't count on happening again."

Sachinn crossed her arms, looking me and Jashi in the eye. "So if you want to use Lecrecius to help on the day you take the throne back, it will have to be before then."

Jashi perked up. "Can you use him to disrupt the network too? Would that work?"

"According to the other rebels we had investigate the matter," said Sachinn, "yes. But it'll only work once, and only for a few hours before the Zendaalans fix the disruption. As we said, only certain Zendaalans have access to the network—for good reason. Our tech people tell us they can send a disruption signal throughout the network that will crash it and disconnect all the officers on the channel until it's repaired. Which again, they estimate would take a few hours. That would be your opportunity to retake the palace while the Zendaalans are uncoordinated."

I looked at Jashi, and she nodded to me. We didn't want to wait and hope another opportunity fell in our laps. Three months. That was how long we had to strike against Dekaar.

I glanced at the chip in my hand. Sachinn followed my gaze and grimaced. "I hope you're ready for what's on there," she said in an uncharacteristically soft voice. She pursed her lips, shaking her head. "I wasn't."

Jashi's eyes widened, and I looked at the chip again, then clenched it in my fist. What we would find on this small device, I was sure, was the whole reason I became a rebel, became Faresh, and was determined to save K'sundi, to save the Half-Dracs. Whatever it was, I would have to be ready.

But somewhere deep inside, a small part of me feared that in spite of all that...I would never be ready for what was on this chip.

THE ZENDAALANS' TRUTH

Jashi *Eloe* Anyua-Omah

Sachinn was right to try and prepare us for what was on that chip she gave us. It shined a light on some things. It made me angry; it made me hate the world and then hate Dekaar for getting us into this mess in the first place. I couldn't understand why he hated the Dragon Kings so much that he would send his own people to hell just to ruin them.

But then I remembered my time with Dekaar and how little he really knew about what the Zendaalans had done in his absence. And it occurred to me that perhaps he *still* didn't know everything they were doing.

The K'sundii, under the influence of the Zendaalans, came to resent the dragon tribe. But Dekaar didn't seem to share those prejudices. He was horrified by the ignorance of his people, disgusted by the fact that the Half-Dracs were forced to live in hiding. He took pride in being a Half-Drac.

I tried to think about the situation from Dekaar's point of view, to put my feet in the shoes of a man who woke up from a thousand-year nap. I thought about how the world looked before he went to sleep, and how he probably didn't expect the world to change by the time he woke up.

Dekaar's hate for the dragons and the Dragon Kings was separate from his feelings about his people. He was strangely infatuated with me, though he hated Kahmel—the one who represented our attempts to reconnect with the Dragon Kings. Kahmel had exactly the mentality Dekaar had been trying to divorce himself from when he was alive—that sort of reverence for the dragons and their Kings. But me, I represented what Dekaar thought he wanted—a K'sundii woman separated from the Dragon Kings and everything they represented. But I didn't think Dekaar realized there *was* no K'sundi without its dragons. What made his people worth ruling over was the very thing he was separating them from by encouraging them to turn from the dragons.

Dekaar hated the dragons, but he loved the Half-Dracs.

He'd instructed the Zendaalans to capture, not kill, the Neo-Dracs they discovered. Dekaar's disturbing speech about zoos crossed my mind. In his own sick way, he admired the Half-Dracs, and even the dragons and the Dragon Kings. He would never want them completely eliminated. He liked his control, but he also required a degree of elegance.

The information on the chip was what the Zendaalans had accomplished on their own, how they'd structured the world to get to this point where K'sundi would always be under their thumb and they would never have to fear our uprising. At the end of the day, the Zendaalans would look out for their own self-interests, not Dekaar's obsessions or complex behavior.

Dekaar believed he had orchestrated a grand plan, but in reality, he was merely a pawn for the Zendaalans' game of complete conquest, a convenient means to an end. They didn't care about Dekaar's sentimental attachments. They would neutralize any threat to their reign, period. They were, as even Dekaar said, crude. Efficient, but their simplicity and totalitarian approach aggravated Dekaar.

When I was finished heaving flames as the anger boiled within me for all that Dekaar and the Zendaalans had done, an idea lit my mind, a spark that grew into a flame. There was a way to turn this information to our advantage, if we played our cards right.

No. Not *we*. This was something only I could do. I was the one who got to know Dekaar's character, his volatile nature. And I knew firsthand how crucial it was to walk that thin line when dealing with him.

We needed to tell Dekaar what we knew. I had a hunch. No, not just a hunch. I was *certain*. Dekaar did not know. And once he realized what his throne truly cost...

I didn't imagine he would resign from the throne. I wasn't so foolish as to believe that. But I did think we could even the playing field in this battle we were trying to mount. Zendaal may have believed they could tame the beast that was Dekaar, fill his head with promises and dreams of conquest.

But in the end, even Dekaar was still a dragon at heart.

And no dragon could ever be truly tamed.

When Dekaar found out what the Zendaalans had been doing all this time, what they'd done to the Neo-Dracs since he ascended the throne—and if my suspicions were correct, even what they'd done to Dekaar, himself—they would find out why they should never have disturbed a dragon's nest in the first place. Because a dragon—ZST, Half-Drac, Neo-Drac, or even dressed as a cyborg—could still breathe fire and ashes.

And no one but us should ever play with fire.

I devised a plan, and I felt confident it would work. But no matter how I twisted the idea in my mind, I knew I would never be able to make Kahmel understand. I knew the risks, but I also knew Dekaar better than anyone else. Without familiarity with the man's character, it would be hard for Kahmel to understand what I understood. I hated it, but I I couldn't tell him what I was about to do. Not until after.

I'd be surprising him again. But he wouldn't be happy with me this time. I just hoped he would understand why I did it and why I couldn't tell him and eventually forgive me.

I was beginning to appreciate his mindset when he'd first become Faresh, wen shouldering so many responsibilities, so many people—

personal feelings had to be set aside when there were lives at stake. He might not forgive me for what I was going to do, but if it saved our people or gave us an advantage for that day of war ahead of us, it was worth it. I was sorry. So sorry. But I knew I had to do this.

All my life, I'd felt like the result of unfortunate events, a leaf in the wind, being tossed from one set of circumstances that controlled my life to another.

For once, I was taking the reins. I was making a decision to steer not only my own future but that of my son's. For him, I would be brave. For him, I would stare down any dragon, even Kahmel. Kai and all the other Neo-Dracs like him were depending on me, and I'd face Dekaar in hell before I let them down.

I knew what I had to do, but I resisted it for days. I hadn't done anything yet, but I couldn't even look at Kahmel without guilt eating me alive. I hated that we were going down the same road we did in the beginning.

I woke up in the middle of the night and looked at Kahmel and Kai. I would come back to them. I wouldn't let Dekaar take me from my family.

And even now, I realized, Kahmel had done so much to protect me all this time. It only felt right that I protect him for once. I knew I was going to be okay. He didn't need to know what I'd done until it was all over. I could spare him that worry. He had enough to worry about for this battle we were planning. And he'd have new worries by the time I got back anyway.

That was what I told myself as I got dressed and snuck out while the rest of the Den was still asleep.

Once I was out of the house, I reached out to my dragons, and after getting an onslaught of backlash, I almost decided to take Comet instead, just because he couldn't talk to me. But the Drake Bond was powerful, and within a few moments, my assurance washed over the traumatic memories they shared of the desperate situation they'd experienced with me. They didn't like it, but they knew why I had to do this and understood why I couldn't tell Kahmel.

Rocket volunteered to escort me, along with Legend. Rocket, because he promised to get me out of the situation at the drop of a hat, if need be. And Legend, because he was the most emotionally stable dragon I had, and I needed to keep a clear head. So I took my red and black dragons, and I nodded without explanation to a curious member of our community on the night shift guarding the Tunnel entrances.

I crossed over, and then I got in contact with the rebels, requesting an emergency escort. Kahmel gave me the clearance to do things like that, and it was the first time I'd ever made such a request. I'd gotten used to conducting royal business with Kahmel, but this felt somewhat alien because it was the first time I'd ever done business with the rebels outside of him. My stomach churned uncomfortably.

The rebels arrived, and I left my dragons beside the Tunnel while I made a quick stop in the capital. I kept my face covered as I rode in the car, but my heart still pounded against my chest as sirens wailed in the distance. The sound had become a permanent part of the background in K'sundi.

And I was about to arrange a meeting with the monster responsible for that.

I met with Sachinn, a single request in mind. I asked her if there was a way to send a message through the Lecrecius bot without the rest of the members on the network knowing where it came from. She gave a complicated answer I didn't really understand, but I got the meaning. It was possible, but she was very confused as to what I was trying to do.

Even so, I made my request and she acquiesced. A message was sent over the private network that only one other person would understand.

Meet me in the desert at these coordinates in an hour. I will be alone. I expect you to be as well. There's something you should know.
- Eloe

HE'S NOT COMING, said Rocket, his unease slipping through me.

I stood in the middle of the desert, a dot in an ocean of sand, a sky of milky twilight above me. My sandals sank into the ground beneath me as my long skirt waved in the light wind of the morning. I crossed my arms, attempting to banish the chill that threatened to seep through my bones.

Rocket's feelings pooled with my own for a moment before I felt Legend growl, bringing me out of my—and Rocket's—thoughts, reminding me of my own self-assurance and telling Rocket to shut up. I thanked him and remembered my grounding exercises. My mantra.

I am here.

I am present.

I am loved.

My mind flashed to the information on the chip, and I added to my mental chant, letting out a puff of flames that warmed me for a moment.

I am here because I'm mad.

I am presently doing something about it.

I am loved, and I love my family.

I'm here to make sure we have our revenge on a world that would let this happen to us.

Those thoughts weren't the kind Kahmel had in mind when he taught me the meditation technique, but they effectively drew me out of Rocket's worried mind and firmly planted me back in the fit of rage that brought me here in the first place.

The sun was rising on golden dunes, and I figured Kahmel had read the note I left him by now. I just hoped he would know I did it for him and Kai.

A shadow shot out from the horizon, making circles in the sky before it finally started its descent. I slipped on a protective visor as Dekaar's dragon stirred up the sand and landed on the ground in front of me with a flourish.

His dragon was massive, at least twice the size of Comet. Its bright orange scales glinted in the sun, and I wondered if it could be an Elemental. If its color was any indication, though, the only element I could affiliate with it was fire. But then again, perhaps it wasn't an Elemental. Dekaar seemed the type to go back to basics. A simple draconian could breathe fire as any other, but in the hands of a master could easily devastate a city. That was the message the massive dragon seemed to emit, and as its owner climbed down, I was sure it was the message I was supposed to receive.

Dekaar was dressed in shadows. He wore a dark mantle that contrasted against the red and gold sash around his shoulders. Rather than acquiesce to modern fashion, he was clad in a dark robe that made me feel like I'd traveled between space and time when I crossed over through the Tunnel, like I was meeting with the past.

And in a way, I was.

"Should I bother asking," said Dekaar in that unnaturally deep tone, cocking his head, "how you got into the Zendaalans' private network?"

"No," I answered, breathing fire. It was the first time we'd met in person since the day he dropped me off in his mansion over four years ago. But unlike then, this time I understood who he was—what he was. Being near him again was like mixing oil and water; it just felt wrong.

But this time, *I* had the advantage. Not him.

I nodded to the mammoth of a dragon behind the new Faresh. "I see you found yourself a dragon without ZST training. Strange, seeing as you abolished Kahmel's old laws."

Dekaar merely shrugged at his hypocrisy. "All of this technological advancement, and still nothing that quite emulates the power one feels in the sky, feeling the wind for one's self. Unlike you" —he glanced at the dragons by my side—"I know what good breeding looks like. And dragons are roaming all over Hemorah nowadays. I searched for a good while before I found him, but I do believe he's suitable."

I soothed my dragons as they bristled, and in that moment I connected to what they were feeling—an overwhelming flood of vicious hatred, all directed toward the man in front of me. I wondered how the dragon beside Dekaar allowed itself to be ridden by him at all.

"Is that so?" I asked, dragging my mind back from my dragons' with effort. *I am here. I am present,* I recited, reconnecting with the moment. "Such a great pick. Have you bonded with him?"

Dekaar chuckled, a smirk appearing on his lips, fingers drumming against the steel that made up his cheek. "I know your husband couldn't have approved of this sham of a meeting," he said, dodging the subject, as I suspected he would. "Here you are, unprotected, showing your cards by revealing to me that you have access to private information our little cyborg friends won't appreciate."

I let him shift subjects and ignored his mention of Kahmel. The subject of Kahmel was in Dekaar's dangerous zone. But the fact that he was already dodging uncomfortable questions was good. I wanted him to be uncomfortable. "You won't tell them," I pronounced firmly.

Dekaar raised an eyebrow with interest, his orange-red eyes glinting.

I gestured to him, with nothing but his dragon to back him up. "You came alone, like I asked, after all."

"This could be a trap." Dekaar folded his hands behind his back and paced to the left. I kept my eyes trained on him, unmoving as he went on. "And if you were so certain I was coming, you should have prepared a trap of your own."

I snorted. "You're late. You think I don't know you spent that time making sure I didn't have backup? And if you have a dragon that'll listen to you, for some reason I can't imagine, you can use the Tunnels and make sure there's no armada waiting for you unseen."

"Cybernetic technology."

I frowned. "What?"

Dekaar leaned toward me, eyes glinting in a way I'd seen before when he delighted in his own atrocities and was waiting for my reaction to them. He raised a hand, and his dragon lowered its huge head toward him. Dekaar stroked its chin. "The Zendaalans have brilliant technology but lack the creativity to use it properly. *ZST*," he spat. "Zendaal's Stupidity Trumps-all, is what it should stand for."

He curved his head against that of his dragon's. "They already had the cybernetic technology to do it, I simply instructed them to use it. The dragon's mind has been altered, parts of it replaced, I don't really know the details. But it responds to Butaah as it should. However, its memory of who I am has been forcibly removed, along with its ability to connect to any other dragon that should tell it otherwise. It is as loyal as any dragon should be without all of the annoying inconveniences."

Dekaar's sadistic manner had me resisting the urge to let the dragons have a good crack at him. They'd never win against the massive beast beside him, though. Rocket and Legend were still adolescent dragons, and that thing was a fully-grown monster of epic proportions. They wouldn't stand a chance. I'd never stand a chance. Dekaar had every advantage against me when it came to expertise. Where I've been training with dragons and my own fire for a mere few years, he had eons worth of knowledge to glean from, trained by people that passed down ancient teachings I could never know.

Seeing I was sufficiently disturbed, Dekaar continued, nodding appreciatively. "I must admit, you're more calculating than you appear. You escaped my mansion right under my nose, in the heart of the Zendaalan capital. I've underestimated you in the past." His eyes glinted with danger. "I won't make that mistake again."

"Good," I said, daring to come nearer. "Then you'll know I'm telling the truth when I say the Zendaalans are lying to you."

A DRAGON IS STILL
A DRAGON ALL THE SAME

Dekaar watched me with laughter in his eyes, like I was a naive child trying to persuade a villainous adult out of his wicked actions by simply saying they were wrong. And I let him laugh at me. I knew what I was doing.

"And that is the reason I won't tell them of our meeting today," he said, ridicule in his tone. "Because I will no longer trust them, for whatever you say they are lying to me about." He held up a finger before I could reply. "I haven't told them about this meeting yet, but only because you intrigued me by using the name I gave you. It surprised me so much, I had to find out why. But I assure you, I have every intention of letting them know about the breach in their security, as well as our meeting. If you don't have a way to leave this realm quickly enough, you'll have an entire squadron on your tail before you can even crest the first dune out of here. I believe you are intelligent, but I can't possibly imagine what you have to say that would change the facts I've laid before you. Now. Impress me."

I swallowed my irritation both at the way he looked at me, like he was looking to be entertained, and especially at the way he almost seemed serious. Despite what he'd said, he believed that whatever I had to say was worth the risk I was taking. He knew I wouldn't have come all this way if I weren't serious.

It didn't matter. It was like Sachinn had said, none of us could have prepared for what was on the chip. And as cocky as Dekaar was acting, he wasn't prepared, either.

"You ordered the Zendaalans to *capture* the dragon tribe members that have developed Half-Drac abilities. Did you know they were killing them instead?"

Anger flashed across Dekaar's features. It lasted a fraction of a second, but it was there, and that was all I needed to know I was right. He had no idea.

"It's to be expected," he said smoothly. But there was frost in his tone. "They are brutes, as I've said. They can hardly be expected to be as elegant as I. But these new Half-Dracs, what are they calling themselves? Neo-Dracs. Their existence is a threat to my rule, and they should be disposed of. The Zendaalans are like a cat that can't manage to play with its food without killing it. They miss out on the fun that way, but that's hardly my problem."

Lies. I knew he was lying because no matter how twisted and heartless the cyborg-K'sundii man was, no matter how many pieces of his body were replaced with glimmering chrome, he could not deceive his natural body. His posture radiated with barely contained rage, and I knew he was waiting to hear the rest of what I had to say, knowing what I'd said couldn't be the end of it. And he was right.

"I wouldn't say they don't play with their food." I cocked my head. I tapped my eWatch and let the screens display in front of him. I watched them from behind, and they still made my insides twist with rage. "Kahmel came close to having this kind of encounter. They don't kill the Half-Dracs right away. They carry out extensive procedures first, taking the bodies apart like a science experiment—oh, perhaps you didn't have those in your day." My voice lowered with rage. "But I think they're similar to the kind of cat you're talking about, except these cats aren't playing. They've been observing. At least, until recently."

Dekaar looked at me through the holographic projection. He wouldn't look at it. Good. So even a monster could be disturbed.

"What would they be looking for?" There was danger in his tone, and it wasn't directed at me.

Satisfied with his veiled disgust, I drew the images back. "What are Half-Dracs, really?" I asked, changing the subject.

Irritation and impatience flooded his demeanor as Dekaar rolled his eyes, huffing. "Half dragons. Surely you know *that*, at least."

"I do," I said, turning the tables on him as I paced to the left. "But the Zendaalans wanted to know more. *What* exactly made us Half-Dracs? They spent centuries trying to figure it out, apparently. Eradication of our race was their ultimate goal, but when that proved difficult, they decided to satisfy their curiosity as they continued their quest for our destruction, tearing apart every Half-Drac they could find, looking for the answer."

"Did they find it?" he asked, trying and failing to keep the shadows out of his tone. The shadows of doubt. The heat of anger, an anger he was maintaining at a simmer.

But I had scarcely begun. By the end, he was going to boil over.

"They did," I said, pulling up more images on my eWatch, mostly of arms, each with a hole in it. Like the scar in Kahmel's arm. "You may be satisfied with knowing you are Half-Drac, but the Zendaalans needed to know where it came from. More precisely, where on our body does this trait originate? It turns out that our bodies are quite similar to the Tree of Life, with a branch that extends throughout the body like a nervous system. But this specific trait is centralized in a very small gland in the bicep." I nodded toward Dakaar's dragon. "Dragons have this same feature, except it's much bigger. That's where our connection to the dragons evolved. Nerves, quite similar to those in anyone else's body, connect to this gland. They extend to our arms, around our mouth, even down to our feet. Those nerves are what create the fire. Pyrokinesis. But right here," I pointed to the spot on my own arm. "That's where our connection to the dragons is. The gland responsible for small amounts of telepathy. For dragons, the telepathic abilities are stronger. For us, even when it's not working on an intentional level, it still receives unconscious signals that reflect in our bodies in various ways."

"All very interesting," Dekaar said, acting bored. "For a medical student, perhaps."

"Did the dragons cut you off?" I knew I was stepping in a tender area.

The flash in Dekaar's eyes showed his switch from calm to very, very dangerous.

But I went on. "Or did the Zendaalans?"

The look of hatred was replaced by a blank stare, but it was no safer than the hatred. "What do you mean?"

I let Dekaar see my rage, turning my lip with a scowl that only revealed a fraction of my disgust. At him. At his blindness. At what he allowed the Zendaalans to do to us. And even what he allowed the Zendaalans to do to *him*. I pointed to his bicep. I'd noticed it before, but I thought nothing of it at the time, thinking it just had to do with the extensive cybernetic implants Dekaar required to stay alive. But now I knew: It was much more than that.

"That patch of metal in your arm. Ever wonder why it's so oddly shaped? An oblong oval in the middle of your skin. You didn't think to ask, I suppose. Well, I'll tell you. They wanted to make sure you wouldn't connect to the dragons or the Dragon Kings again, so they removed the gland that allows you to make Drake Bonds. That's why you can't bond with your dragon, no matter how much you try."

Understanding dawned on him, and I was reminded again that Dekaar and Kahmel shared a silent, dangerous anger. One that was deadlier the quieter they became. It took several moments for Dekaar to speak again.

"All right," he conceded. "You've told me something I didn't know. And I will deal with this information."

"Let me get into some details you should understand," I began. "I'm mostly guessing, but just let me know when I'm wrong. When you stole the parts from the Dragon Kings, you knew the Zendaalans would have the ability to control the world's prosperity. And that, I think, is as far as you survived to see. The first time around."

This time, Dekaar had no clever remark. No snarky comment as he watched me pace to the other side.

"I think you suspected the Dragon Kings' parts would heal them from the sickness they were dying from. The Withering. But the world was cut off from Zendaal when they were in the deepest throes of their illness. When they came out on the other end with fantastic technology, you assumed, with the rest of the world, that it was because of how clever they turned out to be. And so you thought you'd made a good investment, that their brilliance would surely bring you back, even after death. And, as it turns out, you were absolutely right." I gestured to the half-metal man before me, taking pleasure in the way horror slowly crept over him, how he didn't even have the presence of mind to hide it.

And I still wasn't done. "They used the power of the Dragon Kings..." I pulled up more images. A glowing vial appeared on the screen hovering between us. "...through this. It's something installed in every Zendaalan's cybernetic implants, varying in size, of course, depending on the implant. Because apparently they couldn't revive the decayed parts of their bodies without using both technology and the restorative properties the Dragon Kings exude through every part of their bodies, even after they've been amputated. They call the substance Holy Water, and for all intents and purposes, it very well may be.

"I'm sure by moving the Dragon Kings' parts you've slowed their production, but they've been in business for centuries. They have more than enough in storage to last until they've finished neutralizing us Half-Dracs; to last until the danger has passed and they can continue production. Besides, their cybernetic components survive longer than the people they're intended to treat, thanks to your contribution." I nodded to him with a sneer. "They're in no rush to get the Dragon Kings' parts back. But typically, they soak the Kings' parts in a serum, allowing their restorative properties to infuse it until the serum is filled with somatotropin, a hormone that stimulates cell regeneration that the Dragon Kings' parts secrete in enormous quantities. Every Zendaalan with cybernetic parts is walking around with this in their body, completely unbeknownst to them."

Dekaar laughed with a deranged edge. "As if I care what happens to the Dragon Kings or how the Zendaalans use their parts. I suppose part of the Dragon Kings runs through me, keeping me alive. It's not as if I did not suspect it would be required. I didn't care."

"But even *with* the Dragon Kings' parts they couldn't bring you back until now. So they were obviously missing something."

Dekaar froze.

He was afraid to ask, but I'd answer the question for him, anyway. I pulled up another picture, one with mounds of pink flesh stacked on top of each other. At first, I'd had no idea what it was. I wished I still didn't. "They started taking that gland from us when they discovered what it was. The one that connects us to the dragons." I didn't look at the image. But Dekaar couldn't take his eyes off it. "I don't think they know about the Tree of Life, honestly. The Mother."

Dekaar flinched, tearing his eyes from the photo only to stare at me in awe, most likely because he didn't expect me to know it existed.

"But I think they reverse-engineered how it worked," I continued. "After all, if an entire race of people can sense each other's experiences telepathically, imagine what that does for the advancement of their species. They could learn from experiences they didn't have to live. They could evolve from genes they didn't have to inherit. Well," I looked him in the eye, "I'm sure I don't have to explain to *you* how The Mother works.

"So the Zendaalans stole as many of these glands as they could find for two reasons. One, they began to model the communications network I used to contact you, basing it off of how they observed us and the dragons communicating. Using that, they could further their control of the territories they claimed dominion over—and watch you more carefully."

Dekaar's fingers twitched at his sides, and when he smiled, it was devoid of the arrogance from before. It was the clench-toothed smile of a madman. He was on the verge. "So what was the other reason they removed this disgusting gland?"

"Half-Dracs can evolve by shared experiences," I explained again. "Evolution requires two things: survival and reproduction. Genes that come from lessons learned are naturally programmed into the next generation. In our case, that process doesn't require direct relation. A dragon that learns to hunt better in the north will result in a dragon baby that hatches with that learned skill, even all the way in the south." I took a breath to keep my voice from shaking with rage. "But they killed us before we turned eighteen. We, the Half-Dracs, haven't had children together in centuries. They removed the gland that connects us to the dragons, thus sending a message to The Mother through that telepathic link—a message that tells her that having that gland results in the demise of her children. Telling her that in order for us to survive, we *can't* have that gland. Their intention has been to teach The Mother to revoke her connection to her children, that it was the only way for her children to survive. They have been *regressing* our race all this time. And they only brought you back once they knew they wouldn't have any Half-Dracs left to worry about. Or when Kahmel and I threatened their rule, they at least had the tools they needed to finish off the rest of us."

Dekaar heaved fire, so much that the air quivered with heat as flames poured from his mouth, shooting into the sand and curling up toward the brightening sky.

"*Fools*," Dekaar hissed, fire pulsing from his nostrils with every exhale. "What use is the throne with a weakened people? They've spent centuries, *millennia*, cultivating weakness in our people. And they think this is a kingdom I want? What is there left to rule? They themselves are more machine than people. *Blasted fools*."

"We are not allies," I said, climbing on Rocket. I leaned forward, propping my elbow on Rocket's head and regarding Dekaar as he watched me, eyes wild with rage. "And this is still a battle for the throne. You know this. You know we're coming for it."

The prospect actually seemed to calm Dekaar to a degree,

however minute a degree it might be. "I suspected as much when the *Neo*-Dracs emerged." He shook his head. "If it weren't for your discovering the Dens..."

There wouldn't be any Half-Dracs left to fight over, he didn't finish.

I nodded in bitter understanding because we discovered that truth outside of him. In spite of him. And he *dared* to be grateful for our advancements. But I knew accusing him of hypocrisy would have no effect on Dekaar; it was useless pointing it out.

"We will fight for the throne, Dekaar," I said, slipping my riding gear back on. "But it will be between us. Leave the Zendaalans out of a battle between dragons."

Dekaar laughed, a laugh that filled the sky and stung like the sun that was heating up the sand and radiating through the air already. And I knew that whatever he had planned for the Zendaalans wouldn't be pretty. Or quick.It meant my mission was successful. Dekaar knew we were coming, but he'd already known that. And he was sure to prove himself a worthy opponent. But we were narrowing the fight down to an internal matter. Even the Gheresan soldiers joining the battle on our behalf were fighting for their Half-Drac empress.

Regardless of the outcome of our battle, the Zendaalans' hold over the world was about to end. The only question was whether the world would have to suffer the wrath of Kahmel or Dekaar for allowing them to exist in the first place.

"The Neo-Dracs..." Dekaar began.

I watched as his mind put the pieces together. I gripped Rocket's ears, felt him coil within himself, ready to start not when I gave the word, but as soon as the thought entered my mind.

Dekaar looked at me, and I knew he knew. Four years was a long time, and yet no time at all. "You had a child."

"May the best Faresh or Faresha win, Dekaar."

To my surprise, he didn't explode again like I thought he would. The jealousy he usually had for Kahmel made my skin crawl. But, if anything, something like hope sparked in his eye. Like he saw Kahmel in a new light with all that he now understood. Like he was grateful we'd given him a people worth fighting for, a stronger people, because we stood against him and everything he caused.

I understood Dekaar's sick sense of admiration for what it was. He saw what Kahmel and I had built as something worth *taking* from us. We had given him hope that his thousand-year wait was not in vain, if only for what we'd created in spite of him.

Dekaar would work as hard to rob me of everything I'd built as I would work to keep him from it. Dealing with him was a dangerous dance, and I didn't underestimate that.

With a single thought, Rocket was off, Legend trailing not too far behind us.

I wasn't sure what Dekaar had planned for the Zendaalans or when he planned to enact it. But I'd seen those images with Kahmel and the rest of my people. And I read what they'd been doing all this time. All these years.

And I hoped Dekaar would do as he wished with them.

KAHMEL PACED the floor in front of me while I sat on the bed, unable to meet his eyes. We'd stayed like this for at least fifteen minutes. Every time Kahmel stopped as though to say something, he just shook his head and began pacing again.

When I got back, I didn't explain to anyone what I'd done. While our people bustled around me, wondering where I'd been, I asked Nana to take Kai, then went straight to Kahmel and told him we needed to talk. We came here, into our room, and I told him everything. He hadn't said anything to me since. And here we were, an hour later, in the same place we'd been since I finished speaking.

Finally, Kahmel stopped, leaning against the dresser behind him, holding the bottom of his face with his hand. He didn't look me in the eye, either.

"I don't even know where to begin," he said.

I bunched my fists in my skirt, biting my lip.

He passed a hand through his hair. "Not only did you decide to take an incredible risk on your own, without telling anyone, making a huge decision to reveal information straight to the enemy, but you couldn't even tell *me* until after you'd done it all."

"I know," I said. I knew my actions would come with consequences, and I'd face them, whatever they may be.

Kahmel looked up at me then, forehead forming a crease. "Yes, you do, don't you? That's the thing that confuses me the most, Jashi. You knew I'd be upset. You knew what the risks were. I know you. You counted up all of the costs, and you thought it was worth it."

When I finally looked him in the eye, I was startled by how similar it was to looking at Dekaar. Calculating, studying me. To my surprise, the anger in his eyes was suppressed, smothered by his confusion. He was trying to puzzle out what was going through my mind. He knew there was more to the situation than met the eye, and in that, I was grateful. Kahmel really did know me better than anyone else, and scarily enough, it was an understanding shared by no other person I knew but Dekaar.

Kahmel deserved to react to my actions however he liked. But I'd offer him what he was looking for first. "We don't have much time," I said, answering the question he was asking with his gaze. "You're too afraid of losing me. Of losing Kai. I don't blame you, but I couldn't trust you to make the hard decision to let me do what I had to do. I love Kai as much as you do. And because I spent more time with him, I think I deserve to say I love him more."

At that, Kahmel looked a little hurt, but I hoped it made him at least start to think maybe I was on to something after all.

"I would *never*." I looked my husband in the eye so he would know how serious I was. "*Never*. Leave my son to be an orphan. Not if I can help it. And I knew I couldn't explain to you that Dekaar would never hurt me intentionally because *you* would never hurt me intentionally, either. And the two of you are very alike."

Kahmel turned his back to me then, leaning on the dresser. "You have to be joking," he huffed.

"Dekaar taught me everything that has helped us get as close as we are," I said, standing. "He gave me a name the dragons can call me by. He wouldn't let the Zendaalans have me, just like you wouldn't. He used the Zendaalans to get the throne, and he'd let the world go to hell just to have his people to himself—which is what you did when you took the Half-Dracs and brought them to the Dens."

Kahmel still wouldn't look at me, but his death grip on the edge of the dresser had eased.

I came up behind him, placing a hand on his back and tracing it around his side. "What we found out from the information on that chip changed the scope of the battle we're fighting. Dekaar loves his people almost as much as you do." I rested my face against his back. "The difference is, you're willing to do what it takes to make them happy and help them to flourish. If it means they have to hate you or that you have to live in little pocket dimensions for the rest of our lives, you'll do it. But Dekaar only wants to see us chained to *him*. He's vehemently jealous and couldn't stand to share us with anyone, not even the Dragon Kings. But you've always allowed us to be free to do as we wish—even hate you. But because of that freedom, we, your people, love you more than anything."

Kahmel turned to me, pursing his lip into a thin line.

I brought my face closer to his. Forced him to hear me. Not with his ears, but the kind of communication dragons shared, where my words were saturated with all the emotions, history, and love I could convey to him. "You made me your Faresha. And when you did that, I became like you. I don't know if you'll forgive me for what I've done today; maybe none of our people will, but I know I'm right, Kahmel. What we learned last week was enough to make us sick and strengthen our resolve. But more than that, it made me realize this wasn't what Dekaar thought it would mean for him to claim K'sundi's throne for the rest of his immortal life—and the only way it could have been allowed to happen was if he didn't know it was going on."

Understanding eclipsed Kahmel's eyes and the tension melted. He pulled me against him and breathed for a moment, relief rolling off of him, rolling over me, and making me melt into his arms.

"I'm sorry," I said, tears spilling onto his chest.

Kahmel hushed me soothingly. "I get it," he whispered into my hair, kissing me there. He paused a moment, then admitted, "I've been trying to protect you from what you experienced while you were with him. I've been hating him for changing you while you were away from me. I wouldn't even consider the things you learned from him that changed you for the better, even when *you* were willing to accept that your enemy was your greatest help in this battle for our people."

"It's the most confusing thing," I confessed, burying my face into his embrace. "That's why I couldn't tell you. I don't understand it, myself. I realize why dragons communicate with their entire selves because words are so useless sometimes. Being trapped by Dekaar was hell, and I hated being away from you and everyone else all that time. Hated being confined with nothing to do but plot a way to escape." I sighed. "But I also learned more about our history than I could ever learn from an ancient text. Only my dragons truly understand how I feel about my time with him, about how we came to understand each other so deeply, so quickly. I wouldn't expect you to understand, but I also didn't want to hide anything from you. This was the only way I could think of to make the most of what we learned about the Zendaalans from Sachinn. And I'm sorry I had to do it like this."

"You don't have to apologize." Kahmel stroked my hair and wrapped an arm around my waist, gently swaying from side to side. "I understand." He kissed my head again. "I understand."

We stood like that for a while, until I finally pulled away from him, holding him at arm's length. I looked him in the eye. "I did it for you, Kahmel. For our people. Because what we learned can be used for the better."

He rubbed circles into my arm, rubbing our collective fears and worries away as he did. "What do you mean?"he asked gently.

"The Zendaalans should have never tried to contain the dragon people."

Kahmel nodded, pride and ferocity gleaming in his fire-colored eyes.

"This isn't a fight between us and them anymore," I said.

"You're right," Kahmel agreed. "It's a battle for the throne at this point. For the safety of the dragons and Half-Dracs combined, and everything in between."

"And whether it's by our hand or Dekaar's, the Zendaalans' era ended the moment we discovered what they've really been using us and the Dragon Kings for."

"The Blazing Era." Kahmel stroked his chin with one hand while the other remained firmly situated on my hip. "That's what we should call the days after the battle."

"I like that," I said, looking out at the swirling colors of the day sky in the Fire Den.

"I'll tell the rebels what's happened." Kahmel lowered his hand and clutched mine. "And I'll calm them down before they get a chance to get mad at you. I'll remind them that the mother of the Neo-Dracs wouldn't do anything to hurt her children, and what she's done was in their best interest. That will calm them down."

Mother of the Neo-Dracs.

Kahmel had no idea how that title made my heart melt.

Or perhaps he did. His eyes darkened, narrowing as his grip around my waist lowered. "You're right." His expression softened as he placed kisses along the side of my face, down my neck, sending shivers down my spine. "The Zendaalans were fools to try dealing with our people, even one like Dekaar. I just hope I get to be there when he tears them apart. And when he's done with them, we can have a proper battle for the throne."

Kahmel spoke darkness and violence yet touched and kissed with tender affection that made up the complex beauty that was my husband. He pushed me into the bed, and I readily surrendered to his will.

"I promise to adorn you with a much better palace than before," he said, breath hitched. "One filled with people who love you like I do. Filled with people that you can love freely because they'll never leave your side. One that resides over a country that answers to no one but themselves. In a world where your Neo-Drac children will never have to live in fear like we did. Filled with dragons that will bring the world to their feet."

I couldn't answer him, because he smothered me with heated kisses that had flickers of flames, raising the temperature in the room in seconds. And with his touch, he asked me to concede to him. And I acquiesced.

GOD OF GODS

**Dekaar Fetori '*The Traitor*' Kestah of the L'Tagi Clan -
*as called by the dragons***

I am Dekaar. My dragon name was Teridab, but I don't think any of the creatures would acknowledge me by that name anymore. Unlike the K'sundii in this current era, I was quite attached to my dragon name. I don't believe the K'sundii of this generation know what it's like to identify by two names for as long as you can remember. To have two ears, one attuned to your human brethren, the other attuned to your brethren with claws. When I awoke half-deaf, I assumed it was because the dragons had rejected me so completely I'd lost half of my identity. And I resolved not to care because that was the price I was willing to pay to have everything I lived, died, and lived again to achieve.

But to learn that that part of my identity was stolen by the very people I used to take back my throne is...*Le capi veria ghaftiki...*

Ugh. This manner of dictating letters with one's voice is more troublesome than writing, but these Zendaalans practically don't know what paper is, and I won't use a keyboard, so this is what I'm left with. I figured out how to modify the material I'm recording with this device and deleted the last ten seconds because I flew off into a string of curses in Butaah, lost myself, and went about wrecking everything within arm's reach. Now I'm back.

Where was I? Ah, yes. I haven't even gotten to what I've decided to call myself while writing this letter. I don't believe the dragons will acknowledge my dragon name anymore. I have no way to ask and find out, either. Therefore, I finally decided to simply leave my name as the dragons most likely call me, if they deign themselves to call me anything at all. It fits, I think. It's almost as good as a Butaah name. It conveys more than just a word. It is what I did, what I am, and my identity as a half-deaf dragon, stripped of half of himself in more ways than one. Traitor.

I died in my old age, somewhere past eighty. I know I lived a relatively long time because I remember being frustrated with how long it was taking to die. Even at the time, I knew the promise the Zendaalans made would take longer than my first lifetime. I saw my death like one does a nap: an easy way to let time pass without noticing.

When I awoke from my slumber, everything I knew about the world had changed. I imagined the experience should have been somewhat traumatizing. The Zendaalans surrounding me treated me very delicately, like that was the reaction they were waiting for. They spoke very slowly, using some kind of strange device that repeated what they said in my own language. The first thing I did when I awoke, however, was laugh aloud. Life felt glorious. The world around me had changed to accommodate every inconvenience imaginable, to the point of excess.

The dragons I'd left behind were mindless, completely unable to do anything about the betrayal that filled every dragon with hatred for my very being. The reason I had to spend the rest of my earlier life, after my deal with the Zendaalans, in seclusion—I couldn't go anywhere without being chased by the things. I wanted to leave the confines of the world I'd then outgrown, but I didn't think even the Zendaalans could recover my body from the bowels of a dragon.

When I was revived, I was given an enormous amount of knowledge from devices the size of a breadcrumb they called chips, and then I understood the terms they were using, and they no longer had to use their translation devices because I could speak Zendaalan with no effort from myself. They explained how they brought me back. When I died, their ancestors came to retrieve my body and preserve it in their icy mountains, where it laid for a thousand years. When they became capable of reviving my body, they used their technology to replace body parts that could no longer function on their own, restore the look of youth to my flesh, and overall enhance the capabilities of a human being.

My body was half man, half machine, and it felt suiting. Machines, I learned in an instant through their knowledge chips, were devices often given a single function that they would perform repeatedly and reliably for as long as their parts are able to continue. And that felt a fitting allegory for what I had become. My parents, when I was a boy, used to call me stubborn. My brothers and countrymen called me obstinate. I liked to believe I was determined. I had a single goal in mind, and nothing would deter me from it. I would do anything to achieve it. These machines I had emerged into the world with felt well-suited to their master. They and I were of one mind. Mankind was born with functions, much like those of machines. Our destinies. Not all lived long enough to know what theirs were, but I knew mine from an early age.

I was destined to rule. It was my function, and I, like the machines that now kept my body running, only acted to serve that singular purpose.

When I came back into the world, the Zendaalans were shocked by how well I adjusted to the changes. They remarked that the technology they were using to revive the dead was relatively new, and those who died even a few years before they were revived usually found themselves disoriented by how much the world had changed in their absence. I, who had leaped across a gap of a thousand years, didn't even seem fazed.

I knew why, but I didn't bother to let them know because Zendaalans are inelegant and as stupid as they are smart.

But I will leave it here on this record why I was unfazed by the world's changes.

I came from a world where the Dragon Kings made Hemorah prosperous without discrimination. They were the fathers of this planet we call home, and they kept it whole. The dragons that roamed our skies were their children, and the K'sundii, by relation, were their children as well. Some cultures saw the Dragon Kings as gods. If they were gods, we were the demi-gods and the closest the world had to divinity on Hemorah, besides the dragons. But that wasn't good enough for me.

So I killed the gods.

I didn't need the parts I'd stolen from them, because without the gods, we that were most similar to them, being the K'sundii and the Half-Dracs, were the next best thing the world had. I would make gods out of us by ridding our world of the dragons that were our competition.

But the world would never be the same without its original gods. I knew that the moment I stole from all the Dragon Kings, greeting them with a smile as though conducting ordinary business, slicing off their body parts with cold friendliness. I ended the world when I stripped it of its gods. What emerged afterward was a new world completely, one I intended to rule as its new god. I would be god of gods. Like the Dragon Kings ruled their dragons, I would rule the Half-Dracs and whatever dragons remained on the planet.

But *the Zendaalans*. The inelegant, unimaginative, short-sighted, *fools*. (Oh, look, I managed to say it all in K'sundi without slipping into Butaah this time). It was their custom, it appeared, to discover something of infinite value, only to completely miss the point.

(What example can I give that this generation could understand?)

Imagine a dog digging up a bar of gold (gold is still valuable isn't it?), finding no use for it, and then burying it again. That is what the Zendaalans are to the world: dogs that don't understand what they have.

In the time I'd been away, they forgot their place in the world. Perhaps I was partially to blame. Without the gods, they thought of themselves more highly than they ought. And to further the illusion, they made the demi-gods forget who their fathers were.

I...

I never imagined a world where the Half-Dracs didn't know who they were, where the dragon tribes were seen as a scorn, not the warriors they were when I left.

When Eloe told me that, the world I emerged into rocked me for the first time.

Eloe...

In fact, as I think about the past (the recent past, mind you), everything that's ever surprised me has come from her. I named her the Butaah word for heart, and I am glad she kept it. No other name would suit her. She follows her heart, always, and it is what makes her gloriously beautiful. Truly a goddess befitting a god.

Eloe, if you're listening to this, know that my feelings for you are complicated. I despise you. But I hate the world I've forced you to live in. And if I didn't hate you, I'd have made you my queen. But if you *were* ever to be mine, I don't think I'd know how to do anything but destroy you. I think you know that now. That's why you felt safe in coming to me. And you should have. I thank you for what you shared with me that day. It's because of you that I now know the extent of the mess my foolish dogs have made of the world.

The dogs, it appears, forgot for a millennium who their master was. But I shall correct them.

Now, then, to the meat of this letter. I have been waiting for the day Eloe's husband, Kahmel, would come to face me. (I know Eloe will be with him, but I can't think of her as my opposition as much as he. I think people call that sexist now. Ah, well). It occurred to me that perhaps Eloe would fear that her giving me the information would somehow put her at a disadvantage. (Or did I tell her that when she met with me? I think I did. I was wrong. It didn't). But if anything, the information put me, for the first time in over a thousand years, at a disadvantage. Here I am, preparing for war with no soldiers other than myself.

Don't think of the Zendaalans because they're nothing. I shall dispose of them. What I will do to them...well, I'll leave it for the history books to record. *Geh fabi peka.* Let a dragon translate what that means for you, if you want a good laugh. Well, I think it's funny. Some might see it as morbid.

The point is, I have nary a soldier to my name. The K'sundii are useless. They may as well be Zendaalans at this point. The commoners don't ride dragons anymore, and the Half-Dracs are all...

Sorry, I had to cut the recording again.

In short, I am the god of gods, but all the other gods have gone. Either brought to the slaughter, or on the side of my enemy.

Nay, my enemy is the only reason any of the gods are left.

I'd thank Kahmel if it weren't for the fact that he holds everything I lived, died, and came back to possess. I've taken his throne, yet he is the one living among the gods. And I, among dogs.

Still, I am the man who killed the Dragon Kings, for all intents and purposes, for a reason. I am the only Half-Drac left who remembers his true place as a god among men. And Kahmel may have the Half-Dracs, but an army of amnesiac gods is still inferior to what I have at my disposal. The K'sundii may be useless, but the power of technology is still incredible, and I am still a very crafty god who can make use of these idiotic people, even if only as pawns. Kahmel will not underestimate me, nor I him.

Finally, the day has come. I hear the ruckus outside, and I've tuned in to the Zendaalans' network to see what's happening. When I found out, the first thing I did was come in here to make this recording before I do what must be done.

Kahmel, as I expected, came well prepared. It even appears that he and his rebels managed to sneak some Gheresan soldiers across the border, so their numbers have been augmented. I must say, I'm surprised, but then again, Gheres and K'sundi have always been close. Our people have intermarried with theirs for centuries. The Gheresans likely have Half-Dracs among their numbers, even now. Clever of Kahmel to rediscover their connection. Or perhaps he, too, was only following his function. His destiny. And came upon their connection as an unavoidable result. Well done.

I'm going to join the battle soon, but first, I will get rid of our distraction. I must take out the dogs.

I had to record this moment, because it will go down in history. A battle of the gods. What happens today will become a legend that will outlive us all. Perhaps even me.

Regardless of how this battle ends, I leave this record for the world to remember what it has forgotten for much too long.

The dragons are still gods. And we, the Half-Dracs and the K'sundii, are still dragons.

No matter how much time passes, how long we may forget that fact, it will remain true.

For your sake, if we ever fully forget, pray we never remember. Because if and when we do, we will reclaim our place in this world.

And those who took advantage of us at our worst will have hell to pay when the gods of this world exact their revenge.

DAY OF BATTLE

Kahmel Axon Kai of the Omah Clan

The day had come.

We got our people into position. Sachinn led the rebels in bringing the Gheresan soldiers Daoliu promised over to K'sundi. They were now waiting for my signal, lying in wait. But *our people* weren't just the rebels anymore. K'sundii civilians and small businesses kept the Gheresans hidden close to where we were going to move in. The only ones who didn't know what was going to happen today were people who didn't support us. Mainly royal clan members, though even among them we had a fair number of supporters. But government officials and those who worked closely with the Court stayed in the Zendaalans' pockets, and, therefore, Dekaar's.

I knew Dekaar would carry out what he said he'd do with the Zendaalans. But I couldn't imagine what he meant by that.

Jashi and I soared through the air, following our hundreds of dragon riders leading the charge through a Tunnel exiting into the middle of the capital. Rand, Arusi, Asan, and T'shan were all beside us. This wasn't like when we went dragon riding or even when we went capturing dragons for the sake of bettering our defenses. This was war. We were geared up from top to bottom in armored suits, heads covered with helmets that projected a small forcefield to protect the face. Each of us was armed with laser whips, guns, and small knives. Today, we were taking names.

The air shimmered as we emerged in Hashir, directly in front of the Legislation House.

Exclaims of distress met us from many on the streets, but the ones who knew who we were, what we represented, they pumped their fists, cheering us on.

Of course, not everyone was happy to see us.

The K'sundii officers of the Legislation House poured out, rushing into position all about the rounded building, guns trained on us. Their leaders barked orders, staring up at our overwhelming numbers, and called for backup on scratchy radios. The Zendaalans would soon be on their way.

We had some time before that happened, so I laid out the options for them. "This Court," I said, my voice augmented by the technology in my helmet, "has not represented the people it purports to stand for in decades. And these last few years, I didn't care, because you were no longer my problem. But then I heard what you've been allowing the Equalizers to do to those that call themselves the Neo-Dracs, and that does concern me. So I'm back to fix this shitty system and protect my people. You can either stand down or see how mad I really am."

One of the officers stepped forward, marking himself as a leader of sorts. "You'll find no refuge here, Kahmel Omah. You and your people are considered international outlaws. Neither this country, nor any other in the Equalization, will stand for this."

"Well, the way I see it," Jashi said from beside me, leaning lazily against Ocean's head, "we've been marked as criminals for doing absolutely nothing, so we may as well give you a reason."

I chuckled. Typical Jashi.

Before I or the officer could respond, loud protests filled the streets. K'sundii and foreigners alike shouted at the officers flanking the doors of the Legislation House.

A man stepped forward, shouting above the others. "What about the

Half-Dracs? The Zendaalans still won't tell us what they're doing with them. All Kahmel and Jashi have ever done is try to protect us. What have you done? Allowed the Equalizers to do as they wanted with us."

The man received roars of support as the crowd around us grew larger.

I watched the K'sundii officers, muscles tensed and ready. If they moved to fire on us now, they could hit civilians, and I would have to dispose of the threat quickly. The K'sundii were making themselves my people again, and as long as they were mine, they were under my protection.

The officers slowly lowered their weapons.

The civilians around us cheered, but we didn't have anything to celebrate yet. The officers weren't giving in; they were simply waiting for their Zendaalan backers.

Still, we'd take advantage of the situation while we could. I nodded to Arusi, and she led T'shan, Rand, and Asan toward the Legislation House.

"Tell the Court members to evacuate the building," I said. "They're being replaced."

The street roared with applause, and the K'sundii officers, knowing they were outnumbered, stepped aside as Arusi and the others dismounted their dragons at the doors to the Court, laser guns in hand as they flanked the door to the Legislation House. An officer went inside, returning in a few short moments with eight Court members.

The head of them, Roren Monoh, looked at me as he shouted, "You will regret this!" T'shan nudged him, encouraging him to keep moving with his mouth shut.

I closed my eyes briefly to center myself as sirens began to blare, and Zendaalan squadrons descended on us.

They weren't here to talk. They started firing on sight, several of their shots landing close to the people that stood on the ground, supporting us. A few landed on them too.

I figured Dekaar would have his way with them when he was ready, but in the meantime, we had to protect our people.

"Cirssa, it's time to move," I said into my earpiece.

"Understood," she responded.

I sent Huntress into the air, the other dragon riders taking positions around me.

"*K'mhet,*" we called in unison, and our dragons breathed down fire on the attacking Zendaalan ships. Electricity crackled through the air as Comet opened his mouth and roared, sending ships down as sparks flew when the bolts of light made contact. Jashi's other dragons flew close to her, attacking ships on their own. Our dragon riders flew with dragons of their own, some with more than one flying beside them, too, connected with the Drake Bond we now allowed our operatives to perform.

K'SUNDII AND GHERESAN ships took flight around us, firing on the approaching Zendaalans. The clipped language of the Gheresans transmitted over our earpieces, reporting their availability as the ships moved in.

More Zendaalan ships dotted the horizon, converging by the dozens. Bigger ships. Fiercer ships.

We needed to get the civilians to safety.

"T'shan, get Jemmorah and the others to escort the civilians out of the area and tell them to warn the people near the palace too," I ordered.

Cameras flashed from every direction. Everyone in the country knew what was happening now. They had to know what we were after, anyway. And I wasn't interested in hurting my own people.

"Got it," T'shan reported, and three dragon riders diverted from the others and began shepherding the crowd of people that had gathered beneath us, leading them into the safety of nearby buildings.

I made the call just in time, because the Zendaalans didn't give a damn who they hit.

They'd pulled out all the stops. The air thrummed with energy as cannons heated up. Huntress aligned with me, aligned with my intentions, and we avoided laser fire as it blazed the air just beneath us, warming the atmosphere to the point of being sweltering. The side of the building behind me exploded into shards of metal and glass, causing screams to shoot out from below us as people did their best to avoid the shrapnel. Streaks of blood oozed or gushed from some of the peoplesScrapes, burn marks; some injuries worse than others. But the wail in the distance wasn't the sound of ambulances, just more battleships.

I cursed at the political games that had allowed this to happen.

I was damn tired of playing games.

Jashi's voice came over the comm. "Fleets three through six, focus on protecting civilians. The rest of you, defend our positions."

The Gheresans started making distress calls over the channel. The Zendaalans in smaller ships were targeting *them* now, since the dragon riders were proving to be too much for them. Regular laser fire didn't faze dragons much, so they'd turned their firepower on the Gheresans, as their ships were a lot easier to shoot down.

The bigger ships kept us dragon riders busy. Huntress fought to keep ahead of the onslaught. A low buzz vibrated the air with every blast, blazing a smoking trail wherever it made contact. I knew the dragons couldn't take that kind of fire, and so did Huntress.

Some of our fighters went down, their dragons left dead or incapacitated. The smell of burnt flesh filled the air as the blazes continued.

Rand's voice came over the comm. "Kahmel, do you need us to step in?"

"No," I insisted. I needed him and the others to maintain their position at the Court. "We'll call you as a last resort if things get really bad."

"Jashi's down!" called one of the rebels.

I whipped around to see Ocean go down, part of her wing burnt and smoking as she crashed to the ground. Jashi jumped and rolled just in time to avoid being crushed by her own dragon.

"I'm fine," Jashi reported, grunting.

I watched in amazement as she ran to avoid laser fire. Rocket appeared at her side in an instant, and she launched herself on his back and shot back into the air. "Ocean isn't injured too badly, it's just her wing that got clipped. Keep going."

Jashi did not come to play, it seemed. Admittedly, with seven dragons on her side, she might have been the most well-defended operative we had.

She soon proved she was the best operative we had on the offensive as well, as her dragons spread out to protect the Gheresan allies, breathing fire, chucking masses of rock from the ground, and erecting natural forcefields to keep the Zendaalans at bay.

"Someone get Ocean to safety," Jashi said. "I'll do my best to help the Gheresans."

But Ocean didn't want to be coddled. Zendaalan officers approached her on foot, and she made quick work of them, ripping and tearing through operatives as she made her way to the closest building, scaling it at speeds I didn't know she was capable of. She crouched until a Zendaalan ship came close enough, and then she leaped, biting and gnawing as she dragged it out of the sky and ripped the roof off, taking the unfortunate pilot with it as she did.

"Never mind," said Jashi with a sigh.

I let out a tense laugh. "Well, aren't you and your team just a bunch of bad-asses? Where were you in the war with Omani?"

"Uh, working against you for a while. Hope this makes up for it," she said with a chuckle.

Sachinn's voice came over the comm. "Kahmel, more ships closing in on your location. Should we send the feedback surge over the Zendaalan network now?"

I groaned as the sky crowded with more black dots coming straight for us. Below us, T'shan's friends were still trying to get the citizens to safety. The nearby buildings were no longer a safe place, and they had to escort them even farther now. We needed to start moving for the palace. It would lead the Zendaalans away from here —at least most of them. But we only had one chance to use the feedback surge, and only a few hours to make use of the advantage it would give us. It still felt too early to call it in, especially since things would most likely intensify once we got to the palace.

"Not yet," I answered. "Jashi, me and you are going to lead fleets eight, nine, and twelve to the palace, along with fleets A and B from Gheres. The rest are going to stay here and keep our position at the Court. Got that?"

"On it," she said, and Rocket shot in the direction of our old home.

With a thought from me, Huntress headed in the same direction, and a few commands to our people had them following.

But a voice stopped us in our tracks.

Holographic screens lit up all over the city. "I'm late, I know," said Dekaar, his half-cyborg face appearing on every screen in the city, projected against every building, every holographic billboard. No one could avoid his face. "But I had a small matter to attend to. Kahmel Omah." He pursed his lips, as though the name didn't feel right on his tongue. "I'm sorry I don't have a dragon name to call you like I do for Eloe. But I suppose I don't have one anymore either, so that makes us equal in that respect, at least."

The Zendaalan soldiers on the ground and in the air paused as they watched the man they assumed they had in their pocket for the rest of time. The looks of confusion on their faces would have been hilarious if it wasn't so long overdue.

A second voice joined Dekaar's—the woman I spoke with when Jashi was taken, Prexa. She entered the view of the camera, frowning at it and looking at Dekaar. "Dekaar, what's going on here?" she asked in that even-toned voice of hers, silver tongue moving behind her teeth, though anger was clear in the way she clenched her jaw, eyes wild.

Dekaar looked like an older person that wasn't quite used to the new device in front of him. He moved back and forth in front of the camera, waving his hand a few times. "Is this working properly? I believe it is." He sighed. "As much as I love new technology, I also hate it."

Prexa moved to shut the camera off, and even I flinched at how fast the man's hand shot out to catch hers, gripping tight enough to make her knees buckle. "Wh-what are you doing?" she stammered.

Dekaar looked to his side, face lighting with relief, completely disconnected from the woman shaking under his fierce grasp. "Ah, now I can see the city."

The screens changed, flicking to a view of Jashi atop Rocket, looking fierce in her battle gear, the shield in her helmet flickering slightly. The screens blinked again, switching to a view of the Zendaalan battleships suspended in the air, clearly not knowing how to react. Then they switched to me, Huntress breathing heavily, and I was alarmed to see a gash in her arm I hadn't noticed before.

Dekaar was back, grinning, clearly proud of himself. Just looking at his face, you would never think he was holding Prexa against his chest, hand pressed against her mouth as she struggled in vain. He was just pleased to get his setup working.

He looked at Prexa, twisting her to look at her face, and the sick delight in his eye was enough to tell me it had been better for her when he wasn't paying attention to her. "Give me a moment. I need to address this."

He moved quickly, pulling Prexa's arms behind her. Holding her wrists together with one hand, he brazenly unfastened the belt around her pants and used it to secure her arms in place. "This will only take a moment," he apologized to the camera as he continued to wrestle her down off-camera, like the woman in front of him was nothing more than an inconvenience to his HoloCall.

"You know what?" He adjusted the camera to show him and Prexa on the floor. The woman was shaking, pale, as though realizing for the first time what kind of monster she and her people had so heedlessly unleashed upon the world. "This will actually work in my favor."

"What did you do with the security that was posted at your door?" she asked, voice trembling.

Dekaar chewed his lip briefly as he considered the camera, then looked at whatever screens he had to the sides of him, as though the only thing that still occupied his thoughts was making sure everything looked proper on the display. Finally, he straightened, his top half cut off from view until he bent down level with the woman who had her arms tied back to her ankles with her own belt. He grabbed her by the jaw, making her lips pucker as he forced her to look at him.

"The security? I disposed of them." He paused, as though considering it for the first time. "They're probably sitting at the bottom of Egro's stomach. That's my dragon," he added to the camera. He turned back to Prexa, a sly smile turning his lips. "Did you think I didn't know they weren't there *'for my protection'*? It just didn't matter to me because our purposes were aligned at the time. But don't worry, you're very alone, Prexa. Any Zendaalans that try to come for you will meet a similar fate. Egro is very big and very hungry. And so are his brethren."

His brethren? I should have suspected Dekaar would have more than one dragon.

Dekaar brought our focus back to him and Prexa as he squeezed her face, making her cry out in pain and pull against her restraints as her eyes filled with tears. He looked at the camera with the ferocity of a mad man. No. With the ferocity of an angered dragon. "What made you think you could control me?" He was talking to the Zendaalans now. "Did you think I was a simple puppet for you to toy with? A means to get your way in this pathetic mission of conquest? You *foolish, foolish, foolish* people," he said, giving Prexa a hard shake with every insult. "Even a child learns not to play with fire. Yet I find myself having to teach you such a basic principle myself."

A voice came over my earpiece, startling me until I realized it was

Sachinn. "The Zendaalans are withdrawing," she announced, and it was only then that I realized the ships that had us surrounded were pulling back, just as she said. "They're on their way to the palace."

"They have bigger matters to attend to," I said, dumbfounded.

Prexa mumbled something through the streams of tears coming down her cheeks, and Dekaar frowned, annoyance clear on his face. He pushed her away from him, disgusted.

Prexa struggled to look at him, forced to spit her hair out of her mouth as it fell over her face. "We did everything you asked. Why are you doing this?"

Dekaar faced the camera, like a teacher who wanted to make sure the rest of his pupils were paying attention. Below me, I watched as Zendaalan soldiers stood still, staring at the display incredulously, Like they couldn't believe their puppet had the audacity to talk back.

Dekaar, without seeing them, almost looked as though he knew this, and his face shadowed with something murderous. He turned back to Prexa, cocking his head as he looked down on her. "Let me see if I can get this through your *rusted steel* heads. There was no *point!*" He shot to his feet, knocking down a vase from somewhere off-screen, the pieces shattering and covering Prexa's face with scratches and streaks of blood like tears. "There is no *world!*" Dekaar kicked something in his rampage.

We could no longer see everything he was doing, but we could hear the vicious crashing, and the weeping sobs of Prexa as she lay on the floor, subject to whatever came hurtling her way.

"*There is no K'sundi worth having!*" Dekaar continued, crouching down and pulling the woman up by her hair so she was eye-level with him. "There is *nothing* without the Half-Dracs. I *told* you to leave the Half-Dracs alive. I said capture them, torture them, do as you like. But I *told* you not to kill them. You went behind my back. Determined to drive my race to extinction? You never did understand the forces you were dealing with. And I'm going to prove that to you now."

He threw Prexa to the floor, then fumbled with something off-camera. He tapped a screen on the machinery on his arm, then spoke into it, speaking another language.

Butaah, I realized.

I wasn't sure what he was doing, or how he was doing it, but sudden screams pierced the air.

Prexa. The Zendaalan soldiers around us. All screaming.

Sachinn was trying to tell me something, but I couldn't hear her.

Wails came from every direction. All Zendaalans.

It wasn't until I saw the Zendaalans on camera that I understood what was happening to them. Prexa's scream was something primal, an animalistic screech that rang through the air from every screen Dekaar had projected himself onto. With her mouth so wide open, her silver tongue was on full display.

But it was turning black. The small machine in her mouth made a high-pitched whine that surpassed even her screams, the metal eroding in front of my eyes. The tongue writhed in her mouth, like it was a bug dipped in acid rather than a machine malfunctioning.

"What I gave you," Dekaar seethed into the camera, adjusting it so it was no longer tilted down, standing straight as he did, "I also know how to take away." He examined his own metallic hand, watching the way it glinted in the light. "My parts will be just fine. But to anyone else in the world with cybernetic implants, what you're feeling is the life-giving power of the Dragon Kings being revoked from your wretched machinery. After all these years, you didn't think to come up with another power source in the event I turned against you? Pity."

Then, like the matter of the Zendaalans all over the world writhing together in pain was nothing, Dekaar stepped back, clasping his hands behind his back as the woman beneath him continued to shriek in agony. "Kahmel and Eloe. You know where I am. This is now just a battle between us. My cunning against yours." He grinned, cocking his head back. "Come at me."

THE ULTIMATE BOND

Jashi and I led a team of rebels and Gheresans on the familiar path to the palace while a dark chorus played in the background. The cries of the Zendaalans went out from all over.

There was no need to send a feedback surge through the Zendaalans' network. We no longer had a time limit. Dekaar did what Jashi had said he would—this was a fight between him and us now.

We reached the palace to find everything turned on its head. The Zendaalans who had arrived to surround Dekaar were writhing in pain along with all the others all over K'sundi—no, all over the world. I had to focus on the task at hand, because Dekaar wasn't a challenge to be taken lightly, but I glanced at one of the Zendaalans twisting on the ground and recognized the thrashing heap of flesh and metal—the Chancellor who was always pestering Jashi, Dralus. He was outside the palace, chrome hand swirling with dark colors as it made jerky movements, like it was crawling with an infestation of insects. He stared up at me with empty eyes, his one red eye swirling with black as well.

I turned away from the Chancellor.

Dekaar's new reinforcements rose from their hiding places behind the sand dunes in the distance. Massive dragons charged toward us with fury—dragons like Egro, specifically chosen and given cybernetic technology to make them forget who Dekaar was or why they should resist his orders in Butaah.

I jerked my head in a double-take. The massive dragons had riders, ones I recognized. My family. Jashi's parents too.

My brothers Sokir, Jahl, and Segrid rode beside my mother and father. Jashi's parents rose up from behind the dunes, taking their places on the other side. Their faces were grim; they definitely weren't gloating. It looked like Dekaar was calling in their debt. They were the ones who allowed him to take over the throne, claiming him as family, electing him as Faresh when I abdicated. They owed him. And so, they were here, risking their lives to protect him.

So be it.

"Are you all right, Jashi?" I asked over our comm.

Jashi laughed. "I hate my parents even more after having Kai."

My chest ached for her—and for myself, because I knew exactly what she meant. I couldn't imagine doing to our son what our parents did to us. Never.

"They've been dead to me for a while now," she went on. "Today we'll just be making it official."

Dekaar—saving his entrance for last—and his dragon stepped out from inside the palace and shot into the air, level with us. To my surprise, he didn't have a laser. Rather, he carried an ancient weapon —a long scythe that hung by his side and hooked the air behind him. Huntress prickled at the sight of it, a growl emitting from her, echoed by every dragon in the air. And then I realized the significance. It was the same blade he'd used to amputate pieces of the Dragon Kings.

Dekaar's voice reached us, amplified by the helmet on his head. "I'm just curious." He considered the edge of his scythe for a moment. "You still don't know where the Dragon Kings' parts are. What is your plan here?"

I pressed the amplifier on my own helmet. "I'm going to get that information from you, Dekaar. You may choose to tell me yourself, but I doubt you'll do that. So I'm prepared to take the information from you by force."

Dekaar tilted his head, confused. Then his face lit up with understanding. "Ah, sometimes I forget I'm just as ugly as those

Zendaalans suffering all over the world right now." He seemed to ponder it, like he saw the idea as entertaining. "I suppose you *could* do that, couldn't you? My knowledge is just another piece of hardware. Very well. Let's go at it."

We charged.

Sokir went straight for Jashi, and before I could step in, Segrid and Jahl had me flanked on either side.

Jahl sneered, his wide face contorting. "You just couldn't leave well enough alone." His dragon lunged for Huntress and she deftly avoided him.

Segrid's dragon dove from above, claws aiming for me. I shot an arc of fire at my brother, forcing him to dive away from me.

Segrid growled. "What's left for us after this? The Zendaalans are losing all of their power. Everything we worked so hard to build... it's pointless now!" He fired his laser at me.

I snarled,and Huntress batted the blast away, her claws absorbing the hit like I could suck up fire. "I was abandoned by my own family."

Huntress grasped Segrid's dragon in a deadly embrace, their heads level with each other.

I climbed over Huntress's head, lunged for my brother, and held him by the collar as I mounted his dragon. "I spent years on the run, became Faresh, and then spent a few more years on the run. And I'm supposed to feel sorry for you? Rand is the only uncle my son needs. I'd say you should see how a family is supposed to work, but..." Shock eclipsed Segrid's features as he understood what I was saying. Fear entered his eyes. "You don't have that long." I pushed my youngest brother to his death.

"Segrid!" Jahl hurled his dragon at me.

Jahl always was sloppy.

I jumped back onto Huntress, my dragon using her serpentine form to her advantage as she whipped around to face him.

Dekaar swooped in, cutting Huntress off as he flew in between us. "Look at you," Dekaar said, a hungry grin on his face. "I give you a few moments to face your family, and you've already killed one of your brothers." He turned to Jahl. "Focus on the rebel fighters. Kahmel is mine."

Jahl scowled, his face turning red as he hesitated, but he wasn't about to argue with the madman who brought the Zendaalans to their knees on a whim. He flew off to join the fight against the rebels and the Gheresan support ships.

Huntress and Egro circled each other. This was what Dekaar wanted. Everyone I'd brought with me engaged in their own battles—all so Dekaar could have a one-on-one with me.

Good. I tightened my knees around Huntress, eager to face the man who'd kidnapped my wife.

As we circled, each assessing the other for a weakness, dragons emerged out of nowhere—no, they were coming out of Tunnels around the palace—drawing both my and Dekaar's attention away from each other. They flew in droves, like flocks of birds, all of them young.

But why here? Why now?

The young dragons had captured Huntress's attention. I reached for our bond—she wasn't just observing them, she was *listening*.

Jealousy flashed through Dekaar's eyes as he said a word to his massive dragon in Butaan, and the mammoth creature swung a heavy arm at Huntress. I sent an urgent impression to her, knocking her out of her reverie. She swerved just in time because one hit by this beast would decide the fight in an instant.

Huntress, what's going on? I conveyed frantically.

The Dragon Prince has escaped, she said, as though in a trance. She was leaning on my perception of the situation to navigate her flight patterns, rather than using her own senses as she concentrated on something else. I didn't understand. She had the traitor of all the dragons right in front of her. Why would she be focused on what the baby dragons were saying?

"Not quite the dragon trainer I thought you were," Dekaar remarked, his dragon making another deadly swipe at Huntress as we narrowly avoided. "Disappointing."

Huntress, I insisted, hoping to get a better explanation.

Before she could answer, Jashi's voice came over the comm. "Kahmel, all of my dragons are frantic. I can barely understand what they're saying. I think something's—"

Then came another voice. Not Jashi's, not Sachinn's, but Lora's. "Jashi, Kahmel. I just came from the Dens. It's happened again. We can't find Kai."

As if in answer, another flock of dragons emerged from the Tunnels surrounding the palace, shrouding it with their impressive array of colors. And amongst the dragons, coming out from one of the Tunnels, was Kai.

Dekaar looked at me and followed my eyes to Kai. And he grinned.

"No!" I screamed, my shout drowned out by Huntress's roar.

Why would he even be here?

My heart exploded in my chest. I couldn't let Dekaar get near him. But Dekaar's dragon was faster than Huntress. With a single flap of its massive wings, Egro met Kai where he'd emerged from the Tunnel.

"Kai!" Jashi screamed, almost getting knocked out of the sky as her mother's dragon slammed into her. Rocket viciously clawed the dragon and the woman away, knocking them out of the sky, then Jashi and Rocket dashed for our son.

But Kai's dragon was faster than all of us. The infant Wingless slithered out of the grasp of the massive Egro, danced away from Jashi and Rocket, and made a beeline straight for me.

Kai rode his dragon like he'd been born to do it. And I realized, in a way, he was. Huntress paused again, tilting her head. *Listening to Kai.* And then I perceived Huntress's realization, and surprise.

You still don't know what he is, she said.

I frowned. *What are you talkin—*

Think. Her urgency seeped into me. We had no time, and she needed to explain this now. *The dragons coming from the Tunnels.*

They were announcing his entrance. 'The Dragon Prince has escaped,' they said.

The Dragon *Prince.* A term the K'sundii didn't use. But the dragons did. They had Dragon Kings and Queens. And they called Kai the Dragon Prince.

Kai is here to fulfill his purpose. But he needs his father. Bond with him, Faresh.

I didn't understand.

And then I did.

And everything made sense.

The dragons couldn't tell the difference between Kai and another dragon. He *was* a dragon to them. The Dragon Prince.

Kai, on his dragon, flew straight to me, hovering in the air in front of me, waiting.

I couldn't believe what I was about to do.

"*Leh mani stupior.*"

Kai's thoughts aligned with mine and conveyed multiple truths in a single instant as his crude, infantile understanding of the world seeped into my senses. I felt his love for his mother, the way he understood her deeper than an average four-year-old should because he could connect to the dragon elements of her. He knew there was something wrong with his world, that it was incomplete, and his mother was looking for how to complete it. He was looking for it too. That was why he went missing all the time. He was looking for what his mother was looking for. The Dragon Kings' parts. Until finally, he realized he didn't *have* to look for them. Their location was rooted in him, an awareness as natural to him as knowing Jashi was his mother. He could *sense* the Dragon Kings' parts, and he would lead me to them now, if I let him.

I understood why Kai was here, now. How he'd gotten here. Being basically a dragon, he could navigate the Tunnels and Dens much better than we ever could. He knew to come to me because he could bond with me to share the information his four-year-old understanding and vocabulary didn't know how to communicate.

Dekaar's face blazed with fury as his dragon soared toward us for another chance to snatch up my son, the Neo-Drac whom Dekaar was so hungry to rule.

"Take your mother to the Dragon Kings' parts," I told Kai.

He nodded and he and his baby dragon darted off to Jashi.

I spoke to Jashi, leaving no time for her to question. "Kai is going to take you to the Dragon Kings' parts. He isn't just a Neo-Drac, Jashi, he's a dragon. I was able to Drake Bond with him."

Huntress coiled and shot off, intercepting Egro as he and Dekaar pursued Kai.

"I'm going to distract Dekaar while you get them—and end this."

DARK DRAGON GUARDIANS

Jashi *Eloe* Anyua-Omah

I didn't have time to be shocked by what Kahmel said. My son was here and so was Dekaar, and we needed to get out.

Emanon, my father, shouted with evident disgust, "You had a baby?"

Heated anger flashed inside me at seeing his disgust that I'd made another child like myself. The rage increased as my mother Zaranna's face also contorted, repulsed.

"You didn't tell me I had a nephew," Sokir purred.

Flames shot from my nostrils. My dragons pushed through the angry recesses of my mind. *We won't fail the Dragon Prince.*

Infant dragons, it seemed, were quite the little savages.

They swarmed Emanon and Zaranna, forcing my parents to swing and bat at the creatures to defend themselves, unable to communicate with their own massive dragons. Blood poured from their tattered arms.

The hatchlings were *ripping* my parents apart.

Another group of little dragons seized Sokir, crowding all around him, leaving no room for purchase. The infants hauled Sokir up and swung him into the waiting maw of Legend, who was apparently in cahoots with the dragon tykes.

Legend snapped him up in two bites.

While the carnage went on behind him, my son looked to me

with innocent eyes atop his little dragon—a black Wingless that reminded me of Huntress. Kai reached for me, opening and closing his fist like he wanted to show me something.

I saw the sincerity in his eyes. I believed Kahmel. I nudged Rocket on, and we followed my son.

Kai turned and smiled when he saw me following him, and he and his little dragon were off. I was glad to be on Rocket because the little dragon Kai was riding was quick. It darted around the palace, avoiding the mind-controlled dragons Dekaar had lurking everywhere, and took my son directly into the back courts of the building—to a spot that brought up so many memories.

The garden. The little one where Kahmel used to train me in secret. The one I would escape to when I thought I had nowhere else to go. The place that had become a refuge when the pressures of the palace became too much. I'd wanted to show Kai this garden. Only now, he was showing it to me.

Kai didn't need to shout in Butaah for the air to shimmer in front of him. The Tunnel opened for us, and my four-year-old led me through to the other side, along with his team of baby dragons and my group of Drake-Bonded dragons.

My breath caught in my throat and held there.

Stars and whisps of color surrounded us. The Den had no ground, but in the middle of a containment field, the Dragon Kings' parts floated. An eyeball, a horn, a claw, and a wing.

Four massive dragons the size of Egro surrounded the parts, like some mockery of the Dragon Kings. I narrowed my eyes as my breath returned to me; these dragons weren't normal The tops of their heads were encased in dark helmets, leaving only their maws exposed.

No.

The dark helmets *were* their heads. Screens lit up with glowing, angry eyes as we approached. They roared, the robotic tones reminding me of Dekaar's voice.

This was what it took. This was the only way Dekaar could make these dragons go against everything in them to prevent us from saving their Kings. It was like I'd told Kahmel: Dekaar *only* had four years at most to hide the Dragon Kings' parts again. He hid them somewhere close, guarded by the creatures he betrayed, yet the creatures he knew best.

A cold shiver slid down my gut as I looked at them. The only way I could get past them was to kill them. But death was also the only thing that would save them from *this*. This miserable existence any dragon would rather die than carry on.

But what the hell was I supposed to do about Kai?

Trust him, Eloe, came Lily's voice.

Before I could question what she meant, the four massive dragons reacted.

Rocket darted to the side and Kai's dragon followed as a hot blaze of fire shot in the air we were occupying seconds ago.

What did Kahmel expect me to do here? What could I do with four dragons in front of me and Kai at my side? And on the other side of the Tunnel was Dekaar, and I wasn't sure which was deadlier: the dragons or The Traitor himself. And it wasn't like Kahmel could tell me what he had in mind, either.

Kai and his dragon swerved to the side, and more hatchlings burst through the Tunnel, *following him*. The baby dragons flooded the air, splitting up and swarming the massive dragons. *Distracting them.*

Lily said to trust him. To trust *Kai*.

Kai isn't just a Neo-Drac. He's a dragon.

I was able to Drake Bond with him.

Kai is going to take you to the Dragon Kings' parts.

Kai...he knew what was going on better than I did. He knew what I had to do. And he was *helping* me. That was what he came to do, and he wasn't alone. He had the dragons. He could communicate with them.

Yes! chirped Lily. *Trust us. Do what you must.*

Determination filled my little boy's eyes. I didn't think he understood what he was doing, exactly. Dragons acted on instinct. He just knew he was doing as he should. He knew that what was in front of him wasn't right. And he was waiting for me to correct it.

Mama won't let you down.

I thought about the scythe hanging by Dekaar's side. *Perhaps I should take a page from his book.*

Legacy, I conveyed, and felt my dark knight dragon's attention turn to me. *Keep Kai safe. I'll be right back.*

Legacy searched my mind for my intentions rather than ask, and he understood. *Go,* he said. *Leave Kai to us.*

I led Rocket back the way we'd come.

As soon as the world came into focus I hopped off of Rocket's back and ran toward the palace, ducking behind a pillar when I saw Kahmel and Dekaar fighting in the air, Huntress doing her best to avoid the massive beast that gave her no reprieve.

Dekaar showed what years of experience and training could do, sending volleys of fire that blazed past Kahmel by a hair. But not every hit missed, as my husband was covered in scorch marks, and something told me that Half-Dracs weren't impervious to the flames of a skilled Half-Drac fighter.

I swallowed down my worry for him. I had my own hell to deal with.

I raced into the palace, hopping over the moaning bodies of Zendaalan soldiers, forcing myself to stay focused.

I searched the ancient weapons hanging all over the palace walls. I had to find the right one.

Just how many halls are in this palace, anyway? Rocket complained as he shadowed me.

It's a palace, I responded dryly. I slid to a stop in front of a blade with a long, curved edge and pulled it down from the wall, gauging its weight.

I hoped the tainted dragons could forgive my lack of experience. I only hoped I would manage to make their end quick.

Rocket and I dashed back through the halls of the palace, back into the garden. I slung myself onto his back, yelling out for him to open the Tunnel just as Huntress's shriek of pain filled the air.

But Rocket was already moving through the Tunnel, and in a few moments, I was back in the Den.

My mind raced. Kahmel might be losing. I fought the urge to go back to him, knowing the only way to help him was to do what he'd asked me to—end this.

Kai saw me, and the dragons around him reacted. They flew as one before one of the four helmeted dragons—a brown one that reminded me of Gaiena. I thought about her missing horn and damaged heart, and as Rocket brought me up to the neck of the massive dragon, I swung the heavy blade and prayed the Dragon Queen wouldn't regret buying into the hope Kahmel and I had sold her.

Rocket pulled me away as I clung to the handle of the weapon, dragging the blade from the slash I'd made in the thick neck of the dragon, and Royal had to come behind me and finish the job with a mighty swipe of her talons.

The dragon's screen blinked off as the head fell into the infinite abyss that was the Den, the body tumbling after it. And I hoped it found peace.

Kai and his team of hatchlings flew in the line of sight of another huge dragon, this one an angry red. My thoughts flashed to how angry Aithel had been when Kahmel and I first met him and then how easily he let us into his home when we needed him the most.

This time as I brought the blade down, Rocket dived with the motion, putting much more power into the swing. The blade was only long enough to get halfway through, but with a quick swerve, Rocket brought me back around for a final swipe, forging a much cleaner cut for this dragon's end. And it felt like justice.

Kai and the baby dragons flew in front of the third one, a black one. My hand and arm were slick with blood, but determination kept my grip firm. Rocket and I dove into the swipe, Rocket assisting with the cut by gripping the dragon's head with a vicious bite, tearing the flesh with the flap of his wings, pulling the head with him. He flung it into the abyss, and I hoped Averton knew how much I appreciated his warning before Dekaar took me.

The last dragon Kai distracted was white, and as I held the blade up for the last time, I thanked Obellana for making this day possible. For making Kai possible.

My blade fell, and Royal stomped to tear the flesh with the cut, sending the last dragon's head down into forever.

My first thought was how I could possibly hide all this blood from Kai, who so far hadn't turned around to watch me do what I had to do. But he still wasn't looking at me. He and his dragons flocked around the Dragon Kings' parts, crowding and clinging to the protective field like an infestation. The field rippled. They were gnawing through it.

The forcefield flickered, until it faded completely.

The Dragon Kings' parts fell. Dream swooped down, roaring as she erected a half-circle force field that captured the Kings' parts, then flew up, bringing them straight to me.

Please, do the honors, she said.

I frowned. *You want me to take the parts back to the Dragon Kings? Wouldn't it be better from you? I don't even know how to chart a safe path back to them.*

Royal flew before me, chirping, *Kai knows the way. Let him lead you.*

I reached out a tentative hand, touching Obellana's wing.

And instantly I understood how the Zendaalans, and even Dekaar, were able to use them all this time.

I *felt* Hemorah at my fingertips. Awareness of the wing's connection to everything flooded into me, a connection even deeper than the tree of life. It reached and swayed and pulled and flowed to everything within its grasp. I felt the parts of the world where it was blocked, and knew it was as simple as exerting a whim to clear the blockage. I felt where Dekaar was usurping its power.

He had the nerve to use technology to do it. There were little devices stuck to the sides of the Dragon Kings' parts, and he used them to exert his influence, say a word, or a string of commands, and the Dragon Kings' parts, without their proper owners, acquiesced.

I found the connection Dekaar had to them, the thread that kept that unnatural heart pumping.

And I snipped it.

Knowing my job was done and my husband was safe, I withdrew my hand and looked to my Kai, who was smiling from ear to ear, clearly glad we'd done well. I threw off my helmet, unfastened the bloody armor I was clad in, and opened my arms. His dragon lowered him into my embrace, and I hugged him tighter than I ever had in his short life.

"Let's go," I said aloud. "Take me to the Dragon Kings. And then home."

Kai kissed me on the cheek.

Rocket directed his attention to Kai, and we were off.

Kahmel Axon Kai of the Omah Clan

KNOWING what I now knew about Kai changed the entire dynamics of my fight with Dekaar. Before, I was fighting to end him. Now, I just had to buy time.

A good thing, too, because Dekaar's years of training were painfully evident.

I used Butaah like words you spoke to a dog, simple commands that could be easily used to train. Dekaar had entire *conversations*. He spoke, and Egro moved with swift exactness. He may have taken the dragon's memory, but its understanding of the hybrid language the Half-Dracs and dragons established remained intact.

When Dekaar shot bursts of flames, the air around me wasn't just hot. It *tingled.* At one point, Huntress couldn't move fast enough, and he got me in the arm. It burned with the same pain as when Aithel marked me with an oath. It surpassed a burning sensation. The pain radiated through my shoulder and into my bones, and I quickly realized I was outmatched.

Egro fully dominated the air space above the palace, and Huntress struggled just to keep out of range of his mighty swipes.

We have to throw him off guard somehow, I conveyed.

Huntress agreed, though she didn't seem to have any suggestions.

I supposed that left it up to me.

As Egro made another swipe that nearly knocked us out of the sky, I cursed in frustration at the paradox before me. Dekaar, traitor to the dragons, moved more fluidly with his dragon by communicating in Butaah than I could Drake Bonded with Huntress. The only reason his dragon cooperated was because of the cybernetic technology he borrowed from the Zendaalans. He was able to somehow maintain the Zendaalan technology sustaining him and his dragons while the rest of the Zendaalans suffered—but that didn't mean he wasn't vulnerable to the advantage we had in our possession.

"Sachinn," I said into the comm, hoping she was still prepared.

"What is it?" she answered swiftly, to my relief.

Huntress dodged another deadly blow. "I need that feedback surge *now*."

I held my breath, afraid she was going to tell me it was no longer possible, that the rebels who were left in charge of the device had abandoned it when all the Zendaalans were simultaneously crippled. But her voice came back in an instant. "On it."

Dekaar and his dragon buckled. They both grimaced, Dekaar holding a hand to his head and his dragon wailing in agony.

Huntress and I pounced. Huntress flew straight for Egro's neck, making a powerful cut with the rake of her claws.

"No!" Dekaar screamed, making a wide arc with his scythe as Huntress dodged.

I thought we got away.

Until Huntress's shriek filled the air, and I looked down to see her leg falling to the ground.

He'd amputated my dragon's leg.

Heat radiated through my body, rage pulsating through my limbs. That was all Dekaar ever did. He took dragons, people, homes, families, and he chopped them up. Cut them up into little pieces and spread them out for anyone to pick on. And then he got mad when he found himself with nothing left.

I can still...go on, Huntress conveyed.

But I felt the pain ricocheting through her body. Enough was enough.

I pushed Huntress to take me close, telling her to do it anyway when she sensed my intentions and was about to object. She flew in Egro's face, making it hard for him to aim with his raging pillars of fire while he suffered with the pain of the feedback surge. I jumped, landing on the dragon's head.

Dekaar laughed, sneering at the laser pistol at my hip. "Do you really think you can take me with that? I've trained for a lifetime at hand-to-hand combat."

"No." I pulled the knife from my suit. "I'm taking this dragon back."

I plunged the knife into the dragon's head, right between the eyes.

And we dropped from the sky.

I wasn't sure if Huntress could catch me in her current state, but she didn't have to. A Gheresan ship that snuck away from Jashi's parents flew beside me, opening its hood for me to hop in. The Gheresans inside patted me on the back and offered what I could only guess were words of congratulations. But I shrugged them off. This wasn't over yet.

I took control of their navigation and directed the ship down, getting off and telling them to get back in the air as soon as possible. They understood enough and were off without a word. I turned to see Dekaar lifting himself from the body of his weakened dragon.

He hefted his scythe, letting its blade skim the floor of the palace. His head twitched, obviously still affected by the surge Sachinn's people sent up the Zendaalan's network. But the rage in his eyes told me that wouldn't be enough to deter him.

"I will not let you have my throne again," he hissed, assuming a fighting stance.

"It wasn't yours to begin with," I replied, pulling out my laser whip and hoping I could do enough with it to buy Jashi more time.

But Dekaar stopped, his blade dropping from his hand as the light in his eyes dulled. And then he yelled. Screamed. Raged. A single word that echoed a thousand years, *wasted*. "NO!"

Dekaar crumbled slowly. First his legs stopped working, and in his desperation, he stubbornly clawed forward, trying to drag himself by his arms. Then they stopped working too. I stepped to his side, watching as his face twisted in futility. One of his eyes powered down.

With the last of his strength, he shot one hand out, clutching the chest of my armor. I thought he was going to try one more attack, but instead, he pulled me close. "Teridab."

When I frowned, the man repeated what he'd said.

"Teridab. That is to be your dragon name. The meaning has been my torture for longer than any man should suffer. It means loyal. May you live by it, as I never did."

With that, Dekaar faded.

Ocean crawled forward with wicked speed. And snapped him up in two bites.

EPILOGUE

The Diary of Kai of the Omah Clan

My name is Kai, and I'm eleven years old. My parents' names are Eloe and Teridab, Fareshes of K'sundi. Well, they have other names, but those are the ones I prefer.

My parents tell me that when I was young, I helped them save our country.

Personally, I don't remember much of the things they said happened around that time. I just remember playing with my dragon friends all the time. Though I do slightly remember helping Mama do something the dragons said was really important. I remember Mama looked really serious at the time, too. I might have been scared, if it weren't for the dragons telling me we were doing well. Maybe that was what Mama and Daddy were talking about.

Either way, they say that their whole world changed when I was born. The dragons had to tell me they meant *literally*.

It took me a while to realize most people didn't understand dragons the way I did. But then again, I couldn't use lightning like Auntie Cirssa, or change shape like my younger brother, Khes, and none of us quite know exactly what my baby sister Taias can do, but I noticed the way the HoloScreen starts acting up whenever she cries.

I'm a Neo-Drac, which Mama and Daddy say didn't exist before me. They say that some people called the *Equalizers* prevented that from happening before I was born. Whoever they were, they don't exist in Hemorah anymore. Khes says the dragons ate them all, but Mama says they ran away on a spaceship to find a cure for their sickness. But then Daddy whispers that those that didn't definitely got eaten, and Mama hits him.

I don't really know what all of that means, but I'm pretty proud of whatever I did that was so special. I *am* the Fareshiki of K'sundi, after all. And one day, I'm going to become a great leader, just like my parents.

But I'm excited because today my baby sister, Taias, is getting her dragon name. My dragons are excited, too, because they'll finally have something to call her.

For my sister's first birthday, one of my dragon friends offered to be her first. I'm going to surprise Mama and Daddy with him at the party. He's a little bigger than my other dragon friends, but I don't think they'll mind. It is for my baby sister, after all.

Anyway, I have to go now. The party's about to start, and I don't want to be late. I don't want to miss the cake and strawberry ice cream. It's my favorite.

ACKNOWLEDGMENTS

This book was such a struggle at some point as I'd reached a phase where it was hard to approach the blank page, or felt intimidated by the story that lay before me. But the ones that got me through it and encouraged me the whole way through are the absolute best people in my life.

I'm thanking my family; my parents, who have always supported me in my many, *many* hobbies and side projects. My brother, who has always been a silent, yet steady presence in my creative work. When he does speak up, it's always with pride, and I appreciate it more than he could know.

Then there are the people that every adventure story seems to have, and I'm lucky enough to have in real life. The friends I made along the way like Katerina King and Chelsea Lockhart, whose encouragement has always meant the world. They're the most story-book, supportive friends I could ask for.

And finally, anyone and everyone that's read this book. Thank you, thank you, thank you. You're what marks the difference between me just scrawling whatever comes to mind on a random document on my computer. I appreciate everyone that's picked up this book, ebook, or any other form of consuming this story. You mean the world to me, and I hope this story has left you feeling...hopeful. Because that's how I felt when I finished this three-book long journey.

I felt hopeful. And I hope you do too.

ABOUT THE AUTHOR

Celeste Harte is out here making worlds and taking names. She writes books, does professional illustrating under her alter ego, Becky Brown, and even makes video games. Her favorite way to relax is with a good anime or manga, and her favorite games to play range from farming sims to RPG and action games.

This has been an
Immortal Production